20.95

D1059551

AMANDA LESTER

AND THE ORANGE CRYSTAL CRISIS

Also by Paula Berinstein

Amanda Lester and the Pink Sugar Conspiracy
Amanda Lester and the Purple Rainbow Puzzle

Amanda Lester
and the
Orange Crystal Crisis

PAULA BERINSTEIN

This book is a work of fiction. Names, characters, places, and incidents are the product of the author's twisted imagination or are used fictitiously. Any resemblance to actual events, locales, or persons, living or dead, is coincidental.

Copyright © 2015 by Paula Berinstein.

All rights reserved. Thank you for not scanning, uploading, or sharing any part of this book electronically without permission. If you would like to use material from the book (other than for review purposes), please contact the author at paula@writingshow.com.

The Writing Show
P.O. Box 2970
Agoura Hills, CA 91376-2970

www.amandalester.net
www.writingshow.com

ISBN: 978-1-942361-00-8 (softcover)
ISBN-10: 1942361009 (softcover)
ISBN: 978-1-942361-01-5 (ebook)
ISBN-10: 1942361017 (ebook)

Cover design: Anna Mogileva
Text set in Garamond Premier Pro
Printed in the United States of America

For Aden and Ayla

TABLE OF CONTENTS

Acknowledgements   i

Chapter 1	Lestrade, Meet Holmes	1
Chapter 2	Gordon Bramble Explodes	18
Chapter 3	Professor Redleaf's Surprise	30
Chapter 4	Nick's Secrets	47
Chapter 5	Just the Treasure	60
Chapter 6	Amanda Lester, One-man Band	67
Chapter 7	Scars and Bruises	81
Chapter 8	Blackpool	92
Chapter 9	Earthquake!	106
Chapter 10	Mushy Letters and Candy Stashes	118
Chapter 11	The Crystals	128
Chapter 12	Another Dead Body	133
Chapter 13	Stuck	147
Chapter 14	The Magnificent Basements	154
Chapter 15	The Trove of Secrets	170
Chapter 16	Back to the Whatsit	183
Chapter 17	Crystal Weirdness	193
Chapter 18	I'd Like to Thank the Academy	200
Chapter 19	Triboluminescence	214
Chapter 20	Eureka!	221
Chapter 21	An Unexpected Party	229
Chapter 22	The Whatsit	241

Chapter 23	Phone Calls	248
Chapter 24	Overwhelmed	256
Chapter 25	Acoustic Levitation	270
Chapter 26	Couple of Clowns	286
Chapter 27	London	299
Chapter 28	Regrouping	311
Chapter 29	Answers	320
Chapter 30	In Pursuit of a Culprit	330
Chapter 31	Scapulus Holmes, Dreamboat	341
Chapter 32	Windermere	351
Chapter 33	The Quarry	365
Chapter 34	Debriefing	375
Chapter 35	The Detective's Bible	382
Chapter 36	Goodbye to the Crystals	388
Chapter 37	It's a Wonderful Life	396

Discussion Questions for Your Reading Group	405
Acoustic Levitation Is Real!	408
Q and A with Author Paula Berinstein	409
About the Author	412

ACKNOWLEDGEMENTS

Each new book in a series brings opportunities, both to enrich the characters and the story, but also to mess up. If you don't stay true to your vision and maintain continuity, readers will be disappointed. So it is with deep gratitude that I thank my test readers for keeping me honest: Barry Chersky, Jim Cornelius, Cole Crouch, Sudie Crouch, Mary Fritsch-Derrick, Alex Hetzler, Blythe Kropf, Jerry Manas, Aden Mandel, Ayla Mandel, David Mandel, Alyssa Spillar, Keenan Spillar, and Barbara Wong.

My cover designer, Anna Mogileva, is the absolute best! She not only creates stunning artwork, but her ideas make my books and Web site so much richer—and she has a fantastic sense of humor. Thank you, Anna!

My sister, Jan Berinstein, is a technical wizard. Her extensive knowledge of Microsoft Word helped me out of multiple jams. Jan, you're amazing. Thank you!

I can't believe how patient my husband, Alan, is. It isn't easy living with a writer who needs complete peace and quiet, but Alan makes accommodations few others would even consider. In addition he reads every word I write and tells me the absolute truth about my stories. With this book he was quite concerned that I was changing the characters too much and stretching credulity with some of my scientific exaggerations. He won on the character point; Thrillkill and the others are now much more consistent than I originally wrote them. On the scientific matter, well, let's just say that literature is supposed to be larger than life and leave it at that. But because he's Alan, he'll accept my decision with uncommon grace and keep egging me on. I am one lucky woman.

1

LESTRADE, MEET HOLMES

Amanda Lester wasn't ready for what she'd just heard. Life was already weird enough at Legatum Continuatum, the secret school for descendants of famous detectives, in England's Lake District. After the events of the last few months, including her father's kidnapping, two murders, a teacher's disappearance, an explosion, and a criminal plot to corner the world's sugar market, she was battered, fed up, and downright depressed, especially since one of the kidnappers had turned out to be the boy she thought was her best friend. So when she arrived at Headmaster Thrillkill's office on the first day of the new term and overheard one of the teachers say that the school was facing the worst crisis in its history, her first impulse was to run. But when she caught the word "Moriarty," she couldn't help listening, even though she knew eavesdropping was wrong. And that was when all the trouble started, or at least *this* round of trouble.

Moriarty, of course, was the master criminal Blixus Moriarty, whom Amanda had helped catch just a few weeks before. Elegant, brilliant, and cruel, he was at least as dangerous as his infamous ancestor Professor James Moriarty, archenemy of the renowned detective Sherlock Holmes. Even though Blixus was locked away in Her Majesty's Prison at Manchester, nicknamed Strangeways, and his wife, Mavis, in Holloway Castle in London, the detectives who ran Legatum kept him under constant surveillance. And now, it appeared, there was news.

Amanda moved as close to the door as she could without being seen and closed her eyes so she could hear every word.

"I'm starting to think we're out of luck," said one of the teachers. "This is a catastrophe."

"You're overreacting," said another. "There are still places to search. It will turn up."

"Hogwash," said a third. "The Moriartys have it."

"If that's the case," said yet another, "it's gone. It wasn't in their possession when they were captured, or in their rooms here at the school. It must have been destroyed in the fire."

The teacher was referring to the fire that that had killed the Moriartys' son Nick, aka Nick Muffet, and destroyed the sugar factory where their cartel had manufactured deadly sugar-powered weapons—the factory where they had created a virus that tainted their competitors' products. The same factory that had housed Schola Sceleratorum, the secret school for criminals, where Amanda had discovered that Nick wasn't the person he'd claimed to be. The factory where they'd held her father and beat him till he nearly died. That factory, which Nick had deliberately destroyed by igniting the highly flammable sugar dust inside.

"Look," said the evidence teacher. "Whatever happens, we can't alarm the students or the parents. We have to keep this quiet."

"I think we can all agree on that," said Headmaster Thrillkill.

"It wasn't our fault," said the dead bodies teacher.

"No, of course not," said the self-defense teacher. "We did everything in our power to protect it."

"I don't think we did," said the poisons teacher. "If we had, it would be here, wouldn't it?"

"I don't see how you can say that," said the police procedures teacher. "I've got the checklist right here. See? Every requirement followed to the letter up until the 22nd of February. Then boom, gone. What else could we have done?"

"Fault is not the issue," said Thrillkill. "The point is that the situation is dire. We need to correct it immediately. Suggestions?"

This was freaky. Amanda had never heard the teachers talk this way before. She'd never seen them panic, and that scared the wits out of her. These were hardened detectives with years of experience. They'd faced down the world's most evil criminals without blinking. Or had they? What was that crack in Professor Also's armor she'd seen the time someone had mentioned the Khyber Pass? Or when Professor Ducey had slipped and accidentally revealed that someone in his family had been a dirty cop? Even if they'd occasionally made mistakes, she was certain that these people were the toughest in the world—the Navy Seals of detecting—and they were close to unflappable. Except that now they were flapping like a pair of your grandfather's BVDs in a hurricane. The situation was more than unsettling. It was downright weird.

"Hey, you're eavesdropping!"

Amanda whirled around to see that prissy little Wiffle kid standing before her, the one who was always getting on her case about not following the rules. What a Goody Two-shoes he was, always complaining that her behavior didn't measure up to some mythical standard. And here he was doing it again, except this time she *was* eavesdropping, and if he tattled the teachers would be furious.

"Shut up," she said in a stage whisper. "Thrillkill asked me to come to his office."

"Not like this," said the kid, who seemed to have gotten a really bad haircut over the break. His pale red hair looked as if someone had taken a machete to it. "You're not supposed to listen to other people's conversations."

"I'm not listening," she protested. "I'm waiting for a lull."

"Are too."

"Am not."

"Are—"

"What's going on out there?" Headmaster Thrillkill poked his head out. His beard was covered with crumbs. "Oh, Miss Lester, I'm glad to see you. I have a task for you. Will you please stop by my office after your classes? Now off you go." He shooed the two first-years off, then turned back to the teachers and closed the door behind him.

"He's going to give it to you," said the kid. "Wish I were a fly on the wall. Probably something about how you helped that crook Nick Muffet infiltrate the school and—"

3

"You *are* a fly," said Amanda. "You're nothing but a bug, David Wiffle. I feel sorry for you. Go back to your dog poop."

"Ha ha! You wish. You just can't deal with the fact that *I'm* descended from an aristocrat. I'll have you know that my ancestor, Sir Bailiwick Wiffle, was the most popular and successful detective of the 1930s, way beyond . . ."

But Amanda wasn't listening. What was up with Thrillkill? He hadn't taken them to task for their arguing, and he'd given no indication that he thought they'd been eavesdropping. The omission only added to Amanda's worry, especially because he didn't seem to remember that he'd asked her to come to his office in the first place.

What could the headmaster want from her? Did it have anything to do with the argument the teachers were having? She didn't want to know. The man had thawed a bit by the end of last term, but he was still demanding, gruff, and awkward. And yet if she didn't know what he wanted she would be caught unaware by whatever it was, and that might be even more unpleasant.

"And by the way, it wasn't cool what you and that criminal did to me. You got me in a lot of trouble over that kicking thing. I'm not done with you, Lester."

Wiffle was referring to the time he'd accidentally injured Amanda with an errant kick in self-defense class. Despite her antagonism toward him, she had taken the high road and insisted that it was an accident, but Nick, who always came to the rescue, had tried to punch him and ended up twisting his ankle. The teacher had punished the kid anyway, and now he'd never let her forget that there was a permanent note in his file.

"You don't scare me, chicken hawk," she said. She glanced at the clock. "OMG, you're going to be late to class. Can't afford another detention, can you?"

Wiffle took one look and started running toward their observation class. He was so predictable.

Amanda knew she should go too, but suddenly she heard the name "Holmes" from behind the door. Oh brother. It was probably the new kid—Sherlock Holmes's descendant, Scapulus Holmes, whom

4

Thrillkill had mentioned at the end of last term. What was *he* going to be like? And what could he possibly have to do with the missing item? Did they think he had taken it?

It was true that a few short months ago Amanda would have done anything to avoid Sherlock Holmes. And it was true that now she was somewhat less sensitive, although not entirely sanguine, about the man who'd made her own ancestor, Inspector G. Lestrade of Scotland Yard, and by extension *her*, a laughingstock. She had finally decided that she was no longer embarrassed to be the descendant of a police detective known by all to be a dodo. She was pretty sure she had resolved all that. Lestrade wasn't her and she wasn't him. She was going to be the greatest detective ever, as well as the greatest filmmaker, her life's desire, despite her duddy genes. But theory was one thing and practice another. The new kid was probably here, right now, doing his worst. This was getting juicy as well as nerve-racking. She had to find out more.

"Chop, chop," Miss Lester, said Professor Mukherjee, the legal issues teacher, who had suddenly emerged from Thrillkill's office to look for something in the anteroom. "We don't want to be late on the first day of class, do we?"

Nuts. There was no way she'd hear anything now. "Er, no, Professor. I was just . . . I'm on my way."

Oh well. If whatever it was *was* that important, there would be other opportunities to find out about it. Truth be told, Amanda was looking forward to seeing this legendary Holmes. Thrillkill had said that he wanted *her* to show him the ropes. Her! Little did he know that she was the last person who should be doing that. All she'd have to do was take one look at the boy and she'd throw up—a stunt she'd become well known for ever since that first day of spring term when she'd hurled all over poor Simon Binkle's jacket. Fortunately Simon was now a friend, although he could still be irritating in a nerdish sort of way.

But between that incident and the one in the dead bodies, aka pathology, class, where she'd made the entire class puke, she had quite a reputation and didn't want to enhance it. She just knew, though, that this Holmes kid was going to be trouble, although what sort of trouble she wasn't sure. She was pretty sure he'd be arrogant. These sorts of things ran in families: the Wiffle family was arrogant, the Moriarty family was arrogant, Sherlock Holmes was arrogant, ergo their descendants would be the same. She wondered if Professor Ducey, the logic teacher, would buy that argument. It seemed airtight to her.

Suddenly she realized she hadn't had breakfast. In her haste to get to the headmaster's office before class, she'd completely forgotten to eat and she was hungry. Breakfast was officially over as of one minute ago, but she took a chance and snuck into the dining room, making sure to keep an eye out for the new cook, whoever she might be. The previous one had been strict about mealtimes, and if you missed them you were out of luck. Of course the previous cook had also been a mole working on behalf of the Moriarty cartel, so you couldn't go by anything she'd done. Perhaps the new one would be nicer and a bit more lenient, not to mention less crooked.

Amanda hustled as quietly as she could to the dining room, which was next to the stairs leading to the girls' dorm. She looked around, first behind her, then to either side, then whirled around to get a 360-degree view and almost lost her balance. She heard some clunking coming from the kitchen, but there was no sign of the new cook. Was someone coming? Should she chance it?

She tiptoed up to the kitchen door and looked through the round window. No one. The new cook and her assistant must be in the pantry or outside accepting deliveries. She twirled around again, then felt both dizzy and silly. Enough of that. She tiptoed over to the sideboard and grabbed the last roll, sticking it in her bag for a surreptitious getaway. Yay! She'd done it! She stepped out of the dining room as quietly as she could and power walked down the hall toward her first class.

Unfortunately, as soon as she started moving she realized there was no way to consume the loot without anyone seeing, and if they did she'd probably get into trouble. As great a school as Legatum had turned out to be, sometimes it still felt like a prison. Should she duck into a closet and eat the roll? Why not? She opened the door to a supply area, stepped in, tore the thing in two, and stuffed it in her mouth, almost choking in the process. When she'd swallowed the last lump she was so thirsty she knew she'd never make it to class, so she stopped at a water fountain and managed to get water all over her face, hair, and sweater. Great.

Normally she would have noticed the décor and committed it to memory but she was too rushed. With Professor Sidebotham's daily observation quizzes constantly requiring fresh material, Legatum's décor gremlins were always changing the look of the school, and the kids were supposed to note both its present and past states in great detail. Some of the quizzes had been downright unfair though. Like the time when they had to gauge the thickness of dust on a clock. And then there was the time the old woman had wanted to know how many heel marks there were on the Van Helden House common room floor. Amanda knew that detectives had to hone their powers of observation, but sometimes Professor Sidebotham got carried away.

She opened her new class schedule and checked it to make sure she was headed to the right place, barely noticing the camel standing in the main hall. The décor did not normally feature live animals, but the gremlins seemed to have been particularly active over spring break and had gone a bit crazy. They must have been in some kind of "Lawrence of Arabia" mood, which under normal circumstances Amanda would have very much appreciated, "Lawrence of Arabia" being one of her all-time favorite films. Now, however, nothing registered.

Summer Term First-Year Class Schedule

	Monday	Tuesday	Wednesday	Thursday	Friday
8:00-9:15	Observation, Sidebotham	History of Detectives, Also	Crime Lab, Stegelmeyer	Fires and Explosions, Pole	Logic, Ducey
9:30-10:45	Fires and Explosions, Pole	Observation, Sidebotham	Cyberforensics, Redleaf	Crime Lab, Stegelmeyer	Cyberforensics, Redleaf
11:15-12:30	Cyberforensics, Redleaf	Self-defense, Peaksribbon	Logic, Ducey	Self-defense, Peaksribbon	History of Detectives, Also
12:30-1:30	Lunch	Lunch	Lunch	Lunch	Lunch
1:30-2:45	Crime Lab, Stegelmeyer	Sketching, Browning	Disguise, Tumble	Observation, Sidebotham	Sketching, Browning

She checked the first box. Yup. She was going the right way. But as she rushed down the hall, she couldn't stop thinking about not only what the teachers had said, but how they'd said it.

The school was full of tough people. None of the teachers was the least bit shy about expressing him- or herself, and they could be harsh with the students. But she'd never heard them argue like this. Maybe they'd hidden their internal disagreements up to now, but she didn't think so. She was pretty sure they'd always been united in their mission—to produce the best detectives in the world—and their approach to it. Or maybe Thrillkill had always quashed dissent. Whatever it was, she'd never heard a peep before today, not even when she'd overheard Professor Feeney talking about some missing item on the phone last term. At the time, the criminals and their methods teacher had obviously been concerned, but she wasn't arguing with whoever was on the other end. No, this situation was different.

Wait a minute: last term! Whatever it was had been missing for quite a while. Amanda was sure that at least a month had passed since Professor Feeney's phone call, if not longer. If that were the case, why were the teachers talking about it only now? Something must have happened recently. Could it have anything to do with Blixus Moriarty?

He'd been in prison for a month. Might he have pulled something off from there?

As she turned to enter her observation class she almost collided with the door. Everyone was already seated, including David Wiffle, who had obviously eaten breakfast when he was supposed to. She made her way to an empty seat next to her roommate, petite, blind, copper-haired Ivy Halpin, whose golden retriever guide dog, Nigel, wagged his tail at the sight of her. At first she ignored him, but when he looked at her with those soulful eyes she realized she'd been completely distracted and gave him a big hug. This gesture was not lost on David Wiffle, who rolled his eyes. Amanda stuck out her tongue. He mouthed, "Real mature." She turned away.

"Ivy," whispered Amanda. "I have to tell you something important."

"What—is something wrong?" Ivy said so quickly that Amanda started. Ivy was normally the calmest and most together of Amanda's friends. Even when she was concerned about something you could barely tell, but not now.

"Yes, but I don't know what," said Amanda.

"Is it serious?" Ivy reached out and petted Nigel so hard that hair flew off in all directions.

"Yes." Amanda looked around to make sure no one was listening. That Wiffle kid was so nosy.

"Super serious?"

"It could be really bad. I'll tell you after class."

"Is it about Editta?" said Ivy. "She didn't make it to the dorm last night." She looked like she was about to cry.

"She's not here? No, that isn't it."

Amanda looked around. No Editta. Since the whole first-year class took the same courses, their friend from down the hall should have been there. She was probably just late though. Most people had returned from the holiday over the weekend but there were always a few stragglers. Maybe there was a traffic jam on the M1.

"I tried to phone her but all I got was her voicemail," said Ivy. "Five times. I'm getting worried. I don't know why. It's not that late. Are you sure your thing doesn't have anything to do with this?"

"I'm sure. Still, it isn't like her not to show up. You know how superstitious she is. Everything has to be just so or she freaks out."

"Yes. That's what I thought." Ivy twitched in her seat and resettled her butt in her chair. It was a small butt and there was plenty of space to work with.

"I wonder if there's a way to smoke her out." Amanda didn't realize it, but she was mirroring Ivy, wriggling her slightly larger but no longer pudgy butt into her own seat.

"What do you mean?"

"You know how she's always counting things and looking for magic numbers and stuff?"

"Uh huh." That she was. Editta Sweetgum was one of the most superstitious, OCD people Amanda had ever met. The trait seemed to run in her family. From the way Editta described all the odd things her mother believed, she sounded like she practiced voodoo or something.

"How about if we send her three messages one right after the other? When she counts them she'll see how important they are and she'll answer." Ivy tapped the arm of her chair three times to demonstrate. She had a great sense of rhythm.

"I see. A code. Like a light that blinks so many times for yes and so many times for no."

"Exactly."

"Let's do it. Here I—"

Ivy's other roommate, Amphora Kapoor, a tall, chestnut-skinned girl with long dark hair who had just entered and was sitting on the other side of Ivy, turned to them and interrupted with, "Hey, I hate to bring up the topic of Nick . . ."

Simon Binkle, who was sitting behind the girls, leaned forward and said, "Then don't."

"Butt out, Simon," said Amphora.

"You butt out," said Simon.

"I see you're still irritating. Apparently the break did nothing to change that." Unfortunately she was right. Simon could be extremely annoying.

"Apparently it did nothing to change your bad temper." He was right too. Amphora could be tetchy, especially with him. The two were like chalk and cheese.

"Oh, stop it, you two," said Ivy. "What's wrong with you?"

"There's nothing wrong with me," said Amphora. "Ask him." Simon glared at her. "Anyway, I heard they're moving Nick's mother from one prison to another. She's going to be in the same one as his father. I wonder if she'll try to escape. Do you think she could?"

"I would," said Simon. Amphora turned around and gave him a long dirty look. "She has nothing to lose. Lots of prisoners escape. Look at Bosul Fopy and Cowboy Quash. They got away from the two toughest maximum-security prisons in the country. Fopy tunneled under his cell for a mile. A mile! And Quash got away while they were moving him. Of course he had help from his mates, but the Moriartys have lots of friends who aren't locked up. Yeah, she'll give it a go."

"Thanks a lot, Simon," said Amphora. "That was really helpful. What if she comes after Thrillkill, or Amanda?"

This was a thought that hadn't occurred to Amanda. When she'd helped capture the Moriartys she'd thought that was that. It had never occurred to her that either of them might escape. If she'd been thinking from a filmmaker's point of view, she'd have got it at once because the prospect of escape would have added suspense and danger to the story and she would have milked it. But thinking like a detective she'd missed it. Boy, she still had a lot to learn. And BTW, ouch. The thought of either of those two coming after her was terrifying.

"Good morning, class," said Professor Sidebotham. Amanda started. She had been so wrapped up in picturing Mavis Moriarty coming after her with an axe that she hadn't seen the teacher enter the room. Ivy jabbed Amanda with her elbow and mouthed the word "Editta," but because the teacher was watching them Amanda put her phone away without having sent the texts. She'd have to do it later.

Suddenly Simon poked her in the back. "Hey," he whispered. "Did you see that camel?"

"Mr. Binkle," said Professor Sidebotham loudly. "I'm so glad you have volunteered to start the class. Come up here, please. And remove your fedora in the classroom."

Simon was always wearing his fedora now, ever since the first day of school when he'd begun to create his detective's mystique in Professor Also's history of detectives class. The look included said hat and sometimes a red sweater vest. The hat suited him better than Amanda had thought it would, but she still wasn't convinced about the vest, which she felt was too old a look for a twelve-year-old. Maybe not in the UK though. At home in L.A. people would have thought he looked ridiculous. Everyone was more formal here. Everyone but her, that is.

Every time Simon took the hat off you could see that crazy cowlick of his, and then he'd smack his head constantly trying to get it to lie flat. Now he removed the hat and immediately felt for the disobedient hairs. *Slap, slap.* His efforts did no good. He grumbled under his breath and slunk up to the front of the class.

"Stand up straight," said Professor Sidebotham. Simon complied. "That's better. Now, let's do a little exercise. Class, has Mr. Binkle gained in height since last term?"

Last term was about ten days ago. If Simon had grown since then it would be a miracle. Ivy raised her hand. Amanda noticed that the floor around her chair was covered with dog hair.

"Miss Halpin?" said the teacher.

"Simon has grown about a quarter of an inch in the last two weeks," said Ivy. "His voice is coming from a slightly different place now."

Ivy was already an amazing detective. She may have been sightless, but her ears were incredible. She could detect better than any of the other kids just by listening. If she said Simon had grown a quarter of an inch, he had.

"I don't think so," blurted out David Wiffle.

Oh no. Here we go. Amanda sat back in anticipation of the argument to come.

"Mr. Wiffle, from now on wait until I call on you," said Professor Sidebotham. "Now, why don't you think Mr. Binkle has grown?"

"Sorry, Professor. But no one grows a quarter of an inch in ten days."

The class laughed.

"This is a class in observation, Mr. Wiffle," said the teacher. "Not common wisdom."

More laughter. Amanda was particularly gratified to see the thorn in her side taken down a peg, especially by an old lady.

"But aren't we supposed to use everything we know to solve crimes?" said the thorn.

"In general, yes," said Professor Sidebotham, "but this is a class in observation. You must perceive what's around you, not project onto it."

"Yes, ma'am." The Wiffle kid looked more annoyed than usual. He didn't like being wrong, and he *really* didn't like being laughed at.

"What is the answer, Mr. Binkle? You have been keeping track of your height and weight as I instructed, have you not?"

Simon looked like he wanted to sink into the floor. "Yes, Professor."

Amanda leaned over to Ivy and said, "I don't know what his problem is. He looks good." She was right. Simon was tall and trim, albeit a bit geeky-looking.

Ivy whispered back, "Too personal." Amanda nodded, then realized Ivy couldn't see her, so she said, "Yeah. We *are* talking about Simon, aren't we?"

"We're waiting, Mr. Binkle," said the teacher.

"I, um, er . . ."

"Out with it. Have you grown or haven't you?"

"I, uh, yes. I've grown a quarter of an inch since the end of last term."

The students let out a yell—that is, all the students except Mr. Wiffle.

"Gold star, Miss Halpin," said Professor Sidebotham. "Better luck next time, Mr. Wiffle."

This humiliation did not go over well with the Wiffle kid. He groused under his breath and made faces at his freckled friend Gordon Bramble, who was sitting next to him as usual.

"Now then, class," said Professor Sidebotham. "I know you've all seen the camel in the hall. I want you all to text me the answer to this question within ten seconds: one hump or two? Miss Halpin, you may skip this exercise if you desire. Go."

"That's all right, Professor," said Ivy. "I have an answer." She started texting into her specially adapted phone.

Ack! Amanda had no idea. She'd run right past the animal and had barely noticed it. She didn't want to blow another of Professor Sidebotham's pop quizzes. At least she had a fifty-fifty chance, though. She took a chance and texted "1."

"Time," said the teacher. "Let's see what we have. Ten ones, nineteen twos, and what's this? None? Who said none?" She peered out over the class. "I don't like wiseacres."

"But it didn't have any," called out David Wiffle. "It's a flatback highland humpless from Tanzania."

"Actually, he's right," said Simon, thumbing his phone. "And ironically, it was discovered by a biologist named Humphrey something. Pretty good, eh? Hump, Humphrey?" He started to crack up, then stopped abruptly. "I knew that. Why did I say one hump?" He reddened again.

"Well done, Mr. Wiffle. It was a trick question. You passed with flying colors. The rest of you, this is what happens when you let your expectations color your observations. Empty your mind of preconceived notions. Do not see what you expect to see. See what is."

Amphora raised her hand.

"Yes, Miss Kapoor," said the teacher.

"Professor, if there really were no humps, why did you say we're wiseacres."

Oh great, thought Amanda. Now she'd stepped in it.

"Part of my strategy to trick you, Miss Kapoor. Be ever vigilant. Don't let your senses fool you. And on that note, I'd like to announce that we will be using our senses in a very concentrated fashion in one week. We will be going on a field trip to Blackpool."

"Yay!" "Hurrah!" "Cool!" "Radical!" "Sweet!" said the class.

Amanda leaned over to Ivy. "What's Blackpool?"

"It's a huge amusement park-y place. Kind of like Disney World except way bigger and with lots more stuff to do."

"Oh, cool! I love Space Mountain."

"Now, while I expect that you will enjoy yourselves, the purpose of the trip is to practice observing," said the professor, ambling around the room. "You will need to be ready for anything, and I do mean *anything*. I will be presenting observing exercises on the spot. These will count toward your grade, so it will behoove you to pay attention. Mr. Bramble, please put your phone away."

"Yes, Professor. Sorry, Professor," said Gordon Bramble, stuffing his phone in his pocket. Amanda just knew he'd been playing games instead of listening.

"For example, I might ask you to pick out a certain number of items and make a story out of them. Miss Lester, you should be good at that. I'm looking forward to sitting in on your storytelling seminar."

"Thank you, Professor." Amanda beamed. Thrillkill had asked her to present a special storytelling workshop to the class, and she was so excited she couldn't wait.

"Or, I might ask you to give me the backgrounds or attributes of a number of items that have something in common. For example, I want to know where all the blue items within ten feet might have come from. How many of this or that are there? Move your point of view n degrees and tell me how the scene has changed. If you had to testify in court about this or that, what would you say? These are only some of the questions I'll be asking. Others will come as a complete surprise and I expect you to rise to the challenge." She stopped at Prudence Starshine's seat and stared directly at the slender golden-haired girl, who quailed under her gaze.

"You will also describe your methods. I will ask you to write a paper on this topic later. Hearing about how each student works will allow you to try out new techniques and expand on what you see, and later you will look at a given scene the way one or another of your classmates does. So shared experiences will be critical." She glanced from Owla Snizzle to Clive Ng. "Perhaps you, Miss Snizzle, and you, Mr. Ng, will team up." Both kids looked terrified.

"And don't forget to use all of your senses. Miss Halpin, obviously I don't expect you to use your eyes, but I want you to help the other students develop their auditory, olfactory, and tactile senses. In fact I would like you to prepare some lectures on these topics. Please see me at the end of the day to discuss this project."

Ivy grinned for the first time. "Yes, ma'am." Then she turned to Amanda and said, "You're better at this stuff than I am. She should ask you. You notice stuff because of your film training."

"I'm not better," whispered Amanda. "It's just that when you're responsible for every detail of look and feel, you notice everything. But you're naturally better."

"No, I'm not," said Ivy, looking like she'd lost her best friend.

What was up with her? Amanda was starting to worry. She looked around the classroom. "Still no Editta, I see."

"I know," said Ivy. "I don't like this. You don't think her parents pulled her out of school, do you?"

"I don't see why. And even if they did she'd say goodbye."

"Yes, she would. This isn't good."

Suddenly the door opened and Headmaster Thrillkill stuck his head in. He gave a sign to Professor Sidebotham, then entered followed by a nice-looking dark-skinned boy wearing a bow tie and a serious expression. The kid seemed to gleam. The buttons on his blazer glinted like diamonds, the creases in his trousers were impossibly perfect, and he was wearing freshly buffed tasseled loafers. Even his short afro sparkled. He looked like he'd just arrived from the 1950s.

"Sorry to interrupt, Professor," said Thrillkill, "but I have a new student for you. Class, this is Scapulus Holmes."

The room went silent. The boy stood by the door and smiled ever so slightly.

Amanda took in the sight before her. *This* was Holmes? This vision of smugness? Ugh. He was going to be awful—worse than she'd expected. Who dressed like that? He was obviously so self-involved that he couldn't recognize how real people looked and behaved. She wanted to run up and pull that prissy little bow tie off his neck, rub dirt on those too-shiny buttons, and scuff up his look-at-me shoes.

Before she knew it she had blurted out, "OMG, what a dork!" Then, realizing what she'd done, she turned as red as Simon's sweater and bolted from the room, leaving behind a roomful of gaping would-be detectives.

2

GORDON BRAMBLE EXPLODES

Amanda had pulled some stupid stunts in her life, but reacting to Sherlock Holmes's descendant that way was the worst ever. How gauche could she be? She could hear Nick's voice in her head saying, "Good one, Lestrade." He had called her by her ancestor's name when he turned mean, and it had stung like a thousand wasps. She was so ashamed she wanted to die. How could she ever go back into that room? Maybe she should just stow away on another delivery truck, the way she'd done last term when she was trying to find her father, and go home, or anywhere that wasn't Legatum. Her parents had offered her the chance to go back to L.A. and live with relatives. Maybe she should take it and leave this craziness behind.

Actually that might not be such a bad idea. Maybe she didn't belong at Legatum at all. For a girl who prided herself on her observational skills, she had really messed up. How could she have failed to see what Nick really was? Now that she looked back, it was obvious he'd been playing her. Was she that stupid?

Obviously she was. He'd known she was gullible. Out of a class of thirty students he'd singled her out as the one most likely to believe his lies. By spending so much time with her, he'd limited his exposure to others who might have been more skeptical. He must have had highly developed turkey radar. What was it that had made her such an obvious choice? Of course—what else? It was those awful Lestrade genes again.

She heard the door to the observation classroom open and saw Professor Thrillkill come out. Fortunately she was out of his line of sight and was able to duck around a corner without being seen. She tried to make like Ivy and prick up her ears, but her heart was pounding so hard it was difficult to hear footsteps. Still there was the headmaster's voice, joined by another she didn't recognize. She caught the words "Blixus" and "Feeney," but she couldn't make out anything else. She was sure the two of them were discussing the missing item, but she was unable to glean anything beyond that. Nevertheless, the conversation seemed to add proof to her fear that something weird was happening.

She knew she was going to have to face the music so she tiptoed back toward the classroom. Thankfully, Professor Thrillkill and whoever he was talking to had disappeared, but she was still supposed to see him later. Ugh. He'd definitely say something about her outburst. Just when he'd seemed to thaw a little she'd had to go and ruin everything. Typical.

She opened the door slowly to minimize the creaking and stepped back inside. The room was dead still except for Professor Sidebotham's voice. The new student had found a seat. Everyone turned to look at her, obviously embarrassed on her behalf, except for Wiffle and his friend Gordon Bramble, who giggled. She sat back down and drew her body inward, as if to hide in plain sight. Should she say something to Holmes? He was sitting way across the room, paying rapt attention to the teacher. He seemed to be acting like nothing had happened but she couldn't tell for sure. He certainly didn't seem to be brooding, or laughing. He was a complete cipher. Well, wasn't that just like a Holmes—completely wrapped up in himself. Still, she'd done a terrible thing and there would be a price to pay.

"Miss Lester? I asked you a question," said Professor Sidebotham.

The whole class, Holmes included, turned to look at her.

"I'm sorry, Professor. Would you mind repeating it?" Amanda's face felt so hot she thought she could fry an egg on it.

"I said would you please elaborate on my point." The professor looked at her sternly.

"Uh, sure. Er, you were talking about using all the senses instead of just sight." It sounded good anyway.

"That was ten minutes ago, Miss Lester. Please join us in the twenty-first century."

"Sorry, Professor. I was, uh, I didn't hear what you said."

"No, you did not, Miss Lester. You committed a faux pas, which is entirely human, but a detective stands up and accepts the consequences of her actions. She doesn't run away. Being out of the room is no excuse. I'm deducting fifty points from your next test. Is that clear?"

The Wiffle kid was gloating so hard he looked like a mask of himself. Amanda felt that she'd gotten off easy, however, and said, "Yes, Professor. It won't happen again."

"No, it won't. Now, class . . ."

Professor Sidebotham's voice faded out of Amanda's consciousness. Maybe she had been too cocky thinking she was over the whole Holmes thing. She'd just demonstrated that Holmes and his family could still get to her. This was not good.

Except that it wasn't her, it was him. She was the victim. She decided she hated Holmes more than ever. She even convinced herself that it was his fault that Nick had betrayed her and the school. Holmes and his family must have provoked the Moriartys into that whole sugar scheme and made them so angry that they'd had to use their twelve-year-old son to infiltrate the detectives' school. Moriarty was only Moriarty because he had Holmes to play off of. If there were no Holmes, he'd just be an ordinary, run-of-the-mill loser. She seethed so hard she could barely keep it together.

When the class ended Holmes was nowhere to be seen. Amphora ran to Amanda and said, "I can't believe you said that." Although she knew what she'd done was horrific, Amphora's accusing comment got her dander up and she huffed off.

Then Simon came up to her and said, "Way to go, Amanda."

"Don't be mean," said Ivy, who had joined them. "It wasn't the greatest thing to say, but it's not the end of the world."

"It was incredibly embarrassing," said Amanda. "Who's the dork here—him or me?"

"Live and learn," said Simon in his maddening way.

"I think he's cute," said Amphora, rejoining the group.

"You would," said Simon.

"What's that supposed to mean?"

Here we go again. Amanda wondered if those two would ever get along. Probably not.

"Nothing much. You're just a bit moony," Simon said.

"What do you mean moony?" Amphora crossed her arms the way she often did with him.

"You're always mooning over guys, that's all," he said.

"I don't moon. Ivy, do I moon?" Amphora uncrossed her arms and turned to her roommate.

"No, I don't think you moon," said Ivy.

"What do you mean you don't *think* I moon?"

"You don't moon, okay?" said Ivy with uncharacteristic pique. What was up with her? Maybe this thing with Editta was really getting to her.

"What am I going to do?" said Amanda. "I hate that guy. I mean, I don't hate *that* guy because I don't know him, but I hate Sherlock Holmes and everything about him, and—well, I *do* hate that guy because did you see how he looks? He's going to be terrible. And now he knows I hate him and Thrillkill is forcing me to be his big sister and that kid is going to cause me so much grief and what about all the other kids who heard me say that, and Sidebotham too?"

"You're making too much of this," Amphora said.

"Agreed," said Simon, astonishing everyone. He never agreed with her.

"I don't think so," said Amanda. She was pacing now.

"They'll get over it," said Simon. "Anyway, he looked fine to me."

"I don't think he looks bad at all," said Amphora. "It's refreshing when someone pays attention to their appearance."

"Yeah, I saw you noticing him," said Simon. "You looked like a dog discovering a steak." Amphora glared at him.

"He has a lovely voice," said Ivy.

"When did you hear his voice?" said Amphora. She looked startled for some reason Amanda couldn't fathom.

"He said something under his breath," said Ivy. "You didn't hear?"

"No," said Amphora.

"Well, he does," said Ivy.

"You girls are nuts," said Simon, shaking his head and walking off.

"Did you do what we talked about?" Ivy said to Amanda.

"What? Oh, you mean the texts?" She rummaged in her bag. "Got it." She held her phone at the ready. The light hit it at just the right angle and it glinted.

"Yes."

"What texts?" said Amphora, who seemed annoyed at having been left out.

"Have you heard anything from Editta?" said Amanda.

"What? No. Where is she? Why isn't she here?" Amphora seemed to be reading disaster into the question. She did that a lot.

"Exactly," said Ivy.

"We're going to text her three messages in quick succession and see if she answers," said Amanda.

"Oh, I see," said Amphora. "Like a pattern. She'll answer that."

"We hope so," said Ivy. "Amanda, please do it now."

"Okay." Amanda quickly thumbed until she had sent three identical texts in rapid fashion. The girls stood there for a second and

22

stared at the tiny screen. Nothing. "We have to give it some time. Maybe she's busy."

"Yes," said Ivy. "I'm sure that's it."

"Definitely," said Amphora, who didn't look at all convinced.

~◊~

"I need to tell you something," Amanda said to Ivy when Amphora had left. "It's important."

"Something bad?"

"It is bad, I'm afraid," said Amanda. "Maybe very bad."

"Oh no," said Ivy. "You'd better tell me quick."

Amanda explained what she'd overheard before class. As she revealed more and more of the detail, Ivy's expression grew increasingly serious until her brow was deeply creased with worry.

"This isn't good," she said. "We need to do something."

"Do what?" said Amanda. "We don't even know what's missing."

"We have to figure it out fast," said Ivy. "You're right. We've never heard the teachers act like this before. Something terrible is about to happen. Anything to do with the Moriartys can't be good. I need to know more. I'll bet I can pick up something if I nose around."

"Okay. Let's talk about this at lunch. Maybe Simon and Amphora can help."

"If they ever stop fighting. What is it with those two?"

"I don't know. They sure don't like each other."

"No. They don't."

~◊~

23

Amanda, Ivy, and Nigel scooted off to their fires and explosions class. They wished they'd taken it last term, when the school's garage had exploded as part of the class project. As they investigated the explosion and the fire it had started, the kids were unsure what to look for and how to preserve the evidence, but the teachers had structured the exercise to be difficult on purpose. They'd wanted to test the new class's skill at handling an unfamiliar and dangerous situation. In the end, only Holmes House, which was where Amanda, Ivy, Amphora, Simon, Editta, and Nick had been assigned, had cracked the mystery. The other houses, especially Van Helden House, which included David Wiffle and Gordon Bramble, had resented them, going so far as to complain that Holmes House had cheated, which had not gone over well with the powers that be. Holmes House's victory had helped melt Thrillkill's icy exterior and led to him asking Amanda to teach the storytelling class.

The first thing Amanda noticed when she arrived at Professor Pole's classroom was Scapulus Holmes sitting in the first row. Suddenly she remembered that she was supposed to take him under her wing and show him around. There was no way she could do that now. She'd rather be pulled apart by wild camels. Then she had a thought: maybe Thrillkill had forgotten. The kid looked like he could take care of himself just fine. He'd found his way around so far. What did he need her for? *She'd* done all right without a guide. What was the guy, five years old? He was a Holmes. She'd carry on normally and see what happened.

Professor Pole was an affable man in his forties. As a child he had been burned in a house fire, and half his face was scarred and some of his hair missing as a result. If you didn't know him, you might be afraid of him because he looked kind of scary, but once he spoke he was so funny and nice that you quickly forgot.

Not only was Professor Pole fun to be around, he was also brilliant. A physicist by trade, he solved astrophysics problems in his spare time, a pursuit he found relaxing. He also hunted for fossils and had even discovered some dinosaur bones on a dig in Montana. The class promised to be challenging, useful, and fun, and Amanda was looking forward to it, despite the fact that she'd heard it could be dangerous. She was getting used to risk now and wasn't nearly as worried as she'd been a few months before.

"Boo!" yelled Professor Pole while the students were still jabbering among themselves. A couple of the kids dropped things on the floor and one or two clutched their chests as if they'd had a heart attack. "Explosions. That's exactly how they occur. They're strong, sharp, loud, sudden, and almost always unexpected. But you can prepare yourselves for them, and that's one of the things we're going to learn how to do in this dynamite class. Ha ha!" He beamed, obviously proud of his little joke. A couple of the kids groaned, but quite a few of them broke into nervous laughter. Amanda felt her body tense up. She was just sure he was going to try to scare them again.

"You there, Mr. Bramble." Professor Pole motioned to Gordon. "Come up here, please. That's right. Don't be shy."

Gordon Bramble, a me-too sort of boy who normally relied on his friend David Wiffle to take the lead, looked embarrassed and confused, but he managed to get himself to the front of the class.

"Now, I want you to add this liquid to this beaker. Before you do, please put these goggles on." Professor Pole pointed to a clear vessel that contained glittering blue powder. It was sitting in a pan. The liquid he was referring to resided in a smaller beaker that looked like the larger beaker's child. Amanda had visions of Dr. Frankenstein and his monster. What a great film that was with Boris Karloff. She should watch it again.

Gordon took the goggles and nervously fitted them over his eyes. They made him look like a deep-sea diver. He eyed Professor Pole tentatively, as if to say, "Please don't make me do this."

"All right, go," said the professor. Gordon stood stock-still. "It's okay. I promise."

Shaking visibly, Gordon held his arm out as far as it would go and gingerly picked up the beaker with the clear liquid. Then, standing as far away from the large beaker as he could, he poured about a drop into it.

"More," said Professor Pole. "Do the whole thing at once. Upsy daisy."

This baby talk seemed to embarrass Gordon so much that he stood closer to the large beaker and dumped the clear liquid in, whereupon a sparkly blue explosion blasted out of it and overflowed into the pan. It made a snapping sound, like a whip being cracked. It was more show than danger, though. The stuff didn't even get on Gordon's clothes. He winced and turned away, then slowly pivoted around and, seeing what had happened, smiled from ear to ear.

"Awesome," he said. "Can I do it again?"

"Yes, you may," said the professor. "How about a different color? But first, let me explain what just happened. The large beaker contained baking soda with blue dye and glitter. The smaller beaker contained white vinegar. Perhaps you can smell it." Gordon wrinkled his nose and nodded. "The baking soda and the vinegar reacted and caused the mixture to explode. So for you cooks out there, never mix those two ingredients together or you'll have a birthday cake to remember. Now, Mr. Bramble, would you like to do the honors?"

"Professor, Professor," yelled out David Wiffle. "Can I try?"

"You'll get your turn, Mr. Wiffle. Let's see what Mr. Bramble can cook up."

Now that he knew he wasn't going to die, Gordon really got into the experiment. He mixed several different colors of dye and glitter and put them all into the same container. The explosion they created looked like the Fourth of July. He got so excited that he managed to trip. As he started to fall, Scapulus Holmes raced to the front of the room and caught him before he crashed to the floor. Now Gordon was embarrassed again. He murmured a word of thanks and asked if it was okay to return to his seat. Professor Pole nodded.

"Thank you, Mr. Holmes," said the professor. "That was quick thinking."

"Thank you, sir," said Holmes. Ivy was right. He did have a nice voice. He was probably a good singer. As if Amanda cared.

As he turned to go back to his seat, Holmes caught her eye. Oh no. He was probably out to get her after that awful thing she'd said. He stared for a second, then slowly began to smile in a way that seemed to say, "Thanks for the joke." In spite of herself, Amanda felt her lips widen, and before she knew it she was grinning too. The boy gave her a wink. Wait a minute. Was he serious or making fun of her? Whatever he was up to, she would *not* be made a fool of again. She felt herself stiffen. Holmes and Moriarty, Moriarty and Holmes. They were two sides of the same coin. She couldn't believe she'd ever thought the ancestral Moriarty was cool. Well, she was over that bad girl stage. From now on she would give these guys the disrespect they deserved. She frowned. Seeing the change in her, Holmes's face fell and he turned away.

Despite Holmes's odd behavior, and despite the fact that Professor Pole's program that simulated fires and explosions reminded Amanda of the *Explosions!* game Nick was so crazy about, she enjoyed the rest of the class and looked forward to the exercises the teacher had assigned. The students were not to try any more real-life experiments for the first few weeks of the class. Rather, they would simulate various types of disasters digitally, starting with the garage explosion and fire that had kicked off the class project last term. After that they would tackle electrical fires and gas explosions before moving on to dynamite and lightning fires. Professor Pole's graphics were incredibly cool, but the real power of his program was in the physics and chemistry, which he'd worked on in consultation with experts around the world. Later on the kids would do lab experiments, but only if they achieved certain scores on the simulations and with strict safety protocols in place. Everyone was super excited, especially Simon, who started planning all sorts of weird conflagrations. He had some nutty idea about seeing if he could change Earth's tilt so he could fix global warming. Amanda and Ivy were looking forward to seeing *that*.

"You can tease me all you want," he said. "Glitter explosions in a beaker are nothing. The point of all this training is to solve big, important problems. If you must know, I wrote to that professor at UCLA over the break, the one who invented the microscope/cell phone apparatus we used to detect the sugar virus last term. I told him we used the lens from my glasses and it worked great. I asked him if he thinks that's worth an academic paper, and I'm sure he'll say yes."

Simon and Professor Kindseth had discovered a way to turn a cell phone into a powerful microscope using an attachment manufactured on a 3D printer. The only catch had been that they didn't have the proper lens for it, that is until they hit on the idea of using one from Simon's coke bottle glasses. The microscope had worked beautifully, and they had discovered that the cook's pink sugar was actually tainted with a destructive virus.

"That's admirable," said Amanda.

"I'll say," said Ivy. "I'm impressed."

"I think it's nuts," said Amphora, invading their little circle. "You're twelve. There's no way you could publish a scientific paper. Fugeddaboutit." She sounded silly trying to affect a Brooklyn accent with her posh London/Cambridge way of talking.

"I don't care about your opinion, dodo," said Simon. "You know, one day your frivolous behavior is going to come back to bite you. You should get a clue and grow up."

"You're a prat," said Amphora. "I'm going to blow you up in my simulations. It will make the class so much more fun."

"You know what, you two?" said Ivy. "You're getting so predictable you're boring me. I've had enough. Come on, Amanda."

Ivy grabbed Amanda's arm, pulled Nigel's lead, and headed off toward the Holmes House common room. Amanda glanced behind her. Simon and Amphora were still arguing.

3

PROFESSOR REDLEAF'S SURPRISE

Amanda had never seen Ivy so edgy. She was normally the calmest person in the world, but something had rattled her. It couldn't be Editta's disappearance, which wasn't even a disappearance yet. And it couldn't be Simon and Amphora's constant bickering because Ivy was used to that. What was up?

The two girls ducked into the Holmes House common room, which this day had been decorated to look like an airplane hangar. Amanda found it baffling. She didn't know anything about planes, other than what she'd seen on the trip over from L.A., and she couldn't figure out what she was looking at. Ivy dragged her over to a couch and practically threw her down. Nigel sat next to Amanda and let his tongue loll out.

"What's going on?" Ivy demanded. She seemed more impatient than Amanda had ever seen her. Somehow her dark glasses made her look menacing when she was like that, which was weird considering that Ivy was less than five feet tall.

"Are you okay?" said Amanda, staring at her from this angle and that, trying to read her.

"No, I'm not okay. Something bad is going on around here and we have to find out what it is." The reflection from her sunglasses flashed as she moved her head.

"You mean what I told you earlier? How do you know about that?" She leaned in and kept her voice low so their conversation would be private.

"How do I know about anything?" said Ivy too loudly. Amanda jumped back as if she'd been hit. "I've heard stuff. You know how good my hearing is."

"Why didn't you tell me this before?" Amanda tried lowering her voice again.

"There wasn't time," said Ivy softly, getting the message. "I know something is up with the teachers. They're talking about catastrophe. We need to figure out what this is and fix it. They sound like they haven't any idea what to do, and that worries me half to death."

Amanda delivered the nutshell version of what she'd heard outside Thrillkill's office. Ivy kept shaking her head. Nigel wagged his tail against her, *whomp, whomp, whomp,* and she scratched her leg. Between Ivy's red hair and Nigel's golden coat, they looked like life itself against the backdrop of the hangar. Amanda wondered what it would be like to have colored hair. Brown was okay, but it wasn't very interesting.

"Yes, that confirms what I've been hearing," said Ivy when Amanda had finished. "What worries me the most is that the teachers seem so disorganized. I've never seen them like this. Do you think Mavis is really going to escape? If she does, maybe she'll break Blixus out of Strangeways too."

"I don't know," said Amanda. "They've gone up against the Moriartys before. Why should this time be any different?" A thought struck her. Maybe losing Nick had made the criminals more desperate and dangerous. It probably wasn't a good idea to raise the possibility, though. Everyone was sick to death of Nick, and every time she mentioned his name she felt like she was imposing.

"That's what I can't figure out," said Ivy. "Unless they have whatever it is the teachers lost. Do you have any idea what it could be?"

"Not a clue."

Amanda got up and started pacing, then remembered that she had to stay close to Ivy to keep anyone who walked in from hearing their conversation. She caught sight of the new clock Nick had hung up after breaking the old one, which had bothered Amanda with its loud ticking. Nick again. Why did everything have to remind her of him? If this kept up she'd do poorly in her classes. She had to exorcise him. Maybe she should learn to meditate. Or throw darts at his picture. Editta would probably have stuck pins in his effigy. Where was that girl anyway?

"Me either," said Ivy. "We're going to have to do it soon, though."

"Yes. Maybe we should talk tonight."

"Definitely. I'm a little worried about discussing all this in front of Amphora, though. She seems so distracted with all that fighting."

"I know what you mean," said Amanda. "She and Simon have gotten worse. Maybe they stored it all up over the break. Let's meet somewhere we don't usually go and she won't look for us."

"One of the labs?"

"How about the disguise room up on the top floor?" Amanda felt the most at home there. It was a theatrical place, full of costumes, wigs, makeup, and props. A filmmaker's dream.

"Yes, that sounds like a good idea. Eight o'clock?"

"You're on."

Amanda was really looking forward to cyberforensics class. The previous term when she'd needed to get into the Moriartys' computer she'd had no idea how to get past the logon screen. After that she'd promised herself she'd become an expert so that would never happen again.

The class was taught by Professor Redleaf, a white hat hacker of mysterious origin who was rumored to have broken into some of the most sensitive computer networks on the planet. A number of the older students said she came from the Amazon jungle. Others said she had been born in the heart of Africa. She always wore a white hat of one sort or another, Amanda guessed for symbolic reasons, and appeared to be completely emotionless, speaking in a voice that resembled a dial tone. She also seemed to be full of secrets, which wasn't unusual at Legatum, but her manner implied that her secrets were rather more sinister than those of the other teachers. There was an air of magic about her, which was saying something considering that detectives are among the least magical people in the world. What really floored Amanda, however, was that as soon as Scapulus Holmes walked into the class, Professor Redleaf seemed to know him and even smiled at him, whereupon he smiled back and said, "Good morning, Professor. How's that Silver Fern project coming along?"

Showoff! How did they know each other? Did this mean that Holmes was some hacking genius? Was he going to be the teacher's pet? Amanda could feel herself fuming. She realized she was being irrational but she didn't care. Sometimes irrationality was called for, and this seemed like one of those times. Who did he think he was, anyway? Here not half a day and already acting like the great Sherlock.

Professor Redleaf didn't answer Holmes's question out loud, but somehow Amanda got the feeling she had conveyed the answer anyway. Holmes seemed satisfied with whatever invisible message she had delivered and settled in his chair. Professor Redleaf started the class immediately after that, and told them that their project for the term was to divide into teams that would simultaneously try to hack into each other's computers.

Instead of going by the school's houses—Holmes, Van Helden, Dupin, and Father Brown—the students would be assigned randomly using an algorithm Professor Redleaf had written. Amanda was disappointed to find that she wasn't on the same team as her friends, who had been split up as well, but when she learned that she would be working with the Wiffle kid, she just about had a fit, and so did he. Whiny brat that he was, he asked the teacher if he could be transferred, a question Professor Redleaf wouldn't dignify with an answer. Normally Amanda and the kid found themselves competing, and the idea of working together not only didn't sit well with either of them, but seemed to make them hate each other even more. Amanda had no idea how she was going to manage this. The only consolation was that she wasn't on the same team as Holmes and wouldn't have to listen to his bragging. Not that she knew for sure that he would brag. She just figured it was in his genes. That and winking, apparently.

Amanda knew the class was going to be hard, but when Professor Redleaf offered an overview full of unfamiliar jargon (she'd heard of SSL and IP addresses, but that was about it), she realized that it was going to be way more difficult than she'd imagined. She was conversant with a variety of media capture and editing programs, but the technical details that made them all work were another thing. Apparently Amphora was feeling the same way because when Amanda glanced at her, her mouth was hanging open. Ivy seemed unperturbed, thank goodness, and Simon, well Simon was eating the whole thing up with a relish Amanda had seen only when he'd made the smartphone microscope last term. Needless to say, Holmes was smiling as if he knew something the others didn't, which no doubt he did. Oh great. Another freakish Holmes.

Suddenly it occurred to her that perhaps they would *all* emerge from the school as freaks. Look at the kind of observational skills they were developing. They were so attentive and detail-oriented that they might never be able to turn off all that analyzing and would be beset by runaway trivia racing through their heads day and night. And what about the self-defense training? Could they ever walk down a street again without imagining that everyone they saw posed a physical threat? No wonder all the teachers were so weird. This stuff warped a person. It had certainly warped Sherlock Holmes, but funnily enough not her ancestor, G. Lestrade. He was too dumb to get it, and yet his stupidity had saved him and let him live a normal life. Maybe she *should* get out now, before she turned into a freakazoid.

Suddenly she realized that something was going on up front and she was so lost in her own morbid thoughts that she was missing it. Professor Redleaf was standing there staring at her screen with a horrified look on her face. She looked at Scapulus Holmes and said sharply, "Mr. Holmes, please see me after class."

During the rest of the session Professor Redleaf seemed distracted. Everyone was jumpy as a result—except Holmes, who remained stolid. Just watching him convinced Amanda that Simon wasn't the world's most irritating nerd anymore. Holmes had just bumped him out of first place.

The first thing Amanda thought as she headed for lunch was that Professor Redleaf's alarming surprise must have had something to do with the missing item. The second thing was, what was wrong with Ivy? And the third thing was that Editta was still AWOL. What was going on?

When she arrived at the dining room she could see that everything looked different from the way it had earlier. The tables, which had been arranged lengthwise at 8:00 a.m., were now pushed together to form geometric shapes. The sideboards with beverages and condiments now stood smack in the middle of the room and sported bright-colored cloths decorated with abstract designs. The normal silverware had been replaced with clunky implements that were so heavy and awkwardly designed that it was hard to eat with them. And each plate featured a great big hole in the middle. How you were supposed to eat off those was anyone's guess. It seemed that the décor gremlins had lost their minds along with everyone else. Or was this supposed to be a test? Maybe the students were supposed to rig up something before they put food on the plates so it wouldn't drip through. You never knew around here.

Whatever the intent, Simon had solved the problem by placing a glass over the hole in his plate, which seemed to do the trick. The other kids did likewise, except for Holmes, whom Amanda caught sticking a dessert plate under his. Typical. He had to do everything better than everyone else.

After placing a small portion of spinach lasagna around her glass, Amanda said to Ivy, Simon, and Amphora, "Something big is happening."

"Something big is always happening around here," said Simon. "That's what it means to be a detective." The sauce from his lasagna was starting to separate from the solid parts and roll toward the glass. Amanda wondered if it would make it through the hole.

"No, I mean something big and very bad," said Amanda.

"Ah, this must have something to do with Nick, then," said Simon, whereupon Amphora glared at him so hard that he stuck his tongue out.

"Actually, I don't know," said Amanda. "Maybe it does." She didn't like the idea that Nick had wreaked even more havoc than they knew about, but she couldn't discount the possibility.

"Well, what is it?" said Amphora. She hadn't quite managed to get her glass in the right place, and her food was definitely seeking the hole in the plate.

"Something really important to the school is missing and the teachers are going nuts. Thrillkill has completely lost it. When I showed up at his office this morning, he'd completely forgotten that he asked me to be there. He was all, 'Oh, hello, Miss Lester. Fancy meeting you here.'"

36

"Did he have his hair dryer?" Simon said. He was referring to the hair dryer the headmaster always carried in order to melt icicles. He had a morbid fear of them and destroyed them when they crossed his path. This late in the year (mid-April) there weren't any, so Simon's question was obviously designed to provoke rather than elucidate. Was something wrong with him too? Come to think of it, he *was* being more obnoxious than usual.

"Simon, cut it out," said Amanda. "This is serious."

"Sorry," said Simon, looking down at his plate. The food had pooled around the sides of the glass, which were red with marinara sauce. It was getting to be a huge mess.

"Whatever it is, the teachers are fighting because of it." Amanda's food was pooling too. Simon was usually so good with engineering problems. Apparently his solution to this one needed some tweaking, however.

"Which teachers?" said Amphora, looking toward the kitchen.

"Scribbish, Hoxby, Peaksribbon, Mukherjee, I think Pargeter, and some others whose voices I didn't recognize."

"Were they yelling?" said Simon.

"Pretty much, yes," said Amanda, trying to eat faster than the sauce could run. She wasn't winning the battle.

"She's right," said Ivy. "I've been hearing things too." Her plate was nice and neat. How did she do it?

"Oh?" said Amphora. "What things?" She looked at the kitchen again.

"Something important is missing and the teachers are blaming each other," said Ivy. "I don't know what it is or why it matters, but every time I hear them discussing it they act as if it's a disaster."

"Yes, that's what I've gathered too," said Amanda.

"Does this have anything to do with that phone call we heard Professor Feeney make last term?" said Simon, who now had a marinara mustache.

"What phone call?" said Ivy, who didn't.

"When Amanda and I were analyzing the sugar virus in the lab, we overheard Professor Feeney out in the hall talking to someone about something that was missing," said Simon. "She seemed upset."

"That was quite a while ago," said Ivy. "I didn't hear anything last term. I got the impression this was all new."

"It doesn't seem so," said Amanda. "What I can't figure out is why things have exploded now, though."

"We have to investigate," said Simon, who was definitely looking clownish. All he needed was a red nose. "You don't suppose this is another class project, do you?"

"Agreed, and no," said Ivy. "The teachers can be diabolical but this feels like a real crisis. And I've never heard of a second class project for first-years. Fern would have told me." Fern was Ivy's sister, and a fifth-year student. She knew everything about the school and Ivy often relied on her for critical information. "But when we do investigate, we can't let anyone know what we're doing. We don't want the teachers to know that we're aware of whatever it is that's going on, and we don't want to alarm the other students."

"We're going to have to search the school," said Simon. Amanda did not want to see what was under his plate. For that matter, she was afraid to lift her own. She hoped the teachers weren't expecting them to clean the dining room after this little adventure.

"But we don't know what we're looking for," said Amphora. She looked down at her plate. "Don't you think this lasagna is amazing?" Everyone stopped eating and stared at her.

"I think we're going to have to go on the assumption that we'll know it when we see it, like what happened with the class project last term," said Ivy, ignoring Amphora's question. She was referring to the fact that when Headmaster Thrillkill and the teachers had presented the instructions for the class project, they had refused to tell them what the mystery was—only that they'd know it when they saw it. And they had. The garage had exploded in the middle of the night. You couldn't miss that.

"But how big is it?" said Amphora. "What if it's really, really tiny, like a piece of jewelry? How could we possibly find that?"

"It's a problem," said Amanda. "The teachers know what it is, and *they* can't find it. I don't think our chances are very good."

"Do you think we should ask Scapulus to help us?" said Simon.

"I knew it," said Amanda. "You like him, don't you?"

"Sure. Why not? He seems like a smart guy."

"That's your standard for whether you like people?" said Amphora.

"Not completely," said Simon. "But mostly." The implication was clear: he didn't think Amphora was smart and that was why the two didn't get along. Amphora sighed so loud you could have heard her in the kitchen with dishes clattering and the refrigerator cycling.

"So do you?" said Simon.

"What?" said Amanda.

"Think we should ask him."

"Absolutely not."

"I knew it. You're afraid he's smarter than you are, aren't you?"

"SIMON!" said all three girls together, so loudly that everyone in the room, including Holmes, looked at them.

"Keep your voice down," Amanda said. "That isn't true and you know it. And by the way, you've got a red mustache." She indicated where it would be on her own face if she had one.

"I know what I saw and what I'm seeing now," said Simon. "And so what? I mean about the mustache." He felt his upper lip.

"Simon Binkle, you are the most exasperating person at Legatum," said Ivy. Amanda's mouth fell open. Ivy never talked like this. "Shut up. Now look, Amanda doesn't like Scapulus because she doesn't know him yet. In fact I'm not even sure she doesn't like him. What do you say, Amanda?"

"I don't know him," said Amanda, trying to wriggle out gracefully.

"I think he's cute," said Amphora dreamily.

"You think everyone is cute," said Simon.

"Not you," said Amphora.

"STOP IT, all of you!" yelled Ivy. Amanda had never heard her yell. "You're all acting like children. This is serious. Stop being petty and let's figure out what to do." She pushed her plate away. She'd barely touched her food.

By this time the entire dining room was staring at them. David Wiffle looked like he was going to say something but instead broke into a huge grin. Probably planning some revenge or other, Amanda thought. Why couldn't the guy chill out?

"We're all going to have to spy on the teachers," said Ivy. "I don't like invading anyone's privacy, but detectives aren't called snoops for nothing." She grinned. "That was a good one, wasn't it?"

"Very cool," said Amanda. She was glad to see Ivy making jokes. Things had been getting way too serious. "But how are we going to do that? Follow them around until they get together and listen outside their doors?"

"I've got an idea," said Simon. "I can make sound magnifiers. We'll all be able to hear like Ivy."

"Really?" said Amphora. "Aren't you worried they'll catch us?" She pushed her plate away as well, exposing a big red spot.

"Nah," said Simon. "How are they going to tell from so far away?" He lifted up his own plate, took one look underneath, and lowered it again. Amanda was sure the spot underneath was worse than Amphora's, but no more so than her own.

"I don't think it's exactly criminal to listen to people who aren't behind closed doors," said Ivy. "I'm sure they talk in public too." She lowered her glass to Nigel's mouth. The dog lapped loudly. This little ritual always astonished Amanda, who never would have been able to get away with something like that at home.

"I don't even mind listening at doors," she said, "if it's that serious. And I'm pretty sure they won't be watching us to see what we're doing. They seem completely preoccupied."

"I agree," said Ivy. "I'm not worried about being caught. How long do you think it will take to make these things, Simon?"

"Dunno, but I'll start researching right after class. Say, what did you think of Redleaf today?" He popped a marinara-drenched grape into his mouth.

"Very weird," said Amanda. "She looked like someone had just told her World War III had started."

"Agreed," said Amphora. "And she and Scapulus seemed to know each other from somewhere else. Think all of this weirdness is connected?"

"It might be," said Ivy. "We should listen super carefully. But I'm also worried about Editta and I can't see how she could be involved in any of this." She felt under the table. "I'll get you some more water in a minute, Nigel."

"I'll get it," said Amanda, not for the first time. She was always glad to help with Nigel. He was such a sweet dog, and she'd never been allowed to have one of her own.

"Nope," said Simon. "Too flighty."

"She's not flighty," said Amphora. "She's really talented at math."

"Doesn't mean she isn't flighty," said Simon. "All that mumbo jumbo she believes in." He made a gesture. Rather than mumbo jumbo, it looked like he was in pain.

"Okay, that's it," said Ivy. "From now on, any time one of us makes a negative remark, we put 20p in a jar. If you get five nasty remarks, it goes up to 50p."

"That's not fair," said Amphora, eyeing the kitchen door again.

"Why do you keep looking over there?" said Simon, popping another grape into his mouth and chomping for emphasis.

"I'm not looking anywhere," said Amphora, making a face.

"Yes you are. You keep looking at the kitchen."

"I'm just wondering if they're going to bring out anything more interesting. I don't like grapes."

"You don't need anything more interesting," said Simon. "You look good with all that weight off."

"Simon!" yelled Ivy. "Twenty p."

His face fell. "But I complimented her."

"Backhanded compliment. Twenty p. Here, give it to me. I'll set up a jar." She held out her hand.

Simon dug into his pocket and practically slapped the change into Ivy's palm. "Madoff," he said.

"And another twenty p," said Ivy, who was beginning to lose her temper again.

"I think you should go charge David Wiffle 20p," said Simon, crossing his arms.

"He isn't part of this," said Ivy, crossing hers in exactly the same way. How did she know he'd done that?

"He's always insulting people," said Simon petulantly.

"Yes, but he's not our responsibility. Anyway, back to Editta. She hasn't answered your texts, has she, Amanda?"

"No."

"This isn't like her. She doesn't like being left out of things," said Ivy, uncrossing.

"She'll turn up," said Simon, mirroring her. "Probably just has the Monday blues."

"I don't think so," said Ivy. "You don't suppose the Moriarty gang has got hold of her, do you?"

"Don't be ridiculous," said Simon. "What would they want with her? You're starting to sound like her."

"Fifty p!" yelled Ivy. Simon passed the money to her through Amanda this time. She could tell he was getting exasperated as well.

"I don't trust anyone," said Amanda. "Those Moriartys have a lot of connections. Any one of them could have kidnapped her. And by the way, speaking of the Moriartys, how do we know Holmes is who he says he is? Maybe he's another mole." Nick, his mother, the cook, and the doctor had infiltrated the school last term and everyone was paranoid about the possibility of that happening again.

"Yes, how did Nick get into Legatum in the first place?" said Amphora.

"Forgery," said Simon. "And you're not going to charge me 20p for saying that."

"No," said Ivy. "That's perfectly all right to say. I imagine forgery is part of it. That and planting witnesses. It's weird, though. How could the teachers fall for all that?"

"People see what they want to see," said Simon. "Like Amanda wanting Nick to be Prince Charming."

"Fifty p!" said Ivy.

"Hey, no fair. I only had four 20 ps. I've got one more to go," said Simon, folding his arms again.

"We need Editta to keep track of this stuff," said Amphora.

"Will you forgot all those pence and listen?" said Amanda. "How do we know Holmes is who he says he is?"

"Okay, fine," said Simon. "We'll check him out."

"Thank you," said Amanda. "I'll feel better being sure."

"Dahlinks," came a loud voice from the door to the hall. It was one of the décor gremlins. He was wearing a bright red tux. While the two gremlins always wore amazing clothes, Amanda thought this was a bit over the top. "You're all looking mahvelous today," he said.

"Thank you, Mr. Dropoff," said Amphora, beaming. "And you. Nifty threads."

"Thank you, my dear. What's over there, dahlink? Something going on in the kitchen?" He glanced at the door.

"No, sir. Not a thing. Hello, Mr. Updown." She smiled warmly at the second gremlin, who was wearing a torn rainbow-striped T-shirt and ripped jeans.

"Hello, dears," said the second gremlin. "Do you have a moment?"

"Uh . . ." said Simon.

"Yes, of course," said Ivy, motioning to the seat next to her.

"Good," said Alexei Dropoff, dropping into it. "We'd like you to settle a dispute for us, dears. Hello, Nigel, dahlink." He gave the dog a warm look. Nigel wagged his tail.

"Oh, I don't know," said Amanda, who didn't like getting in the middle of people's arguments.

"We'd be delighted," said Ivy. "What's the issue?"

"Well," said Noel Updown, slinking into a chair next to Simon, "you see, one of us thinks you students are more likely to notice our little details on Mondays and Wednesdays, and the other thinks Tuesdays and Thursdays. I won't tell you which of us thinks which so as not to prejudice you."

"You don't have to," said Alexei. "It's obvious which one of us is correct." He gave Noel a smug look.

"Twenty p," yelled Simon. Amphora kicked him under the table. "Ouch."

Ivy elbowed Amphora. "Well, uh, I don't know," said Amphora.

"That's an invalid question," said Simon. "Your assumptions are wrong." There were no grapes left to underscore his statement, so he just bored into the gremlins' eyes with his own.

"Of course they're not wrong," said Noel, sticking his nose in the air.

"Outrageous," said Alexei, turning his head away snootily.

"You're assuming that it's one or the other and nothing else," said Simon. "Or that there's a difference at all. Professor Ducey would fail you." The logic teacher definitely would have taken points off for the gremlins' flawed assumptions.

Ivy was looking like she wasn't sure whether to charge Simon another 50 p. Amanda whispered "Uh uh" into her ear to forestall any punitive action.

"I beg your pardon," said Noel. "That isn't true at all. It's a scientific fact that people do one thing on Mondays and Wednesdays and another on Tuesdays and Thursdays."

"Save us," said Simon. "Another Editta."

"Fifty p," said Ivy, holding out her hand.

"Uh uh," said Simon.

"Uh huh," said Amphora, holding out her own hand.

"I've had enough of this," said Simon. "I've got work to do." He stood up and left the room noisily without looking back.

"Terrible posture, that one," said Alexei. "But now we can address the question properly." He looked disapprovingly at Simon's plate, which he had not bussed.

"Indeed," said Noel. "So what is your answer?" He looked at the three girls.

"Well, sirs," said Ivy kindly, "I would say Mondays and Wednesdays."

"Told you so," said Alexei looking smugly at Noel.

"Not correct," said Noel, giving Alexei a snide look.

"Why do you say that, Ivy?" said Amphora.

"Because we're more keyed up and therefore more alert on Mondays, and we've mellowed out a little by Tuesday, so we're less observant then. Then on Wednesdays, once we've had a chance to adjust to the rhythm of the week, our minds are sharp again."

"Not so," said Noel looking crestfallen. "It's the exact opposite."

"How so?" said Amanda.

"On Mondays you're too traumatized by the change of routine to think straight. By Tuesday you have relaxed. On Wednesday, you congratulate yourself for having such a productive Tuesday, and you let your guard down. Then on Thursday you feel guilty so you buck up again."

"That's quite an interesting analysis," said Ivy.

"And correct," said Noel, folding his arms.

"And incorrect," said Alexei, folding his. Amanda thought they might come to blows.

"Correct."

"Incorrect."

"Gentlemen, gentlemen," said Ivy. "I think both hypotheses have merit. Would you like to conduct a scientific experiment to see which is correct?"

"Absolutely not," said Alexei huffily.

45

"Rubbish," said Noel abruptly.

"Well, then," said Ivy, "I'm not sure there's another way to be certain."

"I am certain already," said Alexei.

"As am I," said Noel. "Thank you for your time. Have a pleasant day." And with that, the gremlins got up and walked out, continuing to argue.

"That was interesting," said Amphora, watching them leave.

"Yes," said Amanda, thinking that if Alexei got marinara sauce on his tux it wouldn't show. "I wonder who's right."

"Simon," said Ivy, barely squelching a giggle. "I just didn't want to say so in front of them."

4

NICK'S SECRETS

With all this unexpected drama going on, Amanda was starting to freak out a little. It seemed as though everything she'd finally started adjusting to was falling apart, and there were signs that things were going to get a whole lot worse before they got better. At least she had her storytelling class to look forward to. This was something she knew through and through, and she was excited by the prospect of sharing the object of her passion.

She'd spent some time preparing at her parents' in London, but with her father still recovering from his kidnapping at the hands of the Moriartys, she'd found it difficult to concentrate. Ever since his ordeal, her father had become a shadow of his former self. He'd lost enthusiasm for his work at the Crown Prosecution Service, a position he'd aspired to all his life, and was talking about quitting and going off to find himself. What finding himself? Herb Lester, scion of the Lestrade family, had spent forever basking in the legacy of his ancestor, prosecuting criminals and making the world a safer place. *That* was his self. What else could there be? At least that was how Amanda's mother looked at it.

Amanda, however, could see his point. To her way of thinking, he'd spent his life in a straitjacket, trying to live up to an ideal that had never existed. The really sad part was that everyone *except* her parents knew what Lestrade really was: a bumbler. To them he was a god, and they had been in thrall to him.

On the other hand, Lila Lester, a successful mystery novelist, hadn't changed at all, or at least not that Amanda could see. Overbearing and opinionated, she was still pushing both her husband and her daughter to do what *she* wanted them to do. No grief, no empathy, no sensitivity whatsoever. In fact she was flourishing now that she had the two of them to talk at, which she did incessantly. If her husband's near death hadn't mellowed her, what would?

With her parents' woes adding to her feelings of loss, Amanda had started digging into her class preparation in earnest on the train ride from London to Windermere. She had devised a brilliant way to get across basic story concepts, which was to use examples from the Harry Potter stories. She'd thrashed around until she'd come up with that one, trying out one dumb idea after another, but now she was getting excited. Harry Potter had everything: a likeable underdog, a powerful and shadowy villain, fascinating supporting characters, high stakes, suspense, a rich world, and FUN. It was perfect! She wanted desperately to get back to it, but with so many distractions she wasn't sure when that would be, especially with Thrillkill wanting something else from her.

After lunch the first-years went to their crime lab class, which built upon the introductory course from last term. Professor Stegelmeyer, never a pussycat at the best of times, was surly and rumpled, which, given that he usually looked like a Marine, was almost alarming. Amanda's lab partner this time was Dreidel Pomfritter, a kid she didn't know very well. He seemed okay, at least so far. Short, with glasses and a dark brown crew cut, he was courteous and competent but not very interesting. Last term she had partnered with Nick and he'd been a blast—for a while, anyway. Come to think of it, maybe it was better that Dreidel wasn't so much fun. Then she wouldn't get attached or sidetracked and everything wouldn't blow up again.

After Crime Lab, Amanda betook herself to Headmaster Thrillkill's office as requested. Surprise, surprise, he seemed distracted. She must have sat there for two minutes, during which time he barely looked at her. Then there was a knock at the door and Scapulus Holmes walked in, whistling. Amanda hated whistling. It was so Huck Finn. Not that there was anything wrong with Huck Finn per se. He was just so read-fifty-pages-by-Friday-and-then-we'll-have-a-test, which she could do without.

At last Thrillkill, glassy-eyed from the effort of staring at whatever had transfixed him, looked up from his computer. "Ah, Miss Lester, Mr. Holmes. Just the two people I want to see." Well of course they were the people he wanted to see. He'd asked them there, hadn't he? Come to think of it, Amanda wasn't sure whether Thrillkill had invited Holmes or the boy was worming his way into her territory unbidden. But about thirty seconds later she found out.

"I have a task for you two," said Thrillkill. Them? Together? This didn't sound good. "I want you to make a training film. You have thirty days." Amanda couldn't believe what she was hearing. Holmes make a film? With her? Why him? What could he possibly know about filmmaking? Then Thrillkill dropped a bombshell. "Miss Lester, I'm afraid you will have to postpone your storytelling class. There isn't time to do both."

What?! That Holmes. This was all his fault. How dare he mess with the one thing she was excited about? What a waste of her talents—working on a training film with some newbie—a kid who wasn't even there last term and couldn't possibly know as much about anything as the rest of the first-years. It was an outrageous request. She felt like screaming.

"Your topic is cyberforensics. I've made a list of the concepts I want you to cover. Please set a time to start work. I expect you to keep me up to date on your progress with a daily report. This is a critical project. Professor Redleaf needs all the help she can get. There's too much important material for her to cover alone. Questions?"

Amanda didn't dare open her mouth for fear she'd lose control. Holmes simply shook his head and said, "No, sir. Thank you, sir." How original.

"Now then," said Thrillkill, "I would like a project plan in forty-eight hours. Understood?"

"Yes, sir," they said in unison, although Amanda was looking at her feet when she spoke.

"Good enough. Mr. Holmes, you are excused." *Mr. Holmes? What about me?* "Miss Lester, I have another job for you." *Oh great. Now what?*

"Now I know this is going to be difficult, but I have complete confidence in you. You will do this because it's critically important, and I know you will put the good of the school ahead of your personal feelings." This did not sound promising. Amanda braced herself.

"I would like you to help search Nick Muffet's room. The school wants to reassess the damage he might have caused. Of course this won't be the first time we've searched it, but we want to be even more thorough. I understand that this will be unpleasant for you, but you knew him better than anyone else. You may be able to spot important evidence the rest of us have missed. Miss Lester?" Amanda was looking down again. Thrillkill lowered his head and peered up at her, trying to catch her eye. It was a gesture of submission, an extremely rare one for him.

It didn't help. Amanda felt herself about to go ballistic. She was the last person who should be searching Nick's room, and it wasn't because girls weren't normally allowed in the boys' dorm. The idea was unthinkable. She couldn't take one more blow. But how could she refuse? Thrillkill had a point. She *was* the best qualified and the detectives did need her help.

But it would be excruciating, especially coming on the heels of the two things that had just occurred: losing her storytelling seminar and having to work with *that* kid. She wouldn't just be searching through a bit of this and that. She would have to look through Nick's most personal possessions.

"When do you want me to do this?" Amanda said, trying to keep her voice steady.

50

"Right now," said Thrillkill. "You don't have any commitments at this instant, do you?"

"No, sir."

"Excellent. Let's begin then, shall we?"

Amanda and Thrillkill made their way to the boys' dorm, which was situated in the southeast corner of the main building. As they entered, the headmaster placed himself in front of her and called out, "Girl in dorm. Make yourself decent," then kept repeating his warning over and over. At one point she caught a glimpse of a boy in his underwear—one of the older students—but it was so quick that it barely registered. As they passed through, boys' heads kept emerging from doorways and she could hear a lot of whispering. She had no idea whether the boys were simply curious or outright mocking her, but she was so miserable she didn't care. Anyway, she'd been teased so much for being Lestrade's descendant that insults didn't bother her anymore—except when Nick had said those awful things. His vitriol had just about destroyed her.

Nick's room was on the top floor. Ever since the tragedy it had stood empty, his two roommates, Philip Puppybreath and Gavin Niven, having moved into David Wiffle's room. Amanda could barely stand to look inside, let alone step over the threshold, but Thrillkill pushed in and she had no choice.

The room was as neat as a pin, although Amanda wasn't sure how a pin could be considered neat. She didn't know if Nick or his roommates had kept things that way or the investigators had straightened everything up before they left. A Batman poster hung on the wall, presumably Nick's, the roommates no doubt having removed whatever decoration they owned. Amanda could see holes in the wall where their pictures might have hung, although those might have been there for years.

The room held three beds, two of them stripped bare. The third was covered with a heavy dark blue quilt with white shapes on it. It looked like the night sky. Amanda thought she could even see the Big Dipper. Nick had good taste.

The room also held three small wooden dressers, three nightstands, three tiny desks, one of which supported a gooseneck lamp, and one not overly generous closet. An uncomfortable-looking wooden chair was nestled under each desk. A large window outfitted with flimsy drapes overlooked the expansive east side of the campus. The room was as bare bones as Amanda's, and especially depressing because of its vacancy.

"This is it," said Thrillkill. "Let's dig in."

It didn't seem that there was much to dig into. The room was so bare that searching it seemed a futile exercise, but Amanda had to do something so she cast around for a suitable starting point.

She didn't want to look through Nick's underwear, if he'd left any, so she started with the closet, which held several school uniforms, three pairs of shoes, a couple of jackets, four casual shirts, and an umbrella. Amanda felt all the pockets and looked inside them. They were empty except for bits of lint, a few pence, and a couple of five-pound notes. She was surprised that the crime scene investigators hadn't removed the money. She looked toward the shelf but couldn't reach it, so she grabbed a chair and climbed up.

The top shelf was incredibly dusty. It looked as if it hadn't been used in ages. That was weird. With space at such a premium, you'd think the boys would have used every nook and cranny, but they'd neglected to avail themselves of this valuable resource. It couldn't have been because they were too short to reach it. Nick, at least, had been considerably taller than Amanda, who was five feet, and she was pretty sure that Philip and Gavin weren't exactly shrimps either. Anyway, there were always chairs to climb onto, but maybe they just didn't have a lot of stuff.

"Find anything?" said Thrillkill, who was rummaging through one of the desks.

"No, sir," said Amanda, standing on her tiptoes. "It's odd, though. This shelf hasn't been used in months."

"Really? How peculiar. Now this is a good example of what to look for. What you fail to find can be just as important as what you uncover. That's a lesson worth remembering."

"Yes, sir."

"Are you sure there's nothing up there?"

"There's a lot of dust," Amanda said. That was true. The dust was so thick that Editta would have insisted on measuring it. "I—wait a minute. There's some writing in the dust. Let me see if I can make it out."

"Do you need a torch?" said Thrillkill, reaching into his coat pocket.

"I have a light on my phone," said Amanda. "Let me get it." She started to get down but Thrillkill was faster. He grabbed her bag and handed it up to her.

"Thank you, sir." She took out her phone and activated the light. "It's . . . oh."

"What is it?" he said.

"It says, 'Dust me.'"

Thrillkill laughed. Amanda didn't think she'd ever seen him do that. "Typical," he said. "They manage to get up there to write in the dust, but heaven forfend they should actually clean the shelf."

"Sir, don't you think it might mean more than that? I mean the writing."

"You think it's a code?"

"I don't know. I'm just trying to keep an open mind."

"Excellent, Miss Lester. Please take pictures of the shelf from a variety of angles and let's get a sample of the dust. The crime scene people have already looked for prints and didn't find anything that shouldn't be there, but it doesn't hurt to do that again."

Amanda processed the shelf using her evidence kit, then turned her attention to the desks. She thought she'd start with the two that probably weren't Nick's. The longer she could delay going through any more of his personal things the better. If she stalled enough, maybe Thrillkill would abort the mission and she wouldn't have to endure the pain of such intimacy.

Not surprisingly, neither of the two desks near the empty beds held anything other than lint. Philip and Gavin must have cleaned those out pretty thoroughly. However when she came to the third, she almost couldn't open the drawers, and not because of her feelings about Nick. They were all stuck. She had to wiggle the top one to move it at all, but when she finally got it free she saw that it was empty.

The second of the three drawers was just as stuck but it was not empty. Inside Amanda found a printed copy of a screenplay entitled "Thaddeus Bott and the Magic Fog." Nick Muffet was listed as the author. It appeared to be a steampunk story he had written, and from the first few lines it looked darn good. She wondered briefly why he hadn't mentioned it, but then realized he'd never told her the truth about anything so of course he wouldn't have. She felt as if she'd been kicked in the stomach—again.

Now to the bottom drawer. Like the first two, this one did not want to open, but it was even more stuck. Amanda couldn't tell if it was blocked or there was something wrong with the sliders.

"Having trouble?" said Thrillkill.

"I can't get the drawer open."

"That's odd. Perhaps the humidity . . ." He yanked on the drawer but it wouldn't open for him either. "Blasted thing. Come on, you." He pulled harder and harder, until all of a sudden the drawer gave way and he fell back on his butt. Amanda wanted to laugh. This was certainly not a position she'd ever seen the headmaster assume. He, however, was unperturbed and said, "There you go, Miss Lester. Have at it."

Thrillkill had pulled the drawer completely out of the desk and Amanda could see that it held an evidence kit full of sample bags, tweezers, a fingerprint kit, and so on—all the items found in every detective's toolkit. In addition, she found the results of the fingerprint exercise she and Nick had conducted that very first day of Crime Lab. There were also some tools, including a hammer, pliers, screwdriver, and Allen wrench. Nick had been handy. It wasn't surprising that he'd owned his own tools.

Amanda dusted all the items for prints, including the screenplay. She would run them through the national database later. She also swabbed everything in case there was any residue that might help paint a better picture of what the Moriartys had been up to. But on the surface none of the stuff looked suspicious.

Then came the dressers. She wasn't looking forward to them. What if Nick had left underwear? That was *way* too personal, although it crossed her mind to wonder whether criminals' underwear looked different from other people's. Dirtier? Torn? With secret compartments? With pictures of spiders or skulls and crossbones on them?

Reasoning that he would have stored such items in the top drawer, she started at the bottom. The lowest drawer contained a few pairs of jeans, which were folded more neatly than she would have expected. Not exactly come-from-the-dry-cleaners folded, but better than most kids would do. She lifted each pair out and examined it thoroughly, cringing all the while. She found a couple of clean handkerchiefs in the pockets, plus a wrapper from some crackers. She remembered the time Nick had offered her saltines and put the wrapper back in his pocket. Could it be the same one? If so, it had been there an awfully long time. There was no way. She was letting her emotions run away with her.

The drawer itself contained some lint but was otherwise clean. With Thrillkill's help, she removed it from the dresser and looked to see if there was anything attached, or any secret compartments. Nothing. The floor underneath was also free of evidence, so she replaced the jeans and the two of them reinserted the drawer.

Next she pulled out the middle drawer. There she found an array of sweaters, which her English friends called jumpers, a word she thought rather peculiar, but then calling cookies biscuits was also strange. She had seen Nick wear every one of these and didn't like looking at them. But the results of this search were the same as the previous one: nothing interesting.

Unfortunately, she had now reached the top drawer. She was tempted to ask Thrillkill to search it for her, but he'd insisted that she look so she figured she'd better do so. Slowly, slowly she pulled the drawer open. Of course she'd been right. It was full of underwear and socks. She thought she'd die. Handle these? She'd never even touched her father's underwear. How could she possibly feel—*feel*—Nick's. She hoped he'd kept it all clean, because she really, really didn't want to deal with it if it wasn't.

She could feel herself start to gag. Luckily she had a couple of gingersnaps with her. She'd begun carrying them everywhere when Simon had discovered that they settled the stomach. Since she was so prone to puking, they'd been a godsend. She popped one in her mouth and waited a minute for it to descend. She was still upset but the nausea was subsiding. Hands shaking, she pulled the drawer out all the way and looked inside.

The first thing she realized was that Nick was indeed well organized. Whether it was his show business training (where had he gotten that anyway?) or just came naturally, it was a relief. All his Y-fronts, T-shirts, and socks were clean and neatly arranged. She breathed a sigh of relief, although her hands were still shaking. She removed each item and examined it thoroughly.

She was able to get the drawer out by herself this time, but when she turned it over, she got a shock. There was something taped underneath—a white letter-sized envelope. She felt underneath the tape and pulled, then squeezed the envelope. Whatever was inside was small, hard, and flat. She opened the envelope to find a memory card. What could that be for?

She gave Thrillkill the card, although she would have preferred to take it to her room and look at it by herself. If it was embarrassing, she might be able to forestall the worst of the teachers' reactions. Her mind raced with terrifying possibilities. She had to know but she didn't want to. What if, what if, what if?

After a quick search of the other two dressers, which were completely empty and free of secret stashes, Amanda stared at the bed. She was no more comfortable riffling through this than Nick's underwear. It was the most personal item of all and she was dreading it. She considered asking Thrillkill if she could skip it but she knew what the answer would be.

She started by looking underneath. There she saw more dust, but unlike the dust on the closet shelf, no evidence of its having been disturbed. She took a couple of samples and stashed them in her bag. She examined the underside of the box spring, crawling under the bed (which precipitated a lot of sneezing) to feel carefully. Nothing there either.

Then, trembling, she gently pulled back the quilt. She examined it top and bottom, side to side. She lay it on the floor and pressed it. Nothing. It was just a quilt. She extracted a scissors from her evidence kit and started to cut. *Snip, snip, snip.* It was torture invading the blanket Nick had pulled over himself every night. With each snip, she felt as if she were cutting herself. She cut and cut and cut until the poor thing was in ribbons but found nothing unusual. Still, she took a couple of pieces for analysis, just in case.

When she had finished destroying, er, searching the quilt, she turned back to the bed. It held the usual bedclothes: a pillow in a case, a blanket, plain white sheets. Amanda pulled back each of the layers to find nothing special. Then, with the same result, the pillow and its case.

When she had removed the pad that underlay the sheets, she stared at the mattress. In the middle was a Nick-shaped depression. She felt as if she would burst into tears. Of course the dent could have been the result of various boys sleeping on the bed over the years, but in Amanda's eyes Nick had created it. She blinked and tried to regain her composure. Then, after a few seconds, she leaned down and started to palpate the mattress, carefully moving along an imaginary grid. Nothing. She knelt and did the same to each of the sides. Still nothing. Now there was only the side that faced the wall. She kneed the mattress away to make room for herself and squatted to feel there too. Right side, nothing. Left side, nothing. Middle—what was that? Something weird was there, sticking out from underneath. It made a crinkling sound when she pressed it.

She pushed the mattress away from the wall to reveal a bit of paper sticking out from underneath. Was that the mattress tag? Oh well, even if it was, she'd better check. If she pulled too hard though, the paper would tear, so she gently lifted up the mattress and carefully removed it. It was all wadded up, but she could tell it was no mattress tag. It looked like a piece of printer paper.

Afraid that the contents might be embarrassing, she slowly unfolded the sheet, pulling a little this way and a little that way to a refrain of *crumple, crumple, crumple, pop.* When she had smoothed the paper out, she was looking at the wrong side. Then she stopped. Maybe she should let Thrillkill do this. No, if it really was embarrassing, she didn't want him to see it before she did. She took a deep breath, flipped the paper over and saw . . . herself! It was a picture of her that Nick had taken one day in the common room. She was smiling and looked as happy as she'd ever been. The composition, lighting, and color balance were all excellent. It was a work of art. But what was it doing under Nick's mattress?!

The discovery threw her for a loop. Why would Nick hide a picture of her? Come to think of it, considering how he claimed to feel about her, why would he possess a picture of her at all? Was it because the

Moriartys were targeting her and he wanted to show the gang what she looked like? Surely that was it. It did seem strange, though, that he'd keep the picture in such an obscure place. Everyone had known the two of them were friends. Why the mystery?

Unless . . . It wasn't possible. Could it be that he really *had* cared about her and it was a memento? He'd always acted as though he did, up until the end, that is, but that didn't mean anything. During their last encounter he'd been false and treacherous. No, this was about a plot that hadn't been implemented, probably related to whatever data was on the memory card, which meant that if Blixus and Mavis hadn't been caught Amanda might be in real danger. Thank goodness they were safely behind bars.

"Sir, I found something," she said.

"Oh?" said Thrillkill. "What have you got?"

She showed him the picture and explained where she'd found it. He didn't react. Amanda wasn't sure she knew what he was thinking and didn't want to, so she said, "I'll bag it. I've found nothing else other than the memory card. No wallet, no phone, no computer, nothing stolen. There's not much to go on."

"We shall see," said Thrillkill. "Perhaps our analysis will turn up something. Let's check a few more things and that will be it for today."

For today? Did he mean he wanted her to come back? She certainly hoped not.

"Thank you, Miss Lester," he said kindly when they had finished. "I know how painful this must have been for you and I appreciate your sacrifice. Now off you go. You and Mr. Holmes have work to do." Amanda breathed a sigh of relief. It seemed he'd completely forgotten that she was supposed to act as the new kid's big sister.

5

JUST THE TREASURE

Amanda was most definitely *not* going to tell anyone what she'd found in Nick's room, not even Ivy. She couldn't face the questions, speculations, and sympathy. Fortunately, Thrillkill would inflict none of these on her. Sometimes his gruffness was actually a plus.

She knew she had to get in touch with Scapulus Holmes, but she didn't want to in the worst way. Maybe Thrillkill would change his mind and cancel the film project. Then she could teach her storytelling class after all. As if. She was engaging in wishful thinking and she knew it.

But before she could text Holmes her phone beeped. He had beat her to it. "Hi! Want to get together?" his message read. Boy, he was friendly. What did he have to be so happy about? Oh right. He was going to be a big shot, making a film at the behest of the big cheese. Ruining her class so he could aggrandize himself. Grump and double grump.

She guessed she'd have to answer him, but decided that it would be in her own sweet time. She made her way back to her room, which like Nick's, was on the top floor, but in the girls' dorm in the northeast part of the school.

When she got there, Amphora and Ivy were nowhere to be seen, so she could enjoy a little privacy. She didn't know what was compelling her, but she decided to look at the video she'd made with Nick last term, the one where they'd explored the secret room. They'd discovered the place in a disused part of the school near the back of the chapel/auditorium when they'd followed the cook, who'd been skulking around.

She opened the video and started to watch. The first thing she saw was the awful yellow slime mold that had feasted on the pink sugar the cook had so carelessly strewn about. Gelatinous and pulsating, it was just as gross on the video as in person. She watched as the camera moved down the stone stairs to the weird little room where the cook had stashed the sugar—and where, together with Mavis Moriarty and the school's doctor, the awful woman had held Amanda's father before moving him to the sugar factory. And then, as they mounted the stairs again, she beheld Nick's face. He had turned around and smiled. Watching him like this was another kick in the stomach. She stopped the film and threw her phone on the bed, then flopped down next to it and sobbed.

After about fifteen minutes she was all cried out and decided to check her email. There, among about a billion notes from her mother and a few inane promotional messages, was a bright, shiny letter from her idol, film director Darius Plover, with whom she'd been corresponding.

You couldn't say that Amanda was in love with Darius Plover, the greatest director in the world, but if you did you wouldn't be far off. She wasn't so much in love with him as with his work. Films like "Scaffold," "Night of the Turkey," and "Plunge" were already classics, and she cited them among her top influences. So when she discovered that he had written her yet another email, she was ecstatic. The message read:

Dear Miss Lester,

I hope this note finds you well and that you are still interested in providing a teen's perspective on my work. (Happy birthday, BTW!) If you are, I have some clips for you to view.

61

These are from my latest film, "Sand," which we are shooting in Morocco. At this link you will find dailies as well as the script. Would it be possible to get your input in the next couple of weeks?

https://www.ploverfilms.com/sand/amanda

If you are too busy with school, don't be afraid to say no. I don't want to distract you from your studies. There will be other films.

As always, thanks for your time and interest.

With sincere appreciation and best regards to my American friend in England,
Darius Plover

Amanda couldn't believe that the great man had actually taken her up on her offer. She didn't know what she could possibly contribute, but he obviously valued her opinion. He was so busy that he wouldn't have bothered if he weren't serious. But this was a huge responsibility! She hoped she wouldn't disappoint him.

Excited beyond belief, she clicked on the link and was taken to a secure cloud. Sure enough, she found the script and several clips. She clicked on the first video.

Against a background of what looked like Egyptian pyramids appeared a large tent with its door parted to reveal a bit of the interior. The camera entered and focused on the two occupants, a grizzled archaeologist and a bearded man who was holding him at gunpoint. Presumably the bearded guy was some kind of terrorist. He was threatening the archaeologist with various torments if he didn't succeed in digging up an ancient scroll. The archaeologist kept telling the armed man that it wasn't that simple, and each time he protested the terrorist would prod him with his rifle.

It was awful! Amanda couldn't believe how poorly the scene had been put together. Sure, it was a rough cut, but it didn't work at all. The cinematography was uninspired, the dialog was terrible, the acting was pathetic, and the story was trite. What was she supposed to say? She couldn't tell the great Darius Plover how she really felt. That would be the end of their budding relationship and she'd be back to minus square one with her filmmaking career, which was on hold anyway. Maybe she should read the script and watch *all* the clips. She might feel different then.

Unfortunately, after doing just that she felt exactly the same. The script was hackneyed, the scenes were poorly shot, and the acting was dreadful. Surely rough cuts weren't *that* rough. Oh great. Now what?

There was only one thing she could do: evade. She could lie about the clips, in which case she wouldn't be doing Mr. Plover any favors, but at least she'd avoid conflict. She could tell him she didn't have the time, in which case he'd probably never give her another chance. Or she could avoid answering altogether, which was about the worst possible course of action. Whatever she did, though, she was not going to tell him the truth. That would be suicide.

She tabled that problem and thought she'd better get back to Holmes. She suggested they meet at lunch the following day and received an instant reply: "Cool. Can't wait." What was wrong with that guy? Why was he so cheerful? If he was going to act like this the whole time, she'd eat her way through a ton of gingersnaps.

After dinner Amanda met Ivy and Nigel in the common room to discuss a strategy for finding the missing item. The hangout still looked like an airplane hangar, but then it would. The gremlins usually changed the décor at night when everyone was asleep. Tomorrow it would look completely different. Amanda wondered what it would be. Sometimes she tried guessing but she was always wrong.

"I like Simon's idea of listening," said Ivy, "but I don't think that's enough. We're going to have to be proactive."

"You mean put together our own theories about what the missing item could be and follow each lead, right?"

"Yes. Exactly. There's a good boy." Ivy rubbed Nigel's head. It was soothing for both of them.

"I'll make a list, shall I?" said Amanda, reaching into her bag.

"Yes, and I'll do the same. Do you have any idea what it might be?"

"Not a clue. I haven't had much time to think about it, and now I've got this film thing with Holmes." She started thumbing a reminder to herself.

"What film thing with Holmes?" said Ivy.

Amanda explained what Thrillkill had asked her to do. Then she said, "I really blew it today. How can I ever face him?" As soon as the words had left her mouth she wished she could take them back. She didn't want to talk about Holmes. Holmes and Nick, Nick and Holmes. If only there were a memory eraser. She was sure she was bringing her friends down with her constant carping about those two.

"You mean Holmes," said Ivy. "How can you ever face Holmes?"

"Yes. I don't know what came over me. I was just so surprised when I saw him."

"Apologize and move on. He seems nice. He'll be cool."

"I don't know how you can always be so optimistic," said Amanda. She felt like she was whining, which she was.

"It's easy. I call it my hidden treasure philosophy. The world is full of beautiful things, but you have to look for them. Searching keeps you too busy to notice the stupid stuff. The harder they are to find, the more satisfying the reward. See what I mean?"

"I guess . . ." said Amanda.

"What's storytelling about? Wondering what's around the next corner, right? If you're curious you won't have time to get depressed or think about Nick Muffet." Amanda started. Just the sound of his name made her jump. "I'm sorry, Amanda, but you need to move on. I know you miss him but he's holding you back."

"I don't miss him," said Amanda.

"I don't mean to be harsh," said Ivy, "but everyone knows you loved the guy. The fact that he hurt you doesn't change that."

"I didn't," said Amanda. "He was just a friend."

Ivy was silent for a moment. Amanda hoped she wasn't going to argue. "Please just try to remember the hidden treasures," she said at last. "It works—especially when you're down."

"Not today, though," said Amanda. "You seem upset. Is it Editta?"

"Actually, it's more than that. Usually nothing gets to me, but sometimes I just know too much because of my hearing and it can be a bit of a burden."

"Really?" said Amanda. "I had no idea. I've been envying you. You're such a great detective and you can do such amazing things, like figuring out the code to get into the sugar factory." Ivy had astonished Amanda with her solution to that problem. After traveling all the way to London to look for her father at the Moriartys' factory, Amanda had been stopped cold by a security keypad and hadn't been able to get past it—until she'd called Ivy, who'd figured out what to press by the sound of the keys.

"Thanks. Sometimes, though, there are things you'd rather not know."

This was a revelation. Amanda had had no idea that being gifted could be such a burden. "Wow. So what do you do?"

"What can I do? I live with them." Ivy no longer seemed upset. Amanda found that odd. Here was a problem her friend had acknowledged, but within two seconds it had ceased to bother her. That hidden treasure stuff must be pretty powerful.

"Ivy, do you think there's something wrong with me?" she blurted out.

"What? You mean because of Scapulus? Of course not. How could you think such a thing?"

"I, uh, no reason."

"You've got to stop beating up on yourself, Amanda. It was an accident. Hidden treasures. Curiosity. Focus on those and you'll be happier."

Amanda pictured a pirate's treasure chest guarded by a fire-breathing dragon. No, that wasn't right. Forget the dragon. It wouldn't exist in Ivy's world. From now, on just the treasure.

6

AMANDA LESTER, ONE-MAN BAND

The next day, Tuesday, Amanda and Holmes met at lunch. They caused quite a stir, the two of them sitting together like that after what she'd said in class. Whispers swirled around the dining room and everyone kept staring at them as if they'd never seen two people eating lunch together. The whole thing annoyed Amanda, but Holmes seemed cheerful and oblivious. He also seemed to be enjoying his food, which consisted of a vegetable curry and fried rice. Amanda had to admit that after last term's fare it wasn't half bad. She hoped she wouldn't put on weight again.

Thrillkill had given Holmes the list of topics he wanted the film to cover. Holmes! Why not her, or at least both of them? When she learned what Thrillkill had done she could barely eat. Maybe she didn't have to worry about her weight after all. Her stomach was so roiled these days that she practically had to force herself—a far cry from her habits in L.A., where she'd been a bit of a glutton.

"This list is exciting," Holmes said, pointing. "I'm glad we're going to do steganography. That's quite interesting."

"Stega-who?" said Amanda. "Why are we covering dinosaurs?"

"It isn't dinosaurs," said Holmes, chewing. "It's the process of hiding data inside an image. When you look at a picture, what you see may not be what you get." He chuckled. Amanda wanted to deck him.

"And look at this. Stochastic forensics. Now that's something we can really sink our teeth into."

She pictured Holmes's teeth growing and growing until he looked like a saber-toothed tiger. "Who-da-what?"

"Stochastic forensics." Whatever *that* was. It sounded like someone throwing up. "It's a method of investigating activities that lack digital artifacts. You use it to look into data theft."

"Right. And how about plunkitography, bozology, and goositude?"

"No, those have nothing to do with—oh, I see. That was a joke." He grinned.

Of course it wasn't. Amanda was feeling especially hostile at the moment, so much so that she had completely forgotten Ivy's hidden treasures and was dreaming up exotic ways to commit the perfect crime with Holmes as the victim.

"So anyway," he said, "I was thinking we could do a short lecture on each topic and then have questions and answers."

"No," said Amanda.

"No? You don't like it?" He looked hurt. He probably wasn't used to people saying no to him.

"No, you don't make films that way." That was sharp. She hadn't meant to be quite so nasty.

"And you know this because . . ."

"I'm a filmmaker." Gosh she sounded haughty. Where was this coming from?

"Ah. The accent. You're from California, aren't you?"

The L.A. stereotypes again. Wasn't there anyone in the world who didn't buy into that? "What's that supposed to mean?"

"You don't have to get so upset. You have a California accent and they make movies in California." He brightened. "I think it's smashing."

She sighed. "That's not the point. The point is that I've been making films since I was three. I know what I'm doing." Should she mention Darius Plover? No, that would be name-dropping. She hated people who did that. It probably wouldn't impress him anyway.

"Splendid! That will be a great help to us." He raised his water glass and toasted her.

Splendid, that will be a great help to us, she mocked in her mind. Well wasn't that just ducky?

"So I'll write the script and you'll direct," he said. "Don't you want to toast?"

"No, and no."

"No? There's water in your glass. Come on." He motioned to her glass. She moved it away.

"Have you written scripts before?" she said leaning toward him. It was an aggressive move rather than an intimate one.

"Well, uh, no." He maintained his straight-backed position.

"Then you can't write the script." She tried to cross her legs and hit the table. "Ouch."

"Ouch?" He looked confused.

"Never mind. You will help me with the content, but I will write the script." She glared at him.

"Well, naturally I'll do the content. I mean, uh, that wasn't nice of me. Sorry. How much do you know about cyberforensics?"

She wanted to say, "Whatever Simon teaches me," but instead she said, "Not much. That's why Thrillkill wanted you on the project."

"Oh," Holmes said. "So I'm just a consulting producer."

"Something like that, yes." She laughed. Where had he picked up the jargon?

"I don't like that," he said. "Why are you laughing?"

"What's wrong with that? Consulting producer is a good position. You get your name in the credits."

"It's peripheral," said Holmes.

"What, you want to be a star?" said Amanda.

Holmes giggled. "No, of course I don't want to be a star. I'll leave that up to you Americans."

"What?!" She could feel her face turning red.

"Don't get your knickers in a twist," he said. "That was a compliment."

Amanda narrowed her eyes and looked him straight in the face. "Look. You may think you're hot stuff just because you're descended from the great Sherlock. You bet I'm American, and we don't think that way. Everyone stands and falls on his or her own merit. So cut it out."

Holmes looked taken aback. "I didn't mean anything. I can tell you're really talented." Amanda wasn't going to let herself fall for that. She glared even harder. "I have to tell you, however, that I don't agree with your approach. Just because I haven't written scripts before doesn't mean I can't contribute. I'm a good writer. I think you'll find me valuable."

Amanda snorted. "We don't have time for you to be valuable. We have a deadline. We need an experienced scriptwriter. That's me. You're the subject expert. Got it?"

"Fine," he said more calmly than most people would have. "If that's what you want, we'll do it your way. However, I'm not the only one around here who has a lot to learn."

This insult so angered Amanda that she got up and stomped out of the room, leaving the plates on the tables rattling. Everyone turned and stared at her. As she clomped through the doorway, she could hear Holmes calling after her, "See you at our next meeting."

Amanda was so distressed by her encounter with Holmes that she didn't see Thrillkill walking toward the dining room and ran smack into him.

"Whoa, there," he said. "Are we late for something?"

"No, sir. Sorry, sir," she said, rubbing her nose where she'd collided with him.

"We have the results from the analysis of Nick Muffet's room," he said. "Mostly inconclusive, I'm afraid. Just two things of interest."

Uh oh. She really didn't want to hear this.

"First of all, that picture on the mattress," he said. "We found fibers on it. We were able to match them to several of Mr. Muffet's outer garments. No surprise there. It was probably in his pocket at some point. As to the memory card, it contains something I think you'll find familiar."

Oh no! What could that be? She felt like covering her ears.

"You made a video of the secret room and the stone stairs leading to and from it. With slime mold all around."

This was a surprise. Why would Nick be hiding a copy of her documentation? "Yes, sir. We made that when we were following the cook last term."

"That was it. Nothing else."

What was going on? Why would Nick have hidden those things? There was nothing particularly secret about them. Unless . . .

"Sir, do you think Nick used steganography on those images?"

"Now that's an interesting idea, Miss Lester. Good thinking. Unfortunately, it isn't possible to do that on a printed picture. We need the digital version, which we don't have. We did look for coded messages in the video, but we didn't find anything."

"Are you sure? Because there can't be any other reason for him to hide those things. They weren't secret."

"I must say I'm rather stumped," said Thrillkill. "Unless, of course . . ."

"Unless what?" she said, hoping he wouldn't say it.

"Unless he was keeping them because of you."

"Me? What about me?"

Thrillkill took off his glasses and looked squarely at her. "I think Mr. Muffet may have had a soft spot for you, Miss Lester."

This was definitely something Amanda did not want to hear. Of course it wasn't true. Thrillkill hadn't been there when Nick had taunted her, bragged about how he'd used her and made a fool of her, tried to get her to kill her own father. Her supposed best friend had laughed in her face, telling her that she'd been gullible and naïve. *That* wasn't a soft spot. The boy was cruel. The only person he had a soft spot for was Nick Muffet.

She tried to put Thrillkill's words out of her mind. The best way to do that, she figured, would be to turn her attention to the missing item. She wondered how Simon was coming along with the listening devices, but Sketching, the last class of the day, was about to start and there wasn't time.

The sketching teacher, Professor Browning, was a beautiful, vibrant American woman who painted striking pictures of caves. Whether they were sea grottoes, mammoth caverns filled with glittering stalactites and stalagmites, or twisty underground tunnels, she seemed as much an expert in speleology as she was in art. Amanda was looking forward to the class. She was good at drawing and wanted to spend more time at it.

When she saw Simon she whispered, "How are you coming along with the listening devices?" He raised his hand and gave her a thumb-finger circle. She breathed a sigh of relief. At least something was going well. She couldn't wait to hear more.

When everyone had taken their seats, the teacher stood in front of the class and seemed to be counting. She frowned. Of course Editta was missing, so the number of students wasn't right. Amanda wondered where her friend was. Her failure to show up was becoming worrisome.

Professor Browning was wearing a black suit with a pencil skirt and very high heels. Her hair was styled in an old-fashioned French roll. She looked very 1960s.

"Good afternoon, class," she said in a way that exclaimed, "I don't fool around, so don't try anything."

"Good afternoon," said the class in ragged but enthusiastic fashion. Somehow she had already won them over. Amanda could feel herself getting excited.

"Let's begin our adventure in sketching. I want you to find one person you don't know well and sit next to them. Go on now—scoot."

Everyone looked around trying to identify the one student they knew the least. Then, in a way that was scarily smooth, they all got up and made a beeline for their choice. No one was left out—except Gordon Bramble. It was as if each person had one and only one "I-don't-know-you" partner they recognized immediately.

Amanda's partner was Clive Ng, a kid known for his interest in rocks. He could always be seen around the school looking at the ground and picking up samples, even when there was snow on the ground. He was rumored to possess an astonishing geode collection and was well liked for his pleasant manner and upbeat attitude. Ivy found herself paired with Amanda's lab partner, Dreidel Pomfritter. Amanda thought that would be interesting. Ivy would be drawing by feel rather than sight. She couldn't wait to see how her sketches turned out.

Simon's opposite number was Owla Snizzle and Amphora's was a tall, skinny girl named Binnie Belasco, who was new this term. Because there was an odd number of kids, Gordon Bramble ended up with Professor Browning.

"Now, class," said the teacher, "I want you to take your charcoal," she held up a piece of charcoal, "and draw your partner's face. You have five minutes. Go."

Amanda stared at Clive and Clive stared at Amanda. He said, "I don't know how to draw." She said, "It's easy. Don't worry," and drew an oval on her pad, a rough outline of the boy's head. Then she blocked out where his features would go. Watching what she was doing, the boy mimicked her until he had a similar oval and lines for where her eyes, nose, and mouth should be.

"I don't know how to do hair," he said, eyeing her long, bushy mane. "It looks hard."

"Don't worry about the hair right now," she said. "Just get the shapes right."

"Okay."

As Amanda filled in Clive's features, he copied her. He seemed to have a talent for drawing after all, because when she looked at his picture she could recognize herself.

"Hey, that's really good," she said.

"Thanks," he beamed. "Yours looks like me too."

"Time!" said Professor Browning after what seemed like thirty seconds. "Put your charcoal down."

All kinds of protests, sighs, and moans permeated the room. Obviously most of the kids hadn't finished. In fact a couple of them hadn't even started.

"Now, before we examine the results of this little exercise," said the teacher, "I want to tell you why we did this. When you are a witness to a crime, or you're investigating one, you will see faces you won't be able to capture with your camera. When that happens you will need to draw them from memory. That's why you need sketching skills. I asked you to select the person you know least well so as to simulate this kind of situation.

"When you know someone, you see them differently from the way you see a stranger. With a stranger you're more objective, and the

74

likeness you make tends to be truer. So, I expect your picture of Mr. Ng, Miss Lester, to be a better one than if you were to draw, say, Miss Kapoor."

Amanda and Amphora looked at each other as if they'd never met.

"We are starting with faces because that is what you will be drawing most often. You will also draw places and things, of course, but those will be easier. Faces are the most difficult and require the most practice.

"Now, let's see how you did. Miss Lester, Mr. Ng, since I've already mentioned you, will you please come to the front with your drawings."

For once Amanda wasn't embarrassed to be called on. Clive seemed a mellow sort and didn't look bothered either. The two of them grabbed their pads and took their places at the front of the room. When Amanda looked out, she could see David Wiffle making faces at her. She felt like making faces back but she wasn't exactly in a position to do so.

"Please hold up your drawings," said Professor Browning.

The pair did as instructed. Oohs and aahs filled the room as the class murmured approval.

"Very nice," said the teacher. "I see you both started by blocking out the shapes and locations of the features, then filled in the detail. Excellent. You may return to your seats."

As she made her way back to her chair, Amanda caught sight of the Wiffle kid making a deprecating gesture. She turned her head away and ignored him.

"Mr. Wiffle," said the teacher. "Will you and Miss Starshine please bring your drawings to the front?"

David Wiffle got up and clomped loudly to the front of the room, followed by a much daintier Prudence Starshine.

"Now let's see what you've got."

Prudence had done pretty well. She wasn't a natural artist, but she'd blocked out the shapes, which gave her drawing a solid foundation. David Wiffle, on the other hand, had drawn only Prudence's eyes and eyebrows in a tight hand that made her look like she was in pain.

"Good start," said Professor Browning. "However, Mr. Wiffle, I think you'll have better luck if you start with the big picture. Block out the shapes and relationships among them before attacking the detail. Nice work, Miss Starshine. I can see the resemblance."

Amanda couldn't, but that was okay. Prudence would do fine. David, on the other hand, would probably continue to think he knew best and produce mediocre work. But what business was it of hers? As long as he stayed out of her way she didn't care what he did.

At the end of class, Professor Browning assigned homework. The students were to practice drawing from memory. She didn't expect them to be completely successful, but the exercise should help them hone their powers of observation (Professor Sidebotham would have approved of that) and get comfortable with their materials, which were to be charcoal and pencil.

As the class was breaking up, Amanda turned to talk to Ivy. When she turned back, there was a mustache on her picture of Clive and she could see David Wiffle laughing. She picked up her pad, caught up with him, and clobbered him over the head. Now she was in for it but she didn't care. It was time that kid learned a lesson, and she was willing to take whatever punishment resulted just to see that happen.

Amanda knew David had provoked her on purpose. It was obvious that he had been waiting for an opportunity to get her expelled, and he may have found it.

"Professor, Professor," he yelled. "Amanda hit me!" He was holding his head and groaning in a way that seemed fake.

Professor Browning came toddling out of her classroom. It was a wonder she hadn't broken her ankle by now the way those heels were so skinny and tall. They *click, click, clicked* on the hard floor in an angry-sounding manner.

"What's happened?" she said. "Mr. Wiffle, are you injured?" She took hold of the boy's hand and moved it out of the way so she could see his head.

"Yes, Professor. I need to go to the nurse," said Wiffle. "Amanda hit me."

"Are you bleeding? Let me see." She felt his head, then turned it this way and that. "No blood. All right. Mr. Bramble," she turned to Gordon, who was looking on with a smirk on his face, "will you please see Mr. Wiffle to the nurse. Now."

Gordon stepped up and winked at David, and the two turned to leave.

"And Mr. Wiffle," Professor Browning called after him, "come see me as soon as you've finished. I'll be in my office."

The two boys left. Amanda could hear them whispering and giggling. Simon, who was standing nearby, shook his head. Amphora and Ivy were trying to pretend they weren't interested and moved a discreet distance away.

"Now, Miss Lester," said the teacher, somehow managing to keep her balance, "tell me what happened."

"I hit him," said Amanda. She could hear a gasp from Ivy and Amphora's direction. "He deserved it and I finally cracked. I'm ready for my punishment." She held out her wrists as if waiting for the handcuffs.

The teacher cracked up. "Good one, Miss Lester. You have a flair for the dramatic. I like that."

Amanda looked at her as if she'd lost her mind.

"I saw what he did to you," said Professor Browning. "He'll be punished. Now I don't condone what you did, but I can understand why you did it. If this happens again, try to be calm. Now off you go. You've got work to do."

Amanda couldn't believe her ears. She could hear more gasps from Ivy and Amphora, whose backs were facing her. Simon was grinning. "I, uh, thank you, Professor," Amanda said.

The teacher smiled and returned to her classroom in a slightly less noisy fashion than the way she'd left it. The four friends and Nigel practically ran to the common room.

"Did you see that?" said Amphora on the way. "Wow."

"I know," said Amanda. "I never expected *that* to happen."

"You Americans stick together, don't you?" said Simon.

"Si-monnnnn," said the three girls in unison. Nigel jumped up on his hind legs and did a little dance.

"Just having you on," he said. "Way to go, Amanda."

Amanda beamed. At least one thing was going her way. Although when David found out, he'd be even more ruthless. He hated their little clique with a passion. If only he would use that energy for something productive, he'd probably make a crackerjack detective.

"You do know he's going to be even more dangerous now," said Amphora.

"Yes," sighed Amanda. "But I think Thrillkill is on my side so I'm not too worried."

She never would have been confident of Thrillkill's support until recently. The man was normally pretty intimidating. Lately, though, he'd been so nice it almost seemed that he'd had a personality transplant.

"Speaking of Thrillkill," Simon said when they'd arrived at the common room, which was decorated like an orchestra pit, "I've worked out how I'm going to make the listening devices. It shouldn't be too long now. I'm going to use the 3D printer to create the parts. I got some open source plans online."

"Oh, wow, that's good," said Amanda. She leaned against the Steinway piano the gremlins had installed, hitting a few keys in the process. They tinkled, *ting ting.* "Oops. Sorry."

"You," came a voice. Everyone looked at the door, even Ivy, who inclined her head. David Wiffle and Gordon Bramble were standing there. "You'd better watch out," said David looking straight at Amanda.

"What are you doing here?" said Amanda. "Aren't you supposed to be at the nurse's?"

"Forget that," said Wiffle. "You hit me and didn't get in trouble. I'm lodging a formal complaint. You're going to be out of here at last." He let out a guffaw.

"I'm glad you think that's funny," said Amanda, "because you're going to need something to keep you going when you find out that *you're* the one in trouble, not me." She pulled a finger across her neck as if to say, "It's the guillotine for you."

"No way," said Wiffle. "You assaulted me. You're dead, Lester. What a great place this will be without you. I can't wait."

"Shut up, David," said Amphora. "You're nothing but a loser. No one likes you."

"And you," Wiffle said to Amphora. "You're going to get in a lot of trouble if you don't stop hanging around that new cook."

"What?" said Ivy, Amanda, and Simon together. They looked at Amphora, who was blushing.

"That's right," said Wiffle. "You didn't know? She's in love with the new cook. I've seen them together."

"Get out of here, David," said Ivy. "Why are you so mean? And you, Gordon. Why do you waste your time with him?" This definitely did not sound like Ivy, who never said a nasty word to anyone. She really must have heard too much of something. She was downright prickly.

"Ha ha," said Gordon. "How little you know. We're planning the most amazing—"

"Be quiet," said David. "It's none of their business."

"Oh really?" said Simon. "What's that? Your new diaper business?"

"Oh for heaven's sake," said Amanda. "What is wrong with all of you? We're thirteen years old, not two. Or at least we're about to be.

Chill out. David, you could be a great detective but you ruin everything for yourself. You should get a clue. Grow up and be competent. That should keep you busy."

"If you only knew," said David.

"Yeah," said Gordon, who never seemed to be capable of speaking for himself.

Both boys stuck out their tongues and stormed out of the common room. Amanda felt a pang of sympathy for them. David really was going to ruin his future if he wasn't careful. And Gordon was going to get himself caught in the undertow. These two boys were headed for failure, and it seemed that there was nothing anyone could do about it.

7

SCARS AND BRUISES

On Wednesday morning Editta showed up at last. No one had seen or heard her go into her room the night before, and no one knew exactly when she'd arrived, but there she was in Crime Lab. She looked terrible—sleep-deprived and red-faced—as if she'd been crying. When the kids asked her what was going on, she simply said she'd had some bad luck and didn't offer an explanation.

"We've been really worried about you," said Ivy. "Are you sure you're all right?" She touched Editta's arm.

"I didn't mean to upset you," said Editta vaguely. "I really am okay."

But she didn't look okay, and she didn't seem it either. Amanda tried not to show it, but she was more worried seeing Editta than she had been wondering where she was.

"What have I missed?" Editta continued. "Anything important?" She didn't seem like she cared.

"Actually, yes," said Simon, removing his fedora. "Something important to the teachers is missing and they're all worried about it. Amanda and Ivy have heard them talking. It seems serious."

"What is it?"

"No one knows," said Simon too nonchalantly. Amanda felt irritated with him. Sometimes he seemed to be taking the problem seriously, but too often he acted like his usual flippant self.

"This isn't good," said Editta morosely. "I knew it would happen."

"You know what would happen?" said Amanda sharply. Did Editta know something about the thing? If she did, she'd better come clean right here and now.

"There were three deaths at the school last term: the cook, the doctor, and the teacher the Moriartys killed. That's incredibly bad luck, especially since they were all murders. Something terrible is going to happen. I just know it. We have to find whatever it is and stop it." Amanda didn't agree with her reasoning, but she was glad to see her friend take an interest.

"Technically it's four deaths," said Simon, assuming Editta's usual role of bean counter.

"You don't need to remind us about that," said Amphora. "Can't you see how upset Amanda is? Anyway, technically it *isn't* four deaths because Nick died in London."

"Can we please change the subject?" said Ivy.

"What's missing?" said Editta, getting the message.

"We don't know," said Amanda, relieved not to have to think about Nick for a few seconds.

"No idea?" said Editta.

"Not really," said Amphora.

"But you know something is definitely not where it's supposed to be."

"Yes," said Ivy. "We've heard the teachers talking about it."

"Why don't you ask them?" said Editta.

"We can't," said Amanda. "They don't want anyone to know. We heard them say so. Who can say what would happen if they knew we knew?"

"It seems a right pickle, doesn't it?" said Editta, turning to the front of the room.

The other kids looked at each other as if to say, "What in the world was *that*?" Ivy sighed so loudly that Amanda knew exactly what she was feeling. She hoped Editta hadn't heard. Not that she would have noticed. She seemed to have relocated to another world.

After lunch came Amanda's favorite class: Disguise. The teacher, Professor Glassina Tumble, onetime costume designer for Hollywood blockbuster films, including some of Darius Plover's, had impressed upon the first-years how important disguise was, especially with facial and gait recognition software now able to see through most attempts to confuse the observer. Because of Amanda's film background, she not only loved disguise but was extremely good at it. Last term she'd got the kids all fired up with her inventive monster makeup, and everyone was looking forward to their new projects.

"Today, class, we're going to start a new unit on bruises and scars," said Professor Tumble. "Given your enthusiasm for bodily flaws, I know you're going to enjoy this topic, but as always, please take it absolutely seriously. Poor disguise isn't just aesthetically offensive. It can kill you.

"Now, some of you may find this unit a bit, well, to be honest, sickening. There will be gore involved. However, you are professionals and I trust you to learn to take disgusting sights, sounds, feels, and smells in stride. Miss Lester, I hear you have a remedy for nausea that may be beneficial to the class."

"Yes, Professor. Gingersnaps. They work very well."

"Excellent," said Professor Tumble. "I understand these are available from the new cook. Is that correct, Miss Lester?"

Amanda had no idea. She hadn't even seen the new cook, and neither Thrillkill nor the teachers had mentioned anything about gingersnaps being available.

"Yes, that's correct," said Amphora out of nowhere.

Simon's head whirled around. Ivy chuckled and Nigel wagged his tail. Gingersnaps helped dogs too.

"Excellent, Miss Kapoor," said the teacher. "Then I urge you to take advantage of this valuable Legatum perk." She giggled. She obviously thought she'd said something funny. Amanda would have agreed with her if she hadn't been distracted by Amphora's comment. Something was going on with her and the kitchen and Amanda meant to find out what it was.

"Now as I was saying, bruises and scars. Yes, Mr. Wiffle." The teacher lifted her chin in David's direction.

"Professor, will we be doing scabs?" said the Wiffle kid.

"Yes. We absolutely will be doing scabs and I expect them to be realistic. Mr. Bramble?"

"Professor, do you want us to do oozing wounds?" said Gordon.

The class laughed. Well, the boys did, anyway. Some of the girls looked a bit pinched.

"Yes, Mr. Bramble. We will be doing wounds of all kinds. Miss Snizzle?"

"Are you going to want us to do pimples?" said Owla Snizzle from Amanda's dorm floor.

Everyone laughed even harder.

"Yes, Miss Snizzle, but not in this unit. Yes, Mr. Binkle?" She looked at Simon, who had risen to ask his question.

"Will we be doing moles and lesions?" said Simon.

More laughter, this time from everyone. The class was really getting into it now.

"The same as I told Miss Snizzle. Yes, but later. Yes, Mr. Holmes?"

Uh oh. Amanda didn't know what Holmes was going to say, but whatever it was she was sure he'd be showing off. She was still feeling guilty about not liking him, but if she was honest with herself she had to admit she couldn't stand him. It wasn't that he wasn't smart and pleasant, except when he'd argued with her about the film. It was that he was too much of those things. She wondered if his flaws, for he had to have some, were anything like his ancestor's. *Sherlock* Holmes had been an egomaniac and a drug addict.

"Professor," said Holmes. "Will we be studying which types of objects make various types of bruises and wounds?"

Now *that* was an excellent question. Amanda couldn't believe how smart Holmes was. She almost reached for a gingersnap, he made her so sick.

"Smashing question, Mr. Holmes. The answer is yes. We will be studying the shapes, colors, depths, and other characteristics of injuries produced by a variety of objects. And I wouldn't be surprised if Professor Sidebotham assigned you some complementary problems to help you round out your experience in this area. Professor Hoxby as well."

"Professor," Holmes continued. "Is it possible for a person with dark skin to seem like they have light skin and vice versa?"

The laughter died out immediately. Everyone seemed shocked that Holmes would ask such a pointed question—every kid of every race and nationality, and there were quite a few different ones in the class. Holmes's mention of race obviously made everyone uncomfortable. Amanda was stunned. Professor Tumble, however, took the query in stride.

"Yes, sir," she said. "Skin color is as much a part of disguise as wigs and facial features. We will be studying how to alter it realistically. And may I say, Mr. Holmes, you have lovely skin. I think we will use you as our model for that unit. You don't have any objection, do you?"

On the contrary, Holmes was loving it. He beamed. "No, ma'am," he said. "Not at all. I'd be honored."

Hate him, hate him, hate him! Where was that gingersnap? He was insufferable and Amanda really was feeling queasy now.

She looked around. Simon's expression and position hadn't changed. He obviously wasn't bothered one way or the other. Typical. Ivy was looking a bit pink, which set off her copper hair in an aesthetically pleasing way but signified that she, too, was a bit perturbed by this discussion. Editta wasn't paying attention, and Amphora was staring at Holmes as if he were Adonis himself. Come to think of it, a number of the girls were getting gooey-eyed. *Oh great. Now he thinks he's a big Casanova.* Amanda reached into her bag and surreptitiously broke off a piece of gingersnap, bent over, and slipped it into her mouth.

Professor Tumble was oblivious to these reactions. She claimed to be hard of hearing, but she was perfectly capable of absorbing what was going on when she wanted to. Amanda suspected that she functioned in a similar way with regard to seeing. As was favored by so many of the teachers, she told the class to divide into teams of two, with each pair taking on a separate issue. At the end of the unit they would present the disguises and the methods they used to create them. The students would then vote on how effective the disguises were.

In theory this approach sounded fine—until Amanda learned that she'd been paired with Holmes. Then it was panic time. She knew throwing herself on the teacher's mercy wouldn't get her anywhere, so she didn't try. She was so upset, though, that she couldn't think of a strategy for handling the situation. She simply started to tremble and hoped no one would notice.

Simon and Amphora had been assigned to work together—a combination destined to create sparks, and not the good kind. Ivy was to work with David Wiffle's sidekick, Gordon Bramble. Never one to take the high road, Gordon was annoyed because Ivy was blind, and he didn't hesitate to show it. However, rather than saying anything to the teacher, he took his annoyance out on Ivy herself. How was he supposed to work with her on something so visual? She was going to ruin his grade, his parents would be upset, and on and on. Ivy had no sympathy for this nonsense and told him to suck it up, whereupon he looked completely shocked and shut his mouth. Editta was stuck with David Wiffle, but she didn't seem to mind. Thinking about her non-reaction, Amanda realized that Editta usually didn't mind anything unless she considered it bad luck, and apparently having to work with David didn't qualify.

Amanda and Holmes were to create acne scars, a prospect that didn't thrill her but excited him no end. Come to think of it, was there anything that didn't excite Holmes? He was so upbeat that sometimes his perpetual sunny mood seemed like an act. At any rate, it was an interesting problem because it involved making depressions in the skin rather than building on top of it. Amanda suggested that they use gelatin or wax as a coating, then make dents with a stipple sponge or spatula knife and cover it all with foundation. Holmes was itching to use latex but realized that it wasn't the right tool for the job. While they were working, he kept talking about zombies, which Amanda normally would have enjoyed, but because he was who he was, she kept finding flaws in everything he said and snapping at him. Rather than snapping back, though, he just laughed and made more zombie jokes until she felt like a zombie herself.

During the exercise Holmes said, "I wrote up a project plan for the film." He made a large pockmark in the wax and nodded approval. He looked like he had a crater in his face. Chicxulub? That was the huge impact crater in Mexico that may have been responsible for the extinction of the dinosaurs. Amanda thought that if Holmes were to appear in public like that, he might see the extinction of whatever social life he had.

"Without me?" She smeared gelatin on her forehead.

"I thought I'd save you some work." He made another depression in his cheek. This one was way too small to have caused an extinction, but it could have created a few tsunamis.

What a liar. Try to make it seem like you're doing this for me while you're really trying to take over.

"Well, you haven't," she said irritably. "I'm going to have to check the whole thing. There may be a lot of rewriting. It would have been easier if you'd let me do it." She was teetering dangerously on the edge of one-man band territory, a place she'd finally left behind after years of pushing everyone away and going it alone. People had warned her that that wasn't healthy and she'd finally made progress in licking the tendency, but Holmes made her want to run screaming back to her comfort zone.

"You just can't let go, can you?" he said cheerfully, despite the Grand Canyon his face was becoming.

"What are you talking about?"

"You. You always have to be in charge." He said it in a not mean way.

"I do not."

"Oh, I think you do. And I understand, really I do. Everyone wants to do things their own way."

"Uh uh."

"It's true and I'll prove it to you. How about if you let me do that for you?" He reached gingerly toward her face.

"What?" She recoiled and dropped her spatula knife. It clattered onto the floor.

"I'll do you and you do me. What say you?" He was grinning as if he were enjoying a private joke. She wanted to pick up the knife and make a mark that could be clearly identified as having come from it and only it.

"No way am I going to do that, Sherlock Holmes," she said, not realizing what she'd called him.

He burst out laughing. "Aw, come on, G. Lestrade. It'll be fun."

"What did you call me?" she said, sticking her pockmarked face in his pockmarked face.

"What did *you* call *me*?" he said, sticking *his* pockmarked face in hers.

"Stop mimicking me!" She picked up the knife and held it toward him.

"En garde," he yelled, holding out his own knife. That was what she and Nick had said to each other when mock fencing last term. Holmes wasn't allowed to say that.

"Shut up!" she yelled. "Get out of my face."

By this time the whole class had stopped what they were doing and was staring at them. Professor Tumble said, "You two, put those knives down at once. We'll have no dangerous activities in this classroom, do you understand?"

"Yes, ma'am," they said in unison, which annoyed Amanda even more. She didn't want to have anything in common with that interloper.

"See that you do," said the professor.

Amanda could feel Simon's eyes boring into her. Wiffle's too. She told herself she didn't care, and in a way she didn't. What she really cared about was her self-image. How could she have regressed back to square one like this? Sure, Nick still haunted her and her father wasn't himself, but she thought she'd evolved. Now she wasn't so sure, and the feeling of failure was getting to her. That Sherlock Holmes. Everything was his fault. He was still reaching out from beyond the grave and she was furious.

Scapulus Holmes said, "Tell you what. Why don't you look at what I wrote? If you don't like it, you can redo it. Just do that for me, would you?"

Why she should do anything for him was beyond her, but she'd been unconscionably rude already. "All right," she said. "I'll look at it after class."

He gave her a big satisfied smile that stretched his pockmarks in all directions. "Thank you," he said. And then he did the unthinkable. He winked at her again.

Before Amanda could read Holmes's project plan, Simon corralled her, Ivy, and Amphora in the hall. "The listening devices will be ready tomorrow," he said in a whisper.

"Yay!" Ivy said, whispering back.

"Hurray!" said Amanda quietly.

"Good," said Amphora loudly, looking as if she didn't believe him.

"Keep your voice down," he said to Amphora. "I'll have them for you before Fires and Explosions. Just wait outside the door and I'll slip them to you." He executed a fancy maneuver that involved turning his back to the girls and flapping a hand behind his butt.

"Sounds like a plan," said Amanda, who thought he looked like a peacock trying to impress a peahen.

"Why do you Americans say that?" said Simon, turning back to them. "Of course it's a plan."

"Why do you put Rs in words that don't have them?" Amanda said.

"I do not," said Simon.

"Right. You don't call me Amander sometimes."

"Nope."

"We do," said Ivy. "You just don't hear it."

"See?" said Amanda.

"No," said Simon. "I don't and you're wrong."

He wasn't quite a maddening as Holmes, but he could still be annoying. Amanda wondered whether he and Amphora would be able to get through the scars and bruises exercises without killing each other. Come to think of it, would *any* of them get through the class without doing each other in?

When Amanda read Holmes's plan she was dismayed to find that it was pretty good. She'd meant to rewrite it, but considering that there was the mystery of the missing item to solve, homework from her other classes to do, and Editta to worry about, she decided to let it stand. She could change it later. She dreaded telling him, though, because he'd just grin at her again with that I-told-you-so expression, and OMG, he might even wink again. Maybe if she texted him she wouldn't have to see that incessant smile and that condescending wink quite so soon.

She pulled her phone out and wrote, "Plan OK."

The answer came instantly: "☺☺☺. You're okay, Lestrade."

No one but Nick ever called her that, and she hadn't liked *that*. She would set him straight right now. She texted back, "It's Lester."

Another instant response: "Yes, and it's Scapulus."

She felt herself go red. There was no way she was going to admit that his reply had served her right.

8

BLACKPOOL

The next morning, Thursday, the girls met Simon outside the Fires and Explosions classroom. He ushered them down the hall and into a huddle, then carefully passed each of them a tiny device. He even gave one to Ivy so she could experiment. It was possible that he'd need to fine-tune the hearing aids, and her input could save him a lot of time.

The devices looked like tiny megaphones. The idea was that they would boost the sound coming in on certain frequencies but not others. So, for example, if someone was playing a tuba in the hall, Simon, Amanda, and Amphora would hear it normally, but if a person was talking, the kids would hear them more loudly than usual. Whether loud would translate into clear remained to be seen. Simon had made only one device per person, so they would have to make do with one boosted ear and one normal one.

"Don't put them in now," said Simon. "We don't want anyone seeing."

"Too late," said Amphora, who had already installed hers. "Hm, you're pretty loud, Simon." She jiggled the device.

"That's one drawback of these," he said, turning his around in his fingers. "There's no adjustment for distance, so voices close to you might be a bit overpowering." He leaned over to Amphora and said, right in her ear, "Like this."

"Ouch!" she said. "Cut that out."

Simon grinned. He loved getting her goat.

"Maybe wear them with an earplug in that ear or something?" said Amanda.

"Hm," said Simon. "Interesting idea. Say, how about cotton? There are plenty of cotton balls in the lab."

"Yes, let's try that," said Ivy.

"Are you going to give one to Editta?" asked Amanda.

"Sure, why not?" said Simon. "She's crazy, but she can still be useful."

"She's not crazy," said Amphora.

"Yeah, she is," said Simon. "She believes in bad mogambo." He put his fingers on either side of his head and made pretend horns, then wiggled them.

Just then Professor Pole appeared and said, "Good morning, everyone. Ready for some fireworks?" The kids stashed their listening devices and followed him into the room, where there was a nice empty seat waiting for Editta, who was nowhere to be seen.

After class there wasn't much time until Crime Lab, but the kids were dying to try out the devices, so they stuck them in their ears as surreptitiously as possible and ventured out into the hall. Amanda could hear some students talking low about twenty feet away, and their conversation was as clear as could be.

"I can't wait to blow up the Sphinx," Gareth Gubb was saying.

"I'm going to explode all those tall buildings in Dubai," said Trevor Gravespoon.

"And Hong Kong," said Arthur Modulo.

Wow, this thing works really well. Simon is a genius. Amanda turned the other way and listened. There were two girls way at the end of the hall, whispering. This time she had to strain her ears a little. She could hear some words but not others.

"Professor . . . in the lab . . . broke it," said a third-year named Polly Pogo.

"Worried . . . never mind . . . he's so cute," said the other third-year girl, Apple Moon.

Amanda wondered who was so cute. Surely they weren't talking about Professor Stegelmeyer, who was so not cute it wasn't funny. Nah, they were probably talking about one of the older boys, like Carlos Fapp or Harry Sheriff. All the girls had crushes on them. Except her, of course. She didn't have time for such folderol.

She ran down the hall and caught up with Ivy and Amphora. "Did you try it?"

"Yes," said Amphora. "It works pretty well. I heard Prudence talking about her stubbed toe from really far away."

"Mine is a bit strong," said Ivy, fiddling with the device in her ear. "But I'm going to try the cotton."

"Mine was great," said Amanda. "At least if you're within maybe twenty or thirty feet. After that it gets a bit spotty."

"What's spotty?" said Simon, joining the group. "Is this something about Professor Tumble's scars and bruises?" Amanda was sure he knew perfectly well it wasn't but couldn't resist the opportunity to be gross.

"No," said Amphora. "We were talking about the listening devices."

"Oh, right," said Simon. "How are they working?" He looked at each of the girls—even Amphora.

"Really well," said Amanda, declining to tell Simon about Apple's crush on Carlos, or was it Harry?

"Mine's a bit loud," said Ivy.

"Right," said Simon. "Well, let's see what happens when you damp it."

"Why would she put water on it?" said Amphora with a disgusted look on her face.

"Not *dampen*," said Simon. "*Damp.* It means to weaken an effect. So if I damp a noise, it isn't as loud."

"That's dumb," said Amphora. "It sounds like you're wetting it."

"Hey, I didn't invent the language," said Simon, holding up his palms.

"Well, you don't have to use it," said Amphora.

Simon gave her a look. "What is wrong with you?"

"Would you two cut it out?" said Ivy. "We have important work to do."

"Anyway," said Amanda, "I think these are going to work out pretty well. Thanks, Simon."

"Yes, thank you, Simon," said Ivy.

Amphora hesitated, then after about ten seconds said, "Yeah. Me too."

The cotton did prove helpful, and the kids listened as much as they could over the next day or so but didn't hear anything earth shattering. They did, however, learn a lot about which kinds of shoes made you look the tallest, which skateboards were hot, and a little too much about Olive Tweedy's skin problems, as well as how Professors Also and Pargeter were feeling about the gremlins (a little uneasy, to be honest; their designs were becoming more and more outlandish, and the two women were concerned that it would be too easy to observe the details). Mostly, though, they heard about the upcoming field trip, which was to take place on Saturday.

This would be the first field trip Amanda's class had taken and excitement was running high. Blackpool was legendary and the kids figured they'd get to run wild. There were now about forty of them in the class, so they would fit nicely on one bus, even counting Professors Sidebotham, Buck, and Ducey, who would be "escorting" them. Amanda thought that was a chicken way of saying "chaperoning," which was what they were really doing.

On the appointed day they all went to the south door, where a dirty, smelly old school bus awaited them. The kids didn't care if it was old and battered except to wonder if its appearance and condition would be on any tests. They were now so accustomed to having to examine everything they saw in so much detail that they were becoming a bit OCD. Perhaps the tendency would pass, though, Amanda thought, in much the same way that medical students lose their hypochondria once they're actually practicing. She certainly hoped so. Some of the kids were becoming hyperactive.

There was much stomping and confusion as they boarded the bus. It seemed that there were no assigned seats, so there was a lot of jockeying for position. Some kids lucked out and others didn't. Amanda, for example, got to sit with Ivy and Nigel, but Simon was stuck with Gordon Bramble, who was most unhappy to have been separated from David Wiffle, who in turn had to sit next to Editta, who, uncharacteristically, failed to count even one thing, freaking out her friends. Holmes ended up next to Amphora, who seemed over the moon about her good fortune and kept giving him goo-goo eyes.

Amanda, Simon, and Amphora weren't wearing their listening devices for two reasons: one, they didn't think there was much possibility of getting valuable intelligence since there were only three teachers with them, and two, the fact that they were at such close quarters would probably make for crossed signals anyway. But Ivy's hearing was as acute as always, and she overheard plenty. Despite the presence of Professors Sidebotham, Buck, and Ducey, there was a lot of gossip about teachers, none of it very interesting except for a rumor that Professor McTavish's parakeet, Angela, had learned to say "Voldemort." Ivy also heard Gordon trying to impress Editta with the amount of weight he could lift ("I could lift two of you without breaking a sweat") and Binnie Belasco telling Clive Ng that she was absolutely fascinated by rocks and would love to go prospecting with him sometime. Ivy kept up a running commentary imparting all of this to Amanda, who was pretty skeptical about ninety percent of what she was hearing.

About a half hour into the journey Professor Sidebotham jerked the kids out of whatever reveries they were enjoying by saying, "Class, we're going to do an exercise now." The students, of course, responded with much moaning and groaning, so she said, "The next person who complains will attend detention for a week," which shut them up abruptly. Then she said, "I want you to examine as many substances on this bus as you can and text me what you find. Go!"

The bus devolved into complete chaos. Kids were looking at seats, the floor, ceilings, and in a couple of cases, each other. They were finding all kinds of stuff, like bits of soil and plant matter, fibers, oil and grease, bits of fingernails, hair (especially Nigel's), pollen, and grape juice. Gordon swore that he had found some lizard skin, but Wiffle told him it was just dead leaves. Simon wondered if Professor Stegelmeyer would want them to analyze everything and captured as much as he could in evidence bags just in case. Holmes was texting madly, which led Amanda to imagine that he'd found more than anyone else, but she decided that was just her antipathy talking. Ivy was at a bit of a disadvantage with all the visual stuff, but her senses of smell and touch were running at full blast, and she too was texting a lot. At one point, Amphora decided that Simon was looking at her too closely and told him to stop. He said he wasn't, and she said, "Well, you're *supposed* to be," which confused him so much that he got dizzy and had to sit down.

Then the two of them got into a heated debate about how to look at a scene. Simon said you were supposed to make multiple passes with your eyes, concentrating on different things each time, while Amphora said no, you're supposed to notice everything at once. Simon said it's impossible to do that and you'll miss things, while Amphora said that his way was like making a bunch of little trips to the store and why not get all the shopping done in one fell swoop. Simon then asked what a fell swoop was anyway, and Amphora responded by declaring that a fell swoop referred to leaping over mountains and fells, but Simon said it probably had to do with felling a tree and watching it topple all at once.

Upon hearing this, the Wiffle kid inserted himself into the conversation and said that they were both wrong—that "fell" in this case meant evil. Amphora looked up the meaning and discovered that David was actually correct for a change, at which point he smirked and started sending texts. What they said was anyone's guess. However, despite their having determined the meaning of one fell swoop, the argument wasn't over. To settle it, the two adversaries decided to conduct experiments to see whose observing technique was more effective, and they seemed to be proceeding apace when all of a sudden the bus lurched and both Nigel and David Wiffle threw up. This led to an unexpected stop after Prudence complained about the smell and said that if they didn't throw away the dirty paper towels they'd used for cleanup that she, too, would hurl.

At last, however, they arrived at Blackpool with everyone's stomach having settled down and Ivy having collected a large amount of money from Simon and Amphora as a penalty for their feuding. As the kids got an eyeful of all the goodies they were about to explore, the bus erupted in a large amount of shrieking and carrying on, which Professor Sidebotham interrupted with an announcement that no recording was to be allowed and they were to work solely from memory. There would be two days of testing after the field trip, so they had better pay close attention. Professors Buck and Ducey each got in a word of welcome cum warning, and the kids were off.

After about ten minutes, during which Holmes kept running up and saying, "Did you see this?" "Did you see that?" Amanda realized that Ivy was observing sounds no one else was noticing. Not only did this revelation help her attune her own powers of audio observation, it also heightened her visual skills because Ivy was always asking insightful questions. For example, she would say, "I'm hearing a loud whine. What is it?" whereupon Amanda would look for the source of the noise. Once Ivy said, "I'm hearing Japanese," and Amanda looked and looked until she saw a Japanese child who had lost her parents and helped her find them. Seeing this, Professor Sidebotham practically did a back flip. She was so impressed with what Ivy was doing that she asked her to create yet another special presentation on audio observing when they got back.

Then Professor Ducey managed to step in some gum, and as he stood on one leg to try to get it off his shoe, he lost his balance and went crashing into Professor Buck, who collided with a bench and ended up face down on the ground. Amanda thought from that position he was getting just about the best look at environmental substances possible and tried hard not to laugh, and Ivy kept nudging her to describe every little detail. The plight of the two male professors was funny enough, but when Professor Sidebotham, she of at least seventy years, attempted to help them up, Amanda couldn't control herself any longer and had to run in the opposite direction and hide her face to keep from being reprimanded. Fortunately, however, none of the professors was badly hurt and the field trip carried on.

After that, everything went swimmingly. Wiffle and Bramble were making up songs to help them remember what they were seeing, which Amanda had to admit wasn't a half-bad idea. Editta had finally started to count things. Simon was mentally deconstructing and reconstructing everything he saw, which was also a good way to remember stuff, and Amphora was sketching. Amanda was used to noticing little details on film sets, so her observing was going well, except that with Holmes interrupting her every three seconds she was starting to lose her place. He too had his methods, which Amanda wasn't quite sure about, but seemed to involve mentally writing Wikipedia entries for the items he saw and cross-referencing them with mental pictures he was snapping and adding to WikiMedia. What really got her, though, was how popular he had become after just a few days. When he wasn't bugging her, the other kids seemed to seek him out and hang on his every word, which Amanda found so distracting that she started to fear she'd blow the tests. All the kids except Wiffle and Gordon, that is, who kept trying and failing to bait him.

Then suddenly Ivy yelled out, "Something is wrong!" She pulled on Nigel's lead and covered him with her body. Amanda was so startled that she froze. Nobody else was paying attention until out of nowhere came two gunshots and Amanda could see a man fall to the ground while another man ran away. The noise startled the other kids and they all yelled and screamed, some of them running toward the scene and others away from it. A couple of security guards began to chase the fleeing man, and within an extremely short time an ambulance pulled up and a couple of paramedics got out and hunched over the victim.

"OMG, it's a murder!" yelled Amphora. Simon was rummaging for his camera, Holmes was edging as close to the scene as possible, Editta was staring into space, Wiffle and Gordon fled, and Ivy was attending to Nigel. Realizing what had happened, Amanda found herself next to Holmes, pushing forward to see what she could. As the crowd surged, she felt herself collide with him and was held there for what seemed like forever as everyone strained to get a look. She was so surrounded by tall people that she couldn't see anything. Finally, realizing that she was too short to see what was going on, Holmes pulled her in front of him and they were both able to see the fallen man lying in a pool of blood with a paramedic compressing his chest. After a minute or so the technician looked at his partner, shook his head, and recorded the time of death. Then he pulled a sheet over the man and stood up.

Amanda was devastated. This was way worse than finding Legatum's cook dead in the pantry with her head in a bag of sugar as she had last term. She'd seen *this* man killed right in front of her eyes. Her heart was pounding and she fought to catch her breath. Holmes turned her around and searched her eyes to see if she was all right. For some reason that caused her to burst into tears and she covered her face in her hands. Then, without warning, she felt herself engulfed in his arms and realized that he was not only patting her back, but hugging her. This liberty so affronted her that she forgot all about crying and screamed, "Stop it!" then disentangled herself and ran back to where Ivy was pulling Nigel's lead so tight that it looked like he was about to lift up off the ground.

"Stupid Holmes," she muttered. "That guy—"

"What?" said Ivy. "Are you all right? What happened? Was that a murder?"

"Yes, and yes," said Amanda. "I'm okay except for what that Holmes did to me, and yes, that guy is dead. They tried to revive him but they couldn't."

"Oh no!" said Ivy, pulling Nigel even tighter, then wrapping him in her arms.

"Say there," she heard from behind her. It was a policeman. "You girls. We'd like to talk to you."

"You would?" said Amanda.

"Yes, ma'am. You're witnesses to a crime. Please come with me."

Amanda had been interviewed by the police before—three times, to be exact. The first was when the cook was murdered. The second was when the doctor was murdered. And the third time was after she'd saved her father from the Moriartys at the sugar factory. Ivy had been interviewed for the same reasons.

The police interrogation added several more hours to the field trip. All the observations they'd been engaged in had to be cut short, but Professor Sidebotham promised them that there would still be an important test on Monday and to review their notes carefully over what was left of the weekend. On the way back the kids were a lot less animated than on the trip out. Some of them looked dazed. Others were crying, and some were making notes. Wiffle and Gordon had managed to sit together this time, and Amanda could hear whispering from their direction. The teachers spent the drive home in a low confab as well, but otherwise all was quiet.

When the bus drew up to the school, Professor Sidebotham surprised the kids by saying, "Class, please go to the Observation classroom and make note of everything you saw from the time you realized someone had been shot. After that I will join you for a brief discussion." That led to a lot of groaning and carping, since it was late and the kids were tired and hungry. But go to the classroom they did. Amanda made as many notes as she could, but after ten minutes she was all written out. Holmes wrote for about thirty minutes, finishing long after everyone else had stopped.

Finally Professors Sidebotham, Buck, and Ducey entered the room. "Send your observations to me now," said Professor Sidebotham. Everyone clicked Send. "Has everyone forwarded their notes?" She looked out. The students all nodded. "Excellent. Now, Professors Buck, Ducey, and I have something to tell you."

Ivy went rigid. Amanda had learned that her friend was a great early warning system and she trusted her instincts. Something was up. Were the police coming out to interview them again? Did they suspect that one of *them* was an accomplice? What could be so important all of a sudden?

"Mr. Holmes, what did you see this afternoon at Blackpool?" said Professor Sidebotham.

"I saw a murder, Professor," said Holmes. "A man was gunned down in front of us."

"Mr. Wiffle? What did you see?"

"The same as Scapulus said, Professor," said David Wiffle.

"Miss Lester?"

"Yes, ma'am," said Amanda. "The same."

"Class? Anyone disagree?"

Everyone shook their head no.

"You are all incorrect," said the teacher gravely. Professors Ducey and Buck were looking dead serious. That was pretty much Professor

Buck's usual way, but Professor Ducey was normally a jolly fellow and he looked weird all stone-faced.

The room buzzed. Finally David Wiffle said, "What do you mean, Professor?"

"There was no murder today," said the teacher.

Ivy elbowed Amanda as if to indicate that she knew what was coming. Amanda looked at her quizzically, but of course Ivy couldn't see her expression.

"It was a fake, arranged by the school," said Professor Sidebotham.

This time, instead of buzzing, the room went deathly still. With the exception of Ivy, Holmes, and Simon, all the kids' jaws dropped. Then, after about sixty seconds David Wiffle called out, "You mean it was a joke?"

"Absolutely not," said Professor Sidebotham. "I mean it was a demonstration, designed to inspire you to observe in a way you haven't before."

"That's not fair!" yelled Wiffle.

"Yeah!" said Gordon.

"How could you do this to us?" said Owla Snizzle, who was practically in tears.

The three teachers stood like monuments, waiting for silence. Then Holmes spoke.

"Good one, Professor!" He grinned from ear to ear, but this show of support did not cause any change in the three teachers. However, Holmes's actions so irritated Amanda that she grabbed hold of Ivy's hand and squeezed hard enough that Ivy cried out. Then she leaned over and said, "See what I mean? He's an idiot."

Ivy whispered back, "Don't be so hard on him. He's got a great sense of humor."

"How can you say that?" said Amanda, wondering if her friend had indeed lost her mind. First she was grumpy and now she was finding insults humorous. She must have forgotten her own advice about hidden treasures. Amanda would definitely have to get to the bottom of this.

Amanda could hear some of the kids whispering about how ruthless the teachers were. Why, last term they'd spent hundreds of thousands of pounds to blow up the school's garage and everything in it just so the first-years would have a mystery to solve. This was getting ridiculous. Sure, they wanted to be detectives, but the teachers' methods were extreme.

"I see you're upset," said Professor Sidebotham. Amanda thought she was about to apologize, but instead she said, "Get over it." A ripple of protest skittered through the classroom. "You heard me," she said. "Do you remember that first day when Headmaster Thrillkill told you that you would not be coddled at Legatum? He meant it. This is how we instruct. You may adapt, or you may leave. The choice is yours."

For an old lady, she was really tough, thought Amanda. And mean as a hyena. But the woman was one of the sharpest people she'd ever met, and so highly regarded that people came to her for help with their toughest cases. Amanda realized that what the teachers had done made a lot of sense, and she relaxed in her seat. Still, she wasn't amused by Holmes's outburst—or his touching her. Who did he think he was anyway?

After Professor Sidebotham dismissed the class so they could go to dinner, the tension was so thick you could have made pockmarks in it. Kids were grumbling, arguing, slinking, shuffling, starting, stopping, and in one case, snuffling. Wiffle and Bramble seemed to be plotting as usual. Simon and Amphora were arguing, and Editta looked like she was sleepwalking. Nigel was acting as if someone had hit him, a condition that seemed to have come on all of a sudden once they'd left the classroom.

Amanda saw some of the kids go to their rooms, others to the various lounges. She, Ivy, Nigel, and Simon made for the dining room. They had just sat down with their plates when out of the blue the room started shaking—and shaking, and shaking, and shaking. As dishes clattered to the floor and glass broke all around them, Amanda knew exactly what was happening. Legatum Continuatum was smack in the middle of a huge, honking earthquake.

9

EARTHQUAKE!

An earthquake in England! Amanda had never expected that. Back home in L.A. she'd constantly prepared for one and her parents had experienced several, but she'd never actually felt more than a few minor tremors. This one was much stronger, and much more powerful and long lasting than the blast that had rocked the school last term when the garage had exploded.

"Get in the doorway," she yelled to everyone in the dining room. She grabbed Ivy and pulled her inside the jamb leading to the hall. "Under the tables now! And stay away from the windows!"

"What are you doing?" yelled Ivy. "Nigel!" She screamed her dog's name over and over.

"It's the safest place," yelled Amanda. "Now stand there and don't move."

Of course only a couple of people could fit inside each of the various doorways, but the rest of the kids were able to make it under the tables without anything falling on them. Nigel was cowering under one of them, squealing with his paws over his eyes, poor thing. Simon had made a dive for him and was holding him to keep him from lunging. He called out to Ivy that Nigel was with him and was okay despite the whining and whuffling. Needless to say, the screaming and carrying on in the dining room was even worse than it had been when the man at Blackpool had been shot, or whatever had really happened to him.

Amanda felt her phone buzz. She wondered if Amphora was all right. There was nothing she could do for her with all this shaking going on, so she ignored the text. It buzzed again. Could it be Thrillkill? If it was, she wasn't in a position to answer. He'd just have to wait.

She could hear loud crashes coming from the kitchen, where it was obvious that pots and pans were falling out of cupboards, probably along with everything in the pantry. Amanda hoped there wasn't anything hot on the stove. She could hear people running up and down the hall and cried out for them to get away from the windows.

Ivy was shaking so hard Amanda had to hold her still. Looking out for her made her forget how scared *she* was. If anything happened to her friend—or her dog—she'd never forgive herself. The shaking must have gone on for twenty seconds—the ground's, not Ivy's, which continued for much longer than that. It was a very long time for an earthquake. The room moved back and forth sharply, and by the time the shaking had stopped all the dishes, glasses, flatware, and just about everything else had fallen and mostly broken.

"Is everyone okay?" Amanda called out.

"No," said a lot of people raggedly.

"Someone is hurt?" she said.

"No, we're not hurt," they said, but they didn't sound convincing.

"Just scared then?" Amanda's background as an Angeleno somehow made her feel as if she should take charge. Even though she hadn't experienced a quake of this magnitude, everyone looked to her as the expert, which compared to them she was. The people she could see were nodding. Despite the vigor of the quake, no one seemed to be injured, although most of the kids were freaking out at least as much as Ivy.

"You obviously know that we just had a huge earthquake and you need to be careful," she said. "There will be aftershocks—lots of them. When that happens, do exactly what you did this time. Stand in a doorway, get under a table, stay away from the windows."

"But what about Nigel?" wailed Ivy.

"Good question," said Amanda. "Simon, can you think of anything?"

"I'll rig up something for him. He might have to stay in a crate for a while."

Upon hearing this, Ivy started to wail even louder.

"I'll keep him with me, shall I?" said Simon. He knew Ivy could manage without Nigel guiding her, but he also knew that she couldn't stand to be away from him.

"I don't know about that," she said.

Just then, Amanda's phone buzzed again. This time Ivy's and Simon's did too. Boy, Thrillkill was quick.

When Amanda finally looked at her phone, she just about screamed. The first two texts, the ones she'd felt as she stood in the doorway, were from Holmes! He was checking to see if she was all right. Didn't he have anything better to do while an earthquake was going on? The guy didn't know when to quit.

The last text, and the ones Ivy and Simon had received, were a blast from Thrillkill telling everyone to keep calm and take precautions. "Do not go to the chapel," he warned. "It isn't safe there."

He was right. The chapel was just about the oldest part of the school and was probably in ruins. Amanda wondered if the rest of the school was even still standing. What if everything had collapsed? What if someone had been killed? As she contemplated these disasters, she finally started to tremble herself.

After several minutes during which no one had the courage to move, one of the older kids stuck his head in the dining room and inquired after them. He told them that a lot of stuff had spilled all over the floors and you could see cracks in the walls. This information was met with additional shrieking, with kids asking whether the school was going to fall down on top of them and demanding to go home to their parents.

Amanda asked the boy whether the cracks were thick or thin. The kid said they were very skinny. Amanda tried to explain that they weren't worrisome, but no one wanted to listen. It seemed that the quake had turned all the kids in the dining room into drama queens.

Then there was a great swish and clatter as the kitchen door opened and a young blonde man ran out with some brooms, which he started handing out with instructions to clear the floors and be careful when walking. He was followed by a tall older man with a Yorkshire accent so thick Amanda couldn't understand him. At first she thought they were two new janitors, but from the way they were talking, she discovered that they were the new cook and his assistant. She didn't know why it had never occurred to her that the cook might be a man, but here he was, and *now* she knew why Amphora had kept looking toward the kitchen. The young guy was a hunk. Whether he was the cook or the assistant she didn't know. Catching Simon's eye, she gestured toward each of the men and made a stirring motion, which Simon answered by pointing to the younger guy. *He* was the cook.

This was certainly something new, and if the earthquake hadn't disrupted everything Amanda would have been eager to question Amphora. As it was, she and Simon told Ivy to stay put with Nigel and started pushing the brooms around the hall, piling up debris near the baseboards. A couple of the other kids joined them, and soon they were running into each other with such enthusiasm that they declared they had invented the game of bumper brooms. Amanda felt mildly guilty enjoying herself in the midst of a disaster, but after a bit of thought she decided there was no harm in making the most of the situation. The main downside was that the brooms coughed up a lot of dust and debris, which precipitated a round of furious sneezing.

Soon the broom wielders were adding flourishes to their game. If you were able to evade an oncoming broom, you got five points. Dodge two at a time and you got extra credit: fifteen points. Steal the debris from someone else's broom and make it your own, five points. Get your own debris back, five points. Hit a pedestrian, minus five points, unless it was a teacher, and then your entire score was zeroed out and you had to start over. Push your broom and debris all the way down the hall without losing anything, twenty points.

A few minutes after the game had started, Simon was in the lead with sixty points. Amanda wasn't doing as well as she'd have liked—ten points. She'd lost points when she hit a couple of kids who had come down from their rooms to see what was happening. Fortunately she'd missed Mrs. Scarper, the matron, who had followed them. Euphoria Mouse, a fourth-year, had managed to accrue forty points and was just about to score a big one when a powerful aftershock hit and the cleanup team ran for the closest doorways. Amanda was really worried about Ivy, so despite the shaking she ran back to the dining room to check on her. Because the floor was so slick, she slipped and fell, practically doing the splits on the gritty surface, but recovered quickly. When she got to the dining room, she could see that Simon had been hit with something—plaster and paint flakes, she thought. He looked like he'd been out in the snow. Then a painting fell off the wall and narrowly missed him because the dummy had left his shelter under the table and was actually standing up. Seeing that he was okay, Amanda kept running toward Ivy and Nigel, who had again taken refuge under a table. Simon followed her and she yelled for him to grab a doorway but he wouldn't listen. The aftershock lasted so long that more paintings fell off the walls and broke. When the shaking stopped, the cook came out again and observed that one of the pictures he really liked had been destroyed. Then he made a reference to his motorcycle, which explained Amphora's attraction even more. Amanda had to admit that he cut quite a dashing figure.

When the shaking stopped, instead of texting as before, Holmes ran in and asked if everyone was all right. Where he had been was anyone's guess, but he seemed fine. Hearing that yes, they were okay, he grabbed a broom. Working quickly, he set up trash receptacles and made short work of the mess, looking cool and collected the entire time. Amanda watched in amazement. She didn't have the energy to resent him but she vowed that she'd indulge in a satisfying I-hate-Holmes session later.

Everyone was still pretty frazzled, but after Holmes's beautifying routine things had calmed down enough that people were starting to comment. Simon kept saying how cool the quake had felt and wow, he had no idea how powerful earthquakes could be. He wondered if Professor Pole was going to talk about this in Fires and Explosions. Not that either a fire or an explosion had occurred, but the quake was close enough that Simon thought he should address the topic. Then he started asking Amanda questions about earthquakes because, after all, she was the expert. He peppered her with so many of them (Isn't there a lot of wasted storage space when you can't put glass things on high shelves?" "What happens to houses that were built before the building codes were upgraded?" "Does American health insurance cover earthquake injuries?" "Do a lot of trees fall down?") that she soon became exasperated and decided to go off somewhere else.

That somewhere else proved to be the Holmes House common room, where she searched for news on her phone. It seemed that the effects of the tremor had been felt all around the UK, and also in Belgium and France, of all things. The strength on the moment magnitude scale, which had replaced the old Richter scale in most places, was a whopping 5.5, the strongest officially recorded in the country since 1931, when a 6.1 quake off the coast at Dogger Bank in the North Sea had rattled the area. The epicenter was located in Aspatria this time, on the north side of the Ellen Valley in Cumberland, about thirty-five miles from Windermere.

Five point five. Wow. That was huge, especially for the UK. There had to be major damage. What had happened to the school remained to be discovered. Amanda shuddered. She couldn't bear the thought of anyone having been killed, or even injured. Even if that weren't the case, with each aftershock things could change. It was terrifying.

As she was contemplating a variety of horrific possibilities, the décor gremlins rushed into the room and began to clear things up. They had decorated the lounge in an alpine lodge style, and there were skis, poles, and antlers all over the place. The basement was a mess too, they said, and it was going to take them weeks if not months to assess the damage and clean it up. Furthermore, some of the reversible walls had been thrashed so they might not be able to keep up the decorating pace they'd set in the past few months. Amanda was relieved. She was tired of Sidebotham's quizzes.

Just as the situation in the vicinity of the dining room looked like it was stabilizing, Amanda received another text. It was Amphora telling her that Thrillkill had broken his leg in the last aftershock. Amphora! How was *she* doing? Amanda texted her back and asked, fortunately to be told that everyone on the third floor of the dorm was fine. She brought Amphora up to date on her own news, purposely neglecting to mention the new cook. There would be time for that later. The next thing she knew was that a rumor had started flying around the school that Thrillkill was dead. However, his appearance on crutches a bit later quickly scotched that one. It turned out that Professor Also had also been injured. Apparently she was completely black and blue and had taken refuge in the nurse's office.

Then Amanda heard a siren. Someone *had* been hurt, or worse! There was such an unreliable grapevine in place at this point that she thought it almost completely useless to ask if anyone knew what was going on, so she ran to the south entrance of the main building and looked out onto the driveway. There, in front of the school, two paramedics were loading Professor Kindseth into an ambulance! He looked unconscious. Professor Buck was standing nearby, supervising.

This was terrible! Amanda was very attached to Professor Kindseth, who was just about the nicest adult on campus. Last term he'd admitted to her that he, too, had wanted to work in the film biz, but his interest lay in cinematography rather than writing and directing, which were Amanda's specialties. Ever since then she'd felt a particular kinship with the little man. Simon would be crushed to hear about his injuries. He and Professor Kindseth had worked so hard to identify the sugar virus and had hit it off so well. Of course Simon wouldn't show his feelings, but he'd be plenty upset.

Amanda watched as the ambulance left with its precious passenger. She'd better check on Amphora—and Editta! How was she? *Where* was she?

She ran down the cleaner but still messy hallway and tromped up the stairs to the third floor. There she found Amphora cowering under her bed, which was a neat trick considering how low the bed was. Fortunately, unlike in Nick's room, there was a minimum of dust underneath, although since the quake, there was plenty everywhere else. Amphora was alternately sneezing, crying, and chattering so hard she had practically bitten her tongue off.

"Are you okay?" said Amanda, bending down to see meet her eyes. "Can you come out of there?"

"N-o, and n-n-n-o," said Amphora, peering out between her fingers.

"It was a 5.5. The epicenter is in Aspatria." It was hard to talk all hunched over like that. Her voice caught.

"N-o w-w-onder! It was p-p-p-ractically u-u-underneath us." Was that a sign of life? Even if all Amphora could express was panic, at least she was talking.

"By the way, we're all fine except that Thrillkill broke his leg and Professor Kindseth just left in an ambulance."

"Oh n-o! Is he d-ead?" Amphora chattered even harder. Amanda reached under the bed and took her hand, which was ice cold.

"I don't think so. I don't really know anything. Where's Editta? Is she okay?"

"I have n-n-n-no idea. Did you l-l-look in her ro-om?"

It was a stupid question. If Amphora had spent the last however long under her bed, how would she know what was going on with Editta?

"No," said Amanda. "Hang on. I'll take a peek."

She opened the door and surveyed the hall, which was so dusty that just looking at it made her want to sneeze. The way was clear, though, so she walked carefully down to Editta's room and knocked. Nothing.

"Editta," she called. "Are you in there?"

Silence.

"Editta?"

"What do you want?" Aha. She *was* in there, although extremely muffled.

"Are you okay? The earthquake was 5.5." She thought her friend might respond better if she mentioned numbers.

"Go away."

"I will if you answer my question." It would be delicate trying to deal with her. Amanda decided to act as non-threatening as possible. "Are you okay?"

"I'm fine." Her voice was weak.

"Can I come in and see?" What if she'd been hit in the head or something?

"Mm."

Amanda took that as a yes. She pushed the door open and peeked inside. Editta was lying on her bed, stomach down, with her hands over the back of her head, as if trying to protect herself. She had it half right. She would have been safer underneath.

"Can you turn over?"

Editta made no move to do so, so Amanda came close and looked at the bit of her face that was showing. She looked uninjured, but who could tell?

"Are you hurt?"

"No."

"Good. Do you want to talk about the quake? I have information."

"No."

"Do you want to talk about anything?" Maybe considering the situation she'd open up about whatever it was that had been bothering her.

"No."

"Do you want something to drink?"

"No."

Amanda thought it best not to push, so she simply said, "Okay. Text if you need me," and left. What was going on? First the teachers, then Ivy, and now Editta. Could whatever was bothering them be the same thing? If so, what was it? She'd better find the missing item, and fast.

Upon returning to her room, where Amphora was making tentative progress toward emerging from her sanctuary, Amanda received a call. It was her mother wanting to find out how she was. Apparently she and Herb had felt the quake too, but much less strongly. After all, London was more than 300 miles from the epicenter.

"Do you want to come home?" said Lila. "I can make you some chicken soup."

"I'm fine, Mom. We're all fine. No one needs chicken soup."

"It's too dangerous. I'm going to come get you."

This was just about the worst idea Amanda could think of and she wasn't about to let it happen.

"Mom, please don't. The teachers are looking after us just fine." This was a bit of a stretch, but how would her mother know that? "The cracks are hairline," which was true, "and I'm pretty sure the structures are sound. They've called the engineers. Really. You don't need to worry. We're on basalt here anyway."

As if. Basalt was one of the safest foundations possible, but she had no idea if that was really the case. She hoped her mother wouldn't look up the geology of Windermere.

"Your father isn't feeling too well," said Lila. "Why don't you send him an email? It might cheer him up."

"Sure. I'll do that right now. What's wrong with him?"

"Same old same old. He's listless. He'll snap out of it, though. I've bought him some videos on PTSD. They give you exercises to do every day. He'll be fine in no time."

Amanda doubted that some video could fix what was ailing her father but she had no intention of saying so. That would just lead to a lot of I-know-what's-best-don't-you-question-me stuff, which she really didn't need, so she mumbled assent and got off the phone as gracefully as she could.

She was dying to say something to Amphora about the cutie pie in the kitchen, but she figured now wasn't the time, so she turned to go back down to the dining room to check on her friends. However, before she could get through the door she got another text from Thrillkill telling everyone to stay in their rooms until further notice. Coincidentally, Ivy and Nigel appeared at just about that time, Ivy having decided that Simon was very sweet to offer to help but she'd prefer to keep Nigel at her side.

Thrillkill's dictum did not sit well. Amanda and Ivy were way too headstrong to allow themselves to be confined. They were willing to clean up the room a bit, but once the place was usable they agreed that they would go out and nose around. At this point Amphora was texting madly with her parents and seemed not to see or hear anything Amanda and Ivy were doing. Ivy pointed at her and then vaguely toward the kitchen, and Amanda took her hand and made a yes sign in her palm. They were wise to Amphora's tricks now, and though neither of them was particularly nosy, they were curious about her little crush.

Amanda, Ivy, and Nigel sneaked down the stairs, although they didn't have to be quite so careful because everyone was preoccupied. When they reached the bottom they noticed several teachers looking around and making notes. Then they heard something disturbing. Professor Snaffle and Professor McTavish were saying that they hadn't seen Professor Redleaf anywhere. She wasn't in her office or her classroom and no one could find her. All the other teachers were accounted for, so this development was particularly worrisome.

Suddenly both Amanda's and Ivy's phones buzzed. What now? Amanda was getting phone shy. Every time a text or a call came through it was something she didn't want to hear. But nothing she had received so far was as bad as this news. Simon was texting them to tell them that Professor Stegelmeyer had found Professor Redleaf under a bookcase and she was dead!

10

MUSHY LETTERS AND CANDY STASHES

Upon hearing the terrible news about Professor Redleaf, Amanda's first thought was that this was another trick meant to test their powers of observation, but after texting back and forth with Simon, she became convinced that the cyberforensics teacher—Holmes's friend—had really been killed.

She was so upset she couldn't think. Ivy burst into tears and clutched Amanda and Nigel at the same time. Nigel was still pretty shook up and seemed to bask in the attention. Simon, however, was texting all sorts of questions, which were hard to ignore. Did the accident have anything to do with the gremlins' placement of the bookcase, and if so, what would happen to them? Was this really a murder meant to look like an accident? What would happen to Professor Redleaf's course? Would Amanda and Holmes still make the film? Amanda was so overloaded and freaked out that she could barely read the texts, let alone consider their implications.

She wondered if there was any way to get news about Professor Kindseth. Surely *he* was still alive, although how could she be sure? Why wasn't Thrillkill letting them know about his condition? Would they have to evacuate the school? And what would happen on Monday, when classes were supposed to resume?

Professor Redleaf's death hit the students hard. No one but Holmes had really known her, but they still took her loss personally. Bonds at Legatum went deep. There was a fierce us vs. them mentality at the school, and Professor Okimma Redleaf had definitely been one of "us."

The next day, Sunday, everyone was dragging around. They'd all been up late because of the earthquake, and the aftershocks during the night hadn't helped them get any rest. Around ten in the morning, Amanda received a text from Thrillkill asking her to come see him. When she arrived, he told her that she and Holmes would have to postpone their film because Holmes was needed elsewhere. He was going to take over Professor Redleaf's class.

Despite the fact that she hadn't wanted to make the film in the first place, this news infuriated her. Who was Holmes to be teaching the class? He was twelve, for Pete's sake. Actually, he might have been thirteen—she didn't know—but in either case, cyberforensics? How could he possibly know enough to teach that? The inconvenient fact that Amanda herself was supposed to teach a class managed to escape her. Holmes was an arrogant twit. *She* was a qualified story expert who had something wonderful to share.

It didn't hit her until about an hour later that this meant her course was back on. Thrillkill hadn't said so, but that was the logical conclusion. When she realized she would be able to teach her storytelling class after all, she pumped the air and ran to tell Ivy the news. Now both girls were lined up to teach. Forgetting the earthquake, the two of them pulsed with energy and started jabbering about tricks for keeping the students on the edges of their seats. Ivy was going to regale them with the story of how she had helped Amanda foil that security keypad by listening to the sounds the keys made, and Amanda was planning to compare and contrast the various villains in the Harry Potter stories to shed light on criminal personalities. This led to their comparing David Wiffle with Draco Malfoy and the discovery of many similarities until Ivy pointed out that David was supposed to be a good guy and Amanda said yes, what had they been thinking.

The rest of the day unfolded in fits and starts while the kids alternately cowered, grieved, and played bumper brooms. Amanda and her group used their listening devices but didn't hear anything helpful. Everyone was preoccupied with the quake, Professor Redleaf, and Professor Kindseth, who had been declared to be in critical condition at the local hospital. Quite a few of the kids wanted to visit him but were told they couldn't do so while he was in intensive care.

On Monday classes were cancelled as building inspectors crawled all over the school. All day Legatum was on high alert as the engineers found this problem and that problem and debated whether they would be able to contain them. Their presence caused the kids to worry even more about what might happen if the school were declared uninhabitable. Where would they go? What would they do? Would there even *be* a school? What did all this mean for the missing object, whatever it was? Maybe it been unearthed in the quake—or buried deeper.

In the end, however, although the damage was extensive, the inspectors miraculously didn't find anything serious enough to close down the school—other than the chapel. Ugly, creepy, and in need of repair, yes. Some things definitely were that. Condemned, however, no. Despite the casualties, everyone declared themselves lucky. A 5.5 earthquake in a place without special provisions in its building codes could have been much more serious.

Still and all, the gremlins' work had now been called into question and the school had to consider earthquake safety in placing items, whether at the gremlins' direction or no. This restriction, of course, threw Alexei and Noel into a tizzy because where objects went was a critical part of design and now they would be limited to a canvas that was inherently out of balance. The two men were occupied from morning till midnight moving, cleaning, storing, and what have you, but that didn't stop them grousing one minute and planning how they might adapt the next. Sometimes Amanda wondered how they could talk so much without becoming hoarse and finally wrote herself a reminder to research the topic.

On Tuesday classes resumed—all except Textual Analysis, that is. With Professor Bill Pickle in jail for having assaulted a commercial rival a few months before, Headmaster Thrillkill had had to look for a replacement, but with all the confusion he hadn't been able find anyone and had had to cancel the class until further notice. This omission, however, affected only the third-year and later students.

Despite the kids' having bumper-broomed pretty well, the school was still thick with dust and debris. Everyone was sneezing and coughing, even Nigel, and Ivy asked Simon if there might be something they could do to protect him. Simon considered acquiring a gas mask, but Ivy said no, Nigel would never wear it. That got Simon thinking about trying to design either a special surgical mask for dogs, or a massive air purifier, or both. In the end, he managed to make a mask out of a muzzle, which Nigel actually tolerated. *That* led him to think about trying to patent it, at which point he decided to consult Holmes, who himself held a patent—some method for finding smoking guns in digital data—and might be helpful. The device worked beautifully and Ivy was immensely grateful. Amanda, however, upon hearing about Holmes and his la-di-da intellectual property, became annoyed despite her love for Nigel, and barked at Simon when he tried to explain what he'd done.

The new doctor—the one who replaced Mr. Tunnel, who'd turned out to work for the Moriartys—was a Chinese woman who was such a whirlwind of activity that Amanda thought she must have been a choreographer in a previous life. She hadn't needed to consult her, but

Amphora and Ivy had—both had bad coughs—and they'd been highly impressed with her medical skills and bedside manner. However, one thing about the doctor, Mrs. Wing, did annoy her, or rather something that happened involving the doctor rather than Amanda personally. When passing by the school's hospital, she heard the doctor conversing in Chinese with Holmes, which she found so annoying she wanted to punch his lights out. (Not the doctor's, of course. Chinese was her native language.) There he was showing off again. How could so many of her contemporaries actually like the guy, especially Simon, who thought he was the bee's knees?

However, some positive developments soon became apparent. The main one was that a number of hidden compartments, cupboards, niches, and even tunnels that had previously been cleverly hidden were now exposed. As a result there was much more to explore than before, and Amanda and her friends felt optimistic about their chances of finding the missing item. Unfortunately, noxious substances had also been liberated, including various spores, weird types of soil and dust, odd species of mold, and long-buried pollen. In fact, the air was so polluted that it was a wonder the engineers had declared the school safe to inhabit. Fortunately, ordinary surgical masks helped protect sensitive noses, mouths, and respiratory systems in the humans. As far as animals were concerned, Simon consulted for Professor McTavish as well as Ivy, and managed to make a special cage filter for Angela, the talking parakeet. This caused him to run to Holmes about a possible second patent application, and he came back yakking his head off about how he was going to file it.

After class Amanda, Simon, Ivy, Amphora, and Nigel spent several hours exploring. They were keen on looking in the basements, which were extensive, and since the earthquake, believed to be even more so. However, they thought it might be best to start at the top of the school and work down, just to be systematic, so up to the top floor they went.

They decided to spread out. Amanda took the north end, Ivy and Amphora the south end, and Simon the middle. This was not exactly an equitable split but it was good enough to start with.

They hadn't searched long when Amphora called out, "You've got to see this." Thinking she might have found the missing thingie, the rest of the team ran to her position, which happened to be deep inside a closet in a disused classroom. When they arrived, they found her standing in front of a tiny compartment that had been hidden behind some shelves containing Christmas decorations. Inside was a metal box, and inside the box was a pile of handwritten letters. Amphora had opened one of them and was reading it with tears in her eyes.

"What's wrong?" said Amanda. This didn't look good. Why was Amphora crying?

"What is it?" said Ivy.

"She's holding a letter and crying," said Amanda, taking Ivy's hand and touching the paper with it. Ivy felt it carefully.

"I can tell she's crying," said Ivy. "I just wasn't sure why. What's wrong, Amphora?"

"It's so sad," Amphora wailed.

"What is?" said Simon, looking skeptical. Amanda just knew what he was thinking. Amphora was creating drama out of nothing. Not that she necessarily disagreed with him.

"These love letters." Amphora held them up. They were written with a fountain pen on blue paper. Fortunately her tears hadn't smeared anything.

"Ooooh, love letters," said Ivy. "Whose are they?" She felt the paper again as if that would answer her question.

"You can't really feel the ink on the paper, can you?" said Amanda.

"Don't be silly," said Ivy. "Of course not."

"You're not trying some voodoo mumbo jumbo, are you?" said Simon.

"Si-monnnnn," said Ivy. "I'm just touching, the same way you'd look at something. It does, by the way, help me to get a feel for how old the paper is. I'd say it's been around for a while, but not centuries or anything."

"You're right," said Simon. "It's newish but not brand new."

"So what does it say?" said Amanda, trying to look over Amphora's shoulder, a futile exercise due to their considerable difference in height.

"It's so passionate," said Amphora. "A guy named Kenneth is spilling his guts to a woman named Charlotte. He's so in love with her he'd live inside a tree if it was the only way to be with her, but she's kind of cold toward him. Well, not cold, but not warm either."

"Let me see that," said Simon, grabbing the letter. "Is there an address or a date or anything?" He scanned the paper.

"No, nothing," said Amphora. "Do you recognize the writing?"

"Uh uh," said Simon. "You?"

"Nope."

"Me either," said Amanda, trying to get a good look.

"Hey, you don't suppose Kenneth is Professor Kindseth, do you?" said Ivy.

"OMG, yes!" said Amphora. "It's got to be."

"Why do you say that?" said Simon, examining the letter back, front, and sideways.

"What other Kenneth is there here?"

The kids thought for a moment. Then Simon said, "There's no other teacher by that name, but how do we know it's a teacher?"

"Who's Charlotte?" said Amphora.

"No clue," said Amanda. "There's no teacher with that name."

"What a cool mystery," said Amphora.

"Yes," said Ivy, "but I don't think these are the missing items. The letters are sad and a bit incriminating, but there's no way these could be throwing all the teachers into such a tizzy. Unless there's some sort of blackmail going on. Do you think there might be?" She reached down and petted Nigel's ears protectively.

"It seems unlikely," said Amanda. "I suppose we could document these and go on, though."

"Yes, good idea," said Ivy.

"I'll do it," said Amphora. "It's such amazing reading."

Simon gave her the kind of look a twelve-year-old boy gives a twelve-year-old girl when she gets all mushy, then left the room.

After that the kids unearthed more hidden compartments than they thought possible. Most of them were empty, though, and after a couple of hours without significant discovery, they thought they'd go down to the dining room for a cup of tea. However, they had barely moved when Amanda called out, "Hey!" When the other kids arrived at her location, a supply closet in a niche in the north hall, she was digging into a deep space stuffed with as many types of candy as you can imagine. Every cubic inch was filled with chocolate creams, red and black licorice sticks, chocolate nut bars, M&Ms, candy corn, chocolate-covered cherries, vanilla fudge, gooey caramels, some kind of marshmallow concoction, dark chocolate bars, mints, Cadbury Roses, chocolate Easter bunnies and Santas, something blue and fruity-smelling, and a whole lot more. The smell was amazing and so hard to resist that Amanda had to fling her arm in front of the stash to keep the others from raiding it.

"What do you think this is about?" she said, trying to remember each variety in case this was one of Professor Sidebotham's setups.

"Who's fat around here?" said Simon.

"Si-monnn," said Amphora and Ivy in unison.

"Well, if you eat this stuff, that's what will happen to you. So it's logical to look for someone who's overweight. Who's fat?"

"No one's fat—anymore," said Amanda. The "anymore" referred to the fact that she, Amphora, and a few of the other first-years had been overweight when they'd started at Legatum, but the previous cook's sugar thefts had reduced the number of calories in the food, and by the end of the term they had all slimmed down.

"Are you sure?" said Simon.

"I can't think of anyone. Can you?" said Amphora.

The kids took a couple of minutes to skim through the images of the students and teachers in their minds, but no one could come up with a name. Even Professor Mukherjee, the legal issues teacher, who had been roly-poly when spring term had begun, had lost weight, which to everyone's surprise made him look rather dashing. Legatum's denizens were all appallingly fit. And so the identity of the owner/manager of the candy stash remained a mystery, at least for the time being.

After their tea break, during which they discovered that the new cook had reinstituted the revered custom of afternoon tea and scones (and grabbed another peek at him—his name was Rupert Thwack), they returned to the third floor. They may have covered a lot of ground, but there was so much more to go that they decided to give it an hour and quit. During that time they found someone's costume jewelry collection, snapshots from an old Halloween party (you don't even want to know), and what Simon referred to as a skateboard graveyard.

The skateboard stash so excited Simon that he lingered over it for a long time. It comprised a huge closet full of broken skateboards of every vintage imaginable. Some were popular makes and models, and others were obviously custom designs. There was a Chocolate Raven Tershy Treehouse deck (very purple) with Spiral wheels, a dark blue Antihero Classic Eagle, and a lime green Roger Snack Attack. Under those he found an ancient Makaha sidewalk board and a G&S Stacey

Peralta Warp Tail. But his favorite was a Zazzle Chronic Monkey, which was painted a bright emerald green and had a picture of a monkey on the deck. He was busting to tell the girls about it, but after Amanda's unfortunate experience on the train to London the previous term, he decided not say anything. Amanda was still fuming about being peed on and had taken an intense dislike to monkeys and apes of all kinds, even King Kong, whose skyscraper scene she had long admired.

Simon found this collection even more baffling than the others they'd come across. Why would anyone keep a bunch of broken skateboards? Someone should fix them. They would be incredibly useful around campus. This place was truly nuts.

After he was able to tear himself away, Simon and the girls continued to scour the third floor but didn't find anything that might qualify as the missing item, which they had started to call "the whatsit." There were, however, two more floors plus endless basements to go, not to mention the gym and various outbuildings. The chapel, of course, was still off-limits, although none of them had ever let a little thing like one of Thrillkill's orders stop them.

11

THE CRYSTALS

The following Saturday, Amanda noticed that Amphora was wearing a necklace composed of a beautiful apricot-colored crystal. It was so striking that she decided she wanted one too and asked Amphora where she'd gotten it.

"If I tell you, you won't believe it," said Amphora, fingering the stone. It sparkled like you wouldn't believe.

"Of course I will," said Amanda, staring at it. It looked like winter, spring, summer, and fall all at once. "Why wouldn't I?"

"You have to understand," said Amphora, "I wasn't doing anything I wasn't supposed to." She seemed awfully nervous. What had she done? Flouted the rules and snuck off to town?

"I know that. But even if you had, so what?"

"No reason," said Amphora. "It's just that . . . well, okay, I did do something I wasn't supposed to. I was out by the chapel. Please don't tell anyone."

"Of course I won't, but why are you worried? You didn't go in, did you?"

"No."

"So what then? Please take me. I'm dying to see what you found. This doesn't have anything to do with gluppy things, does it?"

"Gluppy things" was Amanda's description of the slime mold she and Nick had found in the garden near the secret room where the previous term's cook had hidden her virus-treated pink sugar—the same place the cook and the doctor had held Herb Lester. The things were gross and Amanda didn't ever want to have anything to do with them again.

"No gluppy things. I promise. Ready?"

"Ready. Let's go."

As they worked their way down to the spot where Amphora had found the crystal, Amanda said, "So, the new cook."

"What about him?" said Amphora, reddening.

"He's cute," said Amanda.

"Oh? I hadn't noticed." She quickened her step.

"Come on, Amphora. Everyone knows you have a huge crush on him."

"No I don't." She walked even faster.

"I don't blame you," said Amanda. "He's got a motorcycle and everything."

Amphora stopped and looked at Amanda. "I know," she moaned. "He's amazing. Did you know that he studied with Jamie Oliver?" Jamie Oliver, the boyish celebrity chef, was the coolest guy ever. Even Amanda had heard of him over in the States. Not that he was a boy anymore, but he'd started in his teens and immediately made a huge splash.

"No, I didn't, but it figures. See, that wasn't so bad." Amanda smiled and Amphora visibly relaxed.

"Please don't say anything to Simon," said Amphora.

"I don't have to. He knows."

"Darn it, Amanda. Why did you tell him?"

Amanda looked Amphora full in the face and said, "Thanks a lot. Why would you think I'd do that? Simon has eyes. We all do. It's so obvious it's ridiculous. You need to work on your disguises. That includes not staring at cute guys when you don't want anyone to know you like them."

Amphora sighed. "I can't believe I've been doing that." She looked miserable.

"Well you have, so cut it out. I don't blame you, but if you don't want people knowing, you're going to have to be a better actor than that."

Amphora brightened. "Yes, that's true. Can you teach me?"

Amanda rolled her eyes. "Sure. In my copious free time."

"You don't have to make that film with Scapulus anymore, right?"

"That's true. Okay. We'll meet tomorrow and I'll give you some pointers. Now can we please see where you found the crystal?"

When they arrived at the spot, Amanda saw a huge abyss where a few days earlier a perfectly manicured lawn had graced the space. She found it almost incomprehensible that the inspectors hadn't ruled this place off limits, but there it was, gaping but apparently benign. It was pretty deep in parts, but other sections went only a foot or two down, so she waded in.

"There," pointed Amphora. The place she was indicating was moist and soft.

"You found it just lying there?" said Amanda, whose shoes were already caked with mud.

"Pretty much."

"I wonder if there are more. Let's dig around a bit."

They weren't about to do that with their bare hands, but conveniently there was a gardening outbuilding nearby and it wasn't locked. The girls sloshed their way to it in their muddy shoes, and after rooting around returned with a large shovel and a small trowel.

Working outward and downward from the spot where Amphora had found the crystal, they dug as deep as they could. One would use the shovel for the heavy work and the other would follow with the trowel. In this manner they hoped to avoid damaging any crystals they might find. Amanda filmed as they went, attempting to perform a three-hand job with two and ending up with gunky clothes. Fortunately the camera remained if not pristine, clean enough to do the job.

It didn't take long for them to get results. Within about three minutes Amphora's shovel hit something hard—so much for their two-step digging process—and when they looked they could see more crystals. This encouraged them so much that they spent an hour excavating, and by the time they had worn themselves out they were very close to the secret room.

At that point they had discovered maybe forty crystals, which they had carefully piled up out of the way. Though they were encrusted with mud, each one was as beautiful as the one Amphora had made into a necklace. Amanda bagged and marked them. She was so excited about their findings she could barely contain herself. An unusual discovery and beautiful new jewelry too. She couldn't wait to tell Ivy.

When they had processed all the crystals, something caught her eye. She could see another cavern off the abyss. It seemed to extend way underneath the building, right near the secret room.

"Just a quick peek, okay?" she said.

"All right," said Amphora. "But please make it fast. I'm so tired I'm going to collapse right here."

Amanda stepped back into the crater and carefully made her way to the hole in its side. "It's too dark to see anything," she said, peering in.

"Have you got your light?"

"Of course." The light on her phone had been invaluable in exploring nooks and crannies. In fact, she and Nick had used it to discover the secret room in the first place. She switched it on and shined it into the cavern, which was huge. Suddenly she screamed and dropped her phone in the mud.

Under the building, right next to the room in which her father had been held, stood an upright skeleton, its skull encrusted with dazzling, glowing apricot-colored crystals, and it was staring right at her.

12

ANOTHER DEAD BODY

Amanda was so surprised to see the skeleton that she screamed. It wasn't that she was afraid. She wasn't. And she wasn't exactly thinking, "Oh no, another dead person," but her reflexes were. She didn't know what she'd expected to see, but a skeleton wasn't it. She didn't know why but she thought of Richard III, the medieval king whose body had been found under a parking lot. What had the people who'd discovered *it* thought when they'd first seen it. OMG, was it possible that this was another missing royal figure? Maybe it was even Robin Hood or King Arthur.

"What?!" cried Amphora.

"Eek, eek," Amanda was yelling. She was stomping in the mud so hard it would have been easy for her phone to sink and disappear, which it did.

"What is it?" said Amphora. "Oh no, oh no. I just know it's another body. It is, isn't it?"

"Yes!" screamed Amanda loud enough to wake the thing in the cavern. "It's Robin Hood!"

"What?" said Amphora. "Are you nuts? We have to get Thrillkill."

"Right. Except I've dropped my phone. Oh no, I don't see it. It must be in the mud." She felt around. Nothing.

"I have mine," said Amphora, digging in her pockets. "I'll get him. Who is it really?"

"I don't know. It's a skeleton."

"Aaaaaaah!" yelled Amphora, trying to text but shaking too hard.

"Hang on," said Amanda. "Here it is. Eeeeeew." She'd found her phone way down in the muck. It was in a terrible state, probably as dead as the skeleton. "Here, give me that."

Amphora waded over and handed her phone to Amanda, who punched a message to Thrillkill without remembering to tell him where she was. Oh well. Her GPS would let him know.

"OMG," said Amphora. "A skeleton?" Then, suddenly, she stopped her hysterics. "Wait. That means it's really old, doesn't it?"

Amanda stopped and thought for a second. She was right. The idea of Robin Hood and King Arthur was a bit over the top, but the skeleton did have to be old. Otherwise it would be a body instead of a skeleton. She breathed a sigh of relief. If this were a murder it was an ancient one, and not anything to do with them.

"I think you're right." Then, suddenly remembering what she'd seen, she said, "But it had crystals on it."

"What?" said Amphora.

"The head. It had crystals all over it."

"Hang on. I have to see." Amphora started clomping through the mud.

"I don't think you want to," said Amanda, trying to clean the gunk off her phone.

"But you said it's old. That doesn't bother me so much."

"Okay," said Amanda. "Help yourself. Do you have a light?"

"Yes. Can you give me back my phone?"

Amanda gave Amphora her phone. Thus armed, her roommate tiptoed into the mouth of the cavern. She turned on her light and directed it all around.

"Eeeeek!" she yelled when the light hit the skeleton.

"I told you," said Amanda.

"Wait a minute. Now that I know where it is, I won't be so shocked. I want to see those crystals." She turned the light back toward the body.

"Oooooh, would you look at that? It's gorgeous. I wonder who it is. Do you think it's someone royal?"

"Oh for heaven's sake," said Amanda. "And they tell me *I* watch too many movies." This, of course, was a highly hypocritical thing to say. Suddenly she thought of Darius Plover. She hadn't answered him! When she got out of this mess she would have to write to him or she'd never hear from him again.

Just then Professors Stegelmeyer, Scribbish, Hoxby, and Pole arrived. Somehow their presence lent a sense of order to the scene. They told the girls to stand back while they investigated.

"You haven't touched anything, have you?" said Professor Scribbish.

"Not the body," said Amanda. "We didn't go in there. But we dug up a bunch of these crystals. See? There in the evidence bags."

"Well done," said Professor Scribbish, examining the bags. "Excellent procedure. But what are these crystals?" He held one of the bags up to the light. "Residue from the slime mold?"

That possibility hadn't occurred to Amanda. She wondered if it was true. Could slime turn crystalline? Maybe it could. Simon would probably know. She wished he were there and wondered if she should text him too.

Just then Thrillkill came hobbling around the corner on his crutches. "Have you girls touched anything?" he said upon seeing the mess. "Oh my. That's quite a hole, isn't it?" There was no way *he* was going into the abyss with those crutches.

"It's okay, Gaston," said Professor Scribbish. "They've followed procedure. What do you make of those?" He pointed to the pile of crystals.

Thrillkill looked at the bags. "Nice work, Miss Lester, Miss Kapoor," he said. The two girls beamed. It was about time someone recognized the merits of their explorations. Amanda wondered what he'd think about their findings on the third floor. For all she knew, the candy and skateboard stashes were his. Not the letters, though. Unless

135

Headmaster Thrillkill had a secret identity, he wasn't Kenneth, although all detectives had secret identities—lots of them. Nah. Couldn't be.

"Where did you find all those crystals?" Thrillkill asked. Then he noticed the one around Amphora's neck. "Say, that's not bad. The same?" He nodded toward the pile.

"We think so, sir," said Amphora. "Beautiful, isn't it? I can't see how it can have anything to do with slime mold."

"You'd be surprised," he said, putting her off so much that she removed the necklace and stuck it in her pocket, first encasing it in a baggie. Amanda laughed. Not that she wouldn't have done the same. Thrillkill wasn't known for his tact.

Then he really surprised Amanda. He stepped right into the big hole, crutches and all, and made his way to the mouth of the cavern. He extracted a torch from his pocket and shined it all around the space. When he had located the body, he said, "Hm," then walked inside, along with the other professors. The space was large and it echoed, and Amanda could hear most of what they said, although she had to inch closer to do so. Amphora kept to the fringes with the crystals, as if guarding them from predators.

Suddenly Amanda remembered that she had her listening device with her and stuck it in her ear, turning around to wink at Amphora. Now she could hear every word.

"Not a clue," Professor Hoxby, the pathology teacher, was saying. "I can tell you that it's an adult male, but I won't know anything further until I conduct the autopsy."

Oh no, not another autopsy. Post-mortems were not Amanda's strong suit. Last term she'd got everyone puking in their dead bodies class. But of course the body would have to be examined.

"No, I can't see a cause of death," Professor Hoxby continued. "And I've never seen anything like those crystals before. I wonder—"

"Psssst," said Amphora. "You don't think these crystals could have killed him, do you?" She too had inserted her listening device and could hear everything.

"I don't see how," said Amanda. "You mean you think they might be poison?"

"Yes," said Amphora. "Or some kind of blood sucker. Maybe it got me too."

"I think you'd have known that by now. Do you feel sick?"

"I'm not sure." She took the crystal out of her pocket and threw it on top of the other bags. "Yes, I do. Ugh. I just know the crystals killed that man."

"Amphora, please don't do this. I'm sure there's another explanation. How long have you been wearing that thing?"

"I don't know. A day, maybe."

"Well, then, I think you're fine. If they were that dangerous you'd already be dead." Amanda turned back to the cavern. Professor Hoxby was lamenting the state of the body.

"It's been burned, and whatever clothing wasn't burned has rotted," he said. "The teeth have been smashed in too. Anyone recognize these clothes?"

No one did. It would have been a neat trick to do so. They had been almost completely destroyed.

"The cavern is completely charred," said Professor Pole. "Let's get some samples of that carbon, plus some of this plaster and dust."

"How do you think he got in here?" said Thrillkill.

"Look here," said Professor Pole, pointing to something Amanda couldn't see. "He was walled up."

Amanda felt her stomach lurch. The man had been buried alive? Well, maybe not alive, but in a wall? It was horrible.

"I'll tell you what," he said. "The heat the earthquake released started a fire that burned the body. That fire, together with the pressure, created the crystals. It's quite unusual. Normally you'd need much higher temperatures and more pressure over a longer period of time. I'll need to study this more, but that's my best guess at the moment."

So the power of the earthquake had not only damaged the buildings and released all kinds of gunk into the air, but it had started a fire and created these beautiful crystals? From what, though? Surely not the slime mold. That was long gone.

"I must say that if it weren't so macabre, the sight of this body would be magical," said Professor Scribbish. "Oh, quite ghoulish, but doesn't it look like a fairy tale?"

"I think you're getting a bit carried away, Chris," said Thrillkill. "All I see is a crime scene."

Typical. Thrillkill didn't know the meaning of romance. The closest he ever got to it was his hair dryer and the icicle army he fought with it.

Suddenly Amanda felt a whoosh of air and realized that a bunch of moths had almost flown into her. By golly, if it wasn't already dusk. Could it be? Yes, it was. The moths were heading for the light of the crystals, which had grown stronger as the sky had dimmed. They were attracted by the light of the crystals in the skull! Professor Scribbish was right. The crystals *were* magical. She wondered what Editta would say. Come to think of it, where *was* Editta?

The next task was to remove the body. Amphora did not want to see that, but Thrillkill told her it would be good experience and practically threatened her with some unknown punishment if she were to leave.

Amanda not only didn't mind watching the procedure, but wanted to video it. Despite the sickening nature of the experience, she wanted to learn and was eager to film as much as possible, not only for detective purposes but for her filmmaking. Every chance she got to practice was an opportunity. She'd have to make sure her lighting compensated for the darkening sky though. Filming would be tricky.

"What's this?" Oh great—it was Holmes. He just had to show up everywhere. She was in no mood to talk to him. "Amanda," he called. "Amphora."

"Oh, Scapulus, I'm so glad you're here," said Amphora. "We've just found a dead body. It's awful."

"Here? At the school?" he said. "Who is it?" He craned his neck toward the pit.

"We don't know," she said, shrugging.

"Amanda?" He looked at her.

"Dunno," Amanda said rudely. Holmes looked hurt.

"Who's in there?" he said, pointing to the dark opening.

"Professor Thrillkill, Professor Scribbish, Professor Pole, Professor Hoxby, and Professor Stegelmeyer," Amphora said. Amanda was surprised she could say all that. It was quite a mouthful. She probably would have used last names only. Sometimes Brits were so formal.

"What are those?" he said, pointing to the crystals. "They're quite attractive."

"They're poison," said Amphora, backing away. "You should stay away from them."

"They're not poison," said Amanda. "We don't know what they are, but they're fine."

"No they're not," said Amphora. "I found this one and I made it into a necklace and now I'm sick." She pointed to the necklace.

"Really?" said Holmes, picking up the bag with the crystal and examining it. "What are your symptoms?" He looked her up and down.

"I feel sick to my stomach, my head hurts, and I feel yucky all over. Do I look weird?"

"Not at all," he said. "The crystals quite suit you." She looked startled, then tried to hide a smile. "Did you feel that way before you found the body?"

"Not exactly." She was still trying to hide the grin. This wasn't good. Now she'd start to follow him around the way she did the cook and would never get anything done.

"I think you're feeling ill because you found a body you didn't expect to find," he said.

"Maybe they're radioactive," she said, losing the grin.

"Perhaps," he said, "but unlikely."

"Why do you say that?"

"Radioactive minerals are unstable—"

"Oh no!" said Amphora.

"However," said Holmes, "they break down so slowly that you don't have to worry. Also, they tend to be bright neon yellow or green. Or, they may look like metamicts."

"Meta who?" said Amphora.

"Metamicts. They're opaque and dull, with rounded edges. These crystals don't look like either of those things, but if you're really worried let's test them. I'll get a Geiger counter." He turned and ran back toward the north entrance.

"He's so smart," said Amphora, watching him go.

"La-di-dah," said Amanda, refusing to look.

"Why don't you like him? He's very sweet." Was that a blush? Gosh, Amphora was boy-crazy.

"He's a know-it-all."

"I don't see why you say that. He's just smart. Now if you want to know who's a know-it-all . . ."

"Fifty p," said Amanda.

"You can't do that," said Amphora. "Only Ivy can. And besides, I didn't even say a name."

"I know what you were thinking," said Amanda.

Suddenly a huge "Whoops" could be heard from the opening of the cavern. It seemed that the salvage operation was not going well. Of course considering the state of the skeleton, it was hardly surprising. As soon as the professors attempted to move it, it fell apart. This caused both girls to become nauseous, and because Amanda had used up her last gingersnap and had nothing with which to settle her stomach, she threw up in the crater, causing Amphora to lose her last vestige of control and do the same. This was not good for her image or the evidence. Contaminating the crime scene like that was a huge no-no, and Professor Scribbish took both girls to task. Still, Amanda wasn't sure he was all that unsympathetic because after he had delivered his criticism, he winked at each one of them, confusing her completely. Was it or wasn't it okay to throw up at a crime scene? This was something she'd have to research.

Suddenly it occurred to her that maybe the *body* was the whatsit. The teachers had acted like they didn't know who it was, but what if that was all for the girls' benefit? Maybe they knew all too well. If that were the case, was the fact that the person was dead going to change everything, or had it just been his whereabouts that was the issue? If either was the case, who could be so important that his disappearance would have the teachers practically in crisis?

She thought about Professor Feeney's conversation—the one she and Simon had overheard. It hadn't sounded like she was talking about a person, but maybe she was. They'd accounted for the teacher who'd gone missing at the beginning of spring term, but could there be someone else? She couldn't think of anyone. Maybe Ivy's sister would know. She made a mental note to ask. At the same time, she would speak to Ivy and the rest about the possibility that the body was the thing the teachers had been seeking. She didn't really believe it was, but they had to consider every possibility, no matter how implausible.

Then Holmes came running up. "Here," he said. He was holding a Geiger counter. Was there anything Professor Stegelmeyer didn't keep in his labs? "Let me test those crystals." He waved the Geiger counter over the pile of crystals, including Amphora's, which he'd carefully laid on top. Nothing. "These seem perfectly safe," he said.

"Are you sure it's on?" said Amphora.

"Yup. Absolutely sure." He double-checked the on/off switch.

141

"Maybe it isn't working right."

"I thought about that," he said, "so I brought a sample of a radioactive mineral from the lab."

"Eeeek," said Amphora, stepping away.

"Please don't worry," he said. "I'm just going to test this tiny sample." He took a leaded box from his pocket and opened it, then placed it on the ground. "This is a metamict—the kind of radioactive mineral I mentioned before." The nugget was silver and chunky.

"I don't want to see," said Amphora.

Amanda did want to see, and not only took a good long look, but also snapped a couple of pictures.

"Ready?" said Holmes.

"I'm ready," said Amanda.

"Amphora?" said Holmes.

Silence.

"Okay, here we go," said Holmes. Amanda thought it interesting that he had taken Amphora's silence for a yes. He turned on the Geiger counter and passed it over the metamict. It buzzed. "Hear that?" he said. "It's positive."

"How do I know that's the sample doing that?" said Amphora.

"You're a tough cookie, you know that?" he said, smiling. She blushed again. "I'll show you." He closed the box and passed the Geiger counter over it. Nothing. He looked at Amphora to make sure she'd seen the demonstration. Then he opened the box and passed the Geiger counter over it again. It buzzed.

"You win," said Amphora. "The crystals aren't radioactive. But are you sure that sample is safe?"

"It's fine," he said. "It was open for about twenty seconds." He closed the box, turned off the Geiger counter, and slipped the box back into his pocket.

"Told you," said Amanda.

"So what?" said Amphora. "It's not a sin to be careful."

"You're right," said Amanda. "It isn't." She almost wanted to thank Holmes for calming Amphora down, but she couldn't get the words to come out. Amphora did manage to express her gratitude, however.

"Thank you, Scapulus," she said. "You're a good guy."

Holmes gave her a huge smile, but when he looked at Amanda the smile faded. She could not get herself to express approval of any kind. He looked disappointed but she didn't care. So what if she didn't like him? That was his problem. Anyway, he had charmed the entire rest of the school—even grumpy old Stegelmeyer and Buck. Wasn't that enough?

At last the teachers managed to extract the skeleton from its hiding place and get it into a body bag in a process that was both painstaking and infuriating. Pieces of bone, fiber, and what-have-you kept dislodging, falling, and disintegrating and had to be gathered carefully. This caused a lot of dirt and other matter to be mixed in with the remains, which at first Amanda thought would cause problems in the lab, but then realized that they'd have to analyze it all anyway.

Then came the long, tedious process of evidence collection. Thrillkill wanted the students to learn from the experience, but because inviting all two hundred of them to the scene would undoubtedly result in compromised evidence, he told Amanda that she could text a few people and video the action carefully for the benefit of the rest of the school. They'd set up lights and work into the evening. He also enlisted a few more teachers to help scour the scene. These included Professors Also, Pargeter, and Buck, as well as Professor Browning, who would help the kids with their sketching.

Everyone knew what to look for by this time. First and most important was a murder weapon. Next came fibers, substances that weren't supposed to be there, blood, and anything the murderer or the victim might have dropped or lost, for of course, it was a murder. The man whose skeleton had been found hadn't walled himself up. How he'd died and whether he'd had a hand in his own demise no one yet knew, but that much was clear. Someone, or more than one someone, qualified as a culprit, and they needed ways to identify him or her.

Of course Amanda texted her friends, who were first shocked and then eager to participate. She thought it might be politic to invite David Wiffle and Gordon Bramble as well, and in that way avoid the fits that would ensue if they felt left out. All came running, with the exception of Editta, who had either ignored or not received Amanda's message. When Wiffle and Bramble came running up, they each gave her a most unappreciative look, which made her wonder if she'd done the right thing. She probably hadn't gained any brownie points for her generosity after all.

Professor Scribbish took on the role of coordinator. Of course being the evidence teacher, he would. Before everyone started their search, he patiently explained how they could avoid stepping on each other's toes by assigning territories, reiterated the rules of collection, and told them in no uncertain terms how appreciative he was of their efforts, which got everyone all pumped up. Then he gave the go sign and they were off like a bunch of party kids on a scavenger hunt.

Ivy came up with a couple of observations Professor Sidebotham would be proud of. Come to think of it, thought Amanda, why wasn't Professor Sidebotham there? She should have been one of the first people Thrillkill called. People seemed to be missing all over the place, although Sidebotham's failure to arrive was far less disturbing than Editta's behavior over the past couple of weeks.

Ivy contributed two pieces of evidence no one else had observed: a faint humming coming from the crystals, so low that no one else could hear it, and a sweet smell in the cavern that she swore was aftershave. This, said Professor Scribbish, was most interesting but may have been the smell of decay. Nevertheless, he asked her to write up her findings and characterize them as carefully as possible, just in case.

Another interesting bit of evidence was some bloodstains that David Wiffle found in the bushes. These were difficult to see and he was proud of himself for having discovered them. His friend Gordon showered him with so much praise that Amanda thought Wiffle's head would burst, but maybe it was good for him this once. The poor kid was normally so much less capable than he thought he was that maybe a shot in the arm would calm him down. Of course the blood might belong to a squirrel, but it was still important to collect it and find out.

They didn't find anything else. There was no ID on the body, no label in the clothing, nothing that would help identify it, except, perhaps, its DNA. They found no artifacts that could have belonged to the murderer and no signs of a weapon. Still, they had quite a bit to go on and Professors Hoxby and Scribbish were optimistic that they would turn up something useful.

There was so much to do that Amanda wasn't spoiled for choice: the secret stashes, the missing item, the dead body, her newly resurrected storytelling class, Editta. But the most pressing thing on her mind was Darius Plover and the fact that she'd forgotten to answer his request about the "Sand" clips. This she must take care of immediately or potentially damage her career. She still wasn't sure what she was going to say, but she knew she needed to respond ASAP, so she climbed up to her room and booted up her laptop.

The thing made all the usual clunking, whirring, and half-musical sounds and stood at the ready. She didn't know why she was using it to compose her message rather than her phone. There was something solid about the device that calmed her. Whoever had heard of anything so crazy?

She opened up her mail and reread the director's last message. She'd offered feedback, he'd asked for feedback, and she absolutely *had* to provide feedback.

And suddenly she knew. There was no way she could tell him the truth. Yes, the clips were lousy, and yes, the script was lame, but no, she could not tell him so. She hit Reply and composed a message.

Dear Mr. Plover,

I love the clips! They're exciting, atmospheric, and well-acted. I especially like the one in which the conspirators are meeting in the tent and the camel wanders in. I can't wait to see the finished product!

Sincerely,
Amanda Lester,
Filmmaker.

It was all a lie. The scene in the tent was so grainy you could barely tell there *was* a camel. Furthermore, it was trite. How many films were there in which a bunch of bandits met in a tent out in the desert? Offhand she could think of at least a dozen. What Darius Plover was doing filming such a mediocre script, and filming it badly, she couldn't imagine, but she wasn't going to question him. You just didn't do that.

There. That's done. Now I can breathe. Satisfied that she had saved her career, Amanda sat back and sighed. She could turn her attention to the next problem: her storytelling class. Not only would that be fun, but it would divert her from the gazillion things she *really* didn't want to think about, including Scapulus Holmes.

13

STUCK

The next day was Professor Redleaf's memorial service. Normally they would have used the chapel, but they couldn't because of the earthquake, so they met in the back garden. The kids were crying and the teachers looked solemn. The décor gremlins had dressed in Victorian black with top hats, which some of the kids thought cool and others ridiculous. Ivy had wrapped a black ribbon around Nigel's neck, and Simon had unearthed a black fedora from somewhere and was wearing it along with a black jacket. Even Editta had showed up and was looking suitably funereal, not the most difficult achievement considering her recent behavior. Someone, probably the gremlins, had spent a lot of time picking and arranging flowers, because the makeshift dais was engulfed in them. There were dog violets, bluebells, kingcups, and primroses, all from the school's garden. Fortunately it was too warm for icicles and Thrillkill had arrived sans hair dryer.

Professor Redleaf was too aloof a person to have been beloved, but she was well respected and many people wanted to say a few words about her. Professors Thrillkill, Snaffle, and Mukherjee had much to relate about her cool head, quiet excellence, and dedication. Professor McTavish praised her even though he didn't understand the first thing about her work. And Professor Feeney lauded her ability to penetrate the minds of the world's most dangerous hackers.

When the teachers had completed their eulogies, Scapulus Holmes, apparently the only student who had known her well, mounted the podium and looked out upon the sea of grieving faces. The first thing he said so irritated Amanda that she wanted to run up and shut his mouth.

"Professor Redleaf was my friend," said Holmes.

La di da. Darius Plover is my friend. I don't go around bragging about it.

"We worked together a number of times over the years."

Over the years? Are you kidding? You're twelve.

"I want to tell you about something that happened—"

But Amanda's mental sparring was cut short when suddenly a strong aftershock, so powerful that it threw her over, struck. Holmes grabbed onto the podium, but it wasn't secured and he fell over too. Thrillkill barely managed to steady himself on his crutches, and several people had collided with each other. Others had assumed the strangest positions: crouched on their knees like frogs, balancing like tightrope walkers, leaping with one arm raised like Hermes, the messenger god. Nigel was cowering and leaning heavily on Ivy, who had knelt down and grabbed him around the head and shoulders. People were screaming and wailing—even some of the professors, who tried with varying success to hide their distress. Amanda was so startled that she went numb and couldn't think or do anything.

But her paralysis didn't last long. Once she realized what was happening, she resumed her role of earthquake coach and tried to calm the crowd, explaining what was going on in the hope of taking some of the terror out of the situation. Simon, too, was calm and scientific about the whole thing, as was Ivy this time. These efforts were only minimally successful, however, and there continued to be much carrying on, especially by Editta, who wouldn't stop talking about what bad luck the murder and these aftershocks were. Despite the topic, Amanda was relieved to see her talking again. Maybe there was some good luck in all this chaos too.

But Editta's catastrophizing so infuriated Simon that he said, "So what brings good luck then?" Editta reeled off a whole list of positive harbingers, like white cats, crickets, and chimney sweeps, to which Simon responded, "Fine. I'm going to keep track of these things and show you that your good luck and your bad luck cancel each other out," and started tapping notes into his phone. This so upset her that she appealed to Amphora, whom she knew was not exactly Simon's biggest fan. At this point Ivy interposed herself among the three and said, "Cut it out, all of you. We have to pull together," and Holmes came up and asked if everyone was okay, which precipitated a round of goo-goo eyes from both Editta and Amphora, who had miraculously forgotten how afraid they were. Holmes seemed not to notice, however, and walked back to the podium, from which he told the crowd that he would understand if people wanted to discontinue the service and he'd record his eulogy and post it on the school's intranet, a presumption that infuriated Amanda so much that she fled to her room, one of the few places Holmes could not go.

What did they see in him anyway? Sure, he wasn't bad looking, and he was smart, but so what? A lot of people were smart and nice looking, including, she didn't want to admit it, Nick Muffet, the bane of her existence, or at least the bane until Holmes had assumed the role. That was exactly what Holmes was: a bane. He thought he was so special, always dropping names and acting like a know-it-all. She'd show him. She'd show him that you have to earn respect, not be born to it. She, Amanda Lester, descendant of the worst famous detective in history, would be the best sleuth who had ever lived, proving that you don't inherit excellence. But unlike some people, she wouldn't go around with her nose in the air. Uh uh. She'd be the same modest but amazingly competent person she'd always been.

Once everyone had recovered from the latest aftershock, the school returned to the conundrum of the dead body. Curiosity and speculation were running high, and for once everyone was eager to observe the autopsy, which wouldn't have been the case under normal circumstances. So on Sunday afternoon, because there wasn't room for everyone to attend in person, Professor Hoxby's autopsy of the skeleton was broadcast over CCTV. Some of the older students were allowed into the autopsy room, as was Ivy, who would benefit more from being there than "watching" the proceedings remotely. Amanda and her other friends were to view the procedure in the common room. Just to be on the safe side, several of the students had brought gingersnaps with them. Unfortunately, Holmes had joined the group and for some perverse reason kept looking at Amanda.

Before he began the autopsy, Professor Hoxby explained that some of the results would be delayed. These included extracting the subject's DNA and matching it to known profiles. The same was true for the victim's teeth, for which dental records would have to be sought. However, he would be able to examine the state of the body and look for the cause of death and other clues to the identity of the victim and perhaps even the perpetrator.

The first blow came swiftly. The body possessed no usable fingerprints or teeth. The former were gone, while the latter had been smashed. Someone did not want the identity of the victim known, a safe assumption when you consider that they'd walled up the body so securely that had it not been for the earthquake, it might never have been discovered.

Next Professor Hoxby declared that he could not ascertain the cause of death, although he could see evidence of blunt force trauma to the skull. This, he declared, would not have been forceful enough to kill the man, and there were no wounds, broken or shattered bones, or any other signs of violence upon the body that hinted at what had really killed him. Nor was there evidence of disease. The man had been healthy, of normal height and weight, and between thirty-five and fifty years old. Perhaps the tox screen would reveal something. The man might have been poisoned.

As if those findings, or the lack of them, weren't disappointing enough, Professor Hoxby couldn't fix the time of death. However, based on her sense of smell, Ivy made a guess that the body had been there for a few months, which no one believed because everything else pointed to its having been there for years. However, Professor Hoxby said that he couldn't rule out the possibility that the skeleton was of recent vintage.

The next thing that happened was that Professor Stegelmeyer came into the autopsy room and announced that the victim's DNA wasn't usable. It had degraded due to the heat generated by the earthquake as well as the moist conditions of the compartment. That meant that the school couldn't use DNA to identify the body either. No DNA, no fingerprints, no teeth, no clothing, no recognizable features, no wallet—nothing. All they knew was that they had a middle-aged male of average description on their hands. It was going to be tough to figure out who he was.

The last thing Professor Hoxby did was attempt to remove the crystals from the skull. This feat proved to be impossible unless he cut through the skull itself, which he did not want to do. It was important to keep it as intact as possible for later testing so Professor Stegelmeyer ended up taking the entire structure to the lab, where he would analyze the crystals. Professor Pargeter, the toxicology expert, scurried off to do the tox screen, and the autopsy was over without one person having vomited—a remarkable achievement.

The next thing the school learned was that according to Professor Stegelmeyer's analysis, the crystals were organic and very unusual. Based on these findings, Professors Stegelmeyer and Pole concluded that the crystals had been created at the time of the earthquake. The last time anyone seemed to have gone near the secret room there had been no sign of them, so they had to be new. But exactly how they had been formed and why the two teachers couldn't yet say.

Now Amanda and her friends wondered whether there was any connection between the body and the whatsit, and they decided to do more investigation with that in mind. They still didn't know what they were looking for but they figured they'd know it when they saw it.

But before they could start, Amanda received an email from Darius Plover.

> Dear Miss Lester,
>
> Thank you so much for your quick turnaround. I am delighted that you like the "Sand" clips. I was a bit concerned, but you've put my mind at rest.
>
> I hope you won't consider it too much of an imposition if I send you more clips. I should have something new for you to look at in a few days.
>
> Your friend,
> Darius Plover.

This was not good. If the next clips were bad too, she'd have to lie about *them*. And the next, and the next.

She wasn't a liar, or she never used to be. What did these untruths make her? A friend and supporter, or a villain? Criminals were liars. Amanda was a liar. Nick would have concluded that that made her a criminal in the way he sometimes twisted logic. Would he have been right? What if she ruined Darius Plover's film? He'd lose money. That would make her as good as a thief, wouldn't it?

No way. Lying to help a friend wasn't a criminal act unless your lie was illegal. This wasn't. This lie pumped up Darius Plover's morale and deepened the bond between them. It wasn't actually a lie. It was a little fib. There was nothing criminal or unethical about that, especially since there was no way he'd make important decisions based on anything she said. He'd have to be crazy to let a twelve-year-old dictate his actions.

Amanda breathed a sigh of relief. She wouldn't have to answer him right this minute. And that was a good thing because she had a lot of important investigation to do and her friends were waiting.

14

THE MAGNIFICENT
BASEMENTS

Although Amanda and her friends hadn't searched the first or second floors of the main building, they decided to turn their attention to the basements. These seemed a likely place for secrets. Stretching underneath the school, the gardens, and all the way to the lake, they comprised a vast network of innumerable rooms, niches, cubbies, closets, compartments, and tunnels. In short, they were perfect hiding places.

The basements had so many entrances it was hard to keep track of them. Amanda and her friends selected the one closest to the dining room and waited there for Simon, who had to come all the way from the boys' dorm.

"You can't go in there," said David Wiffle. He and Gordon had sidled up to where the girls were congregated.

"Go away," said Amanda.

"You're not supposed to be down there. It isn't safe, and it isn't allowed anyway," said David.

"Since when isn't it allowed?" said Amphora.

"Since always," said the little prig. "It's in the school rules."

"Is not," said Amphora.

"Is too."

"We don't have time for this," said Ivy. "It's not in the rules and you know it. Now go away."

Gordon cupped his hand and whispered something in David's ear. "Bad idea," said David for all to hear. Gordon whispered again. "You'll get in trouble. Anyway, you don't want to go anywhere *they're* going." Gordon cupped his hand again. "You're nuts," said Wiffle. More whispering, then, "Fine. Do what you want. *I'm* not going to be responsible. Sometimes I really don't understand you, Bramble."

While this little conference was going on, Simon arrived and eyed the two boys quizzically. Ivy was trying to hear what Gordon was saying but her expression indicated that she wasn't getting anything. Simon wiggled his ear but obviously wasn't adjusting his listening device properly because he seemed more absorbed in it than whatever Gordon was saying. Amphora was craning her neck, and Amanda just heard a bunch of *sss sss sss*.

Suddenly Gordon turned to the group and said, "I'm going into the basements with you," at which point the four friends stared at him with their mouths hanging open.

"Uh, yeah, sure," said Simon, who seemed not at all pleased.

"I don't think that's such a good idea," said Amphora in a stage whisper.

"We can't stop him," said Simon with his usual impeccable logic. "It's a free country."

"Nuts," said Amanda. *She* certainly didn't want him.

"Great," said Ivy. "The more the merrier." Amanda wondered if she was actually sending a coded message to David that said, "Ha ha. You can't boss your friend around anymore. Now what are you going to do?" Of course that could have been Amanda's imagination.

Amphora leaned over to Ivy and whispered something. Ivy whispered back, loud enough for Amanda to hear, "Don't worry. He won't find out."

Amanda was horrified. What if Gordon and/or David had heard her? Then they'd know about the whatsit. The possibility that the two boys were wondering what they were doing in the basements in the first place hadn't occurred to her. Troublemakers and prigs they might be, but Wiffle and Bramble weren't *that* stupid. They had to know something was up. But with Darius Plover, Professor Redleaf, Professor Kindseth, dead bodies, mysterious crystals, aftershocks, Holmes, and everything else that had happened in the last few days going on, her brain was overloaded and it didn't occur to her that they might know more than she thought.

"Whatever it is, we know now," said David, which made no sense because they didn't. They only knew there was *something*, but not what the something was.

"Yeah," said Gordon, who seemed to favor that word above all others. "But I don't care. I won't bother you. I want to see the tunnels."

"I told you, that's a really bad idea," said David. "Thrillkill will send you to detention."

"It doesn't matter," said Gordon with moxie Amanda had never seen before. Maybe there was hope for the kid yet. "I'm going."

"Suit yourself," said David. "Just remember, I told you so." And with a tsk tsk, he turned and strutted back down the hall with his back so rigid he looked like a robot.

Gordon just stood there and watched him go with no expression whatsoever. Then he turned to Amanda's group and said, "I'll catch up with you." Amanda was stunned. She'd never expected this kind of behavior from Gordon. He had always been such a toady. Maybe the earthquake had released some weird spores that had gone to his head.

"Don't do us any favors," said Amphora, opening the door to the basements.

When they'd reached the bottom of the stairs the first order of business was to pick a starting place. Since they had no access to blueprints or maps, they were going to have to feel their way. This was one situation in which Ivy's sister, Fern, might have been helpful, but to everyone's astonishment the fifth-year student had explored only a small part of the basements and couldn't describe anything beyond the first few rooms. Amphora wondered if they should make like Hansel and Gretel and leave breadcrumbs so they'd know where they'd been, but Simon pointed out that that wouldn't guarantee that they'd seen everything. Ivy did not penalize him for this statement because it wasn't really arguing. It was a good thing because if she had, he *would* have argued, and then she would have had to fine him.

Ivy suggested an empirical approach by which she, and they with their artificially enhanced hearing, would listen at walls to see if they could tell whether corridors or spaces lay beyond, then find their entrances by calculating exactly where such means of access would have to be. This approach seemed, if a bit tedious, sensible. Amanda expanded on the suggestion by proposing that they map the basements as they go, an idea Simon heartily endorsed and volunteered for. He'd found a special open source mapping program that would be perfect for the job. However, despite these useful strategies, there was nothing in their plan that identified a logical starting point.

Now they were divided. Reasoning that the farthest reaches of the basements would be the most obscure and therefore the most likely places to hide something, Amanda and Amphora wanted to start with them. Ivy and Simon said that just finding those places would waste time and they'd do better to begin with the closest section and work outward. With no one to break the tie, Editta being off who knew where and Gordon not eligible to vote and by himself anyway, they decided to flip a coin. This solution, however, proved to be more difficult than they realized when no one seemed to have one—until Simon came up with a virtual coin.

With heads signifying the closer rooms and tails the farther, he shook his mobile. The coin flew up in the virtual air, flipped a couple of times, clattered to the virtual ground, and wobbled. Everyone clambered to get a good look. Tails it was, and with their lights in place the kids embarked upon the lengthy process of locating the far portions of the basements.

They soon learned that each section had its own personality in the same way as the rooms the décor gremlins arranged. The area at the bottom of the stairs acted as a foyer, a place to introduce the reaches beyond to the "traveler." It comprised a capacious space that looked nothing like a basement. Rather, it resembled one of those lovely rotundas you see on college campuses, with a checkered marble floor, stone archways, massive urns, busts of famous detectives, and a ribbed ceiling. The only way in which it didn't resemble a rotunda was that the ceiling didn't soar, as there was no place for it to go. If it had risen much higher, it would have invaded the first floor of the building, and that would have impinged on valuable classroom space.

Beyond the foyer lay specialized rooms that contained furniture and props grouped in a manner similar to the way movie studios organize their set decorations. Furniture was laid out as an entire room, such as a living room, office, or restaurant. Hand props took their place on shelves with like items, so that you might find an array of light fixtures, vases, or dog food dishes all in one place. Each room was labeled with a general location, and each shelf, cubby, closet, or other division carried its own designation. Presumably the gremlins maintained an index that let them go straight to the desired item rather than having to browse.

Amanda and Amphora were transfixed. When Amanda came across a set of original Lego blocks, she thought it so rare and important that she had to stop and take a picture. Amphora was finding the draperies and upholstery fabrics tantalizing, and the rest of the kids had to pull her away from one particularly charismatic set of emerald green velvet drapes and a gold-and-green brocade fainting couch. Simon was completely impervious to these attractions until he came across a set of action figures that included a G.I. Joe and a variety of Batmans, or as he kept calling them, Batmen, and then they had to pull *him* away. Ivy and Nigel were patient with all this messing around, as usual, even though neither of them could enjoy exploring in the same way the others did.

But for all the fun of the stash, as soon as they'd set out Amanda realized she'd made a mistake and should have voted with Simon and Ivy. There were so many twists and turns, and so many false starts and dead ends, that they made little progress for the amount of time they were spending. It seemed that Amphora was realizing the same thing, for she started to grumble that they weren't getting anywhere. But shortly after the two misguided girls had repented, the group reached a fork in the road, and what a fork it was, for there before them were about a dozen tunnel entrances in a semicircle, ready to receive them. Beyond the entrances they could see rough rock walls.

"Oh great," said Amphora. "Now what?"

"What is it?" said Ivy.

"There are all these tunnels we could go into and they all look alike," said Amphora.

"That's an illusion," said Simon. "There have to be differences. We just need to pick the most interesting one." It occurred to Amanda that Editta would have decided the question by counting and then picking the luckiest number. That would have been her definition of "most interesting."

"Oh, right," said Amphora. "How silly of me not to know that."

"Fifty p!" yelled Ivy. "Stop scrabbling. There are things we can do. Give me your money, Amphora. Right now."

Amphora dug in her pocket and slapped a fifty p coin into Ivy's palm. She and Simon had both started to carry them, even though they continuously protested that Ivy's methods, and occasionally her judgments, were unfair.

159

Nigel looked up at Ivy and whined, as if he wanted to be allowed to choose the opening. "No, Nigel," she said. "I really don't think you'll be able to tell this time." The dog stopped whining and stared at her. Despite the fact that she couldn't see his begging, she knew he was doing it and said, "Don't give me that face. We're going to have to figure this one out for ourselves."

Poor Nigel looked so crushed that Amanda knelt down and gave him a big hug. He responded by licking her nose. As she pulled away she caught Simon smiling. She wasn't sure whether he was laughing at Nigel's impudence, Amphora's frustration, or something else. Since he rarely smiled, this was a big deal. Amanda suspected it had something to do with skateboards.

"I have an idea," said smiling Simon. "Regardless of which tunnels we choose, we'll do better on skateboards than on our feet. It's more efficient."

"Oh right," said Amanda, giving him a look that was harsher than called for. Maybe Amphora's rancor had rubbed off on her, although Simon *could* be oblivious to people's feelings. "How is Ivy going to skateboard?"

"You'd be surprised," said Ivy, a remark that itself caught Amanda off guard.

"What do you mean?" said Amanda.

"I've skateboarded." Could Ivy actually be looking smug? No, it wasn't possible. But she did seem pleased with herself.

"You've skateboarded?" Amanda peered at Ivy to see if she was joking. She didn't seem to be.

"Sure. Why not?"

"How have you skateboarded?" said Amanda.

"Nigel pulls me," Ivy said. She rubbed the dog's ears. Amanda noticed that he seemed to have assumed Ivy's expression. If she hadn't been feeling so skeptical she would have found the similarity funny.

"And you didn't fall over?"

"Nope. He's a genius. You know that." Ivy leaned over and planted a big kiss on Nigel's head. He gazed up at her lovingly and let his long pink tongue dangle out of his mouth. He *was* a smart dog, and extremely well trained. Perhaps he really could pull Ivy along without killing her.

"If you say so," said Amanda. "But we don't know what kinds of surfaces these tunnel floors have. They could be bumpy. Because of the earthquake they might be completely uneven."

"Let me just try it," said Simon. "How about a diagnostic ride?"

"I'll go along with that," said Amphora, astonishing Amanda until it occurred to her that perhaps her roommate's motive was to see Simon fall on his face. It was a good thing Ivy wasn't fining the two of them for what they were thinking.

"Okay," said Simon. "Let me just run back to the skateboard graveyard and grab something."

Amanda had her doubts about whether Simon's idea would work, but she wasn't about to argue. Ivy might fine her as well, and anyway, Simon was pretty good at assessing risk. He probably knew what he was doing.

Because they really had left breadcrumbs, or rather gingersnap crumbs, behind them, Simon was able to get to the skateboard closet on the third floor and back to the clearing inside of ten minutes. When he rejoined the girls and Nigel, he was carrying the monkey board, which looked a bit worse for wear but seemed to be intact.

"Here I go," he said, stepping on the board and shoving off into the tunnel entrance closest to him.

Clomp, clomp, whoops went his skateboard. Then came a loud *thump thud* and the noise stopped. "Oops," he said, his voice echoing.

Amanda ran to see what had happened. There he was a little way down the rocky tunnel standing on the board, nose to the wall. He looked unhurt, but obviously something hadn't worked as expected. "Let me try that again," he said.

Turning the skateboard parallel with the tunnel, he shoved off again. This time Amanda could hear *swoosh swoosh swoosh*, and then *bluck bluck crash*. She ran down the tunnel, noting how uneven the floor was, until she came upon Simon, who again had run into the wall. Fortunately he was still unhurt.

"It seems that the surface is kind of bumpy," he said.

"Ya think?" said Amanda, noting a collection of ruts, potholes, and stumpy bits.

"I think that might qualify as a fifty p fine," he said.

"I'm not part of that deal," she said. "But you're okay and that's the main thing."

He brushed himself off and said, "Of course I'm okay. I've never fallen off one of these things in my life, and you are part of the deal."

"No, it's just you and Amphora, and how many times have you ridden them?" Amanda said. It was the kind of thing Editta would have come out with.

"Billions. Seriously, I know what I'm doing. And no, it's supposed to be all of us."

"Well, as far as I can see, this isn't any more efficient than walking. In fact, it's less so. And forget it. I'm not playing."

"Agreed," he said pleasantly. "I'll have to make some adjustments. Okay, I'll let you off this time."

"Not right now, I hope," she said. "And thank you, oh great and powerful wizard."

"'Course not. I'll do it tonight. It will be awesome. You'll see. You can try one too if you want. You're welcome."

Just then Amanda heard Amphora yell, "Go away." Then she heard, "I won't bother you. I just want to see the tunnels." It was Gordon. "Go that way," she heard Amphora say. "Fine," said Gordon. She could hear the sound of Gordon's feet stomping away.

Amanda and Simon trudged back to the clearing, the roof of which had been carefully painted to look like blue sky graced by a few fluffy white clouds. Amanda thought it looked very L.A. "What was that about?" said Simon.

"Gordon," said Amphora. "He wanted to come with us."

"No he didn't," said Ivy. "He was perfectly content to be on his own."

"How can you believe a guy like that?" said Amphora. "You're too nice."

"It's not a question of believing what he says. I can tell what he's thinking by the tone of his voice. He meant it."

"Oh, right," said Amphora. "When are you going to give that talk on audio observation? I really need that."

"I think we could all use some tips," said Amanda.

"It's almost ready," said Ivy. "But I can tell you right now how I knew Gordon was telling the truth."

"Oh?" said Amanda. "How's that?"

"His voice wasn't shaking and it didn't go up high. If he'd been lying his voice wouldn't have sounded normal."

"Why didn't I think of that?" said Amphora.

"You will," said Ivy.

The regular basements, if you could call them that, benefitted from the gremlins' influence and felt welcoming, but the tunnels were downright creepy, or at least the one the group had chosen was. It was dark, close, knobby, and twisty, with a plethora of tempting tributaries leading off the sides. Amanda couldn't stop thinking about what a great movie setting it would make, and Simon was loving it, but Amphora was freaking out and suggesting that they turn back at two-minute intervals. She kept thinking she was hearing weird noises. Ivy told her there was nothing there but them and that she should take her listening device out, to which Amphora replied that she had removed it ages ago and she was still hearing bumps, shuffling, and banshees wailing. Fortunately Simon kept his mouth shut or Ivy would have collected enough money for them to go out to dinner.

Soon they began to see drawers in some of the walls. These looked kind of like those safe deposit boxes you see in bank vaults. They were about the same size and of similar arrangement. Each one had two locks, just like in the bank. The kids wondered if any of them might contain the whatsit. (What a hunt for a needle in a haystack that would be!) When they had passed hundreds of the things in the tunnel, they came upon various clearings and grottoes that were studded with them. A few of these had collapsed, and despite the danger of falling rock the kids were excited about the prospect of exploring them. It looked like they had pieces of paper inside.

"I wouldn't go in there," said Amphora at one ruined clearing. "It's too dangerous."

"It'll be okay," said Amanda. "If we could make it through the exploded garage we can do this."

"Not the same," said Amphora. "There could be another aftershock."

"Yes, but we'll be in and out in a flash," said Simon. Amanda thought he sounded like he believed he was some kind of superhero, but she had to agree with his logic. The odds of something falling on them in the two minutes they'd be there were minuscule.

"Whatever you guys think is fine with me," said Ivy.

"Let's go," said Simon.

He and Amanda stepped carefully into the collapsed grotto in front of them, took out their phones, and started snapping away. Taking pictures rather than reading the pieces of paper on the spot seemed like a productive use of their time and would allow the others to see the findings too. Amphora kept protesting that there had to be creepy crawly things in there, but neither Amanda nor Simon paid any attention to her. They were so absorbed in what they were doing that they wouldn't have noticed a skeleton tapping them on the shoulder.

"Time," said Amphora suddenly.

Amanda slued around to face her. "Not yet." She turned back to the compartments and kept clicking.

"Yep. Two minutes."

"Thirty seconds," said Simon. "Hang on." He snapped madly, each click coming closer and closer to the previous one. "Ouch! My finger slipped. Hang on."

Amphora tapped her foot, which made a weird uneven rhythm with the clicking of the two cameras. *Tap, click, click, click, tap, tap, click, tap, click click.* After ten seconds she said, "Time." *Click, click.*

"It is not," said Ivy. "Let them work." *Click, click, click.*

"Is too," said Amphora. *Click.*

"You're distracting them," said Ivy. *Click, click, click.*

"Time," said Amphora. *Tap, click, click.*

"Oh, for heaven's sake," said Amanda. "Be quiet. We'll be there in a second." *Click, click.*

"Three seconds," said Amphora. *Tap, tap, click, click, tap.*

"Please," said Ivy. *Click, click.*

"It's dangerous," hissed Amphora. "How would you feel if they were killed?" *Click, click, click.*

"They're not going to be killed," said Ivy. *Click, click.*

"You don't know that." *Click.*

Suddenly Simon and Amanda were standing next to the two girls with broad smiles on their faces. "We got 'em," said Amanda. "Let's go."

Amphora gave them a pout, faced toward the tunnel, and continued to walk. When they didn't follow, she turned around and said, "Are you coming?"

After what seemed like a long time, the kids reached the farthest end of the tunnel, which opened onto the lake. This was not the famous Lake Windermere, but the smaller Lake Enchanto, which was every bit as beautiful but more intimate. Wild peacocks lived around the edges and their calls could be heard at all hours. Amanda had even seen some peachicks on campus. They had the silliest expressions on their faces and they made her laugh.

Between the tunnel and the lake lay three gates one after the other. The middle one was damaged, probably in the earthquake from what they gathered. When the kids looked through, they could see a hidden cove that housed a small dock with a couple of small boats bearing the names Bacon and Eggs tied to it.

Now they faced a dilemma. They had to let Professor Thrillkill know that the gates were no longer secure, but they didn't want him to know they'd been there. If he found out that they'd wandered around in the basements, he'd want to know why, and then they'd have to tell him that they knew about the whatsit, and who knew where that might land them? However the lack of security was a serious problem. If any of the entrances to the school were to be penetrable, criminals could walk right in.

Amphora suggested that they get Gordon to tell the headmaster, which put the other kids off so much that she started to argue and had to pay a hefty fine. They didn't like Wiffle's friend, but they drew the line at entrapment. Aside from taunting them, Gordon had never really harmed them. Maybe he could be redeemed at some point, or even turned. Now that would be something to behold. But it certainly wasn't their first order of business.

"We have to come clean," said Amanda. "Thrillkill is so preoccupied he won't be mad. He'll be glad we told him. It's important to guard the school."

"Maybe we can let him know anonymously," said Ivy. "Type up a note and leave it in his office or something."

"How are we going to get by Drusilla Canoodle?" said Amanda. Ms. Canoodle was Legatum's admissions officer, and she sat very close to Thrillkill.

"Do it after hours," said Simon, sticking a piece of gum in his mouth.

"Isn't his office locked then?" said Ivy.

"No," said Amanda. "He's always there. Especially these days."

"Well, then, there's a good chance of him seeing us," said Ivy.

"Tell one of the other teachers," said Amphora quietly.

The three kids stopped and stared at her. It was an excellent idea, and completely obvious. Why none of them had thought of it they couldn't imagine.

"Professor Also," said Amanda.

"Professor Ducey," said Ivy.

"Professor Tumble," said Amphora.

"Wait a minute," said Simon, chomping on his gum. "This isn't going to work. Telling any of them is the same as telling Thrillkill. We have to tell him. If there are consequences, there are consequences."

This didn't sound like the kid who just last term had been terrified of expulsion. Of course he'd had good reason then. Thrillkill had let him enter Legatum provisionally. The ancestor who qualified him to attend was so iffy that the school had balked at admitting him. Because of that he had almost been kicked out for cutting a class. He had spent the entire term walking on thin ice and had been a bit of a basket case about it. Now he was fearless?

"Look," he said noisily. "I can see you're all skeptical." That they were. Even though you couldn't see Ivy's eyes behind her sunglasses it was obvious that she wasn't subscribing to this point of view. "But if we don't tell him he'll figure it out. If nothing else, Wiffle will tell him, or Gordon. Then he'll think we're covering up something, and you know how much worse that will be. We have to come clean, and the sooner the better. If he doesn't like it, at least we'll know and we won't sit around worrying."

This argument made a lot of sense. Thrillkill would not abide being lied to. Either would any of the teachers. The kids resolved to tell him as soon as they got back.

But before they could get to Thrillkill's office they saw the headmaster talking to Professor Also in the hall. Amanda, Simon, and Amphora stuck their listening devices in their ears and tried to hear what he was saying.

"We've got to do something about that tunnel gate immediately," he said.

"I'll get the construction people here," said Professor Also.

He already knew! What luck. The teachers must have discovered that the gate was broken when they surveyed the school right after the earthquake. Of course. What had the kids been thinking? Did they really think the detectives didn't know what was going on right under their noses?

"Oh, and of course I set up a camera at the entrance," said the headmaster. "We can monitor it."

OMG! A hidden camera had watched their every move at the end of the tunnel. For all Amanda knew, cameras had been hidden all around the basement. Stupid, stupid, stupid. It was a good thing they hadn't lied. Thrillkill would have caught them in the act and that would have been terrible.

The kids looked at each other. These same thoughts were apparent on each of their faces.

"Come on," said Ivy. "We have to figure this out."

No one objected, and the four of them ran into the common room and plopped down on a ratty-looking green sofa. What the décor gremlins were thinking with that one was unimaginable. It wasn't even shabby chic. It was city dump throwaway.

But they didn't have time to contemplate the day's décor. They needed a strategy. If any of the teachers had seen the kids in the tunnels they would want to know what they'd been doing there, and what would they say?

"We have no choice," said Simon, removing his gum and looking for a place to put it. "They already have the proof."

"How do we know they actually record anything?" said Amanda.

"Good question," said Ivy. "Maybe the security guards have a wall of monitors and just watch in real time."

"Maybe," said Amphora, "but maybe not."

"Let's assume they know," said Simon, casually sticking the gum into a pot with a sick-looking plant in it. Amphora gave him a look. "And if they know, they also saw what we were doing. We have to tell the truth."

"Hm," said Amanda. "I hadn't thought of that. You're right. There's nothing to debate. We're stuck. Of course if they don't say anything we're off the hook."

"Then it's a waiting game," said Ivy. "And you know what? I don't care. I'm tired of trying to hide things. It's exhausting."

"You're right," said Simon, pushing the gum deeper into the pot. "Que sera sera. Now let's do something productive. How about looking at those snaps?"

15

THE TROVE OF SECRETS

Amanda and Simon took out their phones and pulled up the pictures from the tunnels. They hadn't bothered to read the pieces of paper from the compartments until now because to do so would have slowed them down. Everyone gathered round and watched as they examined shot after shot.

"These don't say anything," said Amanda, flipping quickly. "What does this mean: 'gutter water'? It makes no sense at all."

"I agree," said Amphora, who was reading the words out to Ivy. "It's gibberish."

"Maybe if we put them together," said Simon, accidentally bashing into Amphora. "But what goes with what?"

"We'd have to input every snippet into a program and let it try to make the associations," said Amanda. "That's textual analysis stuff and Professor Pickle is still in prison. Of course we wouldn't want to ask him anyway. Then he'd know that we know and—"

"It's impossible," said Amphora, elbowing Simon out of their little circle. He elbowed her back. Amanda gave them a cut-it-out look.

"Nothing is impossible if you ask the right questions," said Simon, forcing his way back into the huddle.

"Oh really," she said, jockeying for position. "Ever tried bringing a dead person back to life?"

"Fifty p!" said Ivy. "Pay up—and stop that pushing."

"I've had enough of this," said Amphora. "I don't want to play anymore."

"Then stop making nasty remarks," said Ivy. "And no more shoving." Amphora glared at her, but of course Ivy couldn't see that. Not that she didn't know. Her ability to sense what was going on was downright spooky.

"Getting back to the matter at hand," said Simon, "I'm sure I could come up with a program that would do that, but the data entry would be impossible."

"Even if we just picked a few things and tried them?" said Amanda, still flicking.

"We could try," said Simon, "but the odds are against us. You saw how many compartments there were in that tunnel. There are a lot of other tunnels, which doubtless means an exponentially higher number of snippets. Whatever goes with the ones we found might take years to come up with—assuming that's even how this whole thing works."

"Hang on a minute," said Amanda. "I just had an idea." Everyone leaned toward her. "Professor Snaffle."

"Ye-e-e-s," said Amphora. "I'm not following you." She looked expectant but puzzled.

"Professor Snaffle," said Amanda. "Secrets."

"Ri-i-ight. The secrets teacher. So what?"

"I get it," said Simon, grabbing for Amanda's phone. It flew out of her hand and clattered to the floor. "Those pieces of paper. They're secrets."

"Yes!" said Amanda, reaching for the phone. She was so excited she forgot to take Simon to task. "Exactly. And who is the authority on secrets?"

"Professor Snaffle," said the other three in unison.

"But I don't see—" said Amphora. "You don't expect us to ask her about this, do you?"

"No," said Amanda, examining the screen. She buffed it with her sleeve. "However, we can speculate about what's going on using what we know about her, the school, and the way the teachers operate."

"Okay," said Amphora. "What do you think?"

"Each of the teachers has a specialty."

"Right," nodded Amphora.

"Professor Snaffle's specialty is secrets." Amanda stopped to let the logic sink in. The wheels didn't seem to be turning in Amphora's head, but the others had obviously got the point.

"The pieces of paper are secrets, and—"

"Professor Snaffle must have put them there!" said Amphora.

"Exactly," said Amanda. "And why did she put them there?"

"Because they're Legatum's secrets?" said Amphora.

"Yes!" said Amanda. "Legatum has a trove of secrets."

"Oooooh," said Ivy. "Sounds like Harry Potter. Legatum Continuatum and the Trove of Secrets."

"You laugh," said Amanda, "but I don't think that's so farfetched."

"Say you're right and Professor Snaffle is the overseer of the trove of secrets," said Amphora. "Oooh, I like the sound of that. Anyway, say she put them there. How does that help us?"

"Think of it this way," said Amanda. "The school's secrets are kept in little bits in separate compartments. Professor Snaffle puts them there and makes sure they're safe. Fine, but how does anyone ever use them?"

"They're in code?" said Amphora.

"Actually, that's not a bad idea," said Amanda, "but no. Not exactly. Let's turn it around." Ivy and Simon were grinning. Amphora was on the edge of her seat. "How do terrorists work?"

"You're not saying that Professor Snaffle is a terrorist?" said Amphora, horrified.

"No, of course not," said Amanda. "But think about it. How do terrorists communicate?"

"Well, they don't have a newsletter," said Amphora.

"Correct," said Amanda, waiting for her to go on.

"Well? So what? I don't see . . . OMG, cells! They split themselves into cells and operate independently."

"That's right! And each of these pieces of paper is the same as a cell. None of them knows what the others mean."

"But I don't see . . . wait a minute," said Amphora. "If that's the case, there has to be a master index or something that ties them together. Metadata!" She thought for a moment. "The way anyone knows what these pieces of paper mean is through metadata that's kept somewhere else. Professor Snaffle is in charge of the secrets." She smiled a huge smile. "Professor Snaffle has the metadata, doesn't she?"

"Yuppers," said Amanda. "That was a great syllogism. You get an A in logic."

"I do, don't I?" said Amphora. "Wait till I tell—"

"Wait till you tell who?" said Simon archly.

"No one," said Amphora. "I'm not going to tell anyone."

"You were going to say Rupert Thwack, the cook, weren't you?" said Simon.

"Fifty p!" said Ivy. "Cool it, Simon. She wouldn't tell him. She wouldn't tell anyone."

"Who wouldn't tell anyone what?" said David Wiffle, entering the room. "Say, have you guys seen Gordon? I can't find him anywhere."

"Nope," said Simon abruptly.

"That isn't entirely true," said Ivy. "We saw him in the basements a few hours ago, but he went his own way and we haven't seen him since."

"Something's wrong then," said David, sounding agitated. "He wouldn't just go off like that."

"Why not?" said Simon. Amanda knew he was deliberately baiting the kid. Gordon never went off by himself. He and Wiffle were joined at the hip and Simon wanted to get Wiffle to admit it.

"Because," said David in a surly tone.

"Because why?" said Simon in his usual stubborn manner.

"You're a nosy Parker," said David obstinately. It seemed that he could be just as stubborn as Simon.

"No more than you," said Simon.

"Uh uh," said David.

"Oh for heaven's sake," said Ivy. "You two are a couple of babies. Look, David, I'm sure Gordon is fine. He was quite keen to explore."

"He's not that kind of person," said David, picking at a hangnail. "And for your information, there are still aftershocks going on. It's dangerous down there."

"Oh?" said Simon, seizing on the first point. "What kind of person is he?" He stood up. It was an obvious ploy to intimidate the smaller boy.

"If you must know, he's very sensible." The hangnail was obviously bothering him because the picking got more intense. It didn't seem that he was making any progress toward removing the darn thing.

"Sensible," said Simon, as if to question him.

"Yes." He pulled the hangnail off with a flourish. He looked extremely satisfied with himself. The girls were horrified but Simon betrayed no reaction.

"And how is exploring the tunnels not sensible?" said Simon.

"You don't have to turn this into an inquisition," said David. "Gordon should have been back a long time ago. I think we should send a search party down there."

Simon laughed. "A search party? What do you think this is, the Lone Ranger?" He sounded very snotty. Amanda wondered if David would hit him. That would have made some fight. Neither of the two boys was exactly burly. Simon was tall and thin, and David was short and puny.

Wiffle turned red in the face and crossed his arms. "You're an idiot," he said. "I'm going to Thrillkill."

"Because I said you were acting like the Lone Ranger?" said Simon, deliberately being obtuse.

"Buzz off," said David.

174

"'Buzz off,'" said Simon, mimicking him.

Wiffle leaned forward, stuck his tongue out, and pivoted, then stomped out of the common room.

"Good going, Simon," said Amphora.

"Fifty p," said Ivy.

"Would you stop that?" said Amphora. "He's the one who's argumentative. And anyway, this fining thing is unfair."

"Fifty p," said Ivy. She was being as stubborn as Simon. She sure was testy these days.

"Why don't you cut them some slack?" said Amanda. Realizing that this might have been the first time she'd ever said something mean to Ivy, she gasped. Something had got hold of everyone and was turning them into grumps. Maybe it was the earthquake, although Ivy had exhibited signs before that happened.

"You too?" said Ivy accusingly.

"Ivy," said Simon in a tone Amanda had never heard before, "what's going on? You seem really tense." He looked downright solicitous. Now she was convinced that something strange was in the air.

Ivy burst into tears. "I'm just so worried about everything," she sniffled. "I can't seem to think straight and there's more but I don't want to say."

This confession took the other three by surprise. They looked at each other as if to say, "Did I just hear that?"

After what must have been a minute, Amanda spoke in a tiny voice. "You're stressed, aren't you?"

"Yes," wailed Ivy.

"Everything's changed," said Amphora kindly. "You had certain expectations about Legatum, and nothing is working out the way you thought." She put a hand on Ivy's arm.

"You're right," said Ivy. "All right. I'll tell you, but no comments, okay?" They looked at her as if to say, "Out with it." She sat there for a second, seemingly searching her mind for the right compartment.

Then she grabbed Nigel's head and cradled it and said, "I think I'm losing my hearing."

"What?" said Simon. Everyone leaned forward, although they could hear perfectly well where they were.

"Something's wrong with it," said Ivy. "And by the way, the teachers are going to dissolve the school!"

Amanda couldn't believe what she had just heard. Ivy lose her hearing? That would be a disaster. It would affect Ivy's whole life and potentially ruin her future. No wonder she was upset.

"What do you mean losing it?" she said. Maybe Ivy was exaggerating.

"I mean it goes in and out," said Ivy, breaking into tears.

"How long has this been happening?" said Simon, trying to peer into Ivy's ears.

"I don't know," Ivy sniffled. "A few weeks maybe? Please don't do that, Simon. You won't be able to see anything."

"That long?" said Amphora, moving to hold her friend. "Have you been to the doctor?"

"I, uh, no," said Ivy, wiping her eyes. She leaned into Amphora's embrace.

"Well for Pete's sake why not?" said Simon. He looked embarrassed.

"It comes and goes," said Ivy, her voice muffled as she rested her face on Amphora's shoulder. "It might get better on its own."

Amanda didn't want to say what she was thinking: what if it didn't? How could Ivy jeopardize her greatest gift this way?

"It'll be fine," said Ivy. "The main thing is the school."

The whatsit was so important that the school's very existence depended on it? There was no question that Ivy knew what she was talking about. When her hearing worked it was perfect. So the argument Amanda had heard that first day outside Thrillkill's office was every bit as serious as it had seemed. More, actually.

Now the question was what was to be done about the catastrophe. The kids sat in silence for a couple of minutes. Revealing what was bothering her seemed to have stopped Ivy's bawling, for she had stopped crying completely.

"We have to find it," said Amanda. "And we need to get help for you." She stroked Ivy's hair. Nigel looked up and wagged his tail.

"Absolutely," said Amphora. "You must go to the new doctor. And we have to scour those basements."

"That will take forever," said Simon. "We need a system."

"Simon's right," said Amanda. "We need a system. Let's sit down and make a list of all the possibilities. If we know what the item is, we might be able to find it more quickly."

Just then each of the kids' phones buzzed. A text from Thrillkill had arrived. "Gordon Bramble missing. Last seen in basements. Anyone with knowledge ping me immediately."

Oh great. Wiffle *had* gone to Thrillkill. There was no way Gordon was missing, but here David was making a huge deal out of the fact that his sidekick had finally started to become his own person.

"Weren't there cameras in there?" said Amphora.

"Yes," said Ivy, disentangling herself. After all that hugging she was rather rumpled. "Good thought. They should be able to find him that way."

"Nope," said Simon, who seemed relieved that the hugging and stroking was over. "There weren't very many, and all the ones I saw were broken."

"I don't know if that's good or bad," said Amanda. "It's good because they didn't see us, but it's bad for Gordon." She stopped abruptly. "What am I saying? He's fine. That Wiffle kid is such an attention seeker."

"Yeah, he is," said Simon, "but Gordon doesn't have any sense. He could be lost."

"But how lost is lost?" said Amphora. "The tunnels can't be *that* big."

"Yeah, they are, and . . ." He turned to Ivy. "Don't fine me for disagreeing with her. They really are extensive. You might be surprised."

"You mean he could really get lost in there?" said Amphora.

"Sure," said Simon. "He isn't that bright in the first place, and he doesn't know what he's doing. Those whiny kids always end up getting lost. I'm surprised that didn't happen at Blackpool."

"He had Wiffle with him then," said Amanda.

"Do you really think he's that dumb?" said Ivy. "I thought he was a bit clueless, but he does well in his classes, doesn't he?"

"I dunno," said Simon. "I've never seen his papers. Van Helden House did really badly on the class project last term though."

"I don't think debating Gordon's intelligence is going to get us anywhere," said Amanda. "There really is going to have to be a search party."

"So he wasn't just being the Lone Ranger?" said Amphora.

"Unfortunately no," said Amanda. "For once he actually had a point."

The kids laughed. No joke at Wiffle's expense was ever over the top. He was so irritating that he made himself a target. If only he realized that.

Just then a coterie of teachers walked past the common room door. As they did so, Professor Also stuck her head in and said, "Anyone see Gordon Bramble?"

"Hours ago," said Amphora.

"Where was that?" said the teacher.

"At the big fork in the basements," said Amphora.

"Oh, the glade," said Professor Also. The friends looked at each other. The place where all the tunnels converged was about as far from a glade as you could imagine.

"Uh, right," said Simon.

"Does anyone know if he has his phone with him?" said Professor Also.

No one spoke.

"All right, I think it's time to start looking."

She held her phone and punched in a text. Within about a minute, Professors Buck and Ducey had arrived. They seemed to be the go-to teachers for day-to-day crises. They took off into the basements like a shot.

"Now we wait," said Professor Also.

They waited and they waited and they waited. With each passing moment David Wiffle grew more agitated. He was sure his friend was dead or had fallen into the clutches of some unnamable bogeyman. At first the kids weren't the least bit worried. There was so much to explore down there that who wouldn't spend as long as he could? But when Gordon didn't emerge for dinner, even they became concerned.

"You don't think something really happened to him?" said Amphora, chewing a bit of lettuce. "Mmm, this dressing is wonderful."

"Doubt it," said Simon. "He's just lost. And I don't think it's so great. Kind of vinegary if you ask me." He made a face.

"How about a head injury?" said Amanda. "No, I think Amphora's right. It is good."

"There haven't been any aftershocks since he left," said Simon. "Take mine then." He started to shovel his salad onto Amphora's plate, which caused her to snatch it away and hold it up. The lettuce fell onto the table. "Hey, why'd ya do that? I'm trying to help."

"Simon, you're coming perilously close to another fine," said Ivy.

"Poppycock," he said. "I'm being nice."

"Are not," said Amphora, who was looking unsure about putting her plate back down.

"Just do it, dodo," said Simon. "I'm not going to try helping you anymore."

"Simon, fifty p," said Ivy.

"You know, Ivy, I think you're biased," he said. "Why is it always my fault?"

"It isn't," said Ivy. Amphora looked annoyed and started to open her mouth, but stopped when Amanda shook her head. "Now, getting back to Gordon, I think something could have happened to him. A rock could have come loose."

"If he was knocked out, they would have found him and brought him back," said Simon, pushing his plate away in a way that was obviously intended to annoy Amphora. When anyone even implied that Rupert Thwack's food wasn't four-star quality, she gave them a lecture. His move seemed to do the trick. Amphora looked so mad Amanda fully expected her to stand up and thwack Simon in the nose. "Say, I wonder if he's hiding on purpose."

"Why would that be?" said Amanda.

"To prove a point," said Simon. "I think our friend Gordon is having an identity crisis and he's rebelling against everything and everyone."

"That sounds possible," said Ivy. "Ever since he set off those glitter explosions he's changed."

"Yes, but why would he have to go that crazy?" said Amanda.

"Let's put it this way," said Simon. "If you'd spent half your life hanging around with Wiffle, wouldn't you have lost your mind?"

"Good point," said Amanda.

Just then there was a commotion out in the hall and who should appear but Gordon Bramble himself. He was disheveled and dusty and muttering under his breath. He stumbled into the dining room, getting junk all over the floor.

"Hey, Gordon," called out Simon. "You okay?"

No response.

"Hey, man," said Simon. "Are you all right?"

"Mr. Bramble," said Professor Buck, emerging just behind him. "Snap to."

More muttering, but no acknowledgment from Gordon that there was anyone in the world outside of himself.

"This isn't good," said Ivy. "Hang on. What was that?" She seemed to have heard something Gordon was saying. "You're kidding me."

"What?" said Amanda, Amphora, and Simon together.

"Hoo boy," said Ivy in a low voice. "I think he inhaled some spores or something. He's saying something about having overheard some weird stuff the teachers said."

"What?" the three friends said again.

"I can't tell that well, but it seems to have something to do with the Moriartys," said Ivy.

"Oh great," said Amanda. "Just what we need."

"If the Moriartys are involved, it's serious," said Ivy. "OMG, you don't think they have the whatsit, do you?"

"I'm beginning to think just that," said Amanda. "And if that's the case, it's no wonder they're upset. Even in prison, that family is really dangerous."

Just then David Wiffle stuck his head into the room and started screaming at Amanda's group.

"Do you have any idea how dangerous it is down there? Look at him. He's out of his mind. This is *your* fault. If anything happens to him it will be on your heads. You are completely selfish and irresponsible."

"What's going on here?" said Headmaster Thrillkill, appearing next to the Wiffle kid. "Oh, hello, Mr. Bramble. Are you quite all right?"

Gordon was still muttering to himself. His eyes were glassy.

"Professor," said David, "this is all their fault. They tempted him into the basements."

"Did you do that, Mr. Binkle?" Thrillkill said looking straight at Simon.

"No, sir," said Simon. "We didn't encourage him at all. We just said that we didn't want him with us. If anything, that should have deterred him." He had a point, but it wasn't as well made as it could have been.

"Mr. Bramble, I want you to go to the nurse at once," said Thrillkill. "As for you, Mr. Wiffle, and the rest of you, I want you to settle down. Let's see what the nurse has to say and then we'll worry about what did or didn't happen. Am I clear?"

"Yes, sir," said all five kids, although Wiffle said it in an insolent way.

"Sir," said David. "We're not supposed to be using skateboards on campus, are we?" He gave Simon a sidelong glance.

"I don't see any reason not to," said Thrillkill. "As long as everyone obeys the rules of the road. Now run along. I'm sure you have homework to do."

He removed himself from the room. Wiffle, who was getting really good at noisy exits, once again stomped away, taking Gordon by the shoulders and marching him down the hall toward the hospital. The teachers scattered who knew where, and the four friends were alone once more.

16

BACK TO THE WHATSIT

Even though there was an unidentified body to contend with, the kids felt that finding the whatsit was the most critical problem facing the school, so Amanda decided to make a list of all the terrible things that might happen without it and speculate on what might cause them.

She remembered Professor Feeney's furtive phone call, which was the first time she had heard anything about something not being where it should be. Professor Feeney taught the criminals and their methods class, so maybe the item had something to do with criminals. Of course most things the detectives did had something to do with criminals, so this conclusion was rather a big duh, but what specifically? Could the whatsit be proof of a crime, or something that would lead to a criminal's capture? She wrote:

1. Something to help put criminals away.

Or, it might be a way of fighting criminals. Perhaps it was a defensive technology, like a weapon or a security device. Or perhaps it was an *offensive* technology, like a secret bioweapon. Professor Feeney had said that everything would change if the item fell into the wrong hands. A bioweapon would certainly qualify. The thought of that was *really* scary. Amanda wrote.

2. Offensive or defensive technology.

Perhaps it was something that incriminated the detectives, or harmed them in a legal or financial way. The deed to the school? Money? Compromising photos, dirty secrets? She wrote:

3. Something that could harm the detectives' ability to operate.

Perhaps Professor Feeney meant that if the item weren't recovered the detectives might no longer exist. Did that mean they would all be killed? That was a horrifying thought. Would the criminals infiltrate them more than they had before, or somehow take them over, like a conquering nation? Would the school be destroyed or unable to function? She wrote:

4. The end of the detectives.

She had heard them mention Moriarty. Ivy and Gordon had too. Could Blixus Moriarty have taken the item? If so, where was it? Had the cook or the crooked doctor, Mr. Tunnel, taken it? How about Mavis or Nick? Could it be lying in the factory rubble? The crime scene investigators had already sifted through that. Perhaps they had found something she didn't know about. She had spoken to the nice crime scene woman at New Scotland Yard once before. The woman had called to tell her that after she had set off the fire sprinklers and melted all that sugar, ants had descended on the ruins. It might be a good idea to call her and see what she had to say.

Amanda looked up the number and hit the call icon. The woman she'd spoken to before, Nimba Pencil, answered.

"Why hello, Miss Lester," she said. "Say, I meant to tell you that the ants are gone. The exterminators did a bang-up job."

"I'm glad to hear that," said Amanda. The thought of millions and millions of ants, even all that way away in London, turned her stomach.

She reached for a gingersnap. "I was wondering if it might be possible to get a list of the evidence you gathered. I suppose this must be a rather strange request but—"

"Normally it would be, yes," said Ms. Pencil. "However, in this case I think we can make an exception. After all, if it hadn't been for you, we wouldn't have captured the Moriartys."

And Nick wouldn't be dead.

"We do ask that you keep the list strictly confidential, though," said Ms. Pencil. "Consider this a professional courtesy."

"Yes, of course," said Amanda. "Thank you so much." She was astonished that the woman was practically breaking the rules to do her a favor.

Ms. Pencil texted her a link to a secure storage site and rung off. Amanda entered the site and looked at the list:

Moriarty Sugar Factory Evidence List

Computers, thumb drives.
Industrial equipment and supplies, including trolleys.

Oh boy. This was looking pretty boring. She hoped the list would get more interesting.

Schematics, a dossier on Herb Lester, receipts for sales of the sugar weapons.

These were obviously critical. They shed light on the entire operation and would be important for the upcoming trials of the Moriartys and their cronies. She could also understand why the cartel had kept a file on her dad, but what did it say? Anything related to the missing item? She didn't see what that would be, but it was a possibility. She put a check mark next to "Dossier."

185

A framed wedding picture of Mavis and Blixus Moriarty.

Amanda had never thought about the Moriartys' personal lives. It was weird to imagine this intimate moment. She wondered what Mavis's dress had looked like. They had probably made a beautiful couple. They were both so attractive. No wonder Nick—

Stop it! Why couldn't she stop thinking about him? There were exercises you could do to help you remember, but she'd never heard of anything to make you forget. Unless Editta's mother had some voodoo remedy. Oh for heaven's sake. She was really losing it. She could see why so many of the teachers were crazy. Being a detective made you nuts. Not that she could leave Legatum now with so much at stake. Argh. Back to the list.

Remnants of Schola Sceleratorum, the Moriartys' secret school for criminals: furniture, books, blackboards, refrigerators, microwave ovens, plastic skeletons, grease paint, cameras, film, videotape, disguises, skates, martial arts uniforms, flashlights.

No doubt the grease paint was Nick's. Thinking about him made her angry this time, though, which was a good thing. If she could maintain that feeling maybe he'd stop haunting her. It was infuriating that the criminals had set up a school to train people to be bad. And Nick had been proud of that. What gall.

She wondered what the school had been like. Who would go to such a place? Who taught the classes? It was so hard to imagine the parents sending their kids there the way the detectives' parents did. Was it possible that for every good person in the world there was an evil counterpart? If that were the case, fighting the bad guys would be hopeless. There were too many of them.

No, the thought was crazy. There was no way half the people in the world were bad. Probably more like a thousandth or a millionth of the population. She'd have to discuss this question with Professor Also when things calmed down.

Skateboards.
Bicycles.
Soccer and rugby balls.

Really? The thought of the criminals riding skateboards and bicycles made them seem too normal.

Lab equipment.
Lockers.
Cell phones.
Tablet computers.

It figured that they had labs too. That would have been where they made the sugar virus and its antidote. Was it possible that the whatsit had been kept in one of the criminals' laboratories? She put a check next to that one.

Remnants of the sugar weapons.

Ugh. Those things were so creepy. But related to the whatsit? She didn't see how.

Décor from Moriarty's office.

Now *that* was nice stuff. All steampunky. She had to admit that Blixus had done a beautiful job—every bit as good as the décor gremlins. Maybe he had an artistic streak. Maybe that was where Nick had got his theatrical talents, and would you shut up about Nick already?

Paperback novels, including one or two by Lila Lester: Time and Broken Glass *and* Glare.

Ugh, that was so yucky. Was this part of them surveilling her mother? If so she'd better tell her, although she was sure Lila wouldn't listen.

Was there anything special about those two titles? She tried to remember what the two books were about. She'd only read the first one. *Time and Broken Glass* featured Lila's most popular detective, Neville Vanilla. As Amanda recalled, it was set at Oxford University and featured a group of anthropology students and their teachers. Something about an ancient civilization they were arguing over. She didn't see what that could have to do with the whatsit, and she really didn't understand why the Moriartys would be interested. The second book, *Glare,* was less familiar, but she thought it had something to do with Iceland. What that had to do with anything she couldn't imagine either.

Cars and lorries and their contents. Maps and flashlights, wrenches, pliers, and bolt cutters.

Not surprising, but again, pretty run-of-the mill.

Lunch pails.

Probably smelling of onions. Those guys she'd hid from had eaten so many onions they stunk. That was how she'd been able to follow them and find the school for criminals—and Nick in the wrong place at the wrong time.

Keys.

Now *that* was interesting. Maybe one of the keys opened a safe or locker. She put a check mark next to "Keys."

Weapons: guns, knives, swords, coshes.

Ick, ick, ick.

Lighters.

Like the one she'd used to set off the ceiling sprinklers. Nick had never expected that.

Cigarettes and cigars.

Yick, smelly.

Whiskey and beer bottles.
Ketchup and mustard containers.
Food wrappers.
Food trays, dishes, eating utensils.

More yick, smelly.

Sugar samples.
Chemicals.

The sugar samples would contain the virus the cartel had developed, so they were important. Chemicals fell into the same category. She didn't see how these could be related to the whatsit, but they might be. She checked both "Sugar samples" and "Chemicals," even though the detectives already had some sugar samples on file. Maybe these contained a different virus.

She thought about the list carefully. What were the Moriartys doing with her mother's books? Surely they didn't enjoy reading them. There must be some nefarious purpose to their possessing them. Were they studying her mom?

Was it possible that Nick's cell phone was among the items, with his game *Explosions!* and the link to the film they had been making on it? Maybe she should phone Ms. Pencil back and ask her, although neither the game nor the film was related to her purpose. She was just curious, and she couldn't justify bothering people for that.

What about all the files on the computers? Was it possible they contained something that could lead to the whatsit? Was the data even salvageable after having been drenched in sugar water and burned to a crisp? Maybe she couldn't justify calling Ms. Pencil about Nick's phone, but the computer files were another matter.

She phoned back. Fortunately Ms. Pencil was still there. When Amanda had posed her questions, the woman told her that she was afraid they hadn't been able to salvage any digital data so far, even from the cell phones, but they were still working on it.

Without access to the Moriartys' phones and computers, that avenue was closed. As for the other items, the team might be able to follow them up later but it wouldn't be easy. They'd have to jump through all kinds of hoops with the Metropolitan Police. For now it would be easier to pursue whatever they could get their hands on locally.

Amanda turned her attention back to her own list. The points were pretty vague but they might get the kids thinking. She sent the list to the others and thought about the next step. She kept coming back to the question of what had changed between Professor Feeney's phone call, when the teachers were concerned but not panicked, and now, when they were almost hysterical. Whatever it was couldn't have anything to do with the earthquake because the teachers had been discussing it in Thrillkill's office before the quake had hit. So what was different?

For one thing, most of the students had gone home for spring break. What could have happened during that week to change things? Where did the teachers go over the holiday? Now there was a lead. Amanda and her friends needed to find out where the teachers had been and what they had been doing. Maybe they should pay special attention to Professor Feeney, which would be difficult because she wasn't even their teacher. Amanda wrote:

1. Where were the teachers over the break, especially Prof. Feeney?

That was one lead. Another might have to do with Editta's disappearance, although it was hard to see how. Still, anything out of the ordinary should be investigated.

What did Amanda really know about Editta and her family? She knew that her mother was superstitious. That was where Editta had got that trait. What else? Where *was* Editta for those couple of days? Why wouldn't she say? Could she be ill? Family problems? Something to do with criminals? Amanda wrote:

2. More about Editta and possible connection to whatsit.

What else had changed? Was it possible that there was another mole inside the school and the teachers had hushed up the scandal?

This idea was particularly disturbing because it made her suspicious of everyone, even her friends. That wasn't good. How did she, or anyone, know that people were who they said they were? The school had supposedly checked out Nick and Mavis and they'd missed the truth. What would keep that from happening again? Or . . . OMG! What if the criminals could turn a student or a teacher who had been good to start with bad? How could you tell? Even if Amanda knew what to look for, how could the four of them watch everyone? The prospect was overwhelming. Even so she wrote:

191

3. How can you identify a mole?

Suddenly she got three texts at once, all responding to the list she'd sent. Amphora said, "4." Simon said, "4." Ivy said, "All of the above."

All of the above! Of course. That had to be it. Whatever was missing was so critical that it would affect *everything*, just as Professor Feeney had said.

Amanda looked at the list again. The detectives were the last line of defense against the criminals, and as she'd seen, the bad guys weren't just bent on stealing money. They were also developers and users of weapons of mass destruction. Without the detectives to keep them in line, they would threaten the entire world!

No wonder the teachers were so upset. She still didn't know what had changed, but she was certain that the stakes were even higher than she'd imagined. Maybe it *was* time to hold her nose and do something she really, really didn't want to do. Maybe it was time to ask Scapulus Holmes for help.

17

CRYSTAL WEIRDNESS

Amanda debated about asking Holmes for help. It was unlikely that the four friends could solve the problem of the whatsit alone, but to invite the new kid into their group was a big deal. For one thing, it would put all of them, especially her, in Holmes's debt. For another, it would be humiliating. If he thought she needed him, he'd gloat. And if he said yes, he'd be hanging around even more than he already was. She should probably think the matter through a little longer before committing herself.

But before she was able to reach a resolution, something else happened: the crystals started to exhibit strange properties.

Amphora burst into their room and told Amanda that the crystal she had been wearing had dimmed. They decided they should see if the same was true of the others, so they went to the lab where most of the rest of them had been taken. The same thing had happened. In addition, the color had changed. The beautiful apricot hue had lost some of its saturation and faded to a pale orange. The crystals were still lovely, but they looked like they'd lost their oomph. Amanda could relate to that. She felt the same way.

"What do you think this is about?" said Amphora. "Are they more poisonous now?"

"Would you cut that out?" said Amanda. "You can put it back on, you know. It isn't dangerous." She picked up Amphora's crystal and rubbed it all over her face and hands. "See? Am I sick? No. They're fine."

"Hang on," said Amphora. "You did something." She moved close to the crystal in a tentative way and peered at it. "It looks different."

"It does n—whoa! You're right. It got darker again." Amanda picked up the crystal and held it up to the light. Then she moved it around. "You know, I didn't notice before, but it looks kind of like David Wiffle's hair."

Amphora laughed. "You're right."

"It's not coppery enough to look like Ivy's," said Amanda. "Hers has much more red in it."

"Ivy's hair looks more metallic than this," said Amphora. "This is softer, more of a pastel."

"Yes," said Amanda, "but I don't understand." She put the crystal in her palm and tapped on it. The light got brighter.

"This is really weird," said Amphora. "Do it more."

Amanda hit the crystal against a lab bench. It glowed even more strongly and its color became saturated again. "I wonder if the same thing would happen with the crystals in the skull."

"Let's check with Professor Hoxby," said Amphora. She forgot that she was afraid of the crystal and grabbed it out of Amanda's hand.

The two girls practically ran to Professor Hoxby's office, which was right next to the autopsy room. When they blasted through the door, Amanda noticed that the poor man looked even more purple than usual. She wondered if there was something wrong. Well, besides the whole whatsit thing and the skeleton.

"Ladies," he said, "you seem in a hurry. Is there another body to examine?" He looked almost excited at the prospect.

"No, Professor," breathed Amphora. "It's just that, well, uh, I, you tell him, Amanda."

Amanda thought Amphora should have been the one to ask the questions because it was her crystal, but that was never going to happen so she said," Professor Hoxby, have you noticed any changes in those crystals from the skull?"

"Which skull?" he said, as if there were so many to choose from.

"The one with the body," said Amanda.

"My dear, skulls almost invariably come with bodies. Although occasionally they are separated. You know, there's a wonderful collection of skulls at—"

"The one with the dead body. The one you just autopsied." She was feeling frustrated.

"Oh, that one," he said. "My guess is that he was quite a handsome man."

"Yes?"

"Yes what, my dear?"

Amanda wanted to scream. Was he being deliberately obtuse?

"Sir," she said, "have you noticed any changes in the orange crystals that were stuck to the skull of the body we found under the school on Saturday?"

"Oh, those crystals. That body. I don't know. Shall we take a look?" He sat there so calmly that Amanda wanted to stick a lighter under his butt and get him to react.

She didn't have to, though, because the purple professor arose and motioned for them to follow him to the autopsy room. Normally this would have been a nauseating prospect, but the two girls were so desperate to see what was going on with the crystals that neither seemed to mind.

It took about two seconds to walk from Professor Hoxby's office to the autopsy room. When they got there, though, it seemed that he had lost the key to the cupboard that held the crystals.

"Oh dear," he said. "Wherever did I put that key?" The girls fidgeted so much you could almost hear their bodies hum. "I wonder. Perhaps in this drawer. No. That one? I can't remember."

Amanda spied a key sitting on top of the autopsy table. The idea of touching it was repulsive. She didn't know how the man could handle all that awful stuff, even with gloves. *She* wasn't going to touch it.

"Oh, Professor," she said, pointing to the key. "Is that it?"

"I, uh, oh, there you are, you silly thing," he said. Amanda and Amphora exchanged glances. He picked up the key and examined it. "Yes, I do believe this is the one. I know because it has an especially deep notch about a thirty-second of an inch from the right-most end." The girls rolled their eyes but he didn't see. "Let me just—aha! Treasure unearthed."

He opened the cupboard and removed the crystals, which were sitting in a clear plastic dish. Apparently Professor Stegelmeyer had succeeded in removing them from the skull after all. Amphora held hers up next to them. They were definitely different. The skull crystals were paler and less luminescent than hers.

"Look," she said. "They've faded, just like the others."

"Amazing," said Amanda. "They're still pretty, but they're definitely fainter."

"So they are," said Professor Hoxby.

"But watch this," said Amphora. Forgetting to be afraid, she reached out and scratched one of the skull crystals. It immediately brightened and the orange color came back.

"Oh my," said the professor. "Shall we try another?" He reached out and did the same thing to another crystal with the same result. "This is definitely worth more study. We must involve Professor Stegelmeyer."

That was the last thing the girls wanted. First, they didn't particularly like mean old Stegelmeyer, and second, they wanted to try things for themselves.

"Do you think we could take one or two to the lab and try our own experiments?" said Amanda.

"That's what we're here for," said Professor Hoxby. "I want you to learn as much as you can from this out of body experience. Oh, that was funny." He grinned. Amanda groaned in her head. "Yes, by all means. Would you like to select them?"

Amanda didn't think it mattered which crystals they took, but she said yes anyway. She and Amphora each pointed to a crystal, which the dead bodies teacher bagged and labeled for them.

"Now you know you must sign for these," he said.

"Of course," said Amphora.

"Here is my register. Oh. It *was* here. What have I done with it?" He retraced every step he'd made when looking for the key. "Sorry. Can't find it. Why don't you sign this piece of paper?"

It was an old, crumpled, yucky piece of paper Amanda could swear had blood on it. She grabbed a pair of gloves and the pen he was holding out to her and signed. Amphora did the same, and they left with their prizes.

"Don't forget to send me your report," said the pathology teacher cheerily.

"Of course," Amanda said, then whispered to Amphora, "I'll use purple ink for his copy."

The girls ran to the lab with their treasures. They repeated their previous experiments with the same results. Amphora seemed to have forgotten all about the crystals' potentially deadly properties. Their odd behavior so intrigued her that she couldn't wait to penetrate their secrets.

In fact, she was so excited that she did something completely out of character. She ran to Simon and dragged him to the lab to show him what they'd found. Amanda couldn't believe what she was seeing. Perhaps the crystals did have secret powers. They had certainly effected a change in her roommate.

When Simon heard the news he lit up. "We've got to run exhaustive tests," he said.

"Agreed!" said Amphora in a way Amanda hadn't seen before, especially when talking to Simon, who looked as startled as if a live dinosaur had entered the room and sat down to watch TV.

"We should get started right away," he said.

"I'd like to," said Amanda, "but you know—the whatsit. That's the most important."

"Oh," said Amphora. "Right." She hesitated for a moment and then said, "Do you think we might get something named after us? The Kapoor crystals or something?"

Simon gave her a withering stare. "You've got to be kidding. Is that what you're after? Glory?"

"Not really, but if it happened, wouldn't it be cool?"

"Science is important for what it can do, not who does it," said Simon. "It's not about being a celebrity or massaging your ego."

"I'm not massaging my ego," Amphora said, raising her voice. "I do want to know. Why can't it be both?"

"Hey, you guys," said Amanda, "let's forget about this, okay? If Ivy comes by she'll fine you, and anyway we have more important things to do than squabble."

Simon looked at her appreciatively, but Amphora frowned. "Why do you always cut me off right before I'm about to win an argument?" she said.

"I don't do that," said Amanda. "Where did that come from?"

Amphora moved back and looked at her feet. Amanda knew she was about to dig in and didn't want to waste time trying to placate her. She was about to suggest that they come back to the crystals later when another strange thing happened. Amphora apologized.

"I'm sorry," she said. "I was wrong." Amanda had to stop her mouth from dropping and Simon looked at her as if she were an alien with six heads. "Don't look so surprised. I'm perfectly capable of admitting my mistakes. Sometimes I think you guys don't know me at all." She didn't wait for a response. She turned and walked calmly out of the room.

When she'd gone Simon said, "That was weird."

"I'll say," said Amanda. "I've never seen her like that before. You know, I definitely think something is in the air around here. Everyone is acting really strange. Do you think the earthquake released something?"

"Could be," said Simon. "Except that a lot of this started before then."

"You're right. What then?"

"Who can say?" he said. "I suspect we'll find out though."

18

I'D LIKE TO THANK THE ACADEMY

While the kids were turning their attention to the whatsit, the teachers were hard at work trying to establish the identity of the dead body and the person who had killed him. The most likely suspects were Moriarty's moles—Mavis, the old cook, the crooked doctor, and Nick—so even though the staff had searched their rooms more than once, they did so again, looking for a murder weapon and any evidence that might tie the criminals to the body. Fortunately they left Amanda out this time, or at least they left her out of the search by name. They were still keen on getting the kids involved in a real case, so they encouraged all of them to help look for evidence, following procedure, of course. Professor Scribbish was to supervise their activities.

In the meantime, everyone was concocting theories about how and when the murder had occurred. The victim had to have been someone with access to the school. Otherwise the killer would have had to sneak him in, and that would have been difficult if not impossible. That meant the dead person was probably someone who resided there, or someone who had been there at least once. But no one had been reported missing, so who could it be?

Unfortunately, Amanda and her friends didn't have time to think about all that. Even though the teachers were deeply involved in the case, they were still talking about whatever the whatsit was, and the kids managed to make out some of what they were saying.

One thing the teachers discussed endlessly was where they had already looked. Listening to them was a lesson in the geography of the school because they were constantly naming places the kids hadn't heard of. This struck Amanda as strange because she hadn't realized there *were* that many places she and the others didn't know about. Perhaps they were familiar places with unfamiliar names.

At one point Ivy was listening to Professors Feeney, Snool, and Pargeter, and she heard Professor Snool say something about code names. Whether this was what he'd actually said no one knew. She had not gone to the doctor yet because she was still convinced her hearing would get better on its own. The others weren't happy about her refusal to be checked, but they decided to lay off for the time being. Amanda was actually worried sick, but Simon said at the first sign of real trouble he'd pick her up and carry her to the hospital.

As Amanda strained her ears, she was able to deduce that the teachers had in fact assigned special names to secret places around the school. Knowing this, the team began a Rosetta Stone-like operation in which they tried to figure out which name was attached to which place. One intriguing location was the crypt. Another was the peekaboo. Still another was the cave. The names were as abbreviated and separated from any key to their meaning as the pieces of paper in the trove. If you didn't know what they meant, they were as good as useless.

It seemed, too, that the teachers had given up on the idea that the whatsit had been lost and were starting to conclude that it had been stolen. Of course, as with the murder, the main suspects were the Moriartys. The teachers already knew that nothing of interest appeared on the evidence list from the factory explosion, which affirmed Amanda's conclusion that there was nothing significant to find. That meant that none of the files on the computers or phones was of interest. Also none of the chemicals, sugar samples, medical equipment, or lab equipment. At least all that stuff had been eliminated and they wouldn't have to waste time on it.

The kids also heard a lot of other discussion. For one thing, the papers on informants that had just been turned in to Professor McTavish were excellent, and one was brilliant, but the kids couldn't make out who the author was. Then they heard that one of the teachers wanted to write a new article on predicting criminal behavior based on finger grease left on mobile devices, as well as something about a frantic search for Professor Also's favorite umbrella, which she thought she'd left in the dining room but couldn't find.

But listen as they might, the friends weren't making much progress. And then something happened that insured they wouldn't, or at least Amanda wouldn't. Thrillkill decided that she and Holmes should, in fact, make the training film after all and her storytelling seminar be put on hold again. This news sent Amanda into paroxysms of frustration so pronounced that her stomach hurt for an hour after hearing it. Even gingersnaps couldn't soothe the pain.

Since Professor Redleaf's death. Holmes had been teaching the cyberforensics class and doing quite a job of it, from all the talk among the first-years. Even Amanda had to admit that he was good. He was teaching them how to track people's digital activities, identify and trap hackers, and disable malware, which were, of course, huge topics, but he managed to get across the basic concepts in ways that everyone understood. He was building quite a reputation and Thrillkill was over the moon about his progress.

Amanda, however, felt chaotic. She was now juggling her classes, the murder, the crystals, the whatsit, the training film, Darius Plover, her parents, and Amphora's constant crises, and the stress was beginning to show. However, there was one positive effect: she was too busy to think about Nick.

Unfortunately, she was going to have to focus on the film project now, which would take precious time away from more important things. However, as distracted as Thrillkill was, sooner or later he'd have a fit if she and Holmes didn't produce something, so for once *she* contacted *him* and asked to meet. As usual, she received an instant reply. He was available right then. How about getting a cup of tea and meeting in the Cyberforensics classroom? After running through a number of colorful insults in her head, she figured she may as well get the whole thing over with as soon as possible and said yes.

As she clomped down the stairs, she thought about how she'd like to approach the situation this time. When the two of them had last met they hadn't agreed on anything, but he'd been gracious and had let her take the lead. Maybe she should sit on her aggravation and see if that helped defuse the tension between them. Of course Holmes didn't seem to think there *was* any tension, but as far as she was concerned, the two of them were engaged in a huge power struggle and had been from the first. He had his agenda and she had hers. That was what it always came down to when they were together. She couldn't see how everyone else could like him. He was so difficult.

He reached the dining room the same time she did. He was wearing a bright multicolored sweater Amanda had to admit was really cool. She wondered if he had picked it out himself.

"Hey," he said when he saw her.

"Hey."

"You look nice," he said sweetly.

Amanda looked down at what she was wearing. A blue sweater, jeans, and tennies. Whoop-de-doo. Was he trying to flatter her?

"Uh, thanks," she said. "You look nice too."

"Thanks. I'm really glad Professor Thrillkill changed his mind about the film," he said. "It's going to be fun."

"Right," she said.

"Look," he said, "I know you don't like my approach, so let's back up and talk about what we should do instead. I'm flexible."

Why was he being so nice? He really shouldn't do that. It made it hard to hate him. Unless, of course, he was pulling a Nick and trying to fool her. She wouldn't put it past him.

"Okay," she said cautiously. "Let's give it a try."

"Want to work here?"

Amanda looked around the dining room. It was empty and quiet. No clatter of dishes, no cook running in and out, no students, nothing. "Sure," she said. "Why not?"

He gave her a big grin and found a place at her usual table. Hers, not his. He never sat with her group at meals. Was he trying to invade her territory?

"Uh, how about over there?" she said, pointing to a table in the corner farthest from the hall door.

"Your wish is my command," he said, bowing.

She fought the urge to tell him to stop playing with her and settled herself in the corner. He followed her so closely that she felt claustrophobic.

"Okay," she said, eyeing him suspiciously. "I think the film should tell a story. It should be a worked example that takes the audience through the solving of a problem." She stopped and waited for his reaction.

"Boffo," he said. Boffo? What century was this?

"We should come up with a question that demonstrates as many of the points we're trying to make as possible. However, we shouldn't try to make too many because people will get lost."

"Agreed."

This was too easy. She decided to press. "The problem should be dramatic with high stakes. People like a lot of drama."

"Yes. That makes sense." He paused for a moment, then yelled, "Yeah!" so loud that Amanda almost fell off her seat. "Oops, sorry. I just had to think about it for a second, but I realized this is an amazing idea. You're a genius, Amanda."

Here was a conundrum. She loved being called a genius. It happened about once a century, so she wanted to savor the experience. At the same time, she was afraid he was trying to get on her good side so he could manipulate her and she was afraid to let her guard down. Oh well. Better to be careful. She ignored the comment.

"I'm glad you like it," she said cautiously. "What's a good problem to use?"

"There are so many. Let's make a list."

"You make the list and I'll watch." She had no idea what a good problem would be. She really did need him to take the lead here.

Holmes took out his tablet, stared at it for a moment, and began to type. Thirty seconds later he had a list of nine items. He turned it around and showed it to her. It read:

How to:

- Get into a system when you don't know the ID and password.
- Recover deleted files.
- Trace where a user is located.
- Trace where a server is located.
- Tell what a given user has done (audit trail).
- Stop people from hacking in.
- Set a trap for a hacker.
- Identify and disable malware.
- Find out who's hacked you.

It was quite a list. Amanda was impressed. "This looks good," she said. "Let's pick one. Then we can turn the concepts into characters."

"Sorry?" Well, of course he wouldn't get it. What did he know about storytelling?

"All right, let me give you an example," she said. He seemed to relax. "What if we made an IP address a character the investigator needs to track? The detective tails him or her, goes on a stakeout, that sort of thing."

"Wellll," he said.

"You don't like it?" She could feel herself stiffen.

"An IP address is a thing. It's inanimate. You can't turn it into something with free will."

"Sure you can," she said. "If Terry Pratchett can have a talking chest in his stories, why can't you make a character out of anything you want?"

"That's Terry Pratchett. It's fantasy. This is real." So that was it. The kid didn't have any imagination. This was going to be tough.

"But it makes the story so much more interesting to give things personalities and watch them do things as if they're alive."

"That doesn't apply here. No one will understand the concepts. Anyway, you need explanations. I think we need a voiceover."

Amanda laughed. "Are you kidding? No way. Voiceovers are stupid. You're telling rather than showing the audience what you want to get across. They'll feel like you're trying to lecture them."

"But how can you explain something without a voiceover? Unless we go back to my original idea of lectures and Q and A," he said.

"Easy," she said. "You dramatize it."

"But that isn't enough. This is complicated stuff. You have to explain."

"The dialog and the action will do the explaining. For example, every time an IP address changes, it's like the person you're tailing puts on a disguise and tries to give you the slip."

"No," he said. "An IP address is a location, not a person. It's like the address of your house."

"Sure," she said, "but you can make it into a person or an animal or whatever."

He sat up straight, as if preparing for battle like some kind of knight. This was turning into a big fight just the way she'd predicted. "That isn't programmer culture," he said,

Boy he was dense. "So what? A lot of us aren't programmers."

"You should be," he said. "Programming is a basic skill. Everyone needs to know how to do it."

If Amanda had worn glasses, she would have been peering over them at this point the way Thrillkill sometimes did when he was annoyed. "Not everyone has time to learn to program," she said. "A lot of us have better things to do."

"I see," he said snippily. "And would you not learn to add or subtract because you have better things to do?"

"That's different. You need that to manage money and measure stuff."

Holmes rolled his eyes. "Don't be an idiot savant, Amanda. You need to know a lot more to get along in the world than how to make movies."

This impertinence made Amanda so mad that she got up and stomped all the way to the door. Then she turned around and said very loudly, "When you want to join the human race, Scapulus Holmes, let me know," and left the room.

A few hours later Amanda got a text: "Please come back." So Holmes was going to listen to reason after all. Good. She'd won the argument

as she should have. His position was ultra-dumb and he'd been insulting to boot. She was glad he'd seen the light.

"Pick a problem. I'll block out scenes," she texted back.

"Audit trail," the text came back.

Good choice. The topic was definitely something she could work with. "Can u send points?"

"U got it."

Hurray for our side. They really were making progress now. Maybe they should do the whole project by text. They seemed to get along better that way.

"I'll text Thrillkill w/ progress," she sent.

"Excellent," he texted, adding a smiley face. Apparently all was forgiven. Should she answer? She still didn't like the guy, but maybe a little concession would smooth the process.

She texted him a smiley and sat back to write a quick report for Thrillkill.

"How's the film coming along?" said Ivy when she returned to their room from wherever she'd been.

"Actually okay," said Amanda. "At the beginning I didn't think it would go very well, but he's being pretty nice now."

"Oh?" said Ivy. "Wasn't he nice before?" She sat on her bed. Nigel placed his paw on it. "Okay, Nigel. You can come up." The dog jumped up and leaned on her, causing her to tilt to one side. He was a big animal.

"He's so cute," said Amanda, gazing dreamily at the golden retriever.

"Yes," said Ivy. "He's perfect, isn't he?"

"Well, he thinks he is, but he's actually not," said Amanda.

"What?"

"Oh, sorry. You meant Nigel. I was thinking of Holmes. I mean first I was talking about Nigel. Sorry."

"Scapulus?" said Ivy. "No, of course not. He's a nice guy, and extremely smart, but he isn't perfect. Nigel's the only one who's perfect." She laughed. Amanda was glad to see that her mood had improved.

"I'm glad you said that because everyone else seems to think he is. Holmes, I mean." She couldn't bring herself to use his first name.

"He is popular," said Ivy. "Amphora has a huge crush on him."

"Amphora has a huge crush on everyone," said Amanda, smiling for the first time all day—except for the smiley she'd sent Holmes.

"Yeah. She's going through quite a colorful puberty, isn't she?" said Ivy, giggling.

Now it was Amanda's turn to say, "What?"

"She is," said Ivy happily. "We all are in one way or another. There's no point in denying it, is there?" She seemed her old self again. Maybe her hearing had returned.

"I guess not. Say, speaking of puberty, what do you think is up with Gordon?" said Amanda.

"You mean dumping David?" said Ivy.

"I don't know about dumping," said Amanda. "But he certainly seems to be getting more confident, don't you think?" She reached over and stroked Nigel absently.

"Yeah," said Ivy. "I couldn't believe how much he got into those glitter explosions, and wanting to go into the basements when David kept nagging him about how much trouble he'd get into. I was shocked." She tee heed. Yep. Her hearing must have come back.

"Me too," said Amanda. "What do you think David will do without him?"

"I don't know if Gordon will dump David completely. You think he would?"

"Who can say?" said Amanda. "Weird things seem to be happening around here. Sometimes I think anything could happen. Speaking of which, what's going on with Editta?"

"I don't know," said Ivy. "I did notice that she's actually talking though."

"That's good," said Amanda. "Whatever it is that's bothering her must be getting better."

"Hope so," said Ivy. "I hate for her to be so unhappy. She still won't say anything about what the problem is."

"You don't think it has anything to do with the whatsit, do you?"

"I don't know. We haven't made any progress on that front at all. Which reminds me, what's this about these crystals?"

Amanda brought Ivy up to date on all the latest crystal news, adding that she thought Professor Hoxby was looking more purple than usual, then apologizing because Ivy wouldn't be able to see the difference.

"Don't worry about it," said Ivy. "But this crystal thing is really exciting, isn't it?" She looked just like them with that gleaming orange hair.

It didn't take Amanda long to block out the scenes. Holmes had sent her a list of three points, which was the perfect number. Public speaking coaches tell you to mention no more than three ideas per talk or risk losing your audience. Either the boy was an expert in that too or he had an excellent feel for communication, which confused her, because if he did, why had he argued so much when she'd come up with her fantastic ideas?

When they convened again—it seemed that the far table in the dining room was now "their" table—Amanda explained that they would use motion capture. One of them would be wired with sensors while the other held the camera. They'd put the motion capture together with some digital characters and voila! An animated film.

"I don't think we can manage that alone," said Holmes, scrunching up his face.

"Well, if we can't we'll get help," she said. "Nick can—" She gasped. She was stunned by what had just come out of her mouth. She put her hand to her lips. Then she caught herself and said, "We'll get Prudence or someone to help us. It will be fine."

She sneaked a peek at Holmes. He looked as if someone had hit him. She must have put him in an awful position talking about her dead best friend like that. What could he possibly say?

He sat there for a moment and then said, "Can I see the scenes?"

She pushed her printout over to him. He skimmed it and looked off into the distance. Then he said, "Okay. I'll go with your scenes, but I reserve the right to change them later."

What? She thought he had agreed to go along with her. Why was he being difficult again? "You can't. There's no time. We have to keep on schedule and budget. There's a limit to the amount of fooling around you can do when you're working within constraints. We might be able to fix some things in the editing, but we can't reshoot scenes once they're wrapped."

He stared at her for the longest time. She couldn't tell what he was thinking. Finally he said, "You're the director. I bow to your expertise."

Amanda was gobsmacked. She'd figured he would argue. Now she was thrown off. Was he or wasn't he going to let her direct? Was he letting her get her way now so he could pull the rug out later? The words "What's my motivation?" came to her and she didn't know whether to laugh or cry. That was the question, wasn't it? What made Holmes tick? She had no idea.

Over the next week Amanda wrote the script and set up cameras and lights. Holmes ran here and there, following her around like a puppy and rushing to help her with the heavy stuff. She explained that they would put a green screen behind them and composite the backgrounds in later. She told him how they would frame shots, hit their marks, and use color to tell a story. All of this was new to him and he looked as if someone were performing magic in front of him.

"How did you learn all this?" he said after Amanda had completed a particularly sensitive maneuver with a red fill light.

"I dunno," she said. "I just picked it up. I've always done it. Why are you looking at me like that?"

"Like what?" he said.

"*That*," she said, pointing. "You look like you just ate bad fish."

"Oh, sorry. I didn't realize. No, of course I didn't eat bad fish." He laughed. "Although I quite like fish."

She moved her backlight. "By the way, was something weird going on with Professor Redleaf?"

"She died," he said.

"I know, and I'm so sorry. I meant, well, you seemed to know her. You said so at her funeral. I was just wondering if you knew what happened. She looked really freaked out that first day in class."

"Yes, I knew her. We worked together on a couple of cyberforensics cases."

Amanda was astonished. Holmes was only a kid. "But you're so young. How did that happen?"

"Headmaster Thrillkill is a family friend and he asked for my help on the case. Professor Redleaf and I got along really well."

"I didn't know your family was friends with Thrillkill—I mean Professor Thrillkill."

"Yes. I've known him since I was born," said Holmes.

That explained a lot. Amanda guessed that many of the Legatum families knew each other—and the teachers. Why hadn't that occurred to her before? She wondered how long her own parents had known the headmaster or whether they'd known any of the teachers before she'd entered the school. Of course they'd been far away in the U.S., so maybe not.

"About what happened that day in class," Holmes said. "I don't want to betray a confidence so I'm afraid I can't tell you anything."

What? He had just so much as admitted that something was wrong. This was not good. Was it possible that Professor Redleaf had actually been murdered? Everyone thought she'd been killed in the earthquake, but maybe not. You never knew around here.

"I understand that you want to protect her," said Amanda, "but whatever she saw could be important. She might want us to know."

"I'm sorry, Amanda," he said. "I can't tell you."

She wondered if he was lying. He hadn't done anything to make her think so but people weren't always what they seemed. She'd lied to Darius Plover, and she prided herself on her integrity. If she could do it anyone could. She shouldn't have done that, though. What was she thinking? Maybe she should write back and tell the director the truth. No, if she did that he'd never trust her again. It might be okay to write back and ask him how the film was going, though. She could tell him about the earthquake at the same time.

How had she gotten so sidetracked? She had a film to make. Whether or not it was a training film, and whether or not she had to work with someone she hated didn't matter. She was a filmmaker and this was her business. It was time to get on with it.

213

19

TRIBOLUMINESCENCE

As much as Amanda wanted to wrap the film, before she could do that she got sidetracked again. While she was editing the footage she and Holmes had shot, Amphora texted her and asked her to come to the lab at once with her video camera. Simon was experimenting with the crystals and they were getting amazing results.

When she arrived Simon said, "Let's start over. Amanda, can you video this? I want to document everything." He had laid the crystals out on the lab bench and sorted them into categories.

"Sure, but what did you find?" She peered at the array. Some of the crystals looked as they had when the girls had found them, beautifully luminescent and apricot-colored, but some were darker and some lighter.

"You'll see. It'll be more dramatic this way," he said, fiddling with the placement. He moved what Amanda thought was a pale crystal in with the medium group, then moved it back.

"What's this?" said Amanda. "Am I witnessing a conversion? You've never been interested in drama before."

"Of course I have," said Simon. "You know I like films. Although I have to admit that Spider-Man and Star Trek have gone downhill recently." He moved the crystal back into the medium group.

"Yes!" said Amanda. "I completely agree. I don't know what those directors have been thinking." She caught a glimpse of Amphora. She looked bored. "Amphora, what do you think?"

"Haven't seen them," she said. "I like Daniel Radcliffe."

"Well, sure," said Amanda. "Everyone loves Daniel Radcliffe. That's not the point. What I'm trying to say is that one, if you're going to remake something, improve it, don't ruin it. And two, learn how to do your job properly. I mean honestly, the writing in those pictures is terrible."

"I agree, but can we get back to the crystals?" said Simon. He was lining them up just so.

"Oh, sorry. Sure," said Amanda. "It's just that—"

Suddenly Simon grabbed a crystal and threw it across the room. It hit a wall and fell onto the floor. The three kids rushed to look at it. It had turned a deeper orange and was glowing more brightly.

"Yup," said Simon, looking at it from all angles. "Just what I expected. Oh nuts. You missed recording that, didn't you?"

"Yes, sorry," said Amanda. "How about if you do it again?" She readied the camera.

This time when Simon threw a crystal, Amanda caught the action on video. She captured the crystal's before state, the arc, the splat it made as it flew across the room and hit the wall, and the way it looked afterwards. For the before and after shots, she moved in close.

"Yup," said Simon. "Perfect. Now this time I want to measure the strength of the light before and after." He went to a cupboard and started rummaging around. "And the color temperature. I'm going to need some color sensors."

"Good idea," said Amphora. What was going on? Amphora and Simon getting along? Amanda wondered if Ivy should refund some of their fine money.

"What's that?" said Amanda when Simon had returned with a gadget that looked like a souped-up meat thermometer.

"A lux meter," he said. "That's for measuring the lux count—the intensity of the light. But I didn't find any color sensors. I'm going to have to search for an app and see if I can use my phone for that. At least I can do the intensity right now."

215

He tested the lux meter until he was satisfied that it was measuring correctly. Then he struck, scratched, and bumped the crystals, confirming the results the two girls had got when they'd done the same things. Amanda videoed each experiment and Amphora kept a running log with measurements and descriptions.

"What do you make of this, Simon?" said Amphora. Gosh she was being nice. Well, not nice exactly. Just not mean, which seemed nice when you considered the way she usually treated Simon.

"I'm wondering if the force of the impact is exciting electrons or photons," Simon said. "Does this happen with any other types of light?"

"Doesn't something like that happen with those plastic emergency lights you can carry around?" said Amanda.

"Dunno," said Simon. "I've never seen those. Are they an L.A. thing?"

"Search me," said Amanda. "I just use them. I don't know how they work."

"Well," said Simon, "what makes light brighter?"

"More power," said Amphora. Wow. She was on a roll. Since when did she become Ms. Electrical Engineer? Amanda thought there might be more to Amphora than she'd realized.

"So perhaps the kinetic energy that's being transferred to the crystals is being turned into power and exciting the electrons or the photons," said Simon, who seemed not to have noticed Amphora's transformation.

"Can you explain that slowly?" said Amanda.

"This is what I mean," said Simon. "Kinetic energy has to do with motion. The motion of an object gives it the ability to do work."

"Oh brother," said Amanda. "That's confusing."

"Doesn't have to be," said Simon. "Kinetic energy makes things move. Easy peasey." He stepped around the bench waving his arms in a way that made him look even geekier than he already was. "See? Kinetic energy."

"Okay," said Amanda. "I sort of get it. But what about the light?"

"Ah, that's interesting," said Simon. "Kinetic energy can be transformed into other types of energy, such as electric energy. Ever heard of the piezoelectric effect?"

"No, but if we have some, can I have pepperoni on it?" said Amanda, grinning.

"The piezoelectric effect has to do with generating electricity by applying pressure to something," said Simon. "It was discovered by Pierre and Jacques Curie in the nineteenth century."

"You mean if I press on my forehead I'm generating electricity in my brain?" said Amanda.

"That's an interesting question," said Simon. "I don't know. That would seem weird, wouldn't it? Can you imagine generating electricity every time you press on your forehead? You could do better on Professor Sidebotham's quizzes that way."

"That's cool," said Amphora, poking her forehead. "But I don't feel anything." She pressed so hard that she made a mark.

"You've got a red mark," said Simon. Amphora felt her forehead. "Trust me, it's there." She rubbed at it. "Would you cut it out?" She dropped her hand without argument. Amanda couldn't believe it.

"But here's a really interesting thing," Simon continued. "Certain types of crystals do exhibit piezoelectric effects. And that's what we have here: crystals." He cocked his head toward the display.

"So you're saying that the motion from throwing the crystals is generating the electricity?" said Amphora. She made like she was throwing a ball.

"In a way yes," said Simon. "Hey, is that a softball? You need to work on your pitching. But I think it's not so much the throwing as the impact. In other words, pressure, as I said."

"No, it's not a softball," said Amphora. "Well, it is but it's a pretend one, so it doesn't matter how I throw it. So when we hit or scratch the crystals, they make electricity and glow brighter."

"Exactly," said Simon. "The kinetic energy from your hand is being transferred to the crystals and creating electricity. Or to the imaginary ball."

"But what about the colors?" said Amanda. "Is that electrical too?"

"It's got to be," said Simon. "But in effect, there must be colored bulbs inside. Not bulbs exactly, but something that generates different colors of light."

"Are you telling me that when I press on my forehead I'm making colored lights inside my body?" said Amanda.

"Doubt it," said Simon. "I've never heard of colored light inside a body."

"But sometimes I see blue lights in front of my eyes," she said, rolling her eyes around.

"I think that has to do with the retina," said Simon.

"I do see blue spots when I press on my eye," she said, touching her eyelid.

"I don't think that's the best idea," said Amphora, grabbing for Amanda's wrist. "Don't do that. I mean it."

Amanda removed her finger from her lid. "But if I can make electricity in my eyes, I can shoot laser beams out of them."

"Don't think so," said Simon, "although that would be amazing. The first person I'd zap would be—"

"Don't say it," said Amphora.

"I was going to say David Wiffle," said Simon, turning his imaginary bolts in her direction. Amanda was relieved. She did not want a fight erupting again.

"Not the Moriartys?" said Amphora.

"Them too," said Simon. "Especially them." He shot the imaginary electricity stronger and farther.

"I think I'd go after Professor Sidebotham," said Amanda. "Well, David Wiffle first and then her. You know, another cool thing you could do is make movies inside your head. If you could figure out how to make different colors—"

"That would be sweet," said Simon. "But I really don't think it works like that."

"So the crystals are exhibiting the piezoelectric effect with pepperoni on top," said Amphora. She really seemed to like that joke. "Now what?"

"We need to figure out why they change," said Simon. "I wonder if the pressure is like charging up a battery and over time it gets drained. That might be why the colors fade."

"That makes sense," said Amanda. "Oh wow, do you think these crystals are batteries? I sure could use some more juice for my phone. I have to charge it up all day long."

"It's possible," said Simon. "I'd like to look this stuff up. Hang on." He charged over to the bookcases and started scanning titles.

"Don't you want to look it up online?" said Amphora.

"Nope," he said. "These books are really good. I'll find the information faster here."

Amphora gave Amanda a quizzical look. Amanda shrugged.

"Hm," said Simon after a few minutes. He'd pulled one book after another off the shelves and had been so excited he hadn't put them back. Every surface was covered with them. "It appears that what we're seeing is a phenomenon called triboluminescence. This happens when a material is broken or crushed. On the other hand, piezoluminescence occurs when something is deformed rather than broken, scratched, or rubbed. And sometimes x-rays and other electromagnetic radiation can be emitted."

"Are you kidding me?" said Amphora. "That's dangerous. I told you the crystals were making me sick." She moved away from them.

"You know Scapulus checked that," said Amanda. "There are no x-rays coming off the crystals."

"Are you sure he had the Geiger counter calibrated right?" said Amphora, who had reached the door.

"This is Scapulus Holmes we're talking about," said Amanda. "He's annoying but he's very smart. I can't imagine he didn't check that."

"I don't think he's annoying," said Amphora. "But you're right. I guess they are safe. Should I put my necklace back on?"

"Why not?" said Amanda. "It's beautiful."

Amphora returned to the lab bench and picked over the crystals until she'd found the necklace, then fastened it around her neck. It glowed happily and so did she. "It is lovely, isn't it?" she said.

"Yeah, yeah," said Simon. "Fetching. But we've got to find out more about these things."

"And that isn't the only thing," said Amanda.

"Right, the missing whatsit," said Simon. "How's that coming?"

"It isn't," said Amanda. "Unless Ivy has come up with something. I've been working on the training film, and you guys have been tied up with this."

"Not entirely," said Amphora.

"Oh really?" said Amanda. "What's going on?"

"You'll see," said Amphora.

20

EUREKA!

Over the next couple of hours the three kids learned a great deal about the crystals. They experimented with varying amounts of force and different stressors to see what would happen. The results were exactly as they expected: the more force and stress, the stronger the reaction; the less force and stress, the weaker the reaction.

Then they tried to figure out how long crystals would stay charged up under this and that scenario. They discovered that rubbing them softly made them glow longer with more of an apricot color than when they used a lot of force, which initially made them glow brighter and redder, but seemed to burn them out faster.

"I feel like I'm releasing a genie," said Amphora, rubbing faster.

"If there is one, it's invisible," said Amanda.

"And quiet," said Amphora. "I thought genies were supposed to be talkative."

"Ssh," said Simon. "I'm counting." He was comparing what happened when he rubbed once, twice, and so on, and making notes.

"What if there really is some kind of genie inside?" Amphora continued, ignoring Simon. "Not literally, but maybe something we're not familiar with. Some intelligence."

"Don't think that's possible," said Simon, "although the crystals do seem to release different types of energy depending on the force, motion, and duration of the pressure. Maybe they're some sort of naturally occurring touch screen."

"What about mood rings?" said Amphora. "How do those work? Maybe these are the stones from those."

"You keep going, Simon," said Amanda. "I'll look it up." She stopped her experiment, ran a quick search, and shook her head. "Uh uh. According to this, mood rings never actually worked. Now that I think of it, I'm pretty sure my mom has one in her jewelry box. Next time I go home I'll look. But yeah, they were supposed to be sensitive to heat and change color according to the emotions the person was feeling. But get this: apparently the temperature of the air actually affects the color more than body temperature. Ha! All those gullible people thought the ring was reflecting their mood when actually it was changing when the *room* got hot or cold. How dumb."

"It's not dumb," said Amphora. "I've seen them work."

"It's an illusion," said Simon. "Forget it."

"I'm not going to forget it," said Amphora. "That Wikipedia stuff is wrong. Why are you so negative?"

"I'm not negative," said Simon. "Just realistic. For example, look at this." He put a heat lamp next to a crystal and measured the color and light. Then he put an ice pack next to it and measured again. "No difference. Want me to do that again?"

"No," said Amphora. "What's the point?"

"The point is that your theory is wrong," said Simon.

"The point is that your theory is wrong," she mimicked.

"Shut up," he said, and turned back to his experiment.

"Hey!" said Amanda. "Cut it out. You guys are driving me crazy. You know what I think? I think you're secretly in love with each other."

"Eeeeew," said Amphora, making an awful face.

"Not true," said Simon, looking up from his work. "But why ew, Amphora? I've got a lot to offer."

"Oh really?" said Amphora, looking him up and down. "And what might that be?"

"Oh brother," said Amanda. "I'm sorry I said anything."

"Never mind," said Simon, measuring something. "It takes a real woman to appreciate me."

Amphora bashed her crystal on the bench, whereupon it turned bright red. She stomped over to the bookshelf, grabbed a volume that was sticking out, and clobbered Simon over the head with it. Then she clapped her hands up and down as if to say, "There. That did it," and sat down.

"Owwwwww," said Simon. "What do you think you're doing, you cow?"

"Five hundred pounds," yelled Amanda. "Each."

Amanda had had enough of Simon and Amphora's bickering. She felt slightly responsible for the latest round, however. She shouldn't have suggested that the two were secretly in love. No one took her comment seriously, of course, but even as a joke it irritated them so much that they practically killed each other. It was a good thing a detective didn't have to be a diplomat because Amanda was no good at being tactful.

She thought of calling Ivy to see if she could calm them down. Well, mostly calm Amphora down. Simon was pretty cool and collected for a guy reeling off insults. She felt guilty making Ivy get involved all the time, though. Why was it her responsibility to act as peacemaker?

Maybe they should take a break. Now that the two had started arguing they would be at it the rest of the day. But when she looked up to make the suggestion, there they were watching a crystal together as calmly as if they'd just been meditating.

"It's almost behaving like a pet craving affection," Amphora said. She petted it as if it were a dog or a cat. "Of course it doesn't shed like Nigel."

"Hang on," said Simon. "It's blinking."

Amphora jerked her hand away. "OMG," she said. "It's pink." The crystal was indeed blinking, two blinks at a time, and had changed color again, this time to a pale pink. "It's telling me to keep petting it." She touched it gently again, petting as if it were a delicate bird. The crystal changed color again, back to the apricot color. It was still blinking, two at a time.

"It's communicating!" said Amanda.

"I wonder," said Simon. "It's not out of the realm of possibility. But you do realize that if they can communicate it means they're alive."

The girls looked at each other. Amphora raised her eyebrows and Amanda nodded. He wasn't putting them on.

"Does this mean Amphora has been wearing a living thing around her neck?" said Amanda. As soon as the words had left her mouth she regretted saying them. Amphora would freak out if she thought she'd been wearing a pet. The next thing would be her worrying that the stone would bite her and give her rabies.

"It might," said Simon. "But remember that plants are living things. We're not talking about people here."

"No little gremlins?" said Amanda. "Gosh, I was so hoping for a new kind of house elf or something." She grinned.

"Make fun all you want," said Simon. "But I have a suspicion we might be on the verge of a very interesting discovery."

Amanda didn't doubt it. Simon was really good at science, and he had been inventing devices too. Why, he was almost as knowledgeable as Professor Stegelmeyer already. If anyone could get the crystals to talk, he could.

"Hello there," said Simon, moving his mouth close to a crystal and speaking softly. "Hey, was that a blink?"

"Do it again," said Amphora.

"Helloooooo," said Simon in exactly the same way as before. The crystal remained apricot-colored and blinked.

"Ooooh, it's so cute," said Amphora. "I just know it's alive. There's no other explanation."

224

"You stupid crystal," yelled Simon abruptly at the top of his lungs. The crystal turned pale pink and stopped blinking.

"Oh my," said Amanda. "That's amazing. It *is* alive. Do it again."

Simon repeated the experiment, but this time he yelled, "I am the very model of a modern major general." Same result. "Hm," he said. "I don't think it has anything to do with being insulted. I said something perfectly neutral that time."

"I don't know about neutral, but I see what you mean," said Amanda.

"You should stop yelling at it," said Amphora. "I think you're hurting it."

"Don't be ridiculous," said Simon.

"Seriously," she said. "I think when it turns pink it's telling you to stop. The blinking is like purring. It's happy."

"I think it's time to call in the big guns," said Simon.

"But Professor Kindseth is still in hospital," said Amphora. "Oh, you mean Professor Stegelmeyer. Are you sure you want to do that?"

"Forget Professor Stegelmeyer," said Simon. "We need to get Ivy in here."

After the team had brought Ivy up to speed and she had expressed awe and wonder, Simon said, "Can you hear anything coming from the crystals?"

Ivy motioned for everyone to stand still and be quiet and cocked each ear in turn toward the crystal. "Nope. Nothing. Not like I did back at the pit."

"Hm, not that surprising," he said. "While we were waiting for you, I tried recording them to see if there were any sound waves coming off them, but there aren't."

"They were humming before. Maybe I can get them to hum along," Ivy said. She started singing very softly, close to one of the crystals. It blinked.

"What are you singing?" said Amphora.

"Something I wrote," she sung. She kept singing but changed the words so she could talk to the others at the same time.

"It likes it," said Amphora. "Try something else."

Simon stuck his head in front of the crystal and sang, "Baby, gimme your love" at the top of his voice. The crystal turned pink and stopped blinking.

"Whoa," said Amanda. "It didn't like that at all. Can't say I blame it." She was expecting Simon to take offense at her criticism, but he showed no reaction.

"Sing some more, Ivy," said Amphora. "I really like that song."

"Thanks," said Ivy, and started singing her own composition again. As she did, Amanda got the idea of where the melody was going and started to harmonize. The crystal turned apricot and blinked like a happy kitten. Simon joined in and the blinking stopped. A second or two later the crystal turned pink again.

"You were off tune," said Ivy. "It didn't like that."

"I did that on purpose," said Simon, making a note.

"Yeah, right," said Amphora.

"Don't make me fine you," said Ivy, breaking off the song. "We have important work to do here."

"Sorry," said Amphora.

"You know what I think?" said Ivy. "I think they're behaving like human babies."

"I think you might be right," said Simon.

Amphora and Amanda stared at him. "Really?" said Amphora.

"Sure," said Simon. "Why not? I don't disagree with you guys just for the sake of disagreeing. If you have a valid point I consider it seriously."

"Thank you, Simon," said Amanda. "We appreciate that."

Amphora gave her a look that said, "You don't speak for me," but Amanda ignored her.

"So let's summarize what we know about the crystals so far," said Simon, punching his tablet. "They don't like a lot of force. They do like being petted."

"Isn't that amazing?" said Amphora. She stroked a crystal. It responded immediately. "Oooh, this one likes me. I think I'll name it Melisande." Simon tsked. She picked up the crystal, turned away from him, and cupped it in her hand.

"I'll say," said Ivy. "They're just like Nigel." At the sound of his name the dog looked up at her lovingly.

"We also know that they blink when they like something and turn pink and stop blinking when they don't," said Simon, ignoring Amphora. "And we know that when you hit them they turn red and glow brighter. But after a while, if you leave them alone they fade. We also know that the light they produce is triboluminescence and it's produced by the piezoelectric effect."

"We know quite a lot about them, don't we?" said Amanda, picking one up and holding it to the light. Even in the icky fluorescent purple of the lab's fixtures it gleamed a rich apricot color.

"Yes, we do," said Simon. "And from that information we can posit one, that they're organic, and two, that they're alive and possibly sentient."

"And three," said Ivy, "that they can communicate."

"Yes," said Simon. "And what that boils down to is this: I think we're looking at a new life form."

"OMG," said Amphora, whirling around to face him. "This is amazing. I have to tell—"

"Not so fast," said Simon. "We need to keep this to ourselves for the moment."

"But why?" said Amphora, whining.

"How would you like the Moriartys to find out?" said Simon. "If you thought they were trying to make a killing out of sugar, can you imagine what they'd do with these little guys?"

"You're right," said Amanda, holding the crystal tighter. "We have no idea if there are still moles at Legatum. We've got to keep this quiet. If you're correct, Simon, and these are sentient creatures, they need to be protected."

"Right," said Ivy. "We don't know yet if they can take care of themselves. If they can't, they might easily be abused. No one can know about this."

"Do you think these crystals could be what Professor Feeney was talking about?" said Amanda.

"No way," said Simon, who was still making notes and, it appeared, drawings. "Several of the teachers have seen them, and none of them reacted like they were a big deal. We would have seen or heard something."

"You're right," said Ivy. "These aren't the whatsit."

"So what do we do now?" said Amanda.

"Act like nothing has happened," said Simon. "But continue testing. We need to find out a lot more about these puppies." Amphora smiled. "And don't tell Editta. She's too unstable." He looked carefully at the girls. "What, no objections? You don't think I'm being unfair to her?" All three girls shook their head. "Really? I guess I have a lot more to learn than how the crystals protect themselves."

21

AN UNEXPECTED PARTY

After the kids had concluded that the crystals were alive, their experiments proceeded quickly. They discovered that the little cuties liked cool temperatures, which was very much not like babies. They also learned that they preferred a bit of humidity, which seemed consistent with where they had been found. Simon wondered what would happen if they put the crystals in a cave and suggested that the tunnels would be the ideal place. Amanda thought they should experiment with light sensitivity first to see if that kind of darkness would be harmful to them. They did, and learned that they were extremely sensitive to light. It seemed that they got stronger as the light intensity increased, as long as it wasn't too strong.

None of this information was surprising, but something they observed while testing the crystals' light sensitivity was: the light source they were using dimmed ever so slightly when the crystals were exposed to it. In addition, as they took in light they would turn deep, deep orange and not blink at all. After much testing and questioning the reliability of their instruments, they concluded that the crystals were absorbing light!

Simon put forth the theory that this deep apricot color must be a good thing—more of what they liked. Light was their food, and the more of it they "ate," the healthier they were. If that was the case, then putting the crystals in a cave would harm them. Perhaps the environment in which they'd found them was making them ill.

The idea that whatever light they were eating would diminish as it was consumed gave them pause. Would it be possible for the crystals to absorb so much light that they would visibly dim a bulb? As it turned out, this was exactly what happened, but it wasn't until Ivy connected the dots that they realized the implications. The crystals could be used as weapons to steal light, leaving the victim in the dark! This horrifying thought led to the subject of the Moriartys again, as so many things did, and they resolved even more strongly to guard the crystals carefully.

At one point during the testing, Ivy said that she was hearing an unpleasant noise coming from the crystals. Nigel had pricked up his ears and was looking distressed. Simon said that the crystals were purring, but when he gave them so much light that one of them turned red and blinked out, they realized that too much light could kill them.

That meant several things. First, a certain amount of light made the crystals happy, but above that, it hurt them. Second, their ability to store light was limited. They could hold so much and no more. Third, you had to get the amount of light just right, and what was the optimum amount?

What they had was a living species that could store light and potentially be used as an energy source, but could steal light and possibly be used as a weapon. In addition, the crystals were so sensitive that if you exposed them to the wrong amount of light or the wrong environment, they'd sicken and die. The good news was that you could tell instantly what state they were in just by looking at them. The bad news was, well, obvious.

To make sure they could keep all this information straight, Amanda made a little cheat sheet for all of them, which read:

Apricot: Healthy.
Deep orange: High energy, but also stressed.
Pink: Unhappy.
Red, no color: Dead.

Weak apricot: Ill.
Blinking: "Yes."
Making noise: Distress.

Once they realized the crystals could die, they were more careful. Unfortunately they did manage to kill a few of them. What they learned in the process was that the crystals were capable of containing a large amount of energy for a short time, but if they weren't relieved of it they would die. Unfortunately, the kids hadn't figured out how to drain the excess energy off yet, although they knew in theory that if they used the crystals as a power source, the energy would diminish. Probably not quickly enough though.

"You know what?" said Ivy. "I just remembered that I need to put those drops in Nigel's eyes. Amanda, can you come back to the room with me and help?"

"Sure," said Amanda. They'd been at the experiments for hours, and as excited as she was she could use a break. "I guess you guys should continue without us. Although I hate to miss stuff." She was a bit dubious about leaving Simon and Amphora together, but she told herself she wasn't their keeper.

"Me too," said Ivy, "but I've got to do this." Nigel stood up and wagged his tail. He knew they were going somewhere.

When they got out in the hall, Amanda said, "This is huge."

"I know," said Ivy. "It's a good thing the Moriartys are behind bars. If they got wind of this they'd be trying to steal the crystals. As much as we say we'll protect them, I don't know if we could."

"They'd have to know about them first. A lot of people know they exist, but the four of us—and Nigel—are the only ones who know what's really going on."

"We have to be careful about our notes," said Ivy. "No way do we want them hacked."

"Uh oh," said Amanda, squeezing her new tablet tight as if to protect it.

231

"What?" said Ivy.

"Maybe we should bring Scapulus in on this so he can help us protect our notes."

"Sure. He's trustworthy." Amanda gave Ivy a look she couldn't see. "You don't think so?"

"Who can say?" said Amanda. "He's a royal pain, that's for sure. But I think what you see is what you get with him. Although—"

"You have to forget about him, Amanda," said Ivy.

"I can't," said Amanda. "I've tried. By the way, we are talking about Nick now, aren't we?"

"Yes," said Ivy. "He was a fluke. Scapulus is different."

"What makes you say that?" said Amanda.

"I can hear it in his voice," said Ivy.

Amanda didn't want to say what she was thinking. Why hadn't Ivy heard the dissembling in Nick's voice? "Let's let it sit for the moment," she said. "We don't have to make any decisions right now."

Suddenly everything started shaking. Amanda grabbed Ivy and shoved her into a doorway, then held onto her while the building shook for what seemed like twenty seconds. It was one of the worst aftershocks they'd felt. Ivy was trembling so hard it was difficult for Amanda to tell what was coming from the outside and what was internal. Ivy had adjusted to the aftershocks better than she'd hoped, but she was still afraid. Who wouldn't be? When the ground moves under your feet, nothing is stable. The only safe place is in an airplane flying high off the ground.

Poor Nigel was shaking too. Fortunately when he was scared he'd come close to Ivy and lean on her, so he was under the doorway frame too. Simon never had made him a special protective device, although he had fashioned the breathing mask and it seemed to help. The dog wasn't wearing it now though.

When the shaking had stopped, Ivy said, "That was a bad one."

"Yes," said Amanda. "The worst one yet. I wonder if anyone's hurt."

"We should know quickly," said Ivy. "With all this earthquake stuff going on, people have been communicating really well."

The girls waited a couple of minutes but no texts arrived, so they continued on their way. When they had arrived at their room, Ivy went to look for Nigel's eye drops, and Amanda cuddled with the dog on her bed. She decided to take the opportunity to call her dad. She hadn't spoken with him for a while and she was worried about him.

"Hey, Dad," she said when she'd reached him.

"Hello, dear," said Herb. He sounded breathy.

"How are you?" she said.

A pause. "What's that?"

"I say how are you?" She raised her voice.

"Sorry, it's hard to hear you in this asana. Let me straighten up." What was he talking about? Asana? Wasn't that yoga? "Ah," he said much more loudly. "Those inverted poses are murder. Do you a world of good though."

"Are you doing yoga, Dad?" she said.

"Yup. I'm studying with a fellow from India. Name of Krishna Samosa. Quite a revelation. You should try it."

"You think I should do yoga?" said Amanda. Ivy lifted her sunglasses in a way that said, "What in the world is going on?"

"Absolutely. Change your life."

"Uh, okay, Dad. I will."

"See that you do. You okay?"

"I think so. I mean . . ." He was *not* in a frame of mind to talk. He sounded spaced out. "Yes. I'm good, Dad. Really good."

"I'm glad, Amanda. I've got to go back to my practicing right now, but please find yourself a teacher. Okay?"

"Sure, Dad. I will."

"Namaste."

"Uh, Namaste."

Amanda put the phone down and sat silent for at least a minute. It was the weirdest conversation she'd ever had.

"What was that?" said Ivy finally.

"I have no idea."

"Are you going to take up yoga?" said Ivy.

"Oh, sure. That'll find the whatsit and identify the body and help us figure out the crystals. Are you kidding?"

"Think he's okay?" said Ivy.

"I don't know," said Amanda. "I really don't."

"There are worse things than yoga," said Ivy.

"Not if you're Herb Lester," said Amanda. "He's not a New Age sort of guy. He's Mr. Practical. Well, he does have a passionate side. I never realized that until recently. All his career he's been on a mission to get rid of bad guys and save the world. You have to be idealistic to be like that, don't you? But that's not the same thing as being a hippie." She paused as the very idea hit her. "OMG, my dad is a hippie! I wonder if he has a ponytail. I'm freaking out. I feel like I don't know him anymore. Maybe I never did. Krishna Samosa? Yeesh."

"Give him time," said Ivy. "He's been through a lot."

"Yes, you're right. He probably just needs to get whatever all this is out of his system."

Then Ivy said, "I can't find the drops. Can you help me?"

"Sure," said Amanda. "Nigel can't smell them, can he?"

"I wish," said Ivy. "Don't think so."

But the eye drops were nowhere to be found. The two girls turned the room upside down and after nearly half an hour they still hadn't found them.

"Oh no," said Ivy at last. "What a dummy. I think I left them in the common room. Let's go look."

Girls and dog trundled down to the Holmes House common room. On the way Ivy started to chuckle.

"What's so funny?" said Amanda.

"I'm just a dope," said Ivy. "I should have remembered where I put those things."

"No biggie," said Amanda, stepping into the common room. "I do that stuff all the time."

Suddenly she heard, "Surprise! Happy birthday!" and just about fell over backwards. There in their favorite hangout was the entire Holmes House first-year gang, as well as a bunch of other students she knew, including Ivy's sister, Fern, and the décor gremlins, who seemed to have outdone themselves yet again.

The room looked like the FAO Schwartz toy store in New York. It was stuffed to the gills with plush animals, toy trains, puppets, games, musical instruments, building sets, books, art supplies, balloons, glitter, and the most tantalizing cakes and cookies ever.

"But my birthday isn't till next week" said Amanda. Then she caught sight of Amphora and Simon, who were grinning like Cheshire cats. "You knew about this," she said.

"Yup," said Simon.

"That's why—"

"Never mind," said Ivy. "Let's look at the gifts."

Amanda was astounded to see a huge pile of presents in the corner by the window. Someone, probably Simon, she thought, had stacked them as high as they would go in a tower-like structure that looked as if it would topple any moment. She hoped there wasn't anything breakable inside the colorfully wrapped packages.

"Come look at my cake," Amphora said, pulling Amanda toward the other side of the room.

"You made me a cake?" said Amanda.

Amphora dragged her over to a gigantic cake. It had about a billion layers and was covered with bright blue frosting with curlicues and other decorations in different colors. Half of it was gorgeous, but the other half was lopsided and rickety.

"Ha ha," said David Wiffle, who had crashed the party. "What a stupid cake."

"Shut up," said Amphora. "I worked really hard on that."

"Yeah," said Gordon Bramble, who was back at David's side. Amanda figured they must have made up.

"It's super ugly," said Harry Sheriff, who was attending for some unknown reason. Amanda didn't even know him. If that was the way he behaved, why did all the girls like him so much? "Is that your self-portrait on it?"

"What's the matter with you?" said Amanda. "She put a lot of effort into making this cake. I think it's lovely." Harry Sheriff indeed.

"I'll bet it cost the school a ton of money," said Editta from behind her. Amanda was surprised to see her there, but glad. Maybe she was returning to normal.

"It didn't," said Amphora, who was getting worked up. "And anyway, they can afford it."

"Don't think so," said Simon. "With all the earthquake repairs they have to make, they're going to have to spend a lot."

"Oh, shut up, Simon," said Amphora. "You ruin everything."

Ivy looked like she was about to say something but shut her mouth. Amanda figured this wasn't the time or place to be fining those two and was grateful for Ivy's good judgment.

"You did this all by yourself?" said Editta. She was definitely sounding like her old self.

"I did get a little help," said Amphora.

"Figures," said Simon. "You only made this so you could spend time with *Rupert*. That's why you made it so big. The bigger it was, the more time it would take."

Ivy turned to face Simon and said, "That's it, Simon. I'm not going to fine you for that. I'm going to kick you out."

"You can't do that," said Simon. "You're not Thrillkill. I can be here if I want." He sounded uncharacteristically petulant.

"We're going to have a talk after this," said Ivy. "We need to get some things straight."

"Suit yourself," said Simon, walking off. Then he turned around. "Oh, and by the way, Amphora, your precious Mr. Thwack isn't here because I told him not to come. You should think about someone besides yourself for a change. He could get fired for mixing with the students. Put that in your cake and eat it." He stomped out of the room in a way that was quite unlike him.

"I've had enough too," said Amphora, turning and huffing out after him. "Happy birthday, Amanda. It isn't my fault your party is ruined."

Amanda stared at her. Here her friends had gone to all this trouble to give her a party, and now one by one they were spoiling their own event.

She grabbed a piece of Amphora's cake, which was delicious if a bit aesthetically challenged, and found a seat near the presents. She wolfed down the cake, smearing frosting all over her face, and began to open them. Maybe these people weren't such good friends after all. Well, Ivy was, but the others were giving her so much trouble that they might not be worth hanging around with. Editta was sullen, Amphora prickly and selfish, and Simon rude. Sullen, Prickly, and Rude, attorneys at law. That sounded about right. But not for her. Maybe it was time to find some new friends.

They had chosen cool gifts though. Ivy had given her a book of Irish folktales and said on the card that she hoped they would inspire her filmmaking. Amphora had given her a beautiful bracelet. Editta's package contained, surprise, surprise, a good luck charm. Simon's outsized package contained one of his adapted skateboards, which she thought especially nice for all the effort he'd put into it. Owla, Prudence, Dreidel, and Clive had selected thoughtful gifts as well. Even the gremlins had participated. Alexei had contributed a statue of a peacock, and Noel had picked out a Lucite vase. Amanda suspected that both items had come from the basement. Still, she was chuffed.

Suddenly Holmes entered the room, empty-handed. Amanda didn't remember seeing a gift from him, so he obviously wasn't giving her one. He made a beeline for the food and piled a plate high, saw Amanda in the corner, and left. Left! Without even so much as a "Happy birthday." What was up with him now? She didn't even want to guess. From now on, everything weird that happened would be due to spores. That was the only explanation that made sense and she wasn't going to waste valuable brainpower looking for another one.

Then David Wiffle stomped up to her and said, "Your friend is in trouble now. I told on her."

"What do you mean?" said Amanda, hugging her new skateboard.

"You can't ride that," said Wiffle. "It's too dangerous."

"I can too, and since when do you care about my well-being?" said Amanda.

"I don't," he said. "I mean it's too dangerous for the people who *aren't* skateboarding. They get nervous when they see you coming and run into each other and stuff."

"That's ridiculous," said Amanda. "What did you mean about telling? Who are you talking about?"

"You know who," he said. "That tall roommate of yours who thinks she's so great."

"Amphora? What did you say?"

"I told Professor Buck that she had been in the kitchen with the cook and used school supplies to make an illegal cake."

Amanda was gobsmacked. Illegal cake? What was he, the cake police?

"You little weasel," said Amanda. She felt like bonking him over the head again but knew she couldn't get away with that twice. "What is wrong with you? She was just trying to make me a nice surprise."

"That cook is going to be fired," he said.

"You wouldn't," said Amanda. "You didn't!"

"I did," he said. "You don't get it, do you? If you break the rules, criminals can get in. You should know that better than any of us." He smirked. "It was breaking the rules that got your criminal boyfriend into the school."

"Shut up!" she yelled. "It wasn't my fault."

"Aha, so you admit you let him carry on his nefarious activities. It *was* your fault."

"Was not, was not, was not," yelled Amanda. "You're a hateful little prig and you're going down, David Wiffle."

"What's going on here," said Ivy, materializing with Nigel in tow.

"He's an idiot," said Amanda.

"Nuh uh," said Wiffle. "You're the idiot."

"Shut up!" screamed Ivy. Everyone turned around and stared at her. Wiffle laughed in her face and clomped out of the room yet again.

"Are you okay?" said Ivy.

"Yeah," said Amanda. "I sure hate that guy though."

"You know," said Editta, suddenly appearing, "he isn't such a great detective. Last term his house came in last on the school project. They thought the target of the garage bomber was Professor Pickle and it wasn't. If he's so smart, how did he mess that up? He blamed us for contaminating the evidence, but if he was any good he'd have realized that we didn't and would have solved the mystery just as well as we did."

Amanda gaped. This was the most she'd heard from Editta since last term. What had brought this on? She looked at Ivy, who was also gaping.

"Plus his grades aren't all that good," Editta continued. "I heard him and Gordon talking and neither one of them did all that well in their classes last term. So much for his little rules. They haven't gotten him very far."

Suddenly Simon came running in. He stopped in front of the group and motioned to the door with his head.

"What?" said Amanda.

"Uh," said Simon, "I was just wondering if you'd like a cup of tea." He looked at Editta, then back at Amanda.

"There's tea here, Simon," said Amanda. "Over there." She pointed to a large teapot, which was sitting on the beverage table.

"There's other tea in the dining room," he said.

"Yeah, so?" said Amanda, who was still not happy with him for disrupting her party.

"Just come with me for a second," he said.

"I'll go," said Ivy. "It's getting a bit noisy in here."

"Okay," said Simon. "Come on."

He practically pulled Ivy out of the common room. Editta looked at Amanda and said, "What's up with him?"

"Spores," said Amanda.

22

THE WHATSIT

Ivy was back in about two seconds with Simon trailing behind her. "I hope you had a fun party," she said. "Now it's time to go."

"Yeah," said Simon. "You need to do that whoozit thing."

But they needn't have worried about trying to sneak Amanda out of there. Editta wasn't listening.

"Oh," said Amanda. "Right, the whoozit thing. Would you excuse me a moment, Editta? Thank you so much for the lovely good luck charm. I'm going to find a chain for it and put it on right away."

"You should," said Editta. "It will help you a lot."

Amanda noticed that Editta was wearing one just like it around her neck. Somehow it wasn't doing her a whole lot of good, but Amanda would wear it to please her friend anyway.

Ivy and Simon hustled Amanda out of the common room, and checking around to make sure no one could hear, they told her that Simon had discovered that the crystals were formed from the virus-treated sugar!

"OMG," said Amanda. "That makes perfect sense. We found them where the cook put the sugar, or nearby anyway."

"The slime mold must have moved it around some when it was eating the stuff," said Ivy. "That's why the crystals formed where they did. The earthquake put tremendous pressure on the remaining sugar. There was a lot of heat too, kind of like how diamonds are formed. That's what did it."

241

"I found the virus in them," said Simon. "I used the smartphone microscope Professor Kindseth and I made, and there it was."

"You realize what this means, of course," said Amanda. "Any place the pink sugar was there could be crystals."

"You're right," said Ivy. "I hadn't thought of that. There could be some at the Moriartys' sugar factory."

"Right," said Amanda. "It's a good thing they're in prison and can't go back there. Although wait a minute. The earthquake wasn't strong enough in London to make crystals."

"No," said Simon, "but the explosion and the fire were."

"Oh no!" said Amanda. "I hadn't thought of that. There could be crystals there. Do you think the crime scene investigators found them and—no. I saw the list of evidence. There was nothing about any crystals."

"Maybe they didn't find them," said Ivy. "They could be buried."

"Yes!" said Amanda. "We need to go see."

"I wouldn't worry," said Simon. "The Moriartys aren't going to be able to get them. The police caught them before they'd have time to find them, and they're still in prison. If there are any crystals they'll be sitting there for a long time."

"But just for the sake of argument, let's say the Moriartys—or their associates—did find the crystals," said Amanda. "It wouldn't take them long to discover their properties. They'd want to exploit them. And they wouldn't care that they were living things. They'd take what they could get and just kill them."

"But then they'd have nothing," said Ivy. "That wouldn't be in their interests."

"Yeah, it would," said Amanda. "Because they'd try to make more. And if they succeeded, they'd be breeding this wonderful new life form just so they could abuse and kill it."

"You're right," said Simon. "Technically, that would be genocide."

"Wow," said Ivy. "It would."

The situation was so serious that the three friends wondered if they should tell Thrillkill after all. They knew they'd have to tell Amphora. It wouldn't be fair to leave her out. Editta? Probably not—at least not now. Amanda almost wished they could confide in Professor Kindseth, but that was out of the question. In the end they decided to keep the news to themselves for a while, but they'd have to get to London to explore the ruins of the factory as soon as possible.

They walked back into the common room, where the guests were dispersing. Rupert Thwack had indeed showed up and after wishing Amanda happy birthday, cleared the food with his assistant's help. The décor gremlins insisted on putting the room back in order, and in no time had restored it to its previous state.

Now Editta was the only guest left, and out of the blue she made the oddest comment.

"You know," she said to Amanda, "the charm I gave you will help keep you from losing things. I should have given one to Mrs. Bipthrottle in the library. That way they wouldn't have lost that book."

Amanda and Simon looked at each other. "What book?" said Amanda.

"The one from the library," said Editta.

"You can check books out of the library," said Simon. "That doesn't mean they're missing."

"This one is," said Editta.

"You mean a reference book?" said Ivy.

"Yes," said Editta. "The ones you can't check out."

"That isn't unusual, is it?" said Simon. "Maybe it's on one of the desks. Does it matter?"

"Oh yes," said Editta. "Lots. You see, I counted all the books in the library on the twenty-third of March and there were 4,273. Then when I got back from the break I counted them again. There was one missing. There's a cage area that has a key to it and you have to get permission to go in. I didn't go inside because I could see to count from the outside. But there was definitely a book missing. I could see where it went. The only way you're allowed to take books out of there is if you fill out a special card. I did it once. But there weren't any of those cards on file. I looked three times."

"Why is this so important?" said Ivy.

"The books in the cage are there for a reason," said Editta. "They're super important, and in a lot of cases, rare. They have to protect them."

"So are you saying you think this book is critical to the detectives, or just to the curriculum?" said Amanda.

"The detectives," said Editta. "Have you ever looked at what's in there? There are a lot of important secrets in those books."

The three others looked at each other. Well, Ivy didn't, but she sat up straight and they knew that meant the same thing. Secrets. Of course. The missing book was the whatsit!

They got up and ran to the library, pulling Editta along with them. "What are you doing?" she said.

"Just come with us," said Amanda. "Show us the place where the book is missing."

"There," she pointed when they had reached the cage. There was a large empty space on the top shelf of the bookcase farthest from the cage door.

"Well spotted," said Simon. "I never would have noticed that."

"As I said, I counted them," said Editta. Amanda wondered if Simon was regretting teasing her about all that counting. "I knew from that first. Then I went back and saw the spot."

"And there's no checkout card?" said Ivy.

"Uh uh," said Editta. "Look, here's the place where they go." She led them to a small metal box marked "Special Collection." It was empty.

"But there must be a catalog card for it," said Amanda. "All we have to do is look by the classification number. It should be somewhere between HV and QA."

"Weird them still using a hard copy catalog," said Simon.

"I'll say," said Amanda. "But in this case it should help us."

The four of them went to the card catalog, which was really two catalogs. One was arranged by main entry, that is, author, or if no author, title. The other went by subject. They opened the drawer in the latter that held cards for the middle of the alphabet, which covered HA through QZ. Then they checked the cards for the books on either side of the empty space. There was no card between them, not for H, I, J, K, L, M, N, O, P, or Q. They even looked at a few cards before and after the place where the card should have been. Nothing.

"Oh great," said Amanda. "There's no card."

"We might be able to guess the topic, though," said Editta. "The book on one side is *A History of Codes and Ciphers* and the other is *A History of Scandals*. Oh dear, that doesn't make any sense. I have no idea what it could be."

"Let me think this through," said Amanda. She considered the books on either side. They were both history books, but on two very different topics. What could the connection be between scandals and codes? Of course. They both had to do with keeping and revealing secrets. A code protected a secret, and a scandal made it public. There were those secrets again. They were a big deal to the detectives. Everything seemed to revolve around them.

"Maybe the book has to do with secrets," she said. "That would make sense. Secret communications are vital to detectives. So are breaking criminals' codes. That must be what it is, and if it falls into the wrong hands the criminals will know how we formulate our codes. But why would such a book be in the library, where anyone, including

Mavis Moriarty, could find it? If it's that important, wouldn't it be under lock and key, and if it isn't important enough, why are the teachers panicking?"

"I don't know," said Ivy. "Those are good questions."

"If it is about that," said Simon, "Scapulus could help. Codes are his thing. It's too bad he isn't speaking to us anymore." He looked right at Amanda. She was not going to comment. She was not about to tell him about her aversion to the Holmes family. Only Nick knew about that, and she shouldn't even have told him. Let them think what they liked.

"But here's another question," she said, ignoring Simon. "Do you think it was stolen? It could have been lost. That wouldn't be such a big deal, would it?"

"I don't think we have any way of knowing what happened to it," said Simon. "But we have to assume the worst. We have to figure the Moriartys have it. Anything less wouldn't be such a disaster."

"The Moriartys again," said Amanda.

As they left the library, they ran into Holmes. "Hey, old lady," he said to Amanda.

"Excuse me?" she said, glaring at him.

"You're over the hill now," he said unkindly.

"No more than you," she said.

"Yeah, but I'm a guy," he said. Ivy's mouth dropped. Even Simon looked askance at him.

"So what?" said Amanda.

"So guys can get as old as they want and no one cares," said Holmes. What in the world was up with him? This didn't sound like him at all.

"That party was lame," he said. "You need to have a *real* party, off-campus. You know, a wild party with beer and cigarettes. None of this namby-pamby stuff."

"Have you lost your mind?" said Ivy. "Have all those aftershocks gotten to you, or are all those ones and zeros warring in your head?" This didn't sound like Ivy either.

"Do I take that as a no?" said Holmes.

"You do," said Amanda.

"Suit yourself, Goody Two-shoes," he said, and left.

"What was all that about?" said Amanda.

"I have no idea," said Ivy. "He's usually so nice and polite."

"I think—" said Simon.

Just then Amphora appeared. Her eyes were wild and she looked like she'd just seen another dead body.

"Are you all right?" said Amanda.

"No," said Amphora. "I just overheard Thrillkill. The Moriartys have escaped!"

23

PHONE CALLS

The Moriartys out of prison? They'd joked about it, even half considered it, but Amanda had never actually believed it could happen. Blixus and Mavis Moriarty were considered the most dangerous criminals around. They were in a high-security facility. There was no way.

"What are you talking about?" said Amanda.

"The aftershock," breathed Amphora. She could barely catch her breath. "It damaged the prison so much that they escaped."

"This is terrible," said Ivy. She moved closer to Nigel and hugged his neck.

"We have to find that book," said Simon. He stood up and started to pace.

"What if it isn't the whatsit?" said Amanda, rising as well. She walked over to the window and looked out, but nothing registered. This definitely would not have been the time for one of Professor Sidebotham's quizzes. She couldn't have said what the weather was or whether it was night or day. "If we look for it and it isn't, we could just be wasting time."

"You don't suppose Blixus already has it, do you?" said Amphora, following Simon with her eyes. "The thing went missing before he was caught."

"Oh great," said Amanda, whirling around to face the others. "If you're right and he's out, he could be on his way to get it right now."

248

"I don't think we have any choice," said Simon, slowing down. "We have to find him, the missing book, or both."

"That's a good point," said Ivy. "If we're worried about the whatsit falling into his hands, we need to see what he's got. If he doesn't have it, we're probably safe."

"Do you think he'd return to the factory?" said Amanda. "OMG, if he did, he'd find the crystals."

"We don't know that there are any there," said Ivy.

"But there might be," said Amanda, taking her seat again but sitting on the edge. "So now we have two reasons to go."

"It's not going to be easy," said Simon, speeding up. "Maybe we should search the school again before we worry about that."

"That's a tall order," said Ivy.

"We didn't know what we were looking for before," said Simon. "This time it should be easier. If we see a book, we'll know it's a possibility. Anything else we can forget about."

"Assuming it's the whatsit," said Amanda, getting up again. She moved behind Ivy and rested her hands on the back of her seat.

"Assuming it's the whatsit," said Simon, playing games with his feet. He was touching the toe of one foot with the heel of the other each time he moved forward now.

"So we've got to search all of the rooms, closets, and cupboards as well as the tunnels," said Amphora, who seemed mesmerized by Simon's feet.

"What about the teachers' offices and quarters and the kitchen?" said Amanda, looking where Amphora was looking. There was something steadying about watching Simon's OCD behavior.

"I don't think we need to bother with those," said Ivy. "The teachers will have taken care of their own spaces and the staff's."

"What about the students' rooms?" said Amphora. "We're not supposed to know about this. Is it possible the teachers have been searching our rooms without our knowledge?"

"Wouldn't we catch them at it?" said Amanda.

"Maybe not," said Amphora. "They might think it's safe to do it when we're in class."

"Considering the gravity of the situation, you wouldn't think they'd do nothing," said Simon, stopping in front of the others. He reached out and gave Nigel a tousle. "They probably have."

"I say they haven't," said Ivy. "It's too sensitive. Doing that implies that they don't trust us. I think the parents would be pretty upset if they knew that."

"Let's forget about the students' rooms for now," said Simon. "We can do them later if necessary."

The others agreed, and in the morning they began a systematic search of the school—again. This time they needed even more help if they were to cover all that ground so quickly, so despite his weird behavior of late, they asked Holmes to join them. When he heard that an important book was missing he became agitated and agreed at once. He even said that he was happy to be invited. Seeing these sudden changes in him, Amanda wondered if he might be bipolar.

They split up, with Simon taking the basements, Ivy and Amphora the top floor, and Amanda and Holmes the other floors. Amanda wasn't happy that she was stuck with Holmes again but figured there was no point arguing with something so important at stake. He seemed to be a good searcher—very thorough—but she couldn't bring herself to compliment him. He still irritated her.

As they were combing the classrooms, he raised the issue of the film. "When do you think we can show it?" he said.

"I'm having trouble with the audio," she said. "Also, I keep getting distracted, so I don't know."

"Can I help?"

"Do you know anything about audio or compositing?"

"Not really, but if you show me I can learn really fast."

"I don't have time to show you, Scapulus. I don't understand why Thrillkill didn't assign someone who already knew this stuff."

"Hey," he said. "Shut up."

This astonished Amanda so much that she clamped her mouth shut and stared at him. "What did you say?" she said when she had recovered enough to speak.

"I said shut up. You know what you need? You need a good comeuppance. You're rude and bossy. And I'll tell you what else. I'm tempted to do it myself."

This outrageous behavior so infuriated Amanda that she picked up a blackboard eraser and threw it at him. It hit him in the shoulder and spewed so much chalk dust that both of them sneezed.

"And another thing," he said, "you're not that good."

Amanda froze. "What do you mean I'm not that good?"

"I mean you're not as good a filmmaker as you think you are."

Amanda was shocked. How dare he say such a thing? Was this payback for her outburst that first day? Sure, she'd been thoughtless, but he was being cruel. There was a huge difference.

"That's rich coming from someone whose ancestor was a smug drug addict," she said. "What could you possibly know about making movies?"

Holmes looked horrified but said nothing.

"Struck a nerve, did I?" she said. "How does it feel to be hit where it hurts?"

A million different emotions seemed to pass over Holmes's face. He turned and stormed out of the classroom.

Just as Holmes was leaving, Amanda's phone rang. Her friends rarely called her, so it was probably Thrillkill. She was in no mood to talk to him, but she thought she'd better answer anyway. But when she looked at the caller ID, she saw that the number was unknown. Oh great. Should she answer? Chances were that if she didn't know the caller she wouldn't want to speak to him or her. On the other hand, you never knew with this detective business. She should at least see who it was. She could always hang up.

"Hello?" she said.

"Amanda!" screamed a woman whose voice she didn't recognize.

"Who's this?" said Amanda tentatively.

"It's your cousin Despina, dear," said the woman. "Hill and I are at the guard gate."

"Excuse me?" said Amanda.

"Your dad's cousins, Despina and Hillary Lester. From Liverpool. We're here to show you around the Lake District."

For about the millionth time that day, Amanda's jaw dropped. She had no idea who "Despina and Hillary" were and had no time to waste with them. They were at the guard gate? Was the woman nuts? You don't just drop in on someone you don't know like that.

"I'm sorry," she said coldly. "Do I know you?"

"Of course," fawned the woman. "We visited you in Los Angeles when you were six months old. What a pretty baby you were."

Amanda gagged. Where were her gingersnaps?

"I'm sorry—is it Despina?"

"Yes, darling. Despina and Hill."

"I'm sorry, Despina, but I'm in the middle of something."

"But we're here, dear," said Despina. "Oh, and I must tell you about your cousin Jeffrey. You know he's a detective inspector now. And guess what: he was just transferred from Brixton to Scotland Yard. Isn't that wonderful?"

Amanda had no idea who Jeffrey was, didn't care, and was losing her temper. But before she could say anything, Despina said, "You need to come to Liverpool, dear. We have so much to show you."

"I can't," said Amanda. "Please go away."

This rejection didn't faze Despina one bit. "Oh my. Sorry this isn't a good time, dear. We'll come back later."

Amanda shut off the phone without saying another word. She'd never have to deal with those bozos again. Who cared what they thought? Still, she was shaking. Whether it was from the bust-up with Holmes or the call from her so-called relatives she didn't know. Why was everyone being so difficult?

Then her phone rang again. *Oh no. Not Despina again.* She looked at the phone and saw that this call was from her mother. Could the day get any worse?

She answered the phone and in a hostile tone said, "What!"

"Amanda, is that you?" said her mother. "Why do you sound like that?"

There was no point starting an argument. "Sorry, Mom," said Amanda. "I was distracted. A mouse was nibbling at my foot." Oops. Wrong thing to say.

"What?" screamed Lila. "There are mice at Legatum? I'm going to call Headmaster Thrillkill at once."

Amanda recovered quickly. "It's not a real one," she said. "It's a toy."

She could hear her mother let her breath out. "Oh," she said. "That's all right then. But it sounds frivolous. Who's got a mouse toy? There's studying to do. Maybe I should contact the headmaster after all."

"No, Mom, you don't need to call," said Amanda. "It's an experiment. Everything's fine. We're all studying hard."

"Oh, an experiment," said Lila. "I'm glad. Listen, Amanda, I'm terribly worried about you. You heard about the Moriartys, didn't you?"

Oh brother. Now her mother was going to be hovering. "Yes, we heard."

"Darling," said Lila, "I want to make sure you reread the guide I wrote for the police. That awful Moriarty and his dreadful wife are dangerous. Your father and I are hiring bodyguards, so you're not to worry about us. Your father still isn't that well, but he's under a nurse's care. And by the way, the nurse is fabulous. She's read every one of my books and loves them! Oh, and I'm sending you a copy of my new book, which has a lot of tips and tricks in it that could be helpful to you."

Kill me now. Why does she have to make everything about her?

"And I almost forgot. Your father's relatives in Liverpool phoned and said they're going to call you. They're fabulous people. You'll have a wonderful time with them. Did you know that your cousin Jeffrey was just transferred from Brixton to Scotland Yard? Isn't that exciting?"

Amanda wondered when her mother was going to come up for air. How could she say so much in one breath?

"You know," Lila continued, "Hill is an usher in a magistrates' court and Despina has her own line of clothing for jurors. They're absolutely immersed in law enforcement. Such a wonderful family your dad has."

Where was that gingersnap anyway? Amanda felt around in her pockets. Ah. The cookie had split into pieces but it was still edible. She gulped it down and choked.

"Darling, are you all right?" said Lila. "You're not ill, are you?"

She was, but not in the way her mother thought. "No, I'm not sick." She stepped out of the classroom and made for the nearest water fountain. Her mother probably wouldn't even hear her drink. She turned it on and let the water shoot into her mouth.

"Anyway," said Lila, "now that I know you're all right I feel better. But please keep in touch more. Until those criminals are safely back in prison I'm not going to sleep."

Until Strangeways was repaired they sure wouldn't be going back there, even if the police did manage to catch them. Amanda wondered how the other prisons were holding up. The UK was small, but not small enough that one earthquake, no matter how powerful, could damage all of them. On the other hand, if there were too many prisoners to fit into the country's correctional institutions, what would happen? Would they send some of them to other countries?

She snapped back to the conversation. "Thanks for calling, Mom. I have to go now but I'll text you every day. Okay?"

"Good. Don't forget now."

"I won't. Bye." Amanda ended the call. Her heart was beating as fast as if she'd just completed a hundred-meter sprint. She really had to finish searching. With Holmes gone it would take them even longer.

She finished drinking and was walking back to the classroom when her phone rang again.

If this is that Despina again . . . She looked at her screen. Another unknown. It had to be that woman. She must still be at the gate trying to crash her way in.

Amanda kept walking. The phone stopped ringing. Maybe Despina had finally got the message. Then it started ringing again, still from an unknown caller. Amanda sighed. The only way to get rid of that awful woman was to tell her in no uncertain terms that she didn't want anything to do with her—ever. She answered and heard a man's voice.

"Amanda," he said. "This is Darius Plover."

24

OVERWHELMED

Amanda couldn't believe her ears. Darius Plover was calling *her*? On the phone? Wait a minute. Maybe it wasn't the real Darius Plover. Maybe it was someone playing a joke on her.

"Hello?" she said, pretending she hadn't heard.

"I say it's Darius Plover. I'm calling about the clips."

There was no way anyone else could know about the clips. It had to be him. OMG! But wait a minute. Maybe he was mad at her.

"Amanda?"

"Oh, sorry, Mr. Plover," she said. "I was just so surprised to hear from you. I mean on the phone. I mean, hello?"

"Hello," he said. "Would you like to start over?"

"No, I'm fine. I mean, how are you?"

"Couldn't be better. Thanks for asking. But I'm afraid I've interrupted you."

"Oh no," she said. "Not at all. I've been on the phone all day."

Slap to head. What a stupid thing to say. Now he was going to think she *was* busy and hang up. Of course she was—busy, that is—but never too busy to talk to her idol.

"Shall I call back another time?" he said.

"No!" she said abruptly. "I mean no. This is a great time. "She didn't think she sounded convincing.

"Excellent. Well, then, I'm sorry to interrupt, but I thought I'd try you because I'm on a schedule and I'm anxious to move forward."

"Yes, of course. Schedules are—well, they're very important."
What an idiot. She sounded like a complete dodo.

"I was just wondering if you preferred one of the tent clips over
another. I need to make a decision quickly and you're my focus group."

Oh great. This was a huge responsibility and she didn't like *any* of
the clips. Now what? She had to say something and it had to be nice.
Think, think.

"Uh, I like the one with the red tones the best."

"You do? Good, because I was leaning in the other direction even
though I had my doubts. Now I realize I should be using the deeper
colors."

"Right. Well, I'm really glad I could help you." Gosh, she sounded
like a dork. He probably thought someone else wrote her messages for
her. Surely someone who spoke as poorly as she did couldn't write to
save her life.

"Me too," he said. "I'm ever so pleased. Thank you, Amanda. I'll let
you go back to what you were doing now."

"Sure," she said. "Any time."

"Bye."

"Bye."

That certainly qualified as awkward conversation of the year.
Worse, she hadn't heard what he was saying but had lied to him
anyway. She might have advised him to do the wrong thing! She'd
idolized this man her whole life, and now that she'd actually got to talk
to him she'd blown it. She reached for another gingersnap.
Unfortunately she'd eaten the last one. If she wanted another, she'd
have to go back to her room.

Burping the entire way, she realized that too many things were
hitting her at once. She had to find a way to get rid of some of them, or
at least push them away long enough to deal with the others. What
could she eliminate first? Not the whatsit. It was too important. Not
the crystals. They were dependent on her and her friends for their
survival. Not the film. Thrillkill would drive her crazy if she didn't

finish it. Professor Redleaf's computer? Who knew what that was about? Holmes? He had stomped off. Maybe she wouldn't have to see him for a while. That would help.

As she was heading back to the dorm, she nearly ran into Amphora. She was arguing with David Wiffle.

"I'm much more upper class than you are," Wiffle was saying.

"You don't know anything about India," Amphora said. "My family is Brahmin."

"Who cares what they do there?" said David. "Anyway, *your* highest level is lower than our lowest level."

"Look, peewee," she said. "Indian civilization is way older than yours. We were around before anyone ever heard of the Saxons."

"I'm not a Saxon," said David. "I'm from Cornwall."

"That just shows how stupid you are," said Amphora. "Where you were born has nothing to do with where your ancestors came from."

"Oh yeah? Well you're a lousy detective and you'll never amount to anything."

Amanda didn't know whether to butt in or sneak away and hope they hadn't seen her. After about two seconds' thought she decided it was better if Amphora didn't know she'd heard, and she slunk upstairs as quietly as she could.

She was surprised to find Ivy in their room. Apparently she was taking a break from searching and was putting more drops in Nigel's eyes.

"Hey," she said when Amanda entered.

"Hey." Amanda watched Ivy with her dog for a moment and then burst into tears.

"What's the matter?" said Ivy, running to comfort her.

"Oh, Ivy," Amanda wailed.

"Are you okay?" said Ivy, hugging her.

Amanda sniffled. "It's just—" She wailed some more.

"You're not hurt, are you?" said Ivy.

"No," Amanda sobbed. "Dot hurd."

Ivy patted her on the back, which seemed to have no effect. She leaned down, took hold of Nigel, and pushed him at Amanda, who grabbed onto him and wailed even louder. Nigel looked as if his ears were paining him but he didn't budge.

"I'm not supposed to have this, but you need some tea," Ivy said. She dug out a one-cup water heater from her tiny desk, plugged it in, and filled a mug from a thermos hidden under her desk. When the water was hot enough she immersed a bag of chamomile tea in it and shoved it in Amanda's face. "Drink," she said.

Amanda blew on the liquid, making little ripples on the surface. When she thought it was cool enough she took a sip. "Ouch."

"Oh, sorry," said Ivy. "Burn your tongue?"

"I'b ogay," said Amanda, whose tongue was indeed burned. It would probably feel uncomfortable all day. "I'b zorry. I dode beed to bother you."

"That's all right," said Ivy. "I'm your friend. You're never bothering me."

Amanda took another sip. Her tongue was feeling numb now. "Idz's just dat everything's cubbig at me all at once add I cad get anything settled."

"Tell me," said Ivy.

Amanda's voice started to clear up. "First of all," she said, "there's the whatsit. I'm really worried about it. Now that Blixus and Mavis aren't in prison anymore they probably have it and we're all doomed."

"We're all worried about that," said Ivy, "but the best detective minds in the world are working on the problem. We'll be okay."

"I don't think so," said Amanda. "If that's the case, why are the teachers all freaking out?" The tea was nice. She was feeling better.

"I don't know," said Ivy. "But we can only do what we can do, right? How's the tea?"

"It's lovely, thank you," said Amanda.

"I know you're upset," said Ivy. "But try to remember the hidden treasures." She patted the hand Amanda wasn't using to hold the tea.

Amanda took a long sip. She hadn't thought about Ivy's secret weapon for some time. The idea of giving herself up to her curiosity seemed to help her friend keep her cool. Could it work for her too?

"The treasures, yes. Which reminds me about the crystals. Those are literally hidden treasures, aren't they?" Ivy nodded. "I *am* curious about them, but all I can think of is that Blixus is going to find them and abuse them. We have to save them."

"We will," said Ivy. "I wish I could see them. They must be a sight to behold."

Amanda felt bad for her. Ivy didn't usually complain about her blindness, but she had to feel disadvantaged sometimes. Amanda wished she could wave a magic wand and make her see again. "It's not that easy. We have to get to London, then we have to find the crystals, and what if he already has them?"

"One step at a time," said Ivy. "We'll manage that. We did it before and we'll do it again. Or at least you did. And in the process you discovered what strong stuff you're made of. What else?"

"I couldn't have done it without you, Ivy," said Amanda. "Anyway, these stupid relatives of mine came out of the woodwork and are calling me all day long." She knew she was exaggerating but didn't care.

"What relatives?"

"Oh, some dumb relatives of my dad's. From Liverpool. Well, of course they're dumb. They're Lestrades."

"So's your dad," said Ivy. "He isn't dumb."

"Yes, but he's different," said Amanda. "And then my mother calls and starts hovering. The original helicopter parent. Aaaaaah!"

"Your mother can be difficult," said Ivy, making a cup of tea for herself. The water boiled in seconds with one of those little electric one-cup doohickeys. "That must not have been pleasant."

"No," said Amanda. "Now she wants me to text her every day. She thinks the Moriartys are going to get me."

"It's just a little text, right?" said Ivy. She mashed the teabag.

"Nothing's a little text with my mom," said Amanda.

"You'll handle it. I'll help you. What else?"

"Scapulus. He's driving me crazy."

"Oh, right, Scapulus. Boy, has he changed. He's been acting so weird lately. Do you think this is the real Holmes coming out and the earlier one was just an act?" She blew on the hot tea.

"I can't even tell what's an act anymore," said Amanda. "You are talking to the most gullible person in the world."

"Nick was clever," said Ivy gently. "He fooled all of us." She sipped the tea and flinched. It was still too hot.

"I should have known," said Amanda. "Now I'm wondering if Scapulus is either bipolar or another mole. And by the way, what's with the bad boy act?"

"He's trying to be tough," said Ivy. "I'm guessing he's feeling insecure and wants to look less vulnerable."

"He's acting like an idiot," said Amanda.

"True," said Ivy. "But I think he's scared inside."

"Scared of what?" said Amanda. "He is a Holmes. They don't scare."

"I don't think there's a scared gene," said Ivy. "He's human like the rest of us."

"You could've fooled me. Anyway, who cares about him? The book is important. The crystals are important. Blixus is important. Scapulus is not important." Ivy opened her mouth to say something when Amanda interrupted her. "And then Amphora."

"What about Amphora? *You're* not arguing with her too, are you? I'll fine you." Ivy giggled.

"No, I'm not, but I just heard her having the weirdest fight with David Wiffle in the hall. You won't believe this but they were arguing over who was more aristocratic."

"Oh no," said Ivy, trying the tea again. It seemed to be fine because she took several sips.

"Oh yes," said Amanda. "And then he told her she was a lousy detective and would never amount to anything. She looked like she'd just met a dragon or something."

"That's terrible," said Ivy. "You know how insecure she is."

"I know," said Amanda. "But I think she might be getting worse. Not that David has the best judgment, but that was all she needed to hear. She's already having trouble in Logic. I heard her complain that Professor Ducey was out to get her."

"Professor Ducey? Never."

"I know. I think she's starting to lose it, Ivy."

"Oh great. Just what we need. Say, you don't think she has PTSD from the earthquake, do you?"

Amanda thought for a moment. "I guess it's possible. Everything has been so stressful around here lately. It's amazing anyone is acting normal. Speaking of which—well, not speaking of which exactly, but on the subject of all the stressful stuff, do you think the book—I guess we don't have to call it a whatsit anymore—could be in the secrets trove? How could we possibly search that? There are thousands of compartments."

"Let's think about this logically," said Ivy. "Could the book fit in those compartments?"

"Yes," said Amanda. "Definitely."

"Are you sure?"

"I think so." Amanda picked up a book and tried to estimate its size.

"But you don't know?"

"Well, I, uh . . ." She held up the book and looked at it back and front.

"What are you doing?" said Ivy.

"Measuring," said Amanda.

"And?"

"Hard to say."

"Okay, for the sake of argument, let's say it can," said Ivy. "The next question is, how could it get in one of them?"

"Someone would have had to put it in there," said Amanda. She replaced the book.

"Deliberately?"

"Pretty much, yes."

"And who would do that?"

"Someone with a key?"

"Undoubtedly," said Ivy. "And where are the keys?"

"I have no idea," said Amanda. "Professor Snaffle's office?"

"How many keys are we talking about?" said Ivy.

"Billions. There are two keys for each compartment. Even if one of them is the same for all the compartments, that leaves thousands of unique ones." Somehow it didn't matter that her math was flawed.

"And where could you store thousands of keys?" said Ivy. "I mean, that's a *lot* of keys."

"I don't know," said Amanda, feeling defeated. "We could ask Editta to calculate how much room they'd take up."

"Let's do that later," said Ivy. "But whoever put it there—if someone did—would not only need access to all those keys, wherever they are, but also have to be able to tell which key goes to which compartment."

"What are you trying to say?"

"You know exactly what I'm trying to say," said Ivy. "It isn't practical. I'd say the chances of the book being there are slim to none."

"Think so?" said Amanda. She was relieved. That would have been some project. Of course she still wanted to get into the compartments, but just for curiosity's sake.

"Yes, I do," said Ivy. "So we should look in the more logical places. Of course, that means London."

"Yes," said Amanda. "It does."

Late that night Simon texted Amanda and told her that he had both good and bad news. This sounded intriguing and she knew she wouldn't be able to wait for the details. "Common room?" she texted back.

"CU in 2," he answered.

She wasn't supposed to be downstairs so late, but everything at the school was so chaotic that Mrs. Scarper had given up trying to track the girls. Still, there might be teachers lurking about so it was best to be careful.

She tiptoed down the stairs and snuck into the common room where Simon was waiting for her. He must have been there when he texted her. He couldn't have run from the boys' dorm that fast.

Before she could tell him that she'd rather hear the bad news first— better to get it over with—he said, "Here's the bad news."

"How bad is it?"

"Pretty bad," he said, leaning close. "The only way to save the crystals is to commit genocide. I mean we have to do it."

"What?" she said, pulling back so fast she thought she might have wrenched something. "I thought Blixus would be committing genocide if he made crystals just to kill them."

"He would," said Simon. "Come back here. I don't want anyone to hear."

Amanda leaned in again and felt a pang in her back. She winced and almost fell right into him. His breath smelled like toothpaste. He reached out to steady her. She remembered Nick doing that when they'd found her father's watch in the secret room. She'd been so upset she'd almost collapsed.

"Thanks," she said.

"De nada," said Simon. "But think about it. To save the crystals we'll not only have to rescue whatever existing ones there are, but we'll also have to kill the virus so he can't make any more."

Amanda's eyes widened. "You're not talking about committing genocide on the virus, are you?"

"No," he said. "Not the virus."

She rubbed the sore muscle. "If we stop him from making more, the existing crystals will be the only ones on earth and there can never be any more. Killing the virus means killing the crystals forever."

"You got it," said Simon so softly that she practically had to put her listening device in to hear him. "They'll be extinct. But we don't just have to kill the virus. We have to destroy the formula the Moriartys used to make it so they can't bring it back."

Amanda gasped. Why hadn't she thought of that before? Of course: because Scapulus Holmes, Gaston Thrillkill, and David Wiffle were always in her face, distracting her from what she needed to be doing.

"This is terrible," she whispered. "We lose either way."

"Yes," he said. "But there is good news."

"I could use some," said Amanda.

"The crystals understand language."

"Don't be silly," she said. She leaned in toward him again, careful not to strain the muscle. Maybe she *should* take up yoga as her father had suggested. She caught the smell of toothpaste again. If she could smell him, he could smell her. What if she was stinky? "Hey, is my breath bad?" He shook his head. "Good. You know, it's one thing to blink when they want to be rubbed. It's another to conclude that they understand what we're saying. They're rocks, after all."

"Smart rocks," he said. "I've been doing more testing and they respond to words."

"You mean they respond to tones of voice," she said. "That's not surprising."

"Nope. Words. I was really careful to keep my voice steady, and they changed color and blinked or didn't blink depending on what I said."

"That's nuts. They didn't do that before. Remember when you tested that?"

He shook his head. "'There are more things in heaven and earth, Horatio, than are dreamt of in your philosophy.'"

"You know Hamlet?" Amanda cried. "Oops, sorry. That was kinda loud, wasn't it?" She looked around to make sure no one else had heard, then lowered her voice. "You know Hamlet?"

"Sure, I know Hamlet," said Simon. "I'm English, aren't I?" He gave her a goofy-looking smile. Suddenly a vision of Nick popped into her head. He would have known Hamlet, and it wasn't because he was English.

"Are you trying to tell me that the crystals can understand what we're saying?" she said.

"To some extent, yes. How much I don't know. Not yet, anyway."

"But theoretically they could understand what we're saying about Blixus and the virus and genocide and everything."

"I think that's a bit over the top," said Simon.

"But they could sense our moods and intent from the way we talk, just the way Nigel does, right?" she said.

"I think so," he said. "At least as much as Nigel."

This statement surprised her. Simon loved Nigel almost as much as Ivy did and thought he was the smartest dog in the world. His describing the crystals as being more intelligent than Nigel meant he thought they were geniuses.

"Wow," she said. "Do you think they understand how much danger they're in?"

"Quite honestly, I wouldn't put it past them. They are wicked smart. Please don't do that."

"Do what?" She realized she'd leaned back again and was talking too loud. "Oh, sorry." She huddled again. "Gosh, do you think they'd do well on one of Professor Sidebotham's quizzes?"

"Ha ha," he said. "Although actually, I don't think they'd fail."

"That's a little creepy," she said. "I'd really like to see a demonstration."

"You will. I almost brought one with me, but I remembered I was going to talk about stuff that would scare it so I left it in the lab."

"Yikes," she said. "The thought of Blixus torturing these smart little cuties so he can make weapons out of them, or even use them as energy sources, makes me sick. I feel like running up to the lab and petting them." She was amazed that Simon didn't roll his eyes. He was so not a touchy-feely person. "What do we do about this?"

"You mean about the genocide?" he said.

She flinched. The word "genocide" gave her the creeps. "That and everything else."

"Considering that Blixus is going to kill them anyway if he gets his hands on them, we have no choice. We have to destroy the virus."

"But that's terrible," Amanda said. "Do we really need to do that? What if he doesn't find them?"

"Do you want to take that chance?" He looked at her in a way that said, "No, you don't. You know you have to do this."

Amanda thought for a moment and said, "This is really hard, Simon."

"No one ever said being a detective was easy."

"I didn't even want to be one." She sat back and stared at the badminton net the gremlins had installed for the day.

"But you do now."

"I do now."

"Then you're going to have to toughen up," he said.

She thought she had. She was way tougher than she'd been when she arrived at Legatum a few months before. You had to be or you wouldn't survive. She didn't like the idea that she was still soft. That meant she was vulnerable, and there was no way she was going to let that happen. She opened her mouth to reply but then thought, "What am I going to say?" and stopped.

"There's something else," said Simon. "This is separate, but it's important." He motioned for her to come really close.

Something else? How could there be so many things to deal with at the same time? "Tell me," she said, getting a whiff of peppermint again. "I need to know everything."

"Professor Redleaf's computer. Remember when she looked at it and got upset?"

This *was* a change of subject. She didn't like the sound of it. Anything to do with Professor Redleaf involved Holmes. "Yes. What was that about? You know?"

"I don't know what it was, but I have a hunch."

"Blixus?"

"Could be, but I don't think so."

"The teachers have lots of enemies," she said.

"Yes, they do. But whoever did it and whatever it was, we have to make the data even more secure than it is. Even if they already got hold of some."

"Isn't Scapulus already working on this? He practically admitted to me that Professor Redleaf had been hacked."

"He did? That's interesting because I overheard him saying that they have to solve the hacking quickly or all the school's data will be compromised. It might even be posted on the Web! We would be completely ineffective."

"That's terrible of course, but is the situation any worse than it was when Professor Redleaf saw something?"

"Actually, I think it is," said Simon.

Oh great. Another crisis. "What are you trying to say, Simon?"

"For one thing, I think Scapulus is going to have to spend more time on the project. That means he won't be able to keep helping us look. It might also mean he has to quit the film project. And, he might not be able to help us look for the virus."

As much as Amanda did *not* want to work with Holmes, this wasn't the best news. She felt relieved that she could finish the film without his interference, but they did need his help searching the school, and now that Simon had mentioned it he would be the best person to help them locate and destroy the virus formula. But what was going on with Professor Redleaf's computer? Had Blixus—or Mavis—hacked into it, and if so, what kind of damage had they inflicted? Even scarier, if it wasn't them who was it?

"And?" she said.

"You're going to think I'm nuts," he said.

"I never think you're nuts, Simon. Just argumentative sometimes. Tell me."

"I think Professor Redleaf saw something way worse than Blixus Moriarty. I think the real-life equivalent of Voldemort is out there."

25

ACOUSTIC LEVITATION

Amanda was aware that Simon wasn't one for conspiracy theories. He was the most rational person she knew. So if he had a hunch that Professor Redleaf had seen something terrifying, it was worth investigating. But how? She was sure Holmes had already checked the teacher's browser history and digital activities. If he hadn't come up with anything from that, what else could there be?

She asked Simon if he had developed any theories about what the teacher might have seen, but he hadn't. He couldn't even explain why he thought what he did. This wasn't like him, but she knew him well enough now to trust him. He probably just had to let everything swirl around in his head for a while and then he'd be able to articulate his reasons.

She and Ivy overheard the teachers saying that the last aftershock had damaged parts of the school so badly that they were going to have to block them off and get repair crews in at once. The dorms had been spared, but the administrative area that housed Headmaster Thrillkill's office and the hospital were now off limits. Fortunately there was unused space in the main building, and both departments were to be relocated to the top floor near Professor Tumble's Disguise classroom. The severe damage also extended to the front door, and the south lounge, which belonged to Van Helden House, was touch and go. If Thrillkill were to close it, David and Gordon would not be happy, but then they were never happy, so what did it matter?

It seemed to be a particularly talky day because the kids overheard a lot of other noteworthy stuff as well. For one thing, even though the teachers still weren't mentioning the whatsit by name, they too believed that Blixus might have it and thought they should track him. In fact, they were sending two teachers to London to check the factory ruins and all his known hiding places. This prospect worried Amanda because she knew she was also going and didn't want to run into Professors Scribbish and Feeney, who had been selected for the job. Amphora thought the two teachers would make a cute couple, but Simon told her this was serious stuff and to stop making frivolous comments. Ivy wasn't around or she probably would have fined him.

They also heard a lot of squabbling. Professor Peaksribbon said that he didn't care what anyone said, he was going to make a plan for replacing the whatsit. (He didn't say "book." None of the teachers used that term. They all called the whatsit "it.") Professor Feeney said that she was going to hunt down whoever had taken it and neutralize them. Professor Tumble kept trying to calm the others and urged them to take a wait-and-see attitude. And Professor Mukherjee said emphatically that they should close the school.

It was becoming clear to the kids that the teachers were divided on the topic of the whatsit and that the schism that was forming was starting to tear them apart. They knew they couldn't speak to the teachers about the problem because they weren't supposed to know about it, although how anyone could fail to be aware with all that talk going on was beyond Amanda. What she and the others did know, however, was that the sooner they found the book the sooner the teachers would calm down and be able to direct their energy to other things, like fixing the school.

Of course because they had their listening devices in their ears, they heard a lot of other stuff too, and Amanda was beginning to understand how too much information could wear a person out. Perhaps when she wasn't trying to overhear important stuff, Ivy should put cotton in her ears to tone it down and give herself some peace, assuming her hearing was working better. Amanda was afraid to ask.

But at least some of the talk was funny. The décor gremlins always raised her spirits. At one point she heard Noel say that Alexei's design for the day was so sloppy that he should go back to school. Hearing this, Alexei said that Noel's taste was paleolithic and he should get into a time machine and go where he would be appreciated. Noel countered by saying that Alexei needed a brain refresher, and Alexei, even more unkindly, said that Noel was fat.

One thing she did feel guilty hearing was, wonder of wonders, Holmes being taken to task by Professor Stegelmeyer for a mistake he'd made in Crime Lab. Then later she heard Professor Pole, the nicest person in the world, lose his temper with Holmes over another supposed error. The teachers weren't simply offering constructive criticism. Holmes had done something that had actually angered them, although she couldn't tell what. That such a thing could happen was so startling that Amanda thought she must be hearing wrong, but Ivy confirmed her perception. Either the teachers had gone mad or Holmes was losing his grip. Could it be the stress of teaching the cyberforensics class, or maybe the hacking project, or trying to do both?

Yes, he was under stress, but Amanda decided that the real problem was that Holmes was a jerk. He'd waltzed into Legatum thinking he'd be a star, but he wasn't up to it and now the truth was coming out. When she expressed this opinion to the others, they just looked at each other and said nothing.

Then Amphora found a new piece of evidence. She had been poking around in the area where they'd found the crystals and had even ventured into the cavern where the skeleton had been walled up, when she spotted something shiny. She squatted down and looked at it closely and saw that it was a key. Fortunately she had brought evidence bags with her, so she sealed it up and brought it right to Professor Stegelmeyer for analysis. When this occurred, all the teachers came running to see the new treasure. Amanda hadn't been present, but as soon as she'd left the lab Amphora had run to tell her and Ivy.

"I'm really chuffed," she said, showing them a picture of the key.

"You should be," said Amanda. "The key could tell us who the victim is."

"And the murderer," said Ivy.

"If I tell you something, promise you won't tell anyone?" Amphora said.

"Of course," said Amanda.

"I swear," said Ivy.

"To tell you the truth," Amphora said, "I've been feeling pretty insecure about my skills. I mean you guys all find important clues and figure out what they mean. And Simon is so good in the lab it's intimidating. I feel like a dummy."

"You're not a dummy!" said Ivy. "How can you think such a thing?"

"Yeah," said Amanda. "You contribute as much as the rest of us. Why do you say that?"

"I'm not clever like you," said Amphora. "You guys are always coming up with brilliant ideas and solving difficult problems."

"So are you," said Amanda. "We couldn't have solved the class project last term without you."

"All I did was tag along," said Amphora.

"Not true," said Ivy. "You were the one who researched all the teachers. Without all that deep knowledge we never would have been able to come up with potential perpetrators. And we never would have known that Professor Pickle was involved in that big dispute with Clive Ribchester." Ribchester was Professor Pickle's commercial rival. They both came from pickle-making families and were highly competitive. For a long time the kids had suspected that he'd blown up the professor's car to send a message, but it turned out that Professor Pickle wasn't the bomber's target after all. Amphora had been key in figuring that out too. "You've got the complete dossier on the teachers.

No one else knows half what you do about them. That's hugely valuable."

"It's just a bunch of gossip," said Amphora.

"Uh uh," said Amanda. "You have research skills way beyond what the rest of us can do. We need you."

"Thanks," said Amphora. "I hope you're right. Anyway, I was feeling insecure and I wanted to see if I could be a hero. Maybe I could find something everyone else missed. But also I wanted to see if I could find more crystals. I'm really interested in them."

"And look what happened," said Ivy. "You did." She squeezed Amphora's hand.

"So I did," said Amphora, drifting off into space.

"I can't wait to find out what the teachers think about the key," said Amanda. "I don't know anything about keys. I can't even tell from the shape what kind of lock it goes with."

"Let's go see if we can find out something," said Ivy.

When the girls entered the lab, Professor Stegelmeyer told them that the key probably belonged to some kind of lockbox or chest. Unfortunately no one had yet been able to identify it or link it to a specific individual. The teachers figured that whoever the dead man was, he had swallowed the key and it had fallen into the dirt as the skeleton was shaken during the earthquake. It was frustrating that they still couldn't tell who he was, but now they had new lines of inquiry to pursue. Who would swallow a lockbox key and why? Where was the lockbox or chest and what could be in it? Professor Stegelmeyer told them that he and the other teachers hadn't begun to theorize about those questions yet.

Amanda texted Simon to let him know what was going on. He was very excited about the key and even said something nice about Amphora. He also told her that they'd better get to London as soon as possible. Suddenly Amanda realized that if there were indeed crystals in the wreckage, the sunlight beating down on them might overfill them and kill them. It might even be too late. They'd better skedaddle. They prepared to leave first thing the next morning.

Of course to get to London, Amanda and Simon, who had decided that just the two of them should go or else they'd move too slowly, would have to sneak out of the school. Amanda had been through that before. Last term she'd pretended to be a maid and had stowed away on a delivery vehicle. That strategy, however, had turned into a disaster when the lorry had taken her all the way to Edinburgh, which lay in the opposite direction from the factory in London. As a result, she'd arrived at her final destination when it was dark and had had little time in which to find and save her father before the Moriartys planned to kill him. Luckily, with Ivy's remote help, she'd been able to bypass the security keypad, enter the building, and save Herb Lester in the nick of time.

They weren't going to try that again. This time they'd be sure to get to the train station properly. For transportation they'd use their skateboards, and to keep their mission secret they'd exit the school through the tunnels, first grabbing a few crystals to light their way in case their phones didn't get reception. Except for one thing: they'd have to figure out how to get through the gates at the end. That was such a thorny problem that it almost stopped them, until Amanda ran into Clive Ng, who just happened to be telling a fifth-year student about a technique he was developing to levitate things using sound waves. Bingo! Maybe he could help.

"Hey," said Amanda.

"Whazzup?" said Clive.

"I couldn't help overhearing what you were telling that kid," she said.

"Please don't spread it around. My method isn't completely tested and it's pretty powerful stuff. Not that I don't trust people around here, except what happened last term . . ." He stopped, somehow aware that he'd raised a sensitive subject. He hadn't known Amanda or Nick well, but he'd seen what had happened the day Nick had tried to beat up David Wiffle for accidentally kicking Amanda. He could add two and two.

"How well does it work?" she said.

"Intermittently."

"Would you like to test it in a real-life situation?"

Clive's eyes lit up. "Would I. You know of something?"

"I might," she said, realizing that she and Simon would have to check Clive out before confiding in him. "You're interested then?"

"Absolutely. Hit me."

"Give me a little while. I'll text you."

"Cool," he said. "Can't wait."

When she told Simon, he was ecstatic. "If this works we'll be out of those gates in no time," he said. "But you're right. We have to check him out."

"I know just how to do that," she said. He looked at her quizzically. "Ivy. Fern knows his sister, I think."

As it turned out, Fern knew Clive's sister, Lucky, very well. In fact they were best friends, and when Ivy asked about Clive, Fern told her that he was not only the best guy in the world, but a genius. It almost sounded as if he was another Simon. Amanda imagined the two of them together—Tweedle-Simon and Tweedle-Clive. She hoped they'd get along and not fight the way people who are too alike sometimes do.

But her fears turned out to be groundless. After she and Simon had explained the mission, the two boys started talking a mile a minute, and soon the three were as tight as Amanda's pantyhose before she'd lost weight.

"Do you want me to show you in the lab?" said Clive. "I can do that or we can just go to the gates and give it a try. Do you want to go now? Shall I come to London with you? I'm really excited to see if this works because if it does—"

"I know how to help you patent it," said Simon.

"You're kidding," said Clive. "That would be awesome."

Amanda gave Simon a look. Not Holmes again. Simon ignored her.

"Let's do it now," said Simon. "But I think it's best if only two of us go. We'll patch you in when we get there."

"Sweet," said Clive. "Vamos."

When Amanda got on the skateboard that Simon had prepared for her she discovered a new talent. She'd never thought of herself as athletic, but somehow those Lestrade genes had bestowed upon her the ability to maneuver her board perfectly. Of course Simon had rejigged the boards to glide smoothly over ruts and bumps, which helped a lot, and they were able to race through the tunnels at an astounding speed— except for the times when Amanda insisted on trying fancy moves, with Simon and Clive first applauding her skill and then trying to top her. She wondered if they should extend the bumper-broom game so it could be performed on skateboards. Of course, Thrillkill would never allow skateboards in the halls, but the tunnels would work just as well if not better. Simon agreed that the idea was worth pursuing and Amanda stopped to make a note.

As they breezed through, Amanda wondered about the tunnels they had yet to explore. It seemed that there were more of them than there were veins in the human body. At least that was how it felt. She had no idea how many veins people actually had, but it seemed like a lot. She desperately wanted to get into that secrets trove, whether or not it had anything to do with the missing book.

Clive was amazed when he saw it and said it reminded him of a formation he'd seen on YouTube—some place in the American Southwest. As she once again considered how they might get into the compartments, it struck Amanda that the book might hold the collected secrets all in one place. Simon agreed that that was a possibility, and if *that* was what the book was about, it would be hugely important. No wonder the teachers were freaking out. All their secrets exposed? Yikes. All this was new to Clive, who kept complimenting them on their discoveries. He knew the teachers had been acting strange but he'd thought it was because of the earthquake.

Suddenly Amanda stopped so abruptly that she almost flew off her board. "What was that?" she said.

"What was what?" said Simon, who'd been performing a stunt a ways behind her.

"I heard a voice," said Amanda quietly. "That way." She pointed down a side tunnel.

"Maybe it's one of the teachers," said Simon, whispering. "This might be a chance to gather important intelligence."

Amanda agreed. They picked up their skateboards so as not to make noise and snuck down the tunnel, which was a narrow affair, but not so skinny that they couldn't walk side by side. Still, they hugged one wall so as to remain out of sight. When they had almost reached yet another clearing they stopped. Amanda put her finger to her lips, then pointed. There was Editta, sitting on the ground, sobbing her heart out. In perfect rhythm, Amanda, Simon, and Clive looked at each other as if to say, "Well, what do you know?" Not that Amanda was surprised, except she was. She'd never expected to find Editta hanging around the basements, although when she thought about it, why not? She gestured, "Should we go see her?" Simon shook his head and Clive agreed. She nodded and they tiptoed back to continue their travels.

When they had reached the three gates that led to the lake, they discovered that the broken one had been repaired. Clive told them that would make it easier to get through because the hardware was all nice and new and should move easily.

"Now I can't guarantee this will work," he said as he removed a weird-looking piece of equipment from his backpack. "I don't know if the device can lift pins out of hinges. By the way, you never want to do this around dogs. The ultrasound will break their eardrums."

"We'll remember that," said Amanda. If it came down to a choice between getting past the gates and protecting Nigel, she'd pick Nigel every time.

"What I plan to do is this," Clive said. "I'm going to place a reflector behind each hinge I want to loosen. I'll start with the closest one, obviously, because I'll be able to reach it."

"So you're going to stick something behind each hinge on the first gate, then zap it," said Amanda.

"Correct," said Clive. "When I've lifted all three pins, we'll be able to move the gate from the edges and slip through. Then I'll repeat the process until we've got through all three gates."

"I hope they're not too rusty," said Simon. "They might stick."

"I thought of that," said Clive. "I've got some good old WD-40 with me."

"Excellent," said Simon.

"I've got a camera here that I'll leave after you're gone," said Clive. "That way I can monitor the gates and make sure no one comes through. Then when you've returned we can lower the pins again and voila! Good as new."

"Cool," said Simon. "I'm impressed."

"Me too," said Amanda. "I had no idea you rock people were so versatile."

Clive smiled. "Let me just put this reflector . . ." He reached behind the bottom hinge and placed a shiny piece of metal against the wall of the tunnel. It slipped. He wiggled it and let go. It slipped again. Finally he took a piece of blue tack out of his pack, stuck it on the metal, and pressed the reflector to the wall. "Sometimes you need to get tough with these things," he said. Then he extracted his WD-40 from his backpack and oiled the hinge. The metallic smell was strong and unpleasant.

He moved to a spot a few feet away from the hinge and turned on a laser in his acoustic levitator, then aimed at the point it was making. "Now stand back," he said. "I don't want any unforeseen effects to hurt you."

Amanda and Simon moved to what seemed like a safe distance.

"Okay, now," said Clive. "One, two, three." On three he let go. At first nothing happened, but then they heard the grinding sound of metal on metal and could see the pin rise.

"It's working!" cried Amanda.

"Awesome, man," said Simon.

"Steady as she goes," said Clive. "It's not out yet."

He held the acoustic levitator in place for a full minute, but the pin wouldn't go any higher. Finally he turned it off, laid it down, and whipped out the WD-40 again. After coating the pin with enough of the stuff to disassemble the Eiffel Tower, he returned to his device and aimed again.

This time the pin lifted easily, but as soon as Clive turned the machine off it fell right back down again.

"Okay, it's time to bring in the big guns," he said. He withdrew a large magnet from his pack, stuck it to the wall with blue tack, and repeated the entire procedure. This time when the pin rose it stayed up.

"Wow," said Amanda. "You've thought of everything."

"Nice work," said Simon. "We should do some projects together."

"Absolutely," said Clive, preparing the next hinge.

Within a couple of minutes, he had lifted all three pins on the left side of the first gate and the three kids had pulled the metal toward them and moved onto the second gate—the one the teachers had repaired. As he had predicted, it was a snap to get through that one and they went on to the third.

When they got there, they could see out into the cove and beyond. Just as Clive was about to aim the levitator at the first hinge, Amanda cried out. "Stop!" Clive jumped. "Wait," she said. "There's a dog out there."

Sure enough, a shaggy tan-colored mutt was trotting by. It looked to be alone. Whether it was lost or had just been let out to play they couldn't tell.

The dog stopped at the water's edge to drink. Then, seeing an egret about to land, it got all excited and started jumping around and barking trying to catch the bird, which flew away. Then the dog decided it needed a rest and sat facing the water.

"We can't turn the levitator on with the dog around," said Clive.

"Maybe we can distract it," said Simon. "Hey, dog!"

The dog turned around and looked at the mouth of the tunnel, then went back to whatever it was doing, which was probably attempting to locate the egret.

"Dog!" yelled Clive.

"Hey!" yelled Amanda.

The dog turned around again.

"Go away," yelled Simon.

The dog stood up, stretched, ran to the mouth of the tunnel, and stood there wagging its tail.

"Oh dear," said Amanda. "That wasn't quite what we had in mind." She reached out to pet it through the gate.

"No!" said Simon. "If you do that it will never leave."

"Scram," said Amanda. Nothing.

"Hey, dog," said Clive. "Chase this." He reached in his pack and pulled out a small piece of wood.

"What's that?" said Amanda.

"I use it for digging," said Clive. He reached out through an opening in the gate and attempted to throw the wood. It went about two feet. The dog picked it up and brought it back, laying it on the ground right outside the gate.

"Oh, brother," said Simon. "This is going to take a while. Can you throw it farther?"

"I don't think that will do any good," said Clive. "It will just keep bringing the stick back."

"I have some gingersnaps," said Amanda.

"The last thing you want to do is feed it," said Simon.

"Now what?" said Amanda.

"I guess we wait," said Clive.

At this point, the dog sat down facing them, then scrunched down and laid its head on its paws.

"You'd think three detectives could come up with a solution," said Simon.

"I have an idea," said Amanda.

She took out her phone and called Ivy. After the two had spoken for a few seconds, Amanda held the phone as close to the dog as she could. Suddenly a loud noise came out of the speaker. The dog stood up, yelped, and ran away.

"What was that?" said Clive.

"The devil's interval," said Amanda. "I found out about it when I had to open that electronic key lock at the sugar factory last term. It's a really awful chord that makes people sick. Apparently it works on dogs too."

"Sweet," said Clive.

Now that the dog had run away, Clive was able to lift the last three pins and Simon and Amanda were on their way.

"I'm going to install the camera now," Clive said.

"Awesome," said Simon. "We'll catch up with you later. Thanks, buddy."

"Yes, thank you, Clive," said Amanda. "We couldn't have done this without you."

Clive blushed and turned to put his equipment away.

When they had got through the gates, they waved goodbye to Clive, picked up their boards, and carried them to the dock where the two boats they'd seen before, Bacon and Eggs, were moored. It had always been their plan to take one of them to get to Windermere, but now they weren't sure which to "borrow."

"I think I like the idea of Eggs better," said Amanda.

"I dunno," said Simon. "I think Bacon is in better condition."

"How much better is better?" she said.

Simon got into Eggs and examined it carefully. Amanda wondered how he knew about boats. Perhaps because the UK was an island everyone there did. "Not as bad as I thought," he said. "It needs paint but it looks workable." Then he got into Bacon. "Uh oh," he said. "This isn't good."

"What?" said Amanda.

"There's a leak." He knelt down and poked at something.

"You're kidding. Then how come it's still floating?" She peered over the edge but didn't see anything, so she got in. She still couldn't see anything.

Simon was pointing to a wet spot on the bottom of the boat. "There. It's just damp now but it's going to sink eventually."

"Oh dear," said Amanda. "We certainly don't want that one. It will have to be Eggs."

"I like Bacon better," said Simon.

"If you like it you can take it, but I'm not getting in," she said, climbing back onto the dock.

"Yeah, maybe not. You get into Eggs, and I'll untie it and follow you."

Amanda started to climb into the unleaky boat, tripped, and found herself clinging to Simon to keep from falling into the water. He in turn was so startled that he lost his footing and fell smack onto the dock, elbow first. Both skateboards went skittering down the wooden walkway toward the water. Simon yelled, "No!" and after righting himself, ran after them, only to see his fall into the lake while Amanda's veered off to do the same from another angle. Without stopping he chased the board that was still rolling and dove for it, grabbing it just as it was about to career off the dock. Unfortunately in the process he impaled himself on about a dozen splinters and screamed at the top of his lungs. Meanwhile Amanda sprinted to the site of the first disaster, threw off her backpack, and dove into the water after Simon's board.

To say that the water was cold would be the type of understatement people roll their eyes at, but it was. Somehow Amanda knew this, but being from Los Angeles she expected bodies of water to be a reasonable temperature, not this, which wasn't. The good news, however, was that the water was so shallow that she was able to see pretty well. The only problem was that even though she spotted the board in two seconds, it was entangled in a bunch of weeds, and to get it free she'd either have to hold her breath for longer than was comfortable or grab it with her feet.

She didn't have time to debate the matter. She was too far from the dock to hold onto it while she worked her feet, so she took a huge breath and plunged her head into the water, then kicked herself down to the board. As she'd expected, her first attempt to pull it out of the weeds was unsuccessful, so she yanked even harder but it still wouldn't come loose. She was starting to feel like she was going to run out of air so she propelled herself to the surface for a big gulp, but at the same time she was feeling so cold she thought she was going to freeze to death. Suddenly she saw Simon, blood all over his T-shirt, with a long pole, which he was dangling toward her.

"Grab it," he said. She did and he pulled her to the dock, then held out a hand. She took hold of it and he boosted her up. "You've got to get warm," he said, running toward Bacon and bringing back a blanket. "I won't look, but take off your clothes and wrap yourself in this."

Amanda didn't argue. While Simon turned his back she pulled off her sweater, jeans, shoes, socks, and even her underwear and pulled the blanket tight.

"That's not enough," said Simon. He ran back to Bacon and came back with two more blankets. "Try these."

That was better. She wasn't exactly toasty but she could feel the edge come off the chill. When she was no longer shivering, she peeled off the outer layer and dried her hair as best she could.

"You're all bloody," she said.

"It's nothing," said Simon. "I'll get a T-shirt at the station. The bigger problem is, what are we going to do about your clothes? It will take them forever to dry."

"I hate to say it but we have two choices," she said. "Turn back, or you could get me some dry clothes."

"I don't like the idea of turning back," he said. "On the other hand, if I take the boat into town and back to buy you something, it will take forever."

"There's a better way," she said. "Ivy."

"Oh yeah," said Simon. "I'll text her. She can bring down some fresh clothes and another board and I'll meet her."

"You're probably still worrying about your board," said Amanda.

"You know, now that I think of it, we should have just let the boards go and gone back for some more."

"Never mind," she said. "Let's do that. It will only take a few minutes. I can even come with you to meet Ivy."

"And run into Wiffle?" he said. "I don't think so."

"Good point," she said. "I'll wait here."

She pulled the blanket tighter and watched to make sure Simon wasn't snapping a picture.

26

COUPLE OF CLOWNS

Amanda wasn't used to standing around English docks wrapped in nothing but blankets. She was still wondering if Simon had peeked while she was taking off her clothes. He seemed to have his back to her the whole time, but she'd been preoccupied and who knew if he'd tried? She wasn't thrilled with the idea, but it was better than if Wiffle had been there. Now *that* would have been a disaster.

The whole incident had been ridiculous though. If she hadn't slipped in the first place, they wouldn't have lost Simon's board, he wouldn't have pieces of wood sticking out all over his body, and she'd be dry and comfortably on her way to town.

Keeping an eye out for potential splinters, she walked back down the dock, climbed into Eggs, and waited for Simon to return. It was a warm day for the UK, although not so much for L.A., and she was thawing and drying nicely. She looked out over the sparkling water of Enchanto. Whoever had chosen this setting for Legatum had had good taste. When things settled down she would spend a lot more time appreciating its beauty.

After a while she realized that Simon had been gone a long time. She checked her phone, which was still intact in her backpack, and saw that it had been forty minutes since he'd left. That wasn't good. If he didn't get back soon, it would be too late to return at a reasonable hour and they'd have to scuttle the trip. She sent him a text: "Where R U?" He replied within about three seconds: "Ivy brought wrong board."

Oh boy. Ivy was pretty good at finding her way around and dealing with objects, but she wasn't experienced in the matter of skateboards and even with Amphora's help had picked up the wrong one. Simon had tried to describe what he wanted via text, but neither of the girls could interpret his instructions correctly, so he'd had to climb all the way up to the third floor and dig the skateboard out himself. He was on his way back to the dock as fast as he could go and expected to be there within ten minutes.

Amanda was getting antsy. She didn't mind the itchy blankets, but she remembered what had happened the last time she'd tried to get to London and was worried that they might be delayed again. If that were to happen they wouldn't return until midnight, and despite the fact that the teachers were distracted she didn't want to chance their wrath, which might even lead to a suspension.

She texted Simon again. No answer. He must be on his way. Why did she do that? Answering would just slow him down. What a dummy.

Finally he emerged from the tunnel with his new skateboard and a large black plastic bag, presumably holding dry clothes. He was wearing a clean T-shirt, so he must also have gone back to his room. Actually that was a good idea, even if it did cost them another few minutes, but they'd have to rush now.

He ran to the boat, tossed the bag at her, and turned his back.

"What happened?" she said, throwing off the blankets and putting on the fresh clothes. Uh oh. He'd brought that blue sweater that was way too big for her. Oh well. She'd have to live with it.

"Minor glitch," he said. "Ivy brought the wrong board, so I had to go back upstairs, but I got waylaid by you-know-who and had to get rid of him, and then Thrillkill stopped me and wanted to know how I was getting along in Crime Lab, and then I had to wait for Ivy to get you some clothes, so I thought I may as well get a clean T-shirt, and then I ran into you-know-who again, so it took me longer than I thought it would."

"What did David want?" she said, tying her shoelaces.

"Usual stuff," said Simon. "Not worth mentioning. Don't know why I said anything."

"He really is pathetic, isn't he?" she said.

"I don't know what he's so paranoid about," said Simon. "He's not that dumb. He gets in his own way."

"Yeah," she said. "If he weren't so annoying I might actually feel sorry for him."

"I wouldn't go that far," said Simon.

With Amanda now dry and dressed, the pair got into Eggs extra-carefully and set off. Fortunately the motor worked perfectly and the boat did not leak. After a short time they arrived at a dock close to town and disembarked, then without further incident got onto their boards and skated to the railway station.

"You're good at this," Simon yelled back to Amanda as they barreled along.

"Thanks," she said. As she balanced on her board the wind blew the remaining moisture out of her hair, and when they arrived at the station the only telltale sign of their mishap was the red spots on Simon's arms.

They hopped on a quick train to Oxenholme, then changed to one that would take them to Euston Station in London. As they threaded their way through the London-bound train, Amanda took great care to make sure there weren't any monkeys riding with them. Last time she'd done this she had the misfortune of running into a particularly nasty specimen who'd peed all over her. That was another thing she would not let happen again. But one eventuality she hadn't planned for was another call from her relatives. As soon as she and Simon had sat down, her cousin Despina phoned. Flustered, she made a mistake and picked up.

"Amanda, darling!" said Despina. "How's our little ray of sunshine?" Amanda took the phone away from her ear, pointed to it, and made a gagging gesture. Simon laughed.

"Oh, hello, Despina," she said. "I'm afraid I can't—"

"Darling, we're ready to show you around the Lake District. Are you free at 11:00 this morning?"

Amanda rolled her eyes. "Despina, I—"

"How about if we pick you up then? We'll take a boat ride around the lake and you'll see all the sights. There's a cute little folly—"

"I'm sorry, Despina. I can't go."

"Well, then, darling, how about at noon?"

More eye rolling. "I'm afraid I'm busy then."

"One o'clock? We can still catch a tour boat then." Her voice grew muffled. "What's that, Hill? Tell her what? Oh, right." Her voice cleared again. "Hill says to tell you about the tearoom with the Prince William and Princess Kate plates."

"I can't go today, Despina." Amanda looked at Simon. She hesitated. "I'm going on . . . an elephant ride." Simon gave her a look and she shrugged.

"Oh, that sounds lovely, dear. Where is it? We'll come with you."

It was impossible to get rid of this woman. "I'm sorry. It's for a birthday party. It's private."

"Oh, that's a shame. Is it an African or an Indian elephant?"

What did she care what kind of elephant it was? Pink, polka-dotted, paisley, whatever. "I don't know. I think it's from Tibet." She didn't think there were elephants in Tibet but she didn't care.

"Tibet, darling? Oh, that's lovely. We haven't been there. Would you like to go?"

"Not really. I—"

"How about tomorrow, then?" Surely she didn't mean to Tibet.

"How about next Saturday?" Amanda blurted out. "Not Tibet. I mean Windermere." Making a firm date was the only way to get this woman to stop badgering her. Not that she intended to keep it.

"Splendid! Hill, do you hear that? We're going to see Amanda next Saturday. How about ten, dear?"

"Fine," said Amanda. "Ten. In the morning."

"We'll be at the guard gate then," said Despina. "Be sure to bring your camera."

When did she not have her camera with her? When did anyone not carry a camera these days? Wait a minute. Why did she care? She wasn't going anywhere with those two.

"Oh, and I'll be bringing some pictures of your cousin Jeffrey in his uniform," said Despina. "He looks so handsome."

Amanda didn't care if he looked like Brad Pitt. She had no interest in her cousin Jeffrey or his parents. "Right," she managed to squeeze out.

"I can't tell you how excited we are to finally see you," said Despina. "We can't wait to add your picture to our photo album."

"Uh, me too," said Amanda. "Bye."

She turned to Simon. "You don't have to say it," he said. "I get the picture."

"Well, at least I got rid of her for now," said Amanda. "I'll worry about next Saturday when it gets here."

After a few minutes Simon decided he wanted a sandwich, so they made their way to the concession car and bought two large hoagies. When they got back to their car they could see that someone was sitting in their place—a couple of clowns in full costume.

Amanda turned to Simon and pointed with her chin. "There are a couple of clowns sitting in our seats," she whispered.

"So there are." He came up beside the two men and said, "Excuse me, but these are our seats."

"Not anymore," said the one with the huge blue nose.

"We just got up to get some food," said Amanda.

"Well, go somewhere and eat it," said the other one, who was wearing a spiky orange wig.

"You don't understand," said Amanda. "We were already sitting here." The condensation from her drink was starting to drip.

"Too bad," said blue nose. He turned away and opened his book: *Trinomial Equations.*

"Look," said Simon. "You clowns are going to have to move."

"And who's going to make us?" said orange wig. "A couple of geeky-looking kids?"

"I thought clowns were supposed to be nice," said Amanda. "You're a discredit to your people." The drink was making her fingers freeze.

"Ha!" said blue nose. "Listen to those big words. And you got it wrong, kiddie. It's *de*credit."

"Nuh uh," said Amanda. "Discredit."

"I don't care if it's easy credit," said orange wig. "Off you go." He looked out the window. "Whoa, a Gloster Meteor. Only two of those are still active in the UK. See that, Terry? Hey, you're missing one of the coolest vintage aircraft ever."

"Now see what you've done," said Terry, the blue nose. "I was in the middle of solving this equation and now I've lost my place."

"Who cares about equations?" said orange wig. "This is real life."

"Look, clownie," said Simon. "I don't care if the Hindenburg is out there. She's right. These are our seats and clowns are supposed to be nice."

"Says who?" said Terry.

"Says the rules," said Amanda. Oh no! She was sounding like David Wiffle. Maybe it would be better to do as the clowns had said and find other seats. She did not like what this struggle was doing to her.

"'Says the rules,'" the orange-wigged clown mocked.

"Forget it," said Amanda. She pulled Simon by the arm, which was a neat trick considering that she was trying to juggle her sandwich and the wet drink at the same time. Fortunately all her other stuff was in her backpack or she would have had to manage that too.

"I never liked clowns," said Simon when they were well away from the meanies.

"Me either," said Amanda. "They're grotesque." Two drops of water dripped from her cup and got her jeans on the way down.

"Pop quiz. What makeup was the one with the orange wig wearing?"

"White background, red outline around the mouth, red and blue stripes on the cheeks and forehead, and black around the eyes. Oh, and a fuzzy red nose about the size of my fist."

"Not bad," said Simon. "Although you forgot the eyebrows."

"Oh, right. Red eyebrows. Sorry. Frankly I wasn't impressed. I could do a better job with only two colors."

"Which would be?"

"Red and white, of course. I'll give you a demonstration tomorrow."

They had traversed quite a distance at this point, but the train was so full that they hadn't found any empty seats. Simon was dripping sauce and tomatoes from his sandwich and managed to get food all over his clothes, not to mention the floor. Amanda thought it probably wasn't such a good idea for him to eat while they were walking. Worse, he was sipping from the soda he was carrying in his other hand and was getting Coke all over his face and down his T-shirt. The trail he was leaving would have been helpful for finding their way back had they needed it. She hoped it wouldn't attract ants. At least her drips were sugar-free.

They walked all the way to the last car before they found two seats, which fortunately happened to be next to each other. As soon as they sat down, however, two young toughs came up and said that those were *their* seats.

"Sorry. First come, first served," said Simon. He looked at Amanda as if to say, "If the clowns can do it, we can." She felt torn. While she didn't approve of the clowns' manners, she desperately wanted to get out of the aisle.

"Don't think so," said the one with the tattoo on his neck that said "Inquisition."

"Look, we're sitting here," said Simon. "The seats were empty and we took them." A piece of tomato fell out of his sandwich.

"Well, now they're not," said the one with the ZZ Top beard. "Get up."

"Make me," said Simon.

"Would ya listen to that?" He turned to his friend and laughed. "I wouldn't argue with us if I were you, *laddie*."

At this point Simon was starting to look nervous. Amanda elbowed him and hoped her sandwich wasn't dripping as well. "Come on," she said. "We'll find other seats."

"No," he said. "We're not getting up."

"Look, bozo," said the guy with the tattoo, "we got up for one second. That's not moving. That's a break."

"Well, we did the same thing in that other car, and two clowns came and took our seats," said Simon.

"Yeah, well *you* clowns took ours. Get up." He bumped Simon's drink and it crashed to the floor. Now there would definitely be ants.

"Look what you did," Simon said.

"Tough," said the Inquisition guy. "Get out of our seats."

He pulled back his arm, made a fist, and punched Simon square in the nose. Simon fell to the floor and his food scattered. Amanda got up, put her sandwich on the seat, and turned him over. His nose was bleeding. When she looked up, the two toughs had thrown her sandwich on the floor and taken the seats.

"What's going on here?" The voice was the porter's. "Are you hurt, sir?" he said to Simon.

"I'b gud," said Simon, who was speaking in a muffled sort of way now.

"No you aren't," said Amanda. "That guy punched you."

"Leeb it," said Simon. "I'b fide."

"Officer, those two guys harassed us and punched my friend," said Amanda. She didn't care if she sounded like David Wiffle. There were times when complaining was legitimate and this was one of them.

"That true?" said the porter to the toughs.

"I just touched him," said the guy with the tattoo. "He must be a hemophiliac."

"You decked him," said Amanda. "That was totally uncalled for."

"All right," said the porter after helping Simon up. "You two come with me. I'm sorry, sir," he said to Simon. "Here is a form to fill out if you'd like to make a complaint. And please accept this gauze and antiseptic. Miss, you can find ice at the end of the car."

Simon reclaimed his seat and sat there with his nose up in the air until the bleeding stopped. Unfortunately his face started to turn purple even though he held the ice to it for quite a while. Amanda urged him to fill out the form and make the complaint but he didn't want to.

"Peeble pudge each udder all da time, add eddyway, we hab do keeb a low profile," he said.

"Yes, we do have to keep a low profile," she said. "We're breaking school rules, which we do all the time of course, but we don't want to call attention to Legatum. I don't agree that it's okay to punch people, though."

"Nebber bide" he said.

"What's that?"

"Nebber bind," he said loudly.

"Oh, right. Never mind. Okay." She sat back in her seat. "Do you want some of my sandwich or drink?"

"Dat's okay," he said. "I'll go ged my owd. But you deed to sabe by seat."

"Oh, sure. I'll save your seat. No problem. And if those guys come back I'll just call the porter. But I don't think they'll try again."

When Simon had left to get another snack, Amanda went through her backpack. Her skateboard was there, of course, and a couple of crystals. She had also packed pepper spray, which she'd brought back from her holiday in London as a general precaution. The thought of running into Blixus Moriarty scared her silly. He'd been rough with her when she'd penetrated his territory before, and now that he'd spent time in prison he would be even more dangerous. She had also packed the usual evidence kit, gingersnaps, her phone charger, and the phone itself, which she pulled out.

Finishing her sandwich and drink at the same time, she brought up her film editing program and got to work on the training film. Thrillkill would not be pleased if she and Holmes took any more time with it, and the train ride seemed like a good time to make progress. They had worked up what she thought was a great story about following an audit trail, and she was working on the part where they found the prize at the end of the path.

The example showed how to track down hackers using IP addresses. She had turned it into a story about an explorer—sort of a cross between Marco Polo and David Livingstone with a touch of Lewis and Clark thrown in—who, after following a circuitous route, had found a treasure. In this case the treasure was a smoking gun that proved a crime had been committed, and she showed the explorer opening a chest in which it was hidden. As much as she and Holmes had argued over the direction of the film, in the end he had come around and they were both pleased with the result. She was just about to knit together the scene in which the explorer, one Leaf Mothmore, opened the chest, when Simon returned and said, "How can you edit on that thing?" His voice was beginning to clear up.

"I'm using a program with a cool user interface," she said. "It's pretty easy. You just drag and drop stuff."

"Yeah," he said, "but it's so tiny."

"Not that tiny. You can squodge it so the image gets bigger."

"You people with good vision," he said.

Amanda felt a pang of sympathy and decided a change of subject was in order. "Say, do you have any idea what's bothering Editta? She hasn't been the same since term break."

"Yeah" he said, slurping another Coke. "She's even weirder than usual."

"That isn't nice," said Amanda.

"She's wacko," said Simon. He bit into his hamburger. Another piece of tomato fell out. "Nuts."

"To you she's wacko," said Amanda. "Maybe to her *you're* wacko. Those tomatoes just don't like you, Simon."

"I don't care what she thinks," he said. "Anyway, I don't know what's wrong with her. Probably some dumb superstition thing. I wouldn't worry about it."

"I don't think that's it. She was late coming to school this term. You're not suggesting she thought the date of the first day of class was unlucky?"

"She was?" He unwrapped the burger a little more. Some sauce oozed out and down his finger. "Nuts and lentils."

"What, you didn't notice? Where is your head all the time?"

"For one thing, I was busy watching you make stupid remarks," he said.

"For heaven's sake. Can we forget about that? So I think Scapulus is a jerk. Big deal."

"How could he have been a jerk just by walking into class?" said Simon. He'd got sauce all over his face now.

Point to Simon. She wasn't going to win this one. Maybe yet another change of subject was in order.

"I want to text Amphora and find out what's going on with that key," she said.

"It's not a house key," he said.

"How do you know? Can I have a sip?"

"Wrong shape." He passed her the Coke. It dripped on the sweater she didn't like.

"Okay. I don't know anything about keys. I take your word for it. Let me just write this." She switched to her message screen and dashed off a quick text to Amphora: "Key?" She turned back to Simon. "So what kind of key is it?"

"Dunno." He took a bite of his sandwich. This time he was holding a napkin underneath it and he caught the tomato bits before they could fall onto his lap.

"Could it be a key for a desk drawer or something?" she said.

"It's possible," he said, slurping his drink. "Or maybe a suitcase. Hm, not enough ice."

"You want more ice? I can get some." He shook his head. "So not a door?" she said, sticking her hand under his sandwich to catch a piece of lettuce.

"You don't have to do that," he said. "I got it." She pulled her hand back. Now she was stuck with a piece of lettuce. She grabbed a napkin from Simon's stash and stuck the lettuce in it, then wiped her hand. "It looks kind of small to be for a door. Maybe a cage?" He took another bite. This time nothing dripped out of the sandwich, but he did lick some sauce to keep it from falling.

"Ugh," she said. "I don't like to think of animals being in cages." Should she get up and throw the napkin away or wait till later?

"Could be one of those fighting cages," he said. "Extreme sports."

"Are you kidding? That's just as bad." She paused and thought for a moment. "Do you think you could tell if he did that from the skeleton? Extreme sports, I mean." She grabbed a plastic evidence bag from her pack and put the napkin in it, then stashed it under the seat. It would be okay there till the next time she got up.

"Don't think so," he said, finishing the drink and looking for a place to put the cup. "Well, maybe. But Professor Hoxby didn't say anything about that. Maybe it's from one of those flight cases? Like the kind they use for rock concerts."

"You think the dead guy was a musician?" she said.

"No way of telling," he said, sticking the cup under the seat. "If the body weren't in such bad shape there might be signs that he played this or that instrument, but it's too far gone."

"You mean like callouses or certain muscles that are more developed than normal?" she said. "Here, give me that." She snatched the detritus of the sandwich out of his hand, bagged it, and put it with the other trash.

"Yeah. Like that." He looked under the seat. "Uh, thanks."

Bing! A text from Amphora had arrived: "Nothing."

This was not encouraging. Apparently the key was still a mystery. Amanda texted back: "What about shape?"

Amphora texted back: "Ivy says not house key."

"Tell her great minds think alike," said Simon, reading the text.

Amanda gave him a disgusted look. "She knows how smart you are," she said.

"I'm not bragging," he said. "I'm letting her know we already thought of that."

"Oh, okay," said Amanda, still not convinced of his modesty. She texted, "We know."

"Hey," said Simon, looking over her shoulder. "That's not what I said."

"It'll do," said Amanda. Score one for her. Now they were even.

27

LONDON

Fortunately Amanda and Simon were able to take the tube directly from Euston to Bank Station without having to go through the zoo that was King's Cross. *Unfortunately*, before they left Euston they split up and went to the toilets and lost each other. Amanda kept calling and texting Simon but got no answer. That was weird. Why wasn't he responding? Had something happened to him? Maybe those tough guys had followed them and beaten him up.

After what seemed like forever she became so worried that she called Ivy and Amphora to see if they could get hold of him. After about ten minutes they called her back and said that they couldn't reach him, so she tried Clive, who told her he couldn't get hold of Simon either. Now she was getting so frantic that she wondered if she should call Holmes, although what he could do from a distance she couldn't imagine. After another five minutes of pacing she gave in and phoned him.

When he answered, he seemed incredulous. "Amanda?"

"Yes, it's me," she said. *It's me? We're not "it's me" friends. Why did I say that?* "I'm sorry to bother you, but I have a huge problem."

"Go on then," he said.

"It seems I've lost Simon and he isn't answering calls or texts." She looked around frantically. Still no Simon.

"Where are you?" he said. "I can go look for him."

"Uh, thanks, but that isn't going to help," she said.

"Why not? I'm quick. I can cover the whole school really fast."

"There's a teensy problem about that," she said, pacing.

"What, you don't think I can?" he said. "Why don't you ever think I can do anything?"

"I think you can do a lot of stuff, Scapulus," she said. "But I know you can't do this."

"Thanks a lot," he said. "I don't see why I should help you if you're going to take that attitude."

"We're in London," she said rather loudly. "Oops." She'd almost run into a woman with a walker. The woman, who was about a hundred years old, glared at her and edged forward ever so slowly.

"What?" he said. "You can't be."

"We can and we are. I'll explain later. All I can say right now is that this is really important and I've got to find Simon."

"Where are you?" he said.

"Tube station," she said, not wanting to be specific.

"Well, then, why don't you page him?" said Holmes.

Slap to head. Why hadn't she thought of that? Now what was she going to say? He obviously thought she was the biggest idiot on the planet. Why she cared she didn't know, but for some dumb reason she felt embarrassed.

"That's a good idea," she managed to squeak out. "I'll try that." She felt she needed to acknowledge what had just happened but had no idea what to say. Maybe she should just keep her mouth shut, but the silence on the other end was getting to her. "Thank you, Scapulus. I, uh, I think you're good at a lot of things."

"Thanks, Amanda, but I get it," he said.

This was not the result she'd been hoping for, but she just said "Sorry" and hung up.

She found the information booth and asked for the attendant to page Simon Binkle. Before she could say another word, the woman had picked up a microphone and bellowed, "Mr. Simon Binkle. Please come to the information desk. Mr. Simon Binkle." It was really loud.

Amanda felt even more embarrassed. The woman sat back and stared at her as if she were a space alien.

"Uh, thanks," said Amanda.

Within about thirty seconds Simon came bounding up. "What happened?" he said.

"I don't know," said Amanda. "Where have you been?"

"When I came out of the gents' I couldn't find you, so I waited but you didn't show up. I went to text you, but I forgot my phone when I went back for the clothes, and then when I found a pay phone I couldn't remember your number. It's in my phone but I don't know it by heart."

"I don't understand," she said. "I was right there, just where we said to meet."

"Well, I didn't see you."

"I didn't see you either."

He seemed to take her paging him for granted because he didn't mention it. All he said was, "Let's board this tube and get to the factory. We've lost a lot of time."

When they got off the tube the neighborhood was deserted, as you'd expect on a Saturday. It was now around noon and they had a lot of ground to cover, so they got onto their boards and skated the rest of the way

When they arrived at the wreckage Amanda burst into tears. Despite the fact that she was still furious with him, she couldn't bear to look at the place where Nick had died. Yes, he had lied to her, led her on, and done terrible things, and yes, it was probably the fictional person she really missed. But they'd been so good together. Not that she'd ever forgive him. Not in a million years. She still wished she could scream at him. In fact if Simon hadn't been there she'd have done just that.

"Go on," said Simon, watching her face. "Do it."

She sniffled but didn't look at him. "What do you mean?"

"Yell at him," he said. "It'll feel good." He motioned toward the wreckage with his chin. How did he know?

"You don't think—" she said.

He shook his head. "Do it."

Amanda faced the wreckage, took a deep breath, and screamed, "How could you leave me, Nick Muffet?" That was weird. She hadn't meant to say that. She'd meant to take him to task for lying to her, kidnapping her father, and almost killing him. For laughing at her.

She was breathing hard and her heart was pounding. She turned to Simon. "I'm done," she said. "Let's look for the crystals."

The place was still sticky from the sugar meltdown and there were dead ants all over the place. There was also a huge amount of charred wood and Amanda could still smell a faint burning odor. It was going to be rough searching for the crystals in that mess. She wished she'd thought of a way to keep her shoes from sticking. Then she remembered the evidence bags. They might just fit over them. But when she slipped a bag onto her right shoe, she found that it was too small. If only they'd thought to collect some plastic shopping bags. Oh well. They'd have to clean their shoes later.

They started picking through the mess with Amanda videoing as they went. She opened a channel and streamed the signal back to Clive so he could make comments. He was chuffed and kept asking her to direct the camera here and there. The work was tedious, and at the rate they were going it would take them hours to comb through the rubble, but they couldn't think of a way to make the search go faster.

"Maybe the crystals we brought will sense their countrymen," said Simon, giggling.

"You know," said Amanda, "that's not such a bad idea. Think they'd be able to spot them?"

"It's worth a try," said Simon. "Are you getting this, Clive?" Amanda checked her screen and nodded. He extracted a crystal from his backpack and held it out. Nothing. "That doesn't mean anything," he said. "Maybe it will blink when we get close, assuming there are crystals here in the first place."

She removed a crystal from her stash and held it out, with the same result. "Tell you what," she said. "For the next ten minutes, I'll look on the ground and you hold out the crystal. It's pretty hard to do both at the same time."

"I've got a better idea," said Simon. "I'll attach the crystal to my shoe so I can see it when I look down." He put the crystal in an evidence bag and threaded a shoelace through it, making sure the cord was short enough that the crystal didn't flop around. "What do you think?"

"Looks good to me," said Amanda. "Clive, did you hear Simon? We're relocating the scout crystal to his shoe. Let's roll."

"Cool," said Clive.

They sifted and lifted and dug until their backs were sore, but they didn't find anything. Then, after quite a while spent in this futile activity, Simon stopped abruptly and said, "It's working."

"What's working?" said Amanda, searching a particularly dense bit of wood and plaster rubble.

"It's blinking."

"What?" she cried. "Let me see." Sure enough, the crystal attached to Simon's shoe was blinking its apricot color off and on. "Do you think there are crystals near here? Maybe it's just trying to say that it likes you or something."

"Getting hot," said Clive.

"Dunno," said Simon. He moved the crystal around until it blinked faster. "There!" he said, stepping into some mud. "I can see something."

He grabbed the small trowel he'd stowed in his backpack and dug gently. The crystal on his shoe blinked so fast it looked like a strobe. The color deepened slightly as the crystal got more excited. Amanda thought it looked really cool with Simon's purple nose. She made sure to get a good shot of the two of them. She wanted to try that combination in disguise class.

"Nice camerawork," said Clive.

"Thanks," she said.

Soon Simon had unearthed two perfect crystals. The one on his shoe had settled down and reverted to its normal state, but when he put them close together the scout crystal went back to blinking. Whether because that was the way it communicated with the other crystals or to show its happiness Amanda didn't know.

"Is that amazing or what?" she said. She bent close to Simon's hand to look carefully with both eyes and camera. "They're like their own Geiger counters."

"Yes and no," said Simon. "Obviously they don't blink just because they're near each other. I suspect this one did because it knew we were looking for the others and wanted to let us know we were close."

"They're like dogs," said Amanda. "The blinking is their wagging tail."

"They're pretty amazing," said Simon. He bagged the crystals and put them in his pack. "You do realize what this means, though?"

"What?"

"Professor Pole's theory is correct. The force of an explosion does create the crystals, but only if the virus-treated sugar has been there."

"It's surprising they're not pink," said Clive. "I'll look into it."

"You're right," she said. "But what this also means is that Moriarty might have found them. We have no way of knowing how many crystals are still here, or might have been. And yes, Clive, I thought of that too."

"You're probably right," said Simon. "But let's keep looking. Maybe we'll discover something else. I mean besides more crystals."

A couple of times Simon's warning crystal blinked but they didn't find anything. "Do you suppose there were crystals here and they know it?" he said.

"If they can sense that, they're even more amazing than we thought," said Amanda. "But how are we supposed to be able to tell? They don't leave a residue, do they?"

"I don't know," said Simon. "It doesn't seem likely. We can try swabbing and analyzing what we find in the lab. But it's hard to know where to take a sample."

"I can tell from the video," said Clive. "Hold still."

What was Clive talking about? "Can you zoom in with the sensor crystal and see if it blinks really hard?" she said.

"Let me see," said Simon. He swept the crystal slowly over the place he suspected it was pointing to. "The speed of the blinking is changing. See? Here it goes faster." He positioned the crystal over a place where it looked like the soil had been worked. The crystal blinked frantically. He moved it near another spot that looked undisturbed. The crystal slowed down. "And here it doesn't go so fast. If I didn't know better, I'd say there were some crystals here at one time."

"Okay, let's swab that," said Amanda. "But isn't that weird?"

"I'll say," said Simon. "Of course we have no proof of what's causing the changes in speed. It might be something we haven't thought of. But we should know more when we get these samples into the lab."

"I really think there were crystals here," said Amanda. "There was a ton of the pink sugar—way more than at Legatum. You can't tell me that the explosion didn't turn all that residue into crystals."

"You've got a point," said Simon. "It does seem odd that we haven't found more."

"He's got them," Amanda said. She was a hundred percent sure that Blixus had found the crystals and removed them. If he hadn't missed the few they'd found they might never have known, either.

"You're probably right," said Simon. "And the worst thing is that he probably knows about their special properties. Why else would he have taken them?"

"What is he going to do with them?" said Amanda.

"There are organisms on the crystals," said Clive. "Parasites, I think."

Amanda and Simon looked at each other. "What?" they said together.

What indeed would Blixus Moriarty do if he had the crystals? Amanda just knew he would find a way to make them into weapons. He might turn them into energy storage devices, but doing that would kill them. Either way the crystals would die, leaving Legatum with the only live specimens in the world. She was growing very fond of the little creatures and did not want to see them hurt. Of course she didn't like the idea of Moriarty coming up with new weapons either. But what was this about parasites? How could Clive tell, and what did it mean?

The other immediate problem was the book. It was possible that it, too, was hiding somewhere in the rubble, but because it was only one thing and the crystals potentially many, it would be way more difficult to find. Now they had three tasks ahead of them: the book, the rest of the crystals, and the virus formula. Oh, and the parasites, whatever they were.

"What are we going to do about the book?" Amanda said to Simon, who was still sweeping with the sensor crystal. "We don't have a book Geiger counter to tell us it's here."

"I think we have to assume that Moriarty has it," said Simon. "If it's here, fine—no one has it, and no one can hurt Legatum. But if he's got it he can do a lot of damage, or so it seems. We need to find him first, and then the book."

"I think you're right," she said. "So where do we look? We have no idea where he is or where he's going."

"Let's approach this logically," said Simon, still sweeping. "Where does he live? Does he have a flat? A house? A relative he can go to?"

"I'm sure Thrillkill would have a good idea," said Amanda. "Obviously that's off the table. I wish Professor Kindseth were out of the hospital. He'd probably help us."

"He's doing better," said Clive.

"I'm not so sure he would," said Simon. "He is a teacher. He can't betray the other teachers. Oh, good. Thanks, Clive."

"By helping us?" she said. "All we're trying to do is get their stupid book back for them. And save the crystals. How is that betraying anyone? Thank goodness. Can he have visitors, Clive?"

"Not yet."

"You and I don't think it's a betrayal," said Simon, "but I don't think they'd see it that way."

Amanda thought for a moment. "I wish there were a place to sit down," she said. "I'm tired."

"How about the curb along Factory Road?" he said. "We'd have to walk down a ways, but that would work, wouldn't it?"

"Yes, good idea. Do you mind?"

"Nope. I could stand to sit down for a minute too," said Simon.

"'Stand to sit.' Cool," said Clive.

Simon put the sensor crystal away and the two of them waded out of the debris, which reached halfway down the street, or so it seemed. At last they found a nice stretch of curb and plopped down.

No sooner had her butt touched the concrete than Amanda remembered something. "OMG. How could I have forgotten? One time when the common room was done up like an ocean liner, Nick said he liked sailing. Maybe his dad has a boat."

"Good thinking," said Simon. "The river is right there. Let's check it out. "You still there, Clive?"

"Yup," said Clive. "Take me to the river."

Getting to the Thames was not the easiest thing with all that wreckage between them and it. They would either have to go through or around the mess, and in either case they might be blocked when they got near the water. But eventually they agreed that it would be faster to go around, even if the route was longer.

When they got close they were disappointed to find that there was a solid fence in their way. Simon said they should climb over it, but Amanda peeked underneath and said that the ground dropped off precipitously on the other side.

"At least I can climb up and take a look," he said.

"Show me," said Clive.

"Sorry, Clive," said Amanda. "Can't."

Simon scaled the fence in about two seconds—Amanda wasn't sure how—and was looking at the river. "There's a dock down a ways," he said. "Uh oh."

"What?" she said.

"I think I see him on a boat," said Simon.

"OMG," she said. "We have to get there."

"You're right. There's no way to get there from here. We'll have to find another spot. Come on."

He dropped down from the fence, grabbed Amanda's hand, and pulled her back to the street. He was running so fast she could barely keep up with him. "Skateboards," she yelled.

He stopped for a moment and said, "Right," then pulled his skateboard out of his backpack and started going like the wind. In a few seconds she'd caught up with him, still videoing, and within another minute they found themselves with a clear view of the boat and Blixus Moriarty, who was talking on his phone. The boat was about fifty feet long and looked very old. Amanda wondered if it had once been a fishing boat—or still was. She couldn't imagine the Moriartys casting nets over the side and hauling up tuna or whatever fish lived here. Simon started down toward the dock, but she stopped him.

"Listening devices," she said. "If we stay here he won't see us."

"What listening devices?" said Clive.

"Good idea," said Simon. "Tell you later, Clive."

But even using the listening devices there was too much background noise and they couldn't hear anything Blixus was saying. Neither of them read lips either, nor did Clive, so that was out.

"Do you think he's going off somewhere?" said Amanda. "If he has the book and ends up in Norway or France or something, we'll never get it."

"The Thames leads to the North Sea," said Simon. "Maybe he's heading for the Netherlands."

"Or Germany," said Amanda. "Oh dear, oh dear."

"He might be planning to head up the English coast," said Simon, "or around the south coast to the west of the country."

"You'd know better than me," she said. "I'm not familiar with those places."

"I'm not sure it matters," said Simon. "Even if we knew, how could we follow him?"

"I think we need to sneak on board," said Amanda.

"Yes!" said Simon. "That's what I was thinking."

"Take me," said Clive.

"The only thing is, how are we going to get on the boat without anyone seeing? It isn't that big. And what will we do if we get caught? You can't skate off a boat."

"Yes," said Simon. "We need to think this through."

They stood there for a second and then Amanda said, "Maybe we should wait until it gets dark."

"Okay," said Simon. "But even then, how are we going to find the book or the crystals?"

"The crystals will be glowing and might be easy to spot," said Amanda. "But on such a small boat it's likely we'll run into Blixus, and Mavis if she's there too."

"And they might be in a drawer or something anyway," said Simon.

Suddenly they saw Blixus get off the boat, untie it, and jump back on. The boat was leaving the dock! He was escaping and they had no idea where he was going. Amanda started to run after him, but Simon caught her and shook his head. He was right. There was no way they were going to catch up, and even if they did Moriarty would probably just tie them up. They were sunk. And for all practical purposes, so was Legatum.

28

REGROUPING

Everything was looking bleak now. They'd lost Blixus and the crystals and probably the book, the detectives hadn't identified the dead body or figured out what the key was for, they had no idea who the murderer was, and according to Amphora, who had sent a number of texts while they were searching, Holmes had got nowhere with Professor Redleaf's computer and the teachers were still at each other's throats. The faculty had been arguing so much that Ivy had heard one of them inviting another to a special meeting that specifically excluded "the Punitori." They also told Amanda that a couple who claimed to be her cousins had showed up at the guard gate asking for her—*after* she'd spoken with Despina.

Amanda, Simon, and Clive watched Blixus sail toward the English Channel. They feared the worst and hadn't a clue what to do next. One thing they did know was they had to stop the Moriartys from making more virus-tainted sugar. If they could do that, they could at least prevent them from creating more crystals. That meant that the kids had to get the virus formula and destroy it. But how were they going to do that? Where would it be? Probably on Moriarty's computer. The one Amanda saw in the factory office last term had been blown to bits, and no doubt so had the one in Blixus's office. Nick's computer was with the police, so Blixus couldn't get that, and anyway Nimba Pencil had told Amanda there wasn't anything on it.

Could the formula be on either of the Moriartys' current phones or tablets? Some devices had been destroyed when Nick had blown up the factory, but Amanda was sure they owned more than that. Surely they'd have backups somewhere—probably all over the place. Unfortunately there was only one remedy for the problem: Holmes. Only he could hack their mobile devices now. He and Amanda had ended their last conversation on a sour note, but maybe Simon could convince him to help.

"Simon," said Amanda, "would you mind texting Scapulus and asking him if he'd be willing to help us? Clive, I'm discontinuing the video now."

"OK," said Clive.

"Still not getting along, eh?" said Simon.

"Nope."

"All right. We don't have time for games. But remember, I don't have my phone."

"Oh, yeah. I forgot. You'll have to use mine then. I don't know if he'll answer though."

Simon took Amanda's phone and sent Holmes a text but got no reply. "We could get Ivy to try him," he said. "She isn't fighting with him."

"Good idea," she said. "I'll call her. Or do you want to?"

"You do it," said Simon. "It's your phone."

"Right," said Amanda. She took the phone back and pressed Ivy's icon. The call went straight to voice mail. "Oh great. She's not answering."

Next they tried Clive. He seemed to have put his phone down.

"If you think I'm going to call Amphora—" said Simon.

"I'll do it," said Amanda. But Amphora wasn't answering either. "I can't get hold of anyone. First they send a thousand texts and now they disappear."

"We could always try Wiffle," said Simon, drumming on his skateboard.

"Very funny," she said. "Wait a minute."

"Oh no. You've got that look in your eye."

"Do you think Gordon would help us? He seems kind of different lately." She searched her address book.

"You don't want to tell him what's going on," said Simon. *Drum, drum.* "He'll tell Wiffle and Thrillkill will expel us."

"I suppose you're right," she said. "But he has been acting weird. Not weird exactly. Just more of a person."

"Even so," said Simon, "we can't afford to take the chance." *Drum, drum, drum.*

"I guess you're right. We'll have to wait for someone to get back to us."

"Hang on," said Simon. "Do you see those two guys over there?" He indicated toward the factory wreckage.

"Which two guys?" She looked where Simon was pointing. "Oh, those." She could see two boyish shapes wearing backpacks and dark jackets with the hoods up. Their identities were unmistakable. "OMG, it's Philip Puppybreath and Gavin Niven. What are they doing here?"

"Don't know," said Simon, "but they sure look like they're sneaking around. What could they be up to?"

"I can't imagine. Maybe they're trying to get the book or the crystals back too."

"Those two?" said Simon. "I hardly think so. Wiffle is always complaining about what jerks they are. Ever since the, uh, explosion, they've been rooming with him."

"You can say it, Simon," said Amanda. "I know they used to be Nick's roommates."

"This is just weird," said Simon. "I think we need to get back as fast as possible and find out what's going on."

313

On the train back Amanda said, "Who are the Punitori anyway? Do you think they're connected to the book?"

Simon felt his nose—he'd been doing that ever since they'd boarded the train back from Euston Station. "Interesting name," he said. 'Punitori' means avengers or punishers in Latin."

"You mean like wrestlers?" said Amanda.

"Doubt it," said Simon. "But it does sound like they see themselves as aggressive."

"Do you think these Punitori are some kind of subgroup of the teachers?"

"It's starting to look like it," said Simon. "From what we know, there seem to be several points of view about the missing book and what they should do about it. Perhaps these Punitori represent one of them. "

Just then Amanda received a text from Amphora: "No news re key. Body still unknown."

"Boy," said Amanda, "the teachers aren't getting anywhere with the murder investigation. You'd think they'd have found something by now. I wonder what the problem is."

"Too bad they don't have any DNA," said Simon.

Amanda was half-listening while she texted Amphora back: "How about teachers?" Within a few seconds she received a text back: "Same old."

"What's she saying?" said Simon.

"No change," said Amanda. "Let me just catch them up on what happened here."

"Yup," said Simon.

Amanda sent several texts explaining what they'd seen and done in London. She asked if Amphora and Ivy had any thoughts about where Moriarty might be going. Unfortunately they were as much in the dark as Amanda, Simon, and Clive. They did find it strange that their friends had seen David Wiffle's roommates there though. Amphora said she'd see if she could find anything out about that.

"She's really coming along, isn't she?" said Amanda, sticking her feet on the back of the seat in front of her.

"What?" said Simon, who had removed his skateboard from his backpack and was adjusting the wheels. "You mean Amphora? Coming along how?"

"Last term she seemed a bit lost. Not lost exactly. What am I trying to say? Don't tell her I said this, and don't you say it, but I think she was a bit lazy."

"She's still lazy," said Simon.

Normally Amanda would have jumped all over him for that remark, but instead she said, "I don't think so. At least not as much."

"She's used to having her own way," said Simon. "Her family's got money."

"I gathered that." She didn't want to tell him about Amphora's argument with David Wiffle. The last thing he needed to know was that Amphora had been trying to out-aristocrat the little creep.

"And she's soft," he said. "She doesn't know what to do when things get tough. But she is smart. It's kind of a waste."

Amanda was shocked. Simon had never spoken like this before. "Wait a minute. Did you just say that Amphora is smart?"

"Yes, but don't make a big deal out of it," said Simon. "Lots of people are smart. It doesn't mean anything unless you use it. Look at Wiffle, for example. He's intelligent. He's just a dork. So is Amphora."

Funny he should liken the two. She'd thought that herself but had been afraid to admit it. "I don't think liking boys makes you a dork, Simon."

"I'm not talking about that. I'm just saying she's spoiled."

Bing! A text from Ivy had arrived: "I got into secrets trove!"

Amanda practically dropped her phone. "Look!" she said.

Simon glanced at the phone and said, "Ask her for more detail."

"Siiiii-mon," said Amanda. "Aren't you excited?"

"Not until I know what that means."

"All right. I'll ask her." She thumbed a text and sent it.

Ivy replied that she was able to hear the locks and had been able to pick them. She'd managed to crack several of the compartments but she couldn't read the papers inside. Editta had been with her and had tried to read them but they seemed to be in code. Amanda sent back a congratulatory text. Ivy was amazing. She was probably the best detective in the first-year class.

Simon said, "Yeah!" and Amanda was so surprised that she almost fell off her seat. He wasn't an excitable guy, but for some reason the news had really got to him.

"I'm excited too," she said, "but you do realize that there are thousands and thousands of compartments. How are we going to get into all of them? And how are we going to crack that code?"

"I have some ideas," said Simon. She bet he did. They probably involved Holmes and she didn't want to hear about him. "Speaking of ideas, I'm really jazzed about this skateboard design I came up with. I wonder if I could patent it."

"I don't see why not," said Amanda.

"Thanks. Did you know that Scapulus has a patent?" She knew. She just didn't want to talk about it. Simon could obviously tell because he said, "I'm sorry. I know he bothers you. But not for the reasons you think."

"What's that supposed to mean?" she said.

"Never mind. It's nothing" He went back to fiddling with his skateboard.

Boy, he could be annoying. Speaking of someone who ruined their gifts by being a dork. "What are you talking about? It isn't fair to bring up something and not follow through."

Simon put down the skateboard and looked her full in the face. "The guy is crazy about you," he said, then turned back to his skateboard and twirled another wheel.

"Whaaaaaaat?!" She reached for a gingersnap. "Have you lost your mind?"

"Nope," he said, appearing to be satisfied with the way the wheels moved. "Why do you think he acts so mean to you?"

"What are you talking about?" she said, chewing. The cookie was really dry. She'd have to get some water ASAP.

"He really likes you. He's afraid of being rejected so he acts mean to push you away so you won't hurt him." He stuffed the board back in his pack.

"Give me a break. Wait. He didn't tell you this, did he?" She was going to need to get up.

"Of course not. But I know. I'm surprised you haven't figured it out. And BTW, he's really jealous of Nick." He lifted his left leg and rested his foot on the seat, having to scrunch to get his butt out of the way.

"What do you mean he's jealous of Nick? How can he be jealous of Nick? Nick is dead, and anyway he wasn't my boyfriend. I need to get some water." This was the worst news she had heard all day. Well, not really. Moriarty sailing off with the book and the crystals was much worse, but that was different.

"He was, and Scapulus knows it. He doesn't think he can ever live up to the Nick Muffet legend so you'll never look twice at him. That's why he's been trying to act like a tough guy. So he'll be more like Nick and you'll like him. I'll wait."

Amanda got up and went to the water fountain. She was absolutely fuming and choked trying to swallow the lukewarm liquid. When she returned she plopped herself down so hard that Simon's foot fell off the seat. "Nick was not my boyfriend and Scapulus does not have a crush on me. Where do you get these ideas?" she said.

"Observation," he said, resetting himself.

"You're nuts," she said. "And by the way, eeeeeeew."

"Ew? Oh, I don't know. I think you guys would be good together."

"Aaaagh! I thought you were my friend."

"I am," he said. "And as your friend I think you should go for it."

When they were just a few minutes away from the Windermere station, Amanda said, "Your nose is still purple. How are you going to explain that?"

"Uh, we were practicing our kicks and you accidentally got me?"

"I don't think so. That already happened to me. Too suspicious."

"Well, maybe I was hit by something falling in an aftershock."

"That seems better," she said. "Although they're going to ask you why you didn't report the injury and go to the nurse."

"They won't even notice," he said. "Too preoccupied."

As soon as they returned they went to look for Holmes. He had never answered the text Simon had sent, and they desperately needed his help to destroy the virus formula. It was late but they found him in the Cyberforensics classroom still trying to figure out who had hacked Professor Redleaf's computer. Tired as they were, they were still so agitated that they fell all over each other trying to tell him what was going on.

"Is that what you sent that text about?" said Holmes.

"Yes," said Simon. "Sorry it was on Amanda's phone but I forgot mine."

Holmes looked from one to the other of them but said nothing.

"We have to destroy the virus," said Amanda, hoping he wasn't too mad. He sure looked it. "We really need your help. We need to hack the Moriartys and find it."

"That's very noble of you," he said, "but the security of the school is more important than the crystals."

Well didn't that just beat all. Amanda was furious. The crystals were in pain, and by using them Blixus Moriarty could regain the advantage he'd lost. He was incredibly dangerous and thwarting him was way more important than the school's data, which after all they should have protected better.

"Look, guys," said Holmes softly, "I'm very sorry but I can't help you."

"Okay, man," said Simon. "Thanks anyway."

Amanda glared at him and left him to his project. Crazy about her indeed.

29

ANSWERS

The next morning, Sunday, Amphora told Amanda and Ivy she thought she'd overheard Professor Thrillkill saying there had been yet another murder. The body count at the school was growing uncomfortably high and the three girls became extremely agitated. Nigel must have sensed their distress because he kept whining.

Now Amanda's hands were so full she didn't know what to attack next. She still had to finish the film, she needed to find a way to destroy the virus formula, she had to figure out where the Moriartys were, she had to find out more about the Punitori, there was still the mystery of the dead body to solve and the secret compartments to get into, and now this. Fortunately Amphora volunteered to try to find out what was going on with the murder, leaving Ivy and Amanda to work on the other problems.

Almost as soon as Amphora had set out, Amanda, who was sitting with Ivy in the common room trying to figure out what to do next, received a text: "Nothing," said Amphora. After another few minutes she got another one: "Asked Rupert to keep ears open. Hasn't heard." Amanda looked at Ivy and said, "They must be trying to keep it hush hush, and who can blame them? There have been too many deaths around here."

The next text came in about half an hour: "Wrote names of teachers seen alive. Want list?" Amanda texted back, "What about Prof Kindseth?" Amphora texted, "In hospital."

In the next few texts Amphora sent the list. After thinking a moment Ivy said, "What about Professor Tumble?" Amanda asked Amphora about the disguise teacher, and the next message she received was, "Oh no. Haven't seen her."

Amanda texted back, "Who would want her dead?" Amphora sent, "Can't think of anyone." Then Ivy said she thought the most likely victim was Professor Feeney and had anyone seen her. Amphora texted "No."

"It's got to be her," said Amanda. "You're right, Ivy. She was the one I heard talking about the missing book last term." She texted Amphora and told her what she'd concluded. The next thing she knew, Amphora had run up to Professor Feeney's office, which was empty. However while she was messing around, Professor Also came in and caught her. Now she was sitting in Thrillkill's office waiting for him.

"It's a good thing Simon doesn't know about this," said Amanda.

"Oh, I don't know," said Ivy. "I could collect enough money to pay for a year's tuition."

Amanda smiled for the first time in a while. At least Ivy was joking about her friends' arguing instead of being annoyed.

When Amphora returned from Thrillkill's office she was more upset than she'd been at the news of another murder. "He gave me two weeks' detention," she said. "And by the way, there hasn't been a murder. I got that wrong. Not that I told him I was eavesdropping. I just mentioned that I thought Professor Feeney might be dead, so he called her into his office and she said, 'Obviously not. Whatever gave you such an idea?' So I just said I thought I'd heard something."

"I'm sorry about the detention," said Ivy.

"He was so mad, though," said Amphora. "He said that that no one had died since Professor Redleaf was killed, and I shouldn't have been in Professor Feeney's office without permission, and that if I infringe the rules one more time I'll be suspended for two weeks like my 'friend Simon Binkle.'"

"Oh dear," said Ivy.

"I think he has it in for both me and Simon now, if you want to know the truth," said Amphora. "I hate being lumped together with him. And who is he to threaten me like that? Yes, I shouldn't have been in there, except that I had to find out. He would have done the same thing. Thrillkill, I mean, although I'm sure Simon would have too."

"That's really unfair," said Amanda.

"How would you know?" Amphora said, suddenly turning on her friend. "You always get away with breaking the rules."

Amanda was stunned. "I do not. What a mean thing to say."

"You lead a charmed life, Amanda," she said. "You know you do."

"Where do you get an idea like that?"

"You run down to London whenever you please and you never get in trouble. You break clocks and no one cares. You sneak out in the middle of the night—"

"I do not break clocks," said Amanda.

"All right. Your boyfriend then. But you were with him."

"He wasn't my boyfriend and I didn't like him breaking that clock," yelled Amanda.

"Hey," said Ivy. "People will hear."

"He was not my boyfriend," Amanda said hoarsely. "And I couldn't believe he did that. He didn't even care. I thought it was terrible." Actually, at the time she'd admired Nick for taking matters into his own hands. She hadn't liked the noise of the clock, so he'd climbed up, grabbed it, and broken it to bits. She'd never seen anyone act so quickly or decisively just to please her and she was thrilled. Not that she'd admit it.

"Fine," said Amphora. "Whatever. Anyway, there was no murder, so that's cleared up."

"Look," said Amanda. "I really am sorry about your detention. It wasn't fair, but it could have been worse."

"I suppose so," said Amphora. "But if that Wiffle kid says one thing, or Simon . . ."

"They won't," said Ivy. "If they do, they'll have me to contend with. I think Simon is getting short on money. He'll watch himself."

"I never thought of that," said Amphora. "He can't afford to insult me anymore. I like that."

Bing! Amanda looked at her phone and discovered that she'd received a text from Editta: "Come to library." Perhaps she'd learned something about the missing book.

Amanda, Ivy, and Amphora rushed to the library to find Editta standing there with a card in her hand. "You're not going to believe this," she said. She seemed fine—no sign of distress and no evidence that she'd been crying.

"What is it?" said Amphora, grabbing the card from her.

"Lemme see," said Amanda.

Editta snatched the card back. "It's the book," she said. "It's *The Detective's Bible*, and guess who took it: David Wiffle!"

"No," said the others simultaneously.

"Yes," said Editta. "And look here. He's even assigned a classification number so that it sits between the codes and scandals books. It was misfiled. I found it by accident. Do you believe this?"

The girls were gobsmacked. They were thrilled to finally know what the book was and who had it, but they couldn't for the life of them figure out how any of this had happened. Wiffle? What in the world would he have been doing with the teachers' book, and how long had he had it and not told anyone? Did this mean he was a mole?

Last term they had discovered the existence of *The Detective's Bible*. In fact the target of the bomber in the class project had been just that, but not the original version. The teachers had stashed a facsimile in the garage. The kids had never dreamed that the real one wasn't still safe wherever it was hidden.

Now that they thought about it the whole thing made sense. The answer had been hiding in plain sight. Not that they knew what was in it. They hadn't been able to decrypt the facsimile, which had been burned almost to bits anyway. They did, however, know that the book was important. They just hadn't realized *how* important.

If David Wiffle had taken the book, surely Moriarty did *not* have it and there was nothing to worry about. But David was bound to be in trouble. Didn't he realize what was going on? He could have fixed everything so easily. Why hadn't he? Something didn't add up.

Amanda texted Simon, who joined them at once. He was so glad that they'd solved the mystery that he actually congratulated Editta on her excellent detective work. She was so surprised that she dropped the card and Simon accidentally stepped on it, leaving the tread pattern from his shoe all over it.

Now the task was to find the Wiffle kid. They split up and looked all over the school. Of course only Simon could search the boys' dorm, but he didn't have to. Amanda found David in the gym practicing kicks. While she was waiting for the others she watched him. He had improved since the time he'd kicked her in the nose.

He caught her watching him and said, "Go away. You're distracting me."

"You've gotten better," she said.

For a second he forgot himself. "I have?" he said, looking down at his legs.

"Yes. Nice form." She made a hand-leg gesture.

"You're kidding," he said. "What do you want? I'm not going in the basements with you."

"I have no intention of inviting you to the basements or anywhere else," said Amanda. She leaned back against the mirror with her arms folded.

"Good, because I'm not going," he said. "So what *do* you want?"

"Ah, here they are," she said, seeing that the others had arrived.

"Them?" he said, looking deflated. "What are they doing here?"

"We want to talk to you," said Amanda, motioning to the others to gather round like some kind of gang leader.

"About what?" said David.

"About this," said Editta, shoving the card in his face. Amanda couldn't believe how she'd come to life.

"Where'd you get that?" said David.

"In the library," said Editta. "Misfiled."

"I didn't misfile it," said David. "I put it right where it belonged." Oops. He'd given himself away. Now he couldn't deny having made the card *or* filing it.

"Where's the book?" said Ivy.

"Why do you want to know?" said David, glancing from one to the other.

"Because the teachers are going crazy thinking they've lost it," screamed Amanda. "How could you not know that?"

"Well, I didn't," he said. "And anyway I was trying to protect it."

"What's in it?" said Amphora, stepping forward.

"I haven't the faintest idea," he said. "It's in code."

"The teachers are in a huge dither about it and you'd better produce it fast," said Ivy.

"Okay, okay," he said. "Don't get your knickers in a twist."

"We'll meet you in the dining room," Ivy said.

The kids went to the dining room and poured themselves some tea. After twenty minutes had passed, during which time they'd drunk three cups each, the Wiffle kid hadn't returned, so Simon went to see what was going on. In about five minutes he and David showed up.

"What happened?" said Amphora.

"Can't say," said David. "I don't know what's going on, but the book isn't where I put it." He looked terrified.

"This is not good," said Amanda. "Look again."

"I already did," said David.

"Simon, go with him and make sure he checks everywhere," said Amanda.

The two boys went back to David's room to search some more. Ivy said, "I wonder why there aren't any copies. Or are there? Why is it so important that the teachers have the original?"

"I don't know," said Editta, "but if there are copies, where would they be?"

"Good question," said Amanda. "We've scoured the school and we didn't see any."

"They could be anywhere," said Ivy. "Even hidden inside other book covers."

"Good point," said Amanda. "They're probably around. But apparently the original is the one that counts."

"Weird, though," said Ivy. "If Moriarty got a copy, wouldn't it be the same? He'd still have the content, whatever it is."

"How creepy," said Amphora. "You don't suppose—"

Ivy did one of her lifting up her sunglasses things and Amphora stopped, but Amanda knew what she was going to say. She was going to say that Nick might have taken it and the Moriartys still might have it.

David and Simon still weren't able to find the missing book, but David thought he knew of some other places it might be and went off to search them. He seemed to realize how important it was that he produce it, so Simon let him be. No way would a rule-bound kid like that try to get away with something.

Meanwhile, Editta and Amphora left and Amanda and Simon turned the subject back to the crystals.

"He's got 'em," said Amanda. "He's probably torturing them right now. As soon as he strikes them or tries to fill them with too much light they'll turn red and die. He won't care."

"He's an awful man," said Ivy. "I'm sorry, Amanda. I know how you feel about Nick but—"

"I don't feel that way about Nick anymore," said Amanda. Simon and Amphora looked at each other. "What?" said Amanda. "You know I don't. Ivy!"

"Of course you don't," said Ivy. She didn't sound like she meant it. "Say, do you think the crystals have DNA? They are alive. They'd have to, wouldn't they?"

Amanda and Simon looked at each other. "OMG!" said Amanda. Simon rushed to Ivy and gave her a huge smackeroo right on the lips. Editta and Amphora gaped, but Ivy just smiled. "You're welcome," she said.

Amanda and Simon dashed to the lab, colliding with students and teachers on the way and causing a lot of yelling and cursing. "Call Clive," yelled Amanda. Ivy and Nigel followed at a slower pace. When they got to the lab, Clive was already there and everyone made a beeline for the dead crystal. They laid it out on the workbench and looked at each other. What were they supposed to do now?

"How do you tell if the crystals have DNA?" said Amanda.

"You're thinking the same thing I am," said Simon.

"Of course," she said. "Maybe the crystals that formed on the dead body absorbed the victim's DNA."

"Bingo!" said Simon. "Boy, I wish Professor Kindseth were here. You know, he still isn't doing that well."

"I know," said Amanda. "Have you heard anything today?"

"Uh uh," he said. "Anyone?"

"No," said Ivy. "Not a word."

"Me either," said Clive.

"Hang on," said Amanda. "How about that guide the school made for doing laboratory tests? Let's look it up."

"Good idea," said Simon. "Of course, it's one thing to take cells from something liquid or soft, like tissue or bodily fluids, but the crystals are hard. How could we get samples from them? They don't have jelly centers, do they?"

"Ha ha," said Ivy. "From the sugar?"

"Why not?" said Simon. "They're already so weird anything could happen."

"Yeah, they really are strange," said Amanda. "But cute."

Simon grabbed the school's guide and turned to the table of contents. "I'm pretty sure if we can extract the DNA we can sequence it using these recipes, but I'm not sure how to do that."

"What does the book say?" said Amanda.

"It's pretty involved," said Simon. "Whoa. This is difficult stuff. There's no way we're going to be able to do this alone."

"What are we going to do then?" she said.

"I hate to say it, but we're going to have to go to Professor Stegelmeyer."

"Do we have to?"

"If we want to get this done we do. It's either that or forget it."

"Nuts," she said. "Oh, all right. Let's go."

They marched to Professor Stegelmeyer's office. Fortunately or unfortunately he was in, writing furiously on his computer. Amanda wondered if he might be working on one of his awful novels. Surely not with all these crises going on. He looked up and said gruffly, "What is it?"

"Sir, we need to extract some DNA and compare it against known sources," Simon said.

"You do?" said the crime lab teacher. "Why?"

"Here's the thing," said Amanda, and together she and Simon told him the whole story. Well, not the *whole* story. They certainly didn't tell him they'd been to London.

Professor Stegelmeyer laughed. Amanda had never seen him do that. He had nice teeth. "You've been most enterprising. Very impressive. You did all this alone, did you?"

"Yes, sir," they said together.

"Let's take a look then," he said. Amanda, Simon, and Clive looked at each other as if to say, "What's going on?" "Well, what are you waiting for? Let's get cracking."

When they got to the lab, the teacher looked at the ultrasound machine and the guide and said, "Interesting. Sonication. We won't do it that way."

"We won't?" said Simon. He sounded disappointed.

"Not today. I'll show you how to do that another time. Now let me show you how I usually do it."

He whizzed around the lab, setting up equipment, sticking the crystal with various devices, and making slides, and within a short time they had two different DNA fingerprints. They were all in agreement that one was from the crystal and the other from the body. Now they needed something to compare them with.

Professor Stegelmeyer started up the lab computer. He told them that they would first check the school's database, which included students, faculty, administration, and alumni. Amanda wondered if Nick's DNA was in the database. Simon must have been clairvoyant, or at least seen something in her face, because he looked at her and shook his head no. Checking to see whether Professor Stegelmeyer was looking and concluding that he wasn't, she made a face.

The first search was unsuccessful, but the second one brought up a match. Professor Stegelmeyer stared at the screen for a long time, buried his head in his hands, and said, "Oh no." Amanda and Simon looked at him quizzically. He turned the computer toward them so they could see.

All three kids saw it at the same time. The computer had found a match. The body was David Wiffle's father.

30

IN PURSUIT OF A CULPRIT

Amanda wished they hadn't identified the corpse. It would have been better to let the mystery stand forever than to know what she, Simon, Clive, and Professor Stegelmeyer now knew—that the murdered man was the Wiffle kid's father. She didn't like David, but he didn't deserve to lose his father, especially in such a horrible way.

Professor Stegelmeyer said that they must tell Thrillkill immediately. He didn't want to give him the news via text or phone, so he simply sent "Must see you" and ran off to the headmaster's office. As he departed he told the kids not to say a word to anyone, especially not David. He and Thrillkill would notify the boy.

When the teacher had gone, Amanda turned to the boys and said, "We need to figure out who the murderer is."

"I was thinking the same thing," said Simon. "Do you think—" Bing! All three of them had received texts. Thrillkill wanted to see them.

"He can't be mad, can he?" said Amanda.

"Don't see why," said Simon.

When they arrived at Thrillkill's office, the headmaster, Professor Stegelmeyer, and Professor Also were hunched around Thrillkill's desk, talking low. As soon as they saw Amanda, Simon, and Clive, Thrillkill looked up, pointed to the corner, and said, "Please pull up a chair." Looking at each other as if to say "Now what?" the kids each grabbed one of the cracked green leather chairs Thrillkill kept for guests and scrunched in between the teachers.

"First of all, I want to thank you for your excellent work in identifying the body," said Thrillkill. Amanda exhaled. He wasn't going to yell. "I am going to notify David Wiffle in a moment, but first I would like your help." Their help? That wasn't what Amanda had been expecting. "We would like to conduct a brainstorming session. Who murdered Wink Wiffle and how did it happen?"

"Excuse me, sir," said Amanda, "but you want *us* to help you?"

"Of course, Miss Lester," said Thrillkill. "Why not?"

"Well, uh, I mean, I just thought the teachers would want to investigate," said Amanda.

"We will," said Thrillkill. "But seeing that you three identified the body, we want you to keep going." They hadn't exactly identified the body. Without Ivy they'd never have thought to look for DNA, and without Professor Stegelmeyer they'd still be messing around in the lab, but if he wanted to give them some of the credit, Amanda wouldn't object. "We'll include the rest of the students, of course, but I'd like to keep this quiet for the nonce. Obviously it won't stay that way for long, but let's see if you can make a good start."

"Yes, sir," said all three kids.

"Now," said Thrillkill, "I would like you to stay here with Professor Also and Professor Stegelmeyer and see what you can come up with. I am going to talk to Mr. Wiffle."

He pushed back with a grunt, sending his chair rolling into the bookcase behind him, then hoisted himself onto his crutches, made his way through the door, and closed it behind him.

Without a word of sympathy or foreword of any kind, Professor Also said, "Let's see what you three can do. We're not going to prompt you."

Amanda gulped. She thought it was weird that the teacher didn't at least say, "How awful" or "Poor David Wiffle," but then the teachers were pretty tough. They saw worse than this all the time. She liked Professor Also but she hoped *she'd* never be so heartless.

What should she say? She looked at Simon. He seemed to be concentrating so hard, rolling his eyes back and forth in time to the wheels in his head, that she couldn't tell if he was stumped or had already solved the crime. Clive was staring at the headmaster's desk.

She tried to slow her breathing. *Start with what you know.*

I know that Wiffle's father is dead.

Duh. Yes, we know that. And what flows logically from that?

The body was found at Legatum.

And what questions does that raise?

How did it get here?

Yes, good place to start.

"We need to figure out how Mr. Wiffle got onto campus," she said.

"Yes," said Simon. "Was he killed here or murdered elsewhere and brought here?"

"Let's think about that," said Amanda. "Would he have come here voluntarily and not let anyone know? Or maybe he came to see the murderer but didn't tell anyone else."

"We can check the guard gate records to see when he came through," said Simon.

"Of course he could have snuck in," said Amanda. She looked over at Clive, who gulped. He'd managed to get them by the security gates. Could someone else have done so as well?

"Unlikely," said Simon. "It's pretty difficult. To go through all that implies that he had some nefarious motive and didn't want anyone to know. Otherwise he'd just go through the guard gate."

"Yes," said Amanda. "And if he did have an ulterior motive, what was it? Who could he have been coming to see? Not his son. That wouldn't be cause for sneaking around."

"No," said Simon. "Before we do anything else, let's check with the guard." He looked at Professor Also, who nodded. He took his phone out of his pocket and rang the gate. Amanda could hear the guard's voice. She checked to see if she had her listening device in, but no, he must just have been a loud guy.

"Hello, uh," said Simon. "Is that Merlin? Oh, hi. This is Simon Binkle, first-year? Yes, uh huh. Sure, I wouldn't mind showing you what I did to my board. It's really smooth now. Yeah, you could use it in the fells as long as the path isn't too steep. Listen, uh, would it be possible for you to check some records for me and Headmaster Thrillkill? No, he isn't here right now, but if you'd like to speak to Professor Also . . ." He handed the phone to the history of detectives teacher.

"Yes, Merlin, how are you?" she said. "Yes, uh huh. Yes, do please give Mr. Binkle whatever information he asks for. On my authority, yes. So glad the technology is working properly. Those voice ID devices are very handy, aren't they? All right, I'm giving you back to Mr. Binkle."

Simon took the phone. "Hi." He listened for a moment. "Sure, no problem. I'm looking for information on Wink Wiffle. Can you tell me the last time he was on campus?" He waited a moment. "Really? You're sure?" Another pause. "Sure. How about tomorrow morning? See you then." He hung up.

"I heard that," said Amanda.

"Yeah, my ear hurts," said Simon. "Nice guy, though."

"Care to enlighten us?" said Professor Stegelmeyer. His hearing must not have been so good. Amanda figured you could hear Merlin all the way at the other end of the building.

"Sorry, Professor," said Simon. "Merlin was just interested in my skateboard designs."

"Not that, Mr. Binkle," said Professor Stegelmeyer.

"Sorry, sir. The, uh, the records. Yes. Well, the last time Mr. Wiffle was here was January 6th, the day of the orientation."

So Wink Wiffle had been alive on the day of the orientation. He'd probably come with David to see him off and hadn't been back since, at least not officially.

"We need to tell Professor Hoxby," said Amanda, getting out her phone.

"You mean so he can establish time of death?" said Clive.

"Exactly," said Amanda. "We know Mr. Wiffle can't have been murdered before January 6th. That means he may have been dead for more than three months, but it might be less than that." She punched a text onto her screen and hit Send.

"Professor Hoxby's estimate—and Ivy's—does fall within that time frame," said Simon.

"So it's possible he got onto campus by coming for the orientation," said Amanda. "No sneaking in."

"We could work with that theory, see what we come up with," said Simon.

"It makes the most sense, doesn't it?" said Amanda. "Why would he sneak onto campus?"

"And if he was killed somewhere else, why would the murderer bring him here to bury him?" said Clive. "It isn't logical."

"To send a message, maybe," said Amanda.

"That's a lot of trouble just to send a message," said Simon.

"But not impossible," said Amanda.

There was a knock at the door. "It's Hoxby," said the man on the other side.

Amanda looked at the teachers. Professor Stegelmeyer nodded. "Come in," she said.

Professor Hoxby was so delighted to receive Simon's news about the last day Wink Wiffle had been at the school that he turned a deeper shade of purple than usual. Amanda still had not got used to how ghoulish he was, but she had to admit that he was an excellent pathologist and kind of a nice person if you were able to overlook his weirdness.

He had taken Amanda's text as an invitation to join the brainstorming group. Not that she'd meant it that way, but she guessed it wouldn't hurt. She just hoped he wouldn't talk about too many gory things. She still wasn't used to the whole autopsy routine.

"Shame about Wiffle," he said. "I imagine Thrillkill's quite upset."

"He went off to tell David," said Amanda.

"He and Wiffle were like this," he said, holding up two gnarled fingers.

"Really?" Amanda was surprised. She hadn't imagined Thrillkill being close with anyone.

"Yes, they worked many cases together," said Professor Hoxby. "He's not going to rest until the murderer has been caught."

"You don't suppose it was one of Moriarty's moles, do you?" said Simon.

"I surely do," said Professor Hoxby. "Probably Mavis. I never trusted that woman. There was something shifty about her."

Amanda thought it might not be such a great idea to remind the good professor that if he'd been suspicious of Mavis, he should have said something a lot earlier. If he had, her father might not have been kidnapped and Nick might be alive.

"She certainly had opportunity," she said.

"The doctor too," said Simon. "And the cook. And—" He looked at Amanda. She was sure he was going to say Nick but had caught himself. Unfortunately, Professor Hoxby was not so diplomatic.

"And that kid," said the teacher. "What was his name? Ned?" The room went silent. Professor Hoxby looked around. "What? Did I say something?"

"It's okay, Professor," said Simon. "His name was Nick."

"Let's think about how we're going to approach this now," said Professor Also, butting into the conversation. "I think we need to search the moles' rooms one more time." What would that make it— four times? Five?

335

"I think we should also consider motive," said Amanda relieved at the change in direction. "Why would someone kill Mr. Wiffle?"

"Revenge," said Simon.

"Send a message," said Professor Hoxby.

"Get him out of the way," said Amanda.

"Steal something from him," said Clive.

"Accident," said Amanda.

"Punishment," said Professor Hoxby.

"Isn't that the same as revenge?" said Amanda.

"No," said Simon. "Revenge involves resentment. Punishment is unemotional."

"You think so?" said Amanda. "I thought they were pretty much the same."

"Don't think so," said Simon. "Revenge leads to blood feuds. You kill someone in my family, I have to kill you. Then my relative has to kill someone in your family, then your relative kills someone in my family, and on it goes."

"I see what you're saying," said Amanda. "Then punishment would be fining someone or something like that. Hey, do you think that's what Ivy is doing to you and Amphora?"

"Yeah," said Simon. "That's punishment. There's no emotion involved. It's just a price. It's supposed to change our behavior. Isn't succeeding though. I mean with me and Amphora."

"So punishment changes behavior but revenge is emotional," she said.

"Exactly," said Simon.

"We've got a good list," she said. "If we can put these motives together with the possible suspects, we should be able to figure out who the killer is."

"Unless, of course, we have evidence," said Professor Hoxby. "Then we don't need a motive. Although it's always better if you have one."

"But we don't," said Amanda. "Have evidence, I mean."

"I agree with Professor Also," said Professor Stegelmeyer. "I think it's time we tried again.

There was no way Amanda was going to return to Nick's room. She was sure there was nothing else to be found there, but even if there had been, it was better to let someone else do it. The experience had been awful, and by the way, she still didn't know why Nick had hidden that picture of her or the film they'd made. Not that she had any desire to think about them. In fact, up until this moment she'd completely forgotten about them.

Fortunately no one suggested that she search Nick's room, or anyone's. After the meeting broke up the teachers took care of that themselves, although once David Wiffle had had a chance to digest the news, which he had taken badly, they asked him to come to Mavis's room and look around. When he did he found a ring he recognized as having belonged to his father. This discovery tied Mavis and Wink Wiffle together. How, no one yet knew. Thrillkill, who'd been Wiffle's close friend, had had no idea they'd known each other, if in fact they had. What Mrs. Moriarty would have been doing with Wink's ring they couldn't say.

Now that they had managed to associate the two, they probed Mavis's background even more carefully. Astonishingly, her arrest record was clean, at least up until recently. Her school grades were exemplary, and she'd never even gotten a traffic ticket. She'd either been lucky, amazingly careful, or a late bloomer when it came to criminal activity. Seeing that she'd been married to Blixus for more than a dozen years, the last seemed unlikely. Nor did her family and former neighbors, social media presence, or mobile phone data shed light on the situation. The woman seemed a ghost, but unfortunately she was all too real.

Amanda was dying to know what the deal was with Thrillkill and Wiffle. There was no love lost between Thrillkill and Blixus Moriarty. The same was probably true of Wink Wiffle and Blixus. Perhaps Blixus had put Mavis up to the murder. Whether it was for revenge, to get the man out of the way, send a message, or whatever, she might have done it to please her husband, or to further his business interests. Thrillkill undoubtedly knew a lot more about the whole dynamic between the Moriartys and the detectives than the kids did. Without that missing piece of the puzzle it was difficult for them to speculate much further.

What they had come up with so far was all circumstantial. There was no murder weapon, no physical evidence pointing to the perpetrator, and no concrete motive. All they had was a bunch of stymied detectives and one devastated thirteen-year-old boy.

Then Thrillkill called the group to his office. "I know what happened," he said. "The murder weapon."

"What was it?" said Professor Hoxby. "I'm stumped."

"Icicle," said Thrillkill. There was a rush of breath as the kids gasped. The teachers, on the other hand, nodded their heads.

"It was January," said Professor Hoxby. "Icicles."

"Yes," said Thrillkill. "And no evidence to find. It was brilliant. Just the kind of thing Moriarty would do, although of course, it couldn't have been him personally."

"No," said Professor Stegelmeyer. "It was obviously Mavis." Amanda was glad he hadn't said Nick.

"Because of that business at Uamh Nan Claigg-Ionn, The Cave of Skulls," said Thrillkill. "You know, that's the deepest cave in Scotland."

"Sorry, sir," said Amanda, "but what incident are you referring to?"

"It was a conflict Wink Wiffle and I had with Blixus Moriarty," said Thrillkill. "At the cave. Blixus has had it in for us for a long time, not only because of that, of course, but that was a bit of a watershed." A frozen watershed, it seemed. Whatever had happened, it explained Thrillkill's obsession with icicles and his habit of carrying a hair dryer so he could melt them. "I blame myself for this, though. The incident was my fault. If I'd handled it differently, Wink would still be alive."

"You can't blame yourself, Professor," said Amanda. "Moriarty is evil. He enjoys making people unhappy."

"I appreciate your support, Miss Lester," said Thrillkill, "but in time you will see that there's a lot more to him than that."

"So what probably happened," said Professor Stegelmeyer, "is that Mavis knew the orientation was coming up and she was able to check our files and see that David Wiffle was entering the school. That meant that Wink would be coming to campus and she'd have her opportunity to kill him. The date of the orientation was known. She'd have had plenty of time to plan."

"But could she do all that alone?" said Simon. "I can't believe she could lift the body and wall it up like that."

"I suspect she had help from the doctor and the cook," said Thrillkill. "We were all gone over the Christmas holiday. They would have had a chance to prepare the compartment then."

"Yes," said Professor Also. "She probably anticipated Wiffle's movements based on the orientation schedule. He'd take David to his dorm room, then go to the dining room and get a cup of tea. As he was leaving the chapel after the orientation, she'd have lured him to the back of campus. Her accomplices would have been waiting and they could have killed him there. They might even have got him to go into the gardening outbuilding so as to avoid being seen."

"But if I may ask," said Amanda, "how do you kill someone with an icicle?"

"It would take some planning," said Professor Hoxby. "The best way to do it would be to immobilize him first. Maybe cosh him on the head with something—probably a large icicle so there would be no trace of the weapon. Then take a sharp one and stab him. It might take a few tries. They may have prepared the icicles ahead of time and stashed them in the outbuilding. With the temperature as cold as it was, they wouldn't melt. Then they'd have to hide the body, but with all the activity that day, it would be easy to do that relatively unnoticed. In fact they may have left him in the building and come back later. I suspect they walled him up that night. They selected an obscure place so no one would hear or smell anything."

"But we did," said Amanda. "That first day. Ivy and I heard something in the bathroom outside the chapel. We always thought it was the cook messing around with the sugar, but it could have been Mavis with the body."

"That is possible," said Professor Hoxby. "We have no proof of any of this, of course, partly because the body was so badly damaged that I couldn't find the icicle wounds."

"It sounds like a plausible scenario," said Thrillkill. "Obviously there are others. But it's a useful working hypothesis. And it makes it all the more critical to find out what that ring was doing in Mavis's room."

31

SCAPULUS HOLMES, DREAMBOAT

That evening Amanda got a call from her mother. Her father was not doing well at all, and she thought maybe speaking to his daughter would cheer him up and boost his immune system. But when she tried to hand the phone to her husband, Lila couldn't get him to talk. He claimed he was meditating and couldn't be interrupted.

Amanda didn't take offense at his rejection. Rather, she was worried about him. He had not only failed to recover from his kidnapping, but he was acting like a whole different person. The idea of her father meditating was ludicrous. He wasn't an emotional person. Neither of her parents was. She'd probably never know what horrors he had endured and didn't want to. She just hoped that given time he'd work through the trauma and become himself again.

What *was* upsetting her so much that she couldn't stop thinking about it was Holmes. She was furious with him for refusing to help with the virus. Yes, the hacking problem was important, but if the Moriartys turned the crystals into weapons, a lot of people could lose their lives. She didn't understand how he could fail to see that. She hadn't gotten anywhere by appealing to his sense of right and wrong, so now she would have to play dirty. Seeing how much he supposedly liked her, she *would* try to be his girlfriend as Simon had suggested. She wouldn't tell Simon, though, because he'd act all judgmental. She'd keep the whole thing to herself as long as she could, not even telling Ivy.

She found Holmes in the Cyberforensics classroom as usual. He was staring at his screen with such a look of puzzlement that she almost backed out the door for fear of interrupting something important, but he must have seen her because he looked up, breaking the spell.

"How's it going?" she said.

"Not good," he said, picking up a pencil and fiddling with it. "I can't find anything. I'm no further along than when I started."

"I think you're working too hard," she said.

"There is no such thing as too hard when the stakes are so high," said Holmes.

"Sometimes it helps to take a break," said Amanda. "How about a cup of tea?"

Holmes dropped the pencil. It clattered to the floor, bounced a couple of times, and lay still near his foot. He froze for a second, then reached down to retrieve it. Amanda could hear it rattling around as he kept trying and failing to pick it up. Finally he gave up and sat back in his chair.

"A cup of tea?" he said. "You and me? Now?"

"Sure," she said in her best flirting voice. Not that she thought she had one, but it was probably time to see if she did. "I'm buying."

He eyed her suspiciously, then seemingly satisfied that she wasn't putting him on, stood up and said, "Okay, let's go."

As they made their way to the dining room, Amanda said, "How are you?"

Holmes gave her a sidelong glance and said, "Uh, okay, I guess. How are you?"

She couldn't tell him about identifying the body, so she raised a subject she *could* talk about. "Super," she said. "The film is almost done and I'm so glad we did it. You did a way cool job, Scapulus."

"But I thought—" he said.

"What?" she said. "That I thought you didn't know anything about making films? She put on her most cheerful face. "You didn't, but you obviously do now. You're a really quick study." Then, trying not to choke, she said, "It must be those Holmes genes. Uh, I mean it isn't only your genes." *Dodo!* "You're so smart and so good at everything. I mean I know how hard you work, and you have such good ideas . . ." She thought she'd better quit before she said anything even more stupid, which would have been difficult to do.

"Uh, thanks," said Holmes hesitantly. "I'm glad I could be useful."

"Not just useful." Should she bat her eyelashes at him? Nah. That was a *really* dumb idea. "Critical. I couldn't make a film like that by myself."

"Sure, I contributed a lot of the technical content—"

"Not only that. Your ideas about scene blocking and pacing were amazing. I admit that I had my doubts at first, but I'm so glad we did this together."

"Amanda, are you—"

But they had arrived at the dining room and Amanda interrupted with, "Ooooh, they have lemon today. I didn't think you guys used lemon in your tea."

"We don't normally, but—"

She shoved a cup of tea in his face. "Try it. It's good."

"Uh, thanks," he said, trying not to spill the offering.

"The other thing I wanted to say was that you're doing such a fantastic job teaching the cyberforensics class. I'm understanding the concepts easily. That's difficult stuff. I was struggling until you explained everything."

"You like it?"

"Love it." She stared into his eyes. For a moment he gazed back, then broke off eye contact and gazed off into a corner. She kept looking at him, and in a moment he checked back. When he saw that she was still giving him that look, he got busy with his tea and burned his mouth.

"Good," he said, dabbing at his lip. "I'm glad. I wasn't sure I was explaining things that well. When you know something it's hard to remember what it's like not to know it."

"Yes," she said dreamily.

"I've been meaning to compliment you as well," he said, eyeing her. "You did such great work discovering that those crystals are made from the pink sugar, and also going to London to try to find Moriarty. I don't think I could have done either of those things." As much as Amanda appreciated Simon, she did not want to ruin the mood by pointing out that he had been as responsible for those accomplishments as she had, maybe more. "You're a great detective, Amanda."

Amanda was so flattered and taken aback that she said something so idiotic she couldn't believe it. "Your ancestor was the greatest detective of all." Say what? Her archenemy? Well, not really her archenemy. Moriarty was her archenemy. But Holmes was her nemesis. Was that the same as an archenemy? Oh, who cared. Now she was in for it. She'd never be able to back out of this one.

"Thanks," he said. "He had his good points and his bad points, like all of us." He smiled shyly.

Amanda felt something weird ripple through her body. It was almost as if her heart had skipped a beat. Surely it wasn't that smile. No, of course not, but now that they were chatting without trying to one-up each other, she found herself warming to Holmes. He was gracious when he wasn't trying to be a bad boy. He was also scary smart, and he could be incredibly nice. Okay, she'd admit it—what could it hurt? He was nice-looking too. Actually, more than that. Not that she'd ever confide that to anyone, even Ivy.

Suddenly they couldn't stop talking. He asked her about Los Angeles and listened attentively as she described the exquisite Santa Monica Mountains, the laid-back atmosphere, and the creativity that wafted through the air. She asked him about codes, and he explained all about the differences between those and ciphers and cited famous examples throughout history. And then they were silent, looking at each other as if for the first time.

"I'm sorry," Amanda blurted out.

"It doesn't matter," he said.

"You know what I'm talking about?"

"That first day."

"I didn't know what I was saying."

"It's all right. I knew."

"You were so nice about it."

"It's nothing. Let's forget it."

She searched his eyes. He seemed to be telling the truth. How could he be so generous? "Thank you," she said.

They stayed up late talking, and by the time they went to bed, which was after curfew, Amanda felt like a different person. She found that she really liked him—something she never thought possible, although for some stupid reason she felt that she was betraying Nick, which was beyond ridiculous. But she very much enjoyed the new feelings she was experiencing and was so excited that it took her hours to fall asleep.

The next morning Simon took Amanda aside in the hall and said, "David never found the *Bible*."

"I was coming to that conclusion," said Amanda, stopping under a painting of a nymph. "Now what?"

"I didn't want to bother him, all things considered," said Simon, "but I did overhear him talking to Gordon. He thinks his roommates might have taken it."

"Puppybreath and Niven?" said Amanda. "You think they took it as a joke? They don't get along with him very well, do they?" She pressed a finger to the picture frame. "Whoops. If they dust that for prints—" She was getting carried away. With the teachers constantly turning ordinary objects into evidence she was becoming hyper-aware of everything she touched.

"No, they don't," he said. "To tell you the truth, they're not reliable. I've heard them talking in the locker room, and I wouldn't put anything past those two. And considering that we saw them in London—"

"That's right," said Amanda. "I forgot."

"I have a theory," said Simon, moving to the garden bench the gremlins had placed parallel to the wall.

"Uh oh," said Amanda. "Do I want to hear this?"

"Not really. I think you know what I'm going to say." He crossed his left leg. The bench was too low and he had to bend the other one a lot.

"That they took the book and are planning to give it to Blixus," she said, placing a foot on the bench and stretching.

"*Sell* it to Blixus," said Simon.

"Of course," said Amanda. "Ow. Charley horse. It's worth a fortune to him." She removed the foot and held it while hopping on the other. She lost her balance and crashed to the floor. "Ow!"

"You okay?"

"Yeah, I think so, but my butt hurts."

"There's another possibility that's too awful to think of," said Simon.

"Oh no," said Amanda from the ground. "What?"

"They might be offering it to Blixus as an incentive to take them on," said Simon matter-of-factly.

"No. You can't really think—"

"I don't necessarily," said Simon. "It's just a thought. I'm not saying they're moles or anything. But maybe they see him as some kind of hero. It does happen."

"I know it happens," said Amanda. "Please don't remind me, Simon."

"Not the same thing," he said. He reached out a hand and pulled her up. She rubbed her butt and sat down on the bench.

"I know, but—look, we need to figure this out ASAP. We need to talk to David, for one thing. What kind of mood is he in?"

"Panicked," said Simon. "He's absolutely frantic. I think he's blaming himself. Plus he's really upset about his dad."

"Of course," said Amanda. "It's terrible having to eavesdrop on someone who's in that kind of state."

"He's not going to talk to us," said Simon.

"He might," she said. "People do weird things when they're stressed." She leaned forward and rubbed her butt some more.

"Not *that* weird."

"Does it hurt to ask?"

"He doesn't hate me as much as you," said Simon. "I can try."

"Thanks a lot," she said. "But yeah, you're probably right. What have we got to lose?"

"You look tired. Late night?"

"Shut up," said Amanda. "It's none of your business."

He grinned. She was sure he knew exactly why she'd been up late and didn't like it one bit. "Okay, I'll go find David. I'll text you if I find out anything."

As soon as Simon had left, Amanda texted Holmes. She probably should have waited for him to make a move but she was too excited. "Sleep okay?" she said. That was pretty familiar but it seemed right under the circumstances.

She received a text back immediately. "Not a wink. You?"

She grinned. She didn't care if she never slept again. She was in love with Scapulus Holmes.

A few minutes later she heard from Simon again. "Common room," his text said. When she arrived she found him pacing through the straw the gremlins had strewn on the floor. For some reason they'd got it in their heads to make the place look like a barn. They'd even found the time to build a loft. Amanda would have liked to curl up in it but she had way too much to do.

"Not good," said Simon.

"Would he talk to you?" she said.

"Nuh uh. I overheard him talking to Gordon again. Good little devices, these listening things."

"I feel guilty doing that," she said, drawing with the hay.

"Me too," he said, "but sometimes eavesdropping is necessary."

"Agreed."

"Get this," he said. "David found research on Blixus in his roommates' browser histories."

"How could he get into their computers?" she said, picking up a piece of straw and breaking it in two.

"They left their passwords lying around," said Simon. "Typical. They're pretty sloppy." That they were. Amanda thought of that dusty top shelf in Nick's closet. "They were looking at articles about the prison escapes, for one thing."

"That's not such a big deal," said Amanda, shredding another bit of straw. Simon picked up a particularly long piece and tore it lengthwise. "Everyone here is concerned."

"Yeah, but what were they doing in London? You don't think they were trying to catch him, do you?"

"They might have been," said Amanda. "Maybe they want to be heroes."

348

"Why would they take the *Bible* then?"

"Good point," she said. "This doesn't sound good."

"Especially since I heard David say that the two of them have acted greedy and cut corners before. Even so, he blames himself." He grabbed a handful of straw and threw it.

"He shouldn't have taken the book," she said.

"No, that was dumb," said Simon. "But what's done is done. Now he wants to fix it. He told Gordon he was going to do it alone, that it was his responsibility and he didn't want to get anyone else involved. You have straw in your hair." He reached toward her and pulled a couple of strands off her head.

"What do you think he'll do?" said Amanda, reaching upward and fluffing. Some straw came down in her eyes.

"If it were me, I'd try to find Philip and Gavin," said Simon. "That would be the first thing."

"We can tell David we saw them in London," said Amanda.

"Do you really think it's a good idea for him to go running down there by himself?" said Simon. "Oops. What am I saying? You did, didn't you?"

"I did," said Amanda, "but I'm not David. Not to be conceited or anything."

"No, I get it," said Simon, taking off his fedora and pressing down his cowlick. "He is a bozo. He'd probably get himself killed."

"Okay, we won't tell him," said Amanda. "You should listen some more though. Maybe he'll say something else."

"Yes," said Simon. "Are you sure you're okay? You look like a zombie."

"I'm fine," she said. "Nigel was snoring and kept me awake. No biggie."

"Does he always snore?" said Simon.

She ignored him. "How about if I listen too?"

349

Amanda did listen, and she heard plenty. David told Gordon that he had tried to text his roommates and appeal to their better natures. Not that they had them, because apparently they had taunted him. Then he'd tried phoning with the same result. He hadn't been able to get a useful word out of them, except for one thing. When they were connected he heard what sounded like wind and water in the background. It was obvious to him that they were on a boat.

He told Gordon he was pretty sure it was somewhere near the sugar factory, or that they had got on a boat near there and were sailing somewhere. It was even possible that they were with Blixus, maybe even sailing to the continent. It was a lead, but he had no idea what he was going to do next.

He didn't, but Amanda did. She phoned Holmes.

32

WINDERMERE

By the time Amanda arrived at the statue of Agatha Christie on the north side of campus where they'd agreed to meet, Holmes was already there. He was grinning so much that she was afraid he'd get lockjaw. For that matter, so was she. If this kept up, everyone would know about them within ten minutes, and she didn't want that. The gossip would be unbearable.

"I had fun talking to you last night," Holmes said.

"Me too." She giggled.

"Tonight?" he said.

"Same time, same station." They held each other's gaze for a moment and then Amanda said, "Scapulus, I hope you don't mind, but I need to talk to you about something."

"Anything." He was making puppy dog eyes at her. She hoped he didn't mind a bit of business.

"The missing whatsit. It's the original *Detective's Bible*."

"Ah," he said. "No wonder the teachers have been so upset."

"Yes, and there's more," she said. "We sort of found it except that it's gone again." He looked at her quizzically. "David Wiffle—you know David Wiffle?" He nodded. "David Wiffle took it. He found it in the library."

"He did?" Holmes looked incredulous. "He seems so proper. Why would he take it? But what was it doing in the library? Isn't it supposed to be hidden in some secret place?"

"He is and it is. He thought he was protecting it. The problem is that it's gone, and he thinks his roommates took it."

"Puppybreath and Niven? Why would they do that?"

"We don't know. We think they might be trying to sell it to Blixus Moriarty. Or using it to join his cartel."

"Seriously? I knew they were a bit dodgy, but I didn't think they were as bad as that."

"We don't know that they are," she said. "But there's some circumstantial evidence that implies that's what they've done. Also, we think they might be on a boat. As you know, Simon and I saw Blixus on a boat—in the Thames. Sailing away. We don't know where."

"You think they may be with him?" asked Holmes.

"It's possible. Apparently David tried to get in touch with them, and he heard water and wind or something in the background."

"He told you this?"

"Er, not exactly."

"You didn't eavesdrop?" said Holmes. "Tsk tsk, Amanda." He gave her that crooked smile.

"I'm afraid we did," she said. "What are you smiling at? It was necessary."

"I know," he said. "I just like teasing you." He touched her hair. She felt a bolt go through her. "So you think the roommates are on Blixus's boat with the book and they're headed . . . where?"

"We don't know," she said. "It could be anywhere. Simon and I saw the boat head out toward the North Sea." She sat down on the base of the statue. He joined her and took her hand. Another bolt.

"You're right. That could be anywhere. Europe, either coast of the UK, or in a circle back to the factory."

"You don't think they just went for a joyride, do you?"

"Who can say?"

Bing! Amanda took out her phone. It was a text from Simon: "Teachers looking for Philip and Gavin." She turned to Holmes and said, "The teachers know David's roommates are missing. They've launched a search."

"Do they know they have the book?" he said.

"No. We haven't told anyone we even know what the book is. We wanted to get it back and then tell Thrillkill."

"Let's think about this a second," he said. He looked off into the distance. It was a fine day, and his face was highlighted perfectly in the morning sun. "I've got it. I can hack their GPS and find out where they are."

"Philip and Gavin?" she said.

"Yes." His smile was like Christmas.

"Great idea. But what if they have their phones off?"

"I don't think they will. They need them for navigation. Come with me."

He grabbed her hand again and started to run. She didn't want people to see them like that, at least not yet, so she said, "You go on ahead. I'll catch up."

He looked behind him and said, "Cyberforensics room," then took off. He was a fast runner. By the time Amanda had arrived at the classroom, he was settled amid an array of electronics and was hitting keys at breakneck speed. When she entered he looked up and said, "I've got it. And you're not going to believe where they are."

"Oh, I don't know. In the closet?" She flashed him a smile.

"You laugh, but you're very close," he said.

"They're here at Legatum?" she said. *With Blixus?!*

"Not quite," he said. "They're at Lake Windermere. Let's go."

The campus was still so chaotic that it wasn't difficult to slip away again. This time the whole group went: Amanda, Holmes, Simon, Ivy,

Amphora, Editta, Clive, and Nigel. Holmes had relented on the issue of helping with the virus, but in the short time he'd been working on the problem he hadn't made any progress.

This time they took a bus, which had just started running between the town and the outlying communities. Holmes had grabbed a seat, and as Amanda approached he patted the spot next to him. She glanced around, saw that no one was paying attention, and slipped in beside him. She imagined that the others were buzzing with gossip, but she didn't want to look. As the bus pulled away from the curb, he took her hand. This time she didn't pull away. He smiled at her and squeezed tight. She felt her heart leap.

During the ride, Holmes kept track of the roommates' GPS location and made sure the group disembarked at the stop closest to them. Simon and Amanda had brought their skateboards, but the others didn't have any, which was probably a good thing because they would have been too conspicuous. As they neared the roommates' coordinates, Amanda recognized Moriarty's boat. This was a terrible discovery: Blixus was nearby, as close to the school as she'd ever known him to be!

Now they split up. It wouldn't do for a group of kids and a dog to descend on the Moriartys. While the others hid nearby and Holmes kept trying to hack the virus, Amanda and Simon snuck on board— very carefully.

With each step they listened—hard. Each one of them had inserted their ear device, and Amanda could hear wavelets lap at the sides of the boat, the sound was so clear. They didn't hear anything coming from the deck, so they tiptoed to the door of the cabin and looked through the round window, which was pretty filmy but still gave them a decent view of the interior. There was no sight of Blixus or the roommates, and no sound. Simon pulled a crystal out of his pocket but it didn't blink. He showed Amanda and they shook their heads. It seemed that the crystals, if they ever had been on board, were gone.

Simon opened the door slowly. It creaked a little. Amanda winced. If anyone was there they'd be toast. He stuck his head in, then turned around and shook it. Nothing. Treading softly, the pair entered the cabin, which was old and worn. And then they heard it.

Crunch, crunch, crunch. They looked down at their feet. There was pink sugar all over the floor. It was critical that they not speak so Amanda put her head in her hands to indicate how upset she was. Where there was pink sugar there was the virus, and where the virus was crystals could grow. Amanda's worst fears were being confirmed. Wherever Blixus was, he was trying to make more.

Simon's crystal wouldn't blink. That meant there were no crystals on the boat. But if that was true, where were they? Was it possible Blixus hadn't taken them after all? No, that couldn't be. They had discovered evidence that many crystals had formed at the factory, but they had found just a few. He had to have taken the rest.

It seemed that the boat was deserted, which gave Amanda and Simon a chance to search it. Room by room they scoured the place, looking in drawers, compartments, cupboards, closets, and even checking for secret hiding places, but it wasn't until they came to what looked like a little workshop that they found something. Amanda gasped. Lying on a workbench were two dozen dead crystals and some lab equipment. Now they knew that Blixus *had* taken them, experimented on them, and learned some, if not all of their secrets.

Amanda couldn't understand why, if the criminal had the crystals, he would have come here. Was he planning to use them against Legatum? Yes, that had to be it. He had the *Detective's Bible*, and using whatever information was in it, plus the strength of the crystals, he would destroy them.

If Moriarty had the book, why should they bother to keep searching? No doubt he'd taken it and the crystals to the school. Because the earthquake had caused so much damage, the perimeters weren't as secure as they might be and he could penetrate the campus easily—if not through the tunnel gates, then some other way.

She found Simon searching the sleeping area, pulling out a drawer under one of the trundle beds. "He's got the crystals," she whispered. "Probably the book too. He's going to use them against Legatum."

"Not good," said Simon, feeling under a spare blanket, "but we don't know that he has the book."

"It isn't here," she said. She touched all around the mattress. Ouch. The last time she'd done that . . .

"We haven't finished yet," he said. "Let's make sure." He palpated a spot underneath. "Okay, not there."

"But why would he come here?" She tried the pillow. "Nothing here either."

"Probably to do what you said, but do you really think he and Mavis can bring the entire school down?"

"It depends what's in the book," she said. "We have no idea what it is."

"Let's not panic just yet. We need to be systematic."

"Okay, but I'm getting worried."

"I know," he said. "But he's obviously fallible. We'll find his weakness and stop him."

Amanda was unconvinced, but she returned to her searching. She desperately wanted to text Holmes and tell him about the crystals, but she didn't want Simon asking nosy questions so she continued to search. Between the two of them, they turned the entire boat upside down but they didn't find the missing book. Had Blixus taken it, or did the roommates still have it? Either way, the criminal would have access to whatever was inside, which scared her half to death.

They left the boat and returned to the others, except that they had disappeared. Amanda thought they were going to wait for her and Simon to return, but for some reason they'd gone off.

"What's happened to them?" she said, turning in all directions.

"Dunno, but I'm about to find out," said Simon. He whipped out his phone and sent a text. Within a moment he'd received an answer.

"They're on another boat," he said. "Scapulus found Puppybreath's phone."

"Are David's roommates there?" she said.

"Nope, gone. Maybe they took the other boat and followed the Moriartys. They've probably gone after them."

"But where is everyone?" Amanda said.

"Don't know. Scapulus says they're searching the boat but haven't found anything."

Scapulus. He and Simon seemed to be getting pretty tight. That was awkward. Now Simon would know all her private business, although he seemed to already, so who cared?

"Should we try to find them?" said Amanda, imagining Holmes's smile.

"No," said Simon. "There are too many of them already. We'll just make the group more obvious."

"Right."

Suddenly there came a loud noise from off in the distance. Amanda looked around but didn't see anything. Simon turned around 360 degrees. Another noise. It sounded like an explosion.

"Where's it coming from?" she said.

"Behind us," said Simon. "It's pretty loud with these ear things in. I'm going to take mine out."

"You don't think it's the school, do you?"

Simon listened. There it came again. "Wrong direction," he said. "The explosions are coming from over there." He pointed to a spot behind them and to the left. "Legatum is over there." He pointed to a location south of that.

"What's over there?"

"The old quarry," said Ivy, coming up behind her. Amphora, Editta, Holmes, Clive, and Nigel followed. Nigel did not like the noise. Every time he heard an explosion he whined and clung to Ivy.

"OMG, that's right," said Amanda. "He's blasting. He's trying to make more crystals."

Amanda was certain that they had to get to the quarry and stop Blixus, but she had no idea how to do either. The quarry was way out in the boonies, far off the beaten track. It was too far to reach on foot, and no buses went there. The only thing she could think of was hiring a taxi, but they'd left in such a hurry that no one had brought money with them.

"What are we going to do now?" she said.

"We can't walk," said Ivy. "It's got to be six miles away."

"You think it's that far?" said Amphora. "I'd say closer to three."

"Trust me, it's six," said Ivy. "I can tell from the way the sound attenuates. Anyway, a lot of it is uphill so the skateboards aren't going to do any good."

"What about hitching a ride?" said Amphora.

"You think someone is driving out there?" said Simon. "What a dumb—"

"Don't make me fine you, Simon," said Ivy.

"Sorry," he said. "I'm sorry, Amphora."

What was this—an apology? Amanda couldn't believe her ears. Maybe he really was broke and couldn't afford one more fine. Now *that* was a way to get the two of them to stop fighting. Ivy must have planned the whole thing around Simon's budget, although how did she know his financial situation?

"Thank you, Simon," said Amphora. "You're right, though. Who'd be driving out to the quarry? There's nothing there."

"Call Thrillkill?" said Editta. Everyone turned and stared at her. She'd been so quiet that Amanda had forgotten she was there. It seemed the others had as well.

"Sorry, Editta," said Amanda. "We can't do that. The teachers will go even crazier than they already are. Plus when they find out that David took the *Bible*, they'll expel him."

"Since when do you care about David?" said Amphora.

Amanda glanced at Holmes. Was he jealous? He did have kind of a weird expression on his face. "He's human," she said. "Well, sort of. And he just lost his dad. I'd hate to see him suffer any more."

Holmes looked relieved. "Right," he said. "Let's not add to David's worries."

"I think it's too late for that," said Simon. "If Moriarty has the book he'll be in deep trouble anyway."

"We don't have to add to it," said Ivy.

"So we're back to square one," said Amanda. "What are we going to do?"

"There," said Amphora, pointing. "A tourist tram." She ran toward the vehicle, which was painted a glossy red. It reminded Amanda of those people movers you see at Disneyland. A middle-aged couple was sitting in the front. By the time the rest of them got there Amphora was already flirting with the driver.

"Oh, brother," Simon said.

"Si-monnn," said Ivy.

"I didn't say anything."

"You did, but I'm going to let this one pass. But will you please, for the love of 3D printers, stop it?"

"Sorry," he said. "It won't happen again."

Amanda had her doubts about that. Considering how much Simon and Amphora disliked each other, and considering that they had been paired up for the disguise project and had to spend extra time together, it was amazing they were both still alive.

"I'm sorry," said the driver, a young man with long blond hair who was wearing a Sorrento Beach T-shirt and sandals. Amanda wondered if he'd actually been there. Sorrento was one of her favorite places, although maybe the T-shirt was from Italy, not Santa Monica. He had the right idea, anyway. "I've got to take these people on a tour." He pointed to the very large woman in a flowered blouse and blue pedal pushers and her short, bald husband. The woman was giving Amphora a dirty look. "Anyway, why do you want to go all the way out there?"

"It's really important," said Amphora, batting her eyelashes. Amanda couldn't believe she'd resort to such obvious tactics, although they seemed to be working. The guy was hanging on her every word. "A matter of life and death."

"I might be able to take you, but you'll have to wait until I finish this tour," he said. "Even then I won't be able to wait around. I'll lose my job. In fact, I shouldn't even be thinking about leaving my route. Say, you're the kids from that school up on the hill, aren't you?" He searched Amphora's face. He seemed to want to accommodate her.

"Please," said Amphora. "One of the students is in trouble. We have to save him." She paused and looked him in the eyes. "I'll be ever so grateful." Boy, she was good at this flirting stuff.

"Did you say the school on the hill?" interrupted the large woman.

"Yes, ma'am," said Amphora.

"Is one of you Amanda Lester?" said the woman. She peered at the group, then, for some reason lighting on Amanda said, "Amanda, darling! It's Despina and Hill. Lester. From Liverpool."

Amanda thought she'd just about die. What were *they* doing there? "Uh, hello, Despina," she said. "Hill. I'm sorry, but we've got an emergency."

"Ooooh, that sounds luscious, dear," said Despina. "Isn't it lucky we ran into you? Now we don't have to wait until Saturday. We'll help you. What seems to be the trouble? Oh, but aren't you precious? You look much cuter in person."

Amanda rolled her eyes and looked at Holmes, who was stifling a laugh. "This is dangerous, Despina. I, uh, don't want you to get hurt."

"Nonsense," said Despina. "We're Lesters. You know what that means." She winked.

Yes, Amanda did know what that meant but she couldn't think about her dingdong of an ancestor right now. Blixus was making crystals while they dilly-dallied and they had to stop him.

"She's right," said Hill. He had a high, squeaky voice. "I think you might be pleasantly surprised." This from a court clerk. What did he know about dangerous situations?

"I don't want to be responsible for you getting hurt," said Amanda. "Why don't you take your tour and we'll find some other way to get to the quarry?"

"Quarry, darling?" said Despina. "Is that what all that noise is about?"

"Come on, you guys," she said to her friends. "Let's let my relatives go on their tour. We'll find another way."

"No, you won't," said Despina, suddenly developing an edge. "Young man." She waved at the driver. "Take us to the quarry at once. There's a nice tip in it for you." She waved a five-pound note at him as if that princely amount would convince him to risk his job.

Amanda was so surprised she almost tripped, which would have been a neat trick since she was standing still. The driver looked from one of the group to the other, ostensibly hoping for some kind of definitive solution to his conundrum. Holmes was contorted with giggles, and Ivy was hiding her laughing face in Nigel's fur.

"I said drive," said Despina imperiously. Hill was nodding, obviously pleased with his wife's decision.

That convinced the young man, who seemed to be terrified of the woman. "All right," he said. "I can hear the noise up there. It doesn't sound good. But remember, I have to leave as soon as I've dropped you off. You're sure you're going to be all right?"

"We will," said Amphora. "We won't be if we don't get there, though."

"Hop on," said the driver. Amanda couldn't tell if he was happy or worried. Probably both.

361

The kids boarded the tram, which was arranged in seats of two facing the front. Amanda found herself near the back sitting next to Ivy and Nigel, who were huddled together. Every time there was an explosion, Nigel cowered and buried his head in Ivy's lap. She, in turn, leaned over him so that he was almost completely covered, but her effort to insulate him didn't seem to be doing much good. Despina called out, "Buckle up, dear." Everyone stared at her as if to say, "Now what have you done to us?" Everyone except Holmes, that is, who was laughing his head off. Amanda was glad to see him enjoying himself. He needed to let up once in a while.

"I have pictures of your cousin Jeffrey," Despina yelled back. "Oh, and many nice shots of Windermere. I think you'll especially like the one of a pet monkey we saw."

Amanda didn't want to think about monkeys. She would have been happy never to see one again, even in a photograph. She pretended not to hear.

The driver started the engine with a single *vroom* and shifted into first gear. Suddenly Amanda felt someone come up behind her and plop down. She looked around. It was David Wiffle!

"Have to get to the quarry," he said, panting. "Blixus . . . the book . . . roommates."

Amanda could see Holmes in front of her trying to hack the Moriartys' computers. As the tram rattled toward the quarry he was thrown back and forth. She thought it must be difficult to work that way and hoped he'd manage. If Blixus wasn't stopped soon, he might amass enough crystals to do a huge amount of damage. Not to mention the fact that he'd be torturing and killing more and more of the little creatures.

The six-mile trip seemed to take six hours. Once they had left the town the road narrowed and turned to dirt. The tram kicked up so much dust that the group looked like they'd been in a sandstorm. Simon had to keep wiping his glasses with his shirt, but even that didn't help much. Amanda's eyes were getting sore and poor Nigel was sneezing his head off. Needless to say, all the bouncing was making Amanda nauseous. She may have forgotten to bring money, but she always carried gingersnaps and she ate one now. It worked immediately.

"Any luck, Scapulus?" she said.

"Nope," said Holmes. "Sorry."

"What's that young man doing?" Amanda could hear Despina say. "He seems ever so dedicated."

Holmes ignored her. Everyone did except Hill, who said, "Playing some game, I expect."

"Almost there," called out the driver. The tram was bouncing so much that people were hanging on for dear life. Amanda was glad she'd eaten her cookie.

The tram rumbled through a narrow opening in the road, if you could call it that, and then they saw them. Blixus and Mavis were standing at the far end of the quarry setting off explosions in a bed of pink sugar, although they both looked weird—were they in disguise? Blixus had a mustache, and Mavis was wearing some sort of wig. David's roommates were standing off to the side holding the book and yelling like rabid sports fans.

"It's the book," yelled Amanda.

"I knew it," said David. He stood up in his seat and fell back down as soon as the tram hit another bump.

A white van with its doors open was parked near the Moriartys. A pile of apricot crystals sat on the ground next to it. Pink dust filled the sky, punctuated by glints of apricot-colored light from the crystals that were being created and thrown up in the air. But something else was happening too: the sky was just a little bit darker over the quarry than everywhere else. Amanda hoped it was from the dust, because if it wasn't, it was a sign that Blixus had found a way to force feed extra light into the crystals and they were draining it off from their surroundings. That would have meant that the crystals were indeed capable of stealing light and leaving people in darkness.

The flat floor of the quarry was surrounded by gigantic buff-colored walls studded with blocks of rock and naturally shaped boulders, some of them forming terraces. Tall piles of small rocks and bits of earth-moving machinery dotted the landscape. Off to the right as the tram faced it stood a large pit filled with water. The scene would have been beautiful under other circumstances.

As the tram approached, the kids yelled at the Moriartys to stop. The two of them looked up briefly, broke into laughter, and set off another explosion, throwing more pink dust into the air. David hurled himself off the tram and ran toward them.

"Scapulus, how are you doing?" yelled Amanda. Holmes shook his head. Then she caught sight of something moving behind the roommates. It was tall and dark and looked like a person. Amanda couldn't believe her eyes. There before her, alive and seemingly well, was none other than Nick Muffet.

33

THE QUARRY

Amanda gasped. The shape couldn't possibly be Nick. The dust must have been playing tricks on her eyes. The only problem was that the others were staring too. Editta screamed so loud that Amphora clamped a hand over her mouth. Ivy said, "What is it? What's going on?" Simon froze. David Wiffle, who had been pleading with his roommates to give the book back, stopped and gaped. Despina said, "Who's that when he's at home? Why is everyone screaming?"

Nick smiled and walked toward Amanda. "Hello, Lestrade," he said, when he'd got within speaking range. "Surprised to see me?"

Amanda burst into tears despite willing herself not to, and Nigel licked her hand. Ivy rushed to her side and hugged her. "What is wrong with you, Nick Muffet?" she said. "And what are you doing here? You're supposed to be dead."

"Not quite," said Nick, clearly enjoying himself.

Holmes glanced from Nick to Amanda and back again. An expression of horror crossed his face and he turned away.

Suddenly Nigel broke loose and ran toward the Moriartys. Ivy screamed, "Nigel! Come back here." Simon dashed the fifty yards to the stash of crystals sitting by the van and grabbed some, then banged them together as hard as he could. This action caused beams of light to shoot out of them like lasers as the crystals released the excess light. Simon lifted the crystals, aimed them, and began to zap the Moriartys and David's roommates with bolts of energy. Taking a cue from him,

Blixus, Mavis, and Nick picked up the deepest orange crystals, slapped them around, and started zapping back. David's roommates copied them. Amanda and Clive joined Simon, as did the tram driver, whose name was Eustace. And then something even more unlikely happened: Despina and Hill grabbed a couple of crystals and took their place on the Legatum side. Meanwhile Holmes was still trying to hack the virus, Editta was still screaming, and Amphora was running back and forth waving her arms.

Suddenly a small aftershock hit. Rocks flew into the air, boulders rattled, and even more dust flew about. The battle stopped as the participants fought to stay upright. While the Moriartys were distracted, David took the opportunity to charge Mavis, knocking her down. She screamed, "You little creep! Who do you think you are?" but she had obviously been hurt and was struggling to get up. At the same time Simon zapped Nick, who had been trying to get to his feet as well, and he fell back down.

Amanda took the opportunity to check on Holmes's progress. She ran back to him, looked over his shoulder, and said, "How's it going?"

"Badly," he said. "I'm trying to hack the Moriartys' whole network so I can find all the copies of the formula. I'm working to implant a cybervirus, but I can't quite get—" His jaw dropped. "Oh no! I'm out of juice."

"No!" cried Amanda. "Do you have any kind of power source with you?"

"No. Maybe that van over there. Do you think the key is inside?"

"We can find out, but don't you think Blixus will stop us if we try to do that?" she said.

"How about the tram? I can plug in my charger."

He ran to the tram and turned the key, which Eustace had left in the ignition, but the engine wouldn't start. He tried again. Nothing. Amanda screamed, "Do something, Scapulus!"

"I'm trying," he said. "I hate to say this, but I'm going to need to go back to town."

"How are you going to get there?" she said.

"Good question. Maybe I can hijack the van." He surveyed the situation, then struck out toward the van, carefully skirting the action.

Mavis had recovered from whatever injury she had sustained and the battle had resumed, with Nick going for Simon's jugular, so to speak. He was obviously furious that his former friend had knocked him down and was shooting beams out of the crystals as if they were some kind of automatic weapon. Simon was doing a good job of deflecting them, but he was looking tired and Amanda was worried that Nick would knock him unconscious or worse. With each shot Amanda could see the sky darken just a little more.

Meanwhile Amphora, Editta, and Ivy were following behind Holmes, sneaking round to the van. Not to be left out, Despina and Hill tiptoed after them. When the kids got there they began to take crystals out of the back with the help of Amanda's relatives, who talked nonstop. Amanda would have felt sorry for Hill except that he was as bad as Despina. How they lived with each other she couldn't imagine. While the battle raged, the girls and the Liverpudlians reversed their steps and carried the crystals to the tram, with Hill dropping a few and having to scurry to retrieve them.

David Wiffle was like a machine. He had taken on both his roommates using a combination of martial arts, but they were beating him up badly. Simon glanced in their direction and zapped them royally, which allowed David to get away. Unfortunately that may not have been the best idea because the next thing Amanda could see was David running to the book, grabbing it, throwing it in front of a bulldozer that was sitting next to the pit, getting into the cab, and running over it.

Amanda screamed and ran to the bulldozer. "David, stop it right now!"

"No!" he yelled. "They're not going to have it."

She waited for him to stop while backing up, then before he could move forward again climbed into the cab, flung her arms as far around him as she could, and pulled. "Get off me," he screamed and pushed her away. Holmes looked up from his position inside the van, ran to the bulldozer, and leaped inside the cab. David was exhibiting superhuman strength now: he threw him off too.

At last Ivy yelled, "Nigel, sic!" The dog raced for the bulldozer, leaped into the cab, and jumped up on David, who yelled, "Eeeeeeek!" He pushed Nigel and jumped down, then grabbed the crushed book, hurled it into the pit, and ran off.

"No!" yelled Amanda, jumping into the water. Holmes took one look and leaped in after her.

The water was icky—cold and gritty with a terrible smell—but she barely noticed. Down, down she dove, just as she had when trying for the skateboard back at Enchanto. However this time she wasn't able to find what she was looking for. It was too hard to see. She surfaced, yelled, "Can't find it," and dove down again.

She swam all over the pit, or at least it seemed so, without finding so much as a page. The water hurt her eyes. She could kind of see Holmes zooming around like a fish, but he didn't seem to be having any luck either. She wasn't actually sure she wasn't swimming in circles, as there were no landmarks to go by.

When she couldn't take it anymore she propelled herself to the top. Holmes followed a moment later, holding up his hands to show that he hadn't found anything.

"I can't do this anymore," she said.

"We can try again," he said, diving down for a second go while she treaded water and coughed. Soon he was back again, empty-handed.

The sides of the pit were so steep that they had trouble climbing out. Hill managed to find a foothold near the water and reached out a hand, pulling first Amanda and then Holmes up onto dry land. Simon, Clive, and Eustace were still fighting the Moriartys and the air was still crackling with electricity.

Holmes didn't stop for a moment. He ran back to join the fight, only to hear Simon yell out, "Electricity."

"What?" said Holmes.

"You need juice?" said Simon, releasing a bolt into Blixus's foot.

"Yes," said Holmes.

"Hold up your tablet," said Simon.

"What's that?" said Holmes.

"I say hold up your tablet. Get right over there and don't move."

Holmes raced back to where he'd left the tablet, ran to the spot Simon had indicated, and held it up. Simon took aim and let out a soft beam of light, which hit the USB port. The tablet burst into life, lights flashing, startup noises sounding, screen painting. "We got it!" Holmes yelled.

"Thought it might work," said Simon, dodging a blast from Mavis.

Holmes handed the tablet to Amanda, who was still recovering from her foray into the pit, grabbed Simon's crystals, and faced Nick. Nick laughed and said, "Who are you?"

"You know perfectly well who I am," said Holmes.

"Oh, so that's it, is it?" said Nick. "You look like you're pretty tight with Lestrade there, Holmes. Better watch out. She's trouble."

Nick pulled a glowing orange crystal out of his pocket, aimed it at Holmes, and let go with an electric blast that knocked the shorter boy to the ground. Simon stopped zapping Blixus for a moment and threw Holmes a crystal, which gave off such a crackle of light that it knocked Nick back and nearly into the pit. Holmes got to his feet and let go with another blast, but Nick recovered his footing and got off his own bolt right before it hit him. Holmes went flying. When Holmes regained his balance, he zapped Nick three times in a row and sent him right, left, then right again.

The two boys were glaring daggers at each other—Holmes and Moriarty, Moriarty and Holmes, just as their ancestors had done a century before. Amanda, Editta, and Amphora screamed on the sidelines, and Ivy kept yelling, "What's going on?" Despina and Hill joined Simon, Clive, and Eustace in their fight against Nick's parents, which was a sight to behold, and David Wiffle had returned from wherever he'd run off to and was struggling to hold his ground against his roommates. As the combatants blasted each other over and over, the crystals began to turn red and wink out. Seeing that the weapons were failing, Amanda and Amphora ran to supply the Legatum fighters with fresh ones, which made Amanda want to cry, or would have done if she'd had time to think.

The fighting kicked up so much dust that sometimes it was hard for the foes to see each other. The fact that the sky above the quarry was like twilight now didn't help. More than once Amanda and Amphora were almost hit by friendly fire, and Despina accidentally grazed Eustace, causing a long, narrow part to form on the right side of his yellow mane. Nigel didn't like the dust at all and he pulled Ivy back to the tram, which was parked sufficiently far away from the action to remain if not pristine, at least less dusty than everything else.

Blixus had succeeded in creating more crystals, but their numbers were declining at an alarming rate. Amanda feared that soon they'd be extinct, or at least they would if Holmes could destroy the virus formula. Of course he was otherwise occupied, so the threat was minor for the moment, but if and when the tide turned, chances were that the crystals would either die out entirely or end up as a crippled race. It was a lose-lose situation and Amanda wasn't sure which outcome would be worse.

When Simon, Clive, and Eustace had initially begun to zap the Moriartys, both sides had been defending territory. Now the violence took on a personal tone, as David fought for his honor and Nick and Holmes sought to annihilate each other for reasons both contemporary and historical. Blixus and Mavis simply seemed to find the whole thing funny, which enraged Despina so much that she charged Mavis and managed to knock her over again. Blixus got his revenge easily by tripping Hill as he raced to join his wife, knocking him onto his nose, which immediately turned purple and grew to the size of a small eggplant. Despina wheeled around and tried to blast Blixus but dropped her crystal, which Blixus kicked out of the way, causing her to run after it. She made an easy target and he nicked her in the butt. Meanwhile Puppybreath and Niven were taunting David, yelling, "Where are your knickers, Little Lord Fauntleroy?" and "An electron is bigger than your brain." David took each insult as if it were a slap, and hurled back lame retorts like, "Your ancestors are stupid" and "You can't talk to me like that—I'm a Wiffle." Amanda had never felt so sorry for him. In all the time he'd been at Legatum, he'd learned nothing about relating to other people.

Suddenly Clive yelled, "Amanda, can you cover for me?"

She ran to where Clive was standing, dodging blasts from Mavis, and grabbed his crystals from him.

"Thanks," he panted. "I've got an idea."

Amanda stood up straight and began to fight. Out of the corner of her eye she could see Clive run all the way to the tram and get on. She couldn't imagine what he was doing. Then, wheeling around to evade a blast from Philip, she saw him running toward the group with his pack on his back. What in the world?

Clive blew past her and she could see him dance past orange beams until he had come to the base of one of the walls at the far side of the quarry. Finding a foothold, he began to climb, higher and higher until he'd stopped above what looked like a loose congregation of boulders. She could see him remove a couple of reflectors from his pack and place them within the grouping. Then he climbed back down, found a spot with a direct line of sight to the reflectors, and laid his pack on the ground. The next thing she knew he had removed his acoustic levitator and aimed it at one of the reflectors.

"Clive, watch out for Nigel!" she yelled.

"Oh no," he yelled back. "Get him away."

"Ivy," Amanda screamed, "get Nigel out of here."

Ivy grabbed Nigel, turned him toward the road, and commanded, "Run!" He took off like a shot and pulled her almost at a speed she couldn't manage until the two were completely out of sight.

"All clear," Amanda yelled to Clive.

"Thanks," he said, and aimed the levitator once more. "Now get out of the way!" A spot from his laser materialized on the edge of one of the boulders. Amanda was beginning to get the idea and it wasn't pretty. Clive was going to create an avalanche!

Before she could say anything more the boulder began to move, and within a few seconds it had hit another boulder and another. Soon all the boulders were tumbling down onto the quarry floor. Amanda dived for Simon, who was so absorbed in the fight that he hadn't heard Clive, and pushed him as hard as she could. "Get out of here!" she screamed. Simon looked up, caught sight of Clive, grabbed Amanda's hand, and tore out of there.

As the boulders fell, the noise became deafening. It sounded like a hundred King Kongs. The Moriartys looked up to see a storm of rocks coming toward them and scattered in three directions. David and his roommates dashed for cover, and Eustace made a beeline for the wall to the right of the boulders, which was safely out of their path. Hill and Despina looked like deer in headlights, but Amanda pulled away from Simon, ran back to them, grabbed their hands, and tugged them out of the way.

The descending rocks tumbled like bowling pins. They scattered all over the quarry, flying into the air when they hit the ground and each other hard and fast. They bashed earthmovers, flew into the pit, and nearly decimated the white van, which was miraculously spared. It must have taken them ten minutes to come to a stop. At least that was how it felt. When they did, the pit into which David had thrown the book was completely covered. There was no way to get past them now short of using a crane.

Everyone was injured. Almost everyone was bleeding. They were all bent over, panting. Clive was in the worst shape of all, having been closest to the falling rocks. He had a cut on his head and looked dazed. Amanda worried that he might have a concussion.

She looked around. Something about the avalanche had made her madder than ever, released something in her. How had it come to this?

How had the best friend she'd ever had become so rotten? Where was all that violence coming from? She picked up a crystal, faced Nick, and zapped him so hard he fell onto his shoulder. "Ouch," he yelled from the ground. "Big mistake, Lestrade."

He got up, rubbed his shoulder, and let out a blast so strong that it propelled Amanda right into Holmes, who oofed, grabbed Amanda's crystal, and shot beams at Nick from both hands at once. Nick dodged them, laughed and shot back a line of hits, sending Holmes to the right and Amanda to the left. "You shoot like a girl, Holmes," he taunted. This made Amanda so mad that she loaded up on crystals and sent out a double-strength arc that got Nick in the stomach. He recoiled so far back that he collided with his father, who was in the process of collecting fresh crystals and almost fell over but managed to stop himself just in time.

"What is wrong with you?" Blixus said to his son, who was clutching his stomach. "How can you let Lestrade get the better of you? Get over here now."

Nick hesitated, looked back at Amanda, then fixed his gaze on Holmes and said, "This isn't over." His father pushed him and he stumbled to the van. Amanda couldn't stand seeing Nick like this. No matter what he was or how he'd behaved, the indignity was too much to bear. She yelled to Blixus, "You killed Mr. Wiffle."

"Wink is dead?" he said.

"You know perfectly well he was murdered," said Amanda.

"Really?" said Blixus. He seemed genuinely surprised. "Well, well. It wasn't me, but whoever it was I'd like to thank him."

Amanda felt confused. Was it possible Blixus hadn't killed Wink Wiffle after all?

She turned to Nick. "You didn't—" He shook his head. For some reason she believed him. He hadn't killed David's father either.

They stared at each other for so long that it felt like time had stopped. Finally she spoke. "Why?"

"Don't be naïve," he said. "You know why."

He turned and all three Moriartys got into the vehicle. Then they sped off, raising a plume of dust so irritating that everyone who was left sneezed ten times in a row.

As the van raced toward the road, Editta dashed out in front of it and screamed, "Nick! Take me with you!" The van screeched to a halt. The back door opened and she threw herself in. Then, to everyone's horror, the door closed and the van sped away.

They were all so shocked and exhausted that no one said a word. Holmes kept looking at Amanda, who was staring at the spot where the van had stopped. Ivy and Amphora were holding each other with Nigel in between. David limped off into the boulders. Simon supported Clive and walked him back to the tram. Despina and Hill tended to their injuries while Eustace sat on a rock feeling his scalp. Puppybreath and Niven were nowhere to be seen. It was so dark that if they were more than a hundred feet away, no one would have been able to see them.

Suddenly Holmes said, "The virus!" and ran for his computer. It was so dusty that he had to wipe off the screen, and for a moment it seemed that the keys wouldn't work. Then he yelled, "Got it!" It took a couple of seconds for his words to register.

"You hacked it?" said Simon at last.

"Yes," said Holmes. "I got into the whole network. Unless he's got the formula somewhere off the grid, it's gone."

Amanda burst into tears. Holmes looked at her with pain in his eyes, closed the computer, and walked away.

34

DEBRIEFING

The kids retrieved the remaining crystals from the tram. They glowed a lovely orange in the darkness, but Blixus had stuffed them so full of light that Ivy could hear their pain and covered her ears. Amanda, Simon, Clive, and Amphora each took one at a time onto their laps and caressed them gently until they had turned a healthy apricot once more and their sounds of distress abated. As the excess light drained off, the sky grew just a little bit brighter. Ivy exhaled with relief and Nigel stopped trying to hide his head. The kids wrapped the crystals in Simon's jacket and placed them on an empty seat. Nineteen had survived.

Eustace managed to get the vehicle started again and drove them all the way to the school. On the ride back no one said a word—not even Despina Lester. Holmes sat by himself and Amanda cuddled up with Ivy and Nigel. Amphora sat behind Eustace and leaned her head back. Simon attended to Clive, who was definitely not in good shape. Hill and Despina sat together in the last row with their eyes closed. They had searched for David and his roommates to no avail.

When they had returned to Legatum, Simon took Clive to the hospital and the other friends plopped down in the common room. It turned out that Clive didn't have a concussion, but both of them needed to be patched up and by the time the two boys returned, an hour had gone by. Now it was time to turn their attention to the elephant in the room.

"We have to tell Thrillkill," said Amanda. "We can't keep this from him."

"I wish we didn't have to," said Amphora. "He'll kill us."

"It doesn't matter," said Ivy. "We're going to have to take whatever punishment he gives us. Whatever it is, it can't possibly be as bad as what he's going to do to David."

"I don't know," said Simon. "Thrillkill and David's father were tight."

"Yes," said Amanda, "but the *Bible* means the survival of the school. Or it seems to, anyway. Thrillkill is responsible for lots of people. He's not going to sacrifice everything for one friendship."

"I didn't even know Thrillkill had friends," said Clive. Everyone looked at him. It seemed they hadn't expected such a remark from nice, quiet Clive.

"He doesn't seem like the type, does he?" said Amphora, giggling.

"You never know about people," said Simon.

"What's that supposed to mean?" said Amphora.

"Nothing," said Simon.

"Where's Scapulus?" said Ivy, who seemed not to have noticed the two arguing again.

"Dunno," said Simon. "I haven't seen him since we got back. He didn't answer my text. Anyone hear from him?" He looked at Amanda, who shrugged.

"That doesn't sound good," said Amphora. "I hope he at least went to the nurse. He was beat up pretty bad."

"I don't think he did," said Simon. "We didn't see him there, did we, Clive?"

"I didn't," said Clive.

"If we don't hear from him soon, can you see if you can find him, Simon?" said Ivy.

"Yeah, sure," said Simon.

"We'd better go," said Amanda. "I want to get this over with."

Thrillkill bent over and rested his head in his hands. Then he punched his phone. "It seems we have a problem," he said to whomever was on the other end. "Yes, now." He rung off.

"We're going to mount a search for Wiffle, Puppybreath, and Niven," he told the kids. "And then we're going to go after the book. It has to be there. What we're going to do about Miss Sweetgum I don't know. You're sure she's with the Moriartys?"

"She was," said Amanda. "Whether she still is we don't know."

"Did you get a license plate?" said Thrillkill. There was a knock at the door. "Follifoot?"

"Yes." So that was the teacher Thrillkill had called. It was a good choice. Professor Buck was strict, but he was tough, well organized, and always had your back, although he hadn't been at all nice when Amanda and Nick had found the pink sugar in the secret room. He'd really taken them to task for leaving a murder scene, even though what they'd found by doing so had turned out to be critical.

"Come in."

Professor Buck entered the office and closed the door behind him.

"We've got three students missing up at the quarry," said Thrillkill. "And one with the Moriartys."

"With the Moriartys, sir?"

"Yes, Miss Sweetgum. Apparently she's run off with them."

"You mean it was voluntary?" said Professor Buck.

"So it seems," said Thrillkill. "Some kind of misguided infatuation. I'm about to notify her parents."

Professor Buck whipped out his phone and made a call. "Quarry. Three students. Now." He put his phone away and said, "About Miss Sweetgum."

"Yes," said Thrillkill. "White van. License plate, children?"

Amanda hated being called a child. She certainly didn't feel like one.

"No, sir," said Simon. "Maybe Scapulus got it."

"Your classmate was kidnapped by the most dangerous criminal in the country and you didn't get the license plate, Mr. Binkle? Let's get Holmes in here at once." He sent off a text.

"It wasn't his fault, sir," said Amphora. The other students looked at her with their mouths open. Ivy gasped.

"And why didn't *you* get the plate, Miss Kapoor?" said Thrillkill.

"It all happened so fast," said Amphora. "We'd been fighting, and David had destroyed the book, and—"

"What book?!" said Professor Buck. "Please tell me you don't mean what I think you mean."

"I'm afraid so, Professor," said Amphora. "The original *Detective's Bible.*"

"You mean you found it?" said Professor Buck incredulously.

"David did, actually," said Amphora. "But his roommates stole it and tried to give it to Blixus Moriarty, and . . ."

"What?!" thundered Professor Buck. "Do you mean to tell me that two Legatum students got hold of the *Bible* and gave it to our worst enemy?"

"They tried to," said Amphora. "But David took it away from them. Unfortunately, he kind of lost his mind and drove a bulldozer over it, then threw it in a pit full of water."

"And where is it now?" said Professor Buck coldly.

"We think it's still down there," said Amanda. "Scapulus and I tried to dive for it but we couldn't find it."

"So Moriarty might have doubled back after you left and got it," said Professor Buck.

This possibility hadn't occurred to Amanda. It was a horrifying thought.

"We don't know," said Amanda. "He might have. He was so mad at Nick, though—"

"Nick Moriarty?" said Professor Buck and Thrillkill at the same time.

"Uh, did we forget to tell you that?" said Amanda.

"You're not telling us that Nick Moriarty is alive, are you?" said Thrillkill.

"I'm afraid so," said Amanda.

Thrillkill and Buck looked at each other as if to say, "What *else* aren't you telling us?"

"Let me get this straight," said Professor Buck. "Blixus and Mavis Moriarty escaped from prison. For some unknown reason they ended up at a quarry near here and kidnapped Editta Sweetgum. Their son, Nick, who died in the explosion at their London factory a couple of months ago, magically came back to life and showed up there with him. Meanwhile, one of our students stole Legatum's most prized and critical possession, and two of our other students stole it from him and almost gave it to our worst enemy. However, the first student ended up destroying the book, and now all of those people are missing."

"Yes, sir," said Amanda weakly. "That's part of it, anyway."

"Part of it?" roared Professor Buck. "You mean there's more?"

There was another knock at the door. "Mister Holmes?" said Thrillkill.

"Yes, sir," said Holmes from outside the door.

"Come in and sit down," said Thrillkill.

Holmes entered and sat on the far side of the group, next to Professor Buck. He avoided Amanda's eyes. Clive looked from one to the other and a light bulb seemed to go on.

"Mister Holmes," said Thrillkill. "Your classmates are telling us about what happened at the quarry. Did you by any chance manage to get the license plate of the Moriartys' van?"

"No sir," said Holmes.

"Let's see, you're going to tell me there was too much going on, are you?" said Thrillkill.

379

"Well, sir, there was a lot, but actually there's no excuse. I take full responsibility."

Amanda couldn't believe Holmes could be so generous. She grabbed Ivy's hand. Ivy squeezed and she squeezed back.

"You cannot take responsibility for what the other students did or didn't do, Mr. Holmes," said Thrillkill. "Let's not grandstand."

Holmes looked stung. Amanda felt sorry for him.

"There is one thing, sir," said Holmes.

"What's that?" said Thrillkill.

"It's possible someone else got the plate."

"Someone else?" said Thrillkill. "What someone else?"

"The tram driver," said Holmes. "Or Amanda's relatives."

"What?!" Thrillkill exploded. "What tram driver? What relatives?"

"My cousins from Liverpool, I'm afraid," said Amanda. "You see, we were at the lake searching the boats—"

Thrillkill stood up and stared at the students one by one. Then in a very controlled voice he said, "What boats?"

Amanda's phone rang. The number was unknown but somehow familiar. Then she remembered: Despina! "I think this might be important, sir," she said to Thrillkill. He nodded.

"Hello," she said. "Despina, is that you?"

"Yes, darling," said Despina. "Are you all right?"

"Yes. Are you and Hill?"

Thrillkill let out a huge sigh.

"We're fine, dear. Well, not exactly fine. We're at the doctor's. However, I remembered something that might be important."

"What's that?" said Amanda.

"I've got the license plate of that van for you."

Amanda let out a whoop. Thrillkill gave her a dirty look, so she said, "She's got the plate, sir." Thrillkill stopped glaring and made a motion that said, "Get on with it, already." "ME56BLX," she said slowly as Despina read out the number. Holmes scrambled to make a note of it.

"Thank you, Despina. You've been incredibly helpful. I'll call you later, okay?"

"Yes, excellent, dear," said Despina. "Oh, Hill says that boyfriend of yours is very handsome."

Amanda felt herself go limp. She did not want to hear about Holmes. She did not want to see Holmes. She did not want to talk to Holmes. She did not want Holmes to talk to her.

And then a thought struck her: was Despina talking about Holmes, or Nick?

35

THE DETECTIVE'S BIBLE

Professor Buck sent divers to the quarry to look for the *Bible*. He also sent a team out to search for David Wiffle, Philip Puppybreath, and Gavin Niven. They removed the boulders and dragged the pit but found no sign of the book there or anywhere in the area.

They discovered David Wiffle a short way away sitting against a boulder. He was scratched, bruised, and dusty. When they approached him he said nothing but came with them willingly. They tracked the roommates to the road but their footprints disappeared. Whether they were with the Moriartys or had gone somewhere else the rescuers couldn't tell. The boat they'd stolen was still tied up at the lake, as was Blixus's. The teachers searched both but found no clue as to where they or the Moriartys had gone. They did discover Nick's fingerprints all over the Moriartys' boat. It appeared that he'd been hiding out there since the explosion.

Thrillkill didn't punish David. He said the boy had been through enough. His father was dead. He destroyed the book out of loyalty to the school, taking it in the first place to try to help the detectives. Now he had withdrawn and wouldn't show his face. Even Gordon Bramble couldn't get a word out of him, although he did take meals up to David's room. Mostly they remained uneaten though.

If the teachers had been upset before, now they were hysterical. It wasn't just that the *Bible* was missing. It had been destroyed, or so it seemed. They had lost their holy grail. Without the *Bible* to unify them they seemed to lose their compass and began to fight openly. It was now obvious that they had split into two factions:

The Realists. They believed that the *Detective's Bible* was the undying symbol of their organization and without it they were lost. They wanted to discontinue the school. The members of this group were:

> Browning. Sketching.
> Mukherjee. Legal issues.
> Hoxby. Pathology.
> McTavish. Police Procedure.
> Pickle (although still in prison). Textual Analysis.
> Pole. Fires and Explosions.
> Scribbish. Evidence.
> Sidebotham. Observation and Research.

The Punitori. They were militant and wanted to take back what was theirs. They aimed to hunt down the perpetrators of the assumed theft and "neutralize" them. They'd recover the *Bible* and resume their operations. Their members were:

> Also. History of Detectives.
> Feeney. Criminals and Their Methods.
> Snool. Weapons.
> Pargeter. Toxicology.
> Buck. Profiling.
> Stegelmeyer. Crime Lab.
> Ducey. Logic.
> Peaksribbon. Self-defense.

The last group, which wasn't exactly an official division, was those who abstained. They were:

Thrillkill. Headmaster.
Snaffle. Secrets.
Kindseth (still in the hospital). Photography.
Tumble. Disguise.

Amanda wondered about the Punitori. How did they propose to recover the *Bible*? It had to have been destroyed. There was no way you could crush it with a bulldozer, drown it, and come up with anything but pulp, if even that. And did they really plan to neutralize two first-year students—boys who were obviously a bit misguided but who were probably redeemable?

Amanda and her friends still didn't know what was actually in the *Bible*, of course. Perhaps there were facsimiles around that contained the same critical information. If that were the case, they could still use it and nothing would actually be lost. It wasn't clear whether facsimiles existed, though, or where they might be if so.

What they did know what that the teachers didn't want the parents or the other students to find out what had happened to the book, although some of the teachers were advocating coming clean. They'd already cautioned Amanda and her friends to keep their mouths shut. They were afraid the students would leave the school and the whole enterprise would die. Ivy had heard Thrillkill and Professor Also worrying about money and recruitment. But the worst thing about losing the *Bible* was the prospect of the Moriartys having access to it. The very thought was scaring the teachers stiff. Amanda thought Professor Scribbish had even lost some hair, which he could afford, but still wasn't good.

Then Amphora heard something that resolved a longstanding question, and not in a good way. There were no copies. Whatever was contained in the *Bible* was gone. Now the kids knew that the secrets trove in no way duplicated the book. That was something else entirely—something seemingly off the teachers' radar.

But there was more to the book than it seemed. The physical object was unique—so special that it could never be replaced. It had been hand-written by Legatum's founder, Lovelace Earful, upon the school's founding in 1887, which of course made it irreplaceable. But apparently Mr. Earful had added secret features that rendered the book priceless. Detectives had labored to find this information for more than a hundred and twenty years with absolutely no luck. The thing was a combination of the Holy Grail and the Dead Sea Scrolls, and without it they had lost their foundation.

A couple of the teachers claimed that they could remember some of the information in the *Bible* and had written down what they could, but the bulk of the content had been lost. No wonder they were going crazy. If they couldn't find it they had several choices: attempt to recreate the information, start over from scratch, or do without.

The immediate result of the book's loss was that if someone like Moriarty had the information, they'd be on level playing ground with the detectives. If no one did and the teachers did recreate the information, they'd have a leg up again. Some of the teachers argued that they had to try to do that just in case. Others figured that it was too late. This defeatist attitude so angered the Punitori that they almost came to blows with the Realists right there in the main hall. In fact at one point, elderly Professor Sidebotham beaned middle-aged Professor Also over the head with her tablet, sending the history of detectives teacher to the nurse, who fortunately knew nothing about the book and couldn't take sides.

One thing no one was mentioning was that if the Moriartys had the *Bible*, the fact that it was in a very difficult code might render it useless to them. They all knew better. The criminals had access to some of the world's best cryptographers and they'd crack the code one way or another. Whether they could decipher what legions of detectives had been unable to do was another question.

At last one of the teachers raised the idea of taking protective measures. This was Professor Ducey, whose practice of logic wasn't limited to the classroom. He claimed that whether or not the Moriartys had the book, the detectives should act as if they did and do so at once. But what measures would that protection consist of?

Amanda and her friends thought about this question long and hard. Without knowing what was in the book it was difficult to know how to defend Legatum, but they resolved to try.

"We have to find Blixus," said Ivy.

"Maybe Scapulus can hack him again and we can find out from here," said Simon. "He did get into their network."

"It's worth a try," said Ivy.

She texted Holmes, but when he came to the common room and heard what they were trying to do he shook his head. "It won't work."

"Why not?" said Amphora, who was still flirting with him but in a less conspicuous way.

"They've disconnected everything," he said. "After we destroyed the virus formula the whole network disappeared."

"You didn't do that?" said Ivy.

"No," said Holmes. "It wasn't anything I did. They obviously figured out we'd got in there. I'm sure they've recreated the network, but I have no way of finding it."

"Then it's going to have to be in person," said Ivy.

"What's going to have to be in person?" said Holmes.

"We need to find Blixus," said Simon. "We need to get that *Bible* back."

"You think he has it and it's intact?" said Holmes.

"Dunno," said Simon, "but we have to find out. The school is going to fall apart if we don't."

"I'll go," said Holmes.

"We're all going," said Simon. "Right?"

"Right," they all said, although Amanda didn't relish the thought of going anywhere with Holmes now.

"But where do we look?" said Amanda.

"Where indeed?" said Simon. "Any ideas?"

Complete silence.
"I guess we have some research to do," said Ivy.

36

GOODBYE TO THE CRYSTALS

Before they tackled the problem of locating Blixus, Amanda and Simon turned their attention to the remaining nineteen crystals. They called Clive in as a consultant.

"We should put them underground," said Simon. "They need to be in their natural habitat."

"And it has to be a special type of soil," said Clive.

Amanda and Simon stared at him. "What do you mean?" said Amanda.

"They need to be in contact with a blacksniff parasite," said Clive.

"A what?" said Amanda.

"It's a class of parasites that lives in the soil around here. It seems to like the crystals."

"A parasite on crystals?" said Amanda.

"They are alive," said Simon. "That makes sense. What are they for?"

"I'm not sure exactly," said Clive. "They do something to the crystals that make them thrive. I saw them with my special app when you were streaming that video to me from the factory. I'm not sure if they clean the surface of the crystals or nourish them somehow. But they can't live underground without them."

"I thought they ate light," said Amanda.

"They do," said Clive. "This might be another nutrient they need. I'd have to experiment to know for sure, but they've been through enough. I don't want to poke and prod them anymore."

"That explains a lot," said Simon.

"What do you mean?" said Clive.

"I'll bet the soil where Mr. Wiffle's body was found is full of those things. That's why they did so well there. At the factory too."

"You're right," said Clive. "This area has loads. There weren't that many on the London crystals though."

"Are you telling me that if Blixus had made more crystals and there had been no parasites, they would have died?" said Amanda.

"Yes," said Clive. "And get this: I sampled some of the dirt at the quarry, and it was all wrong. The ones he was making would never have lasted."

"But he didn't care about their health," said Amanda.

"No," said Simon. "Make 'em and milk 'em. That was all that mattered to him."

"But we have access to the right kind of soil around here, right?" said Amanda. Clive nodded. "Where would be the best place?"

"There's a little niche in the tunnels that would be good," said Simon. "A part under the lake. Don't you think that would work?"

"I do," said Clive. "The environment is perfect. Legatum is sitting on top of a unique ecosystem."

"Are you sure they'll be safe there?" said Amanda.

"Yes," said Simon. "We'll bury them where no one can see them. And if there's another earthquake and the alcove collapses, they'll still be fine. They like that kind of soil."

"Can we visit them?" said Amanda.

"I think that can be arranged."

On the way to bury the crystals, Amanda, Simon, and Clive stopped to look at the secrets trove. They were proud of Ivy for figuring out how to get into the compartments, but the job before them was monumental. How were they going to get into all those compartments and read all those coded secrets? They were already spread so thin and there were thousands of secrets to obtain and read. It wouldn't hurt to look at some of the ones that had been exposed by the quake and its aftershocks though.

They didn't know what the odds were of finding it, but within the first few secrets they looked at they saw something about the Cave of Skulls. This was the place where Thrillkill and Wink Wiffle had run into Blixus Moriarty. The kids were dying to find out what had happened there. Whatever it was might have led to David's father's death, and if they could follow the story they might even be able to find the perpetrator *and* figure out what went with the key Amphora had found. They pawed the open compartments nearby but couldn't find another mention of the incident, at least not one they could decipher. Because so much of the trove seemed to be encrypted they couldn't tell.

"If these secrets have nothing to do with the *Bible*, what do you think they are?" said Simon.

"I'm guessing they have to do with various cases," said Amanda. "What else would be so important and take so much room?"

"DNA," said Simon.

"You're kidding," said Amanda. "You don't think the detectives keep people's DNA codes locked up here, do you?"

"Not really but you never know," said Simon.

"What about the national DNA database?" said Clive.

"The trove could be for people who aren't in the database."

"Why on earth would they have that?" said Amanda.

"To compare with evidence they find," said Simon.

"Seems a weird way to store the information," said Amanda. "I'm guessing that's not it."

"Some kind of intelligence, maybe?" said Clive.

"That's possible," said Amanda. "But it's not in a very usable form, is it?"

"There's obviously more here than meets the eye," said Simon.

"There always is with this place," said Amanda. "So are we ruling out the possibility that these are lines from Professor Stegelmeyer's novels?"

The two burst into laughter. It was the first time they'd done that in days. Clive searched their faces.

"You don't want to know," said Amanda.

When they'd found the place Simon had selected, the kids buried the crystals and said goodbye. As they placed dirt over them, the crystals blinked their farewells, then glowed apricot. Amanda felt tears sneak into her eyes and rubbed them away.

"I'm glad we were able to save some of them," she said. "It's terrible that there will never be more now that the virus formula is gone."

"We're now custodians of the race," said Simon. "It's a big responsibility."

"What if something happens to us?" said Amanda.

"I've already taken care of that," he said. Amanda looked at him quizzically. "I stuck a secret in a compartment. They'll figure it out eventually."

When they returned from their mission they were delighted to see Professor Kindseth walking down the hall, even if he was using crutches. He had been released from the hospital but was still weak.

When Simon showed him his work from the 3D printer, he was thrilled. However when they told him about the factions the teachers had split into, he became very agitated. He wouldn't verify or deny anything they claimed they knew, though, because the dispute was a matter for the teachers. Amanda could not imagine him taking sides and hoped he would remain neutral.

There was still no news about the mysterious key. The detectives hadn't found anything in Wink Wiffle's house or office that it might go with. His wife didn't know anything about it, and neither did David, who was trying to cooperate as much as possible while staying out of sight. Simon had even suggested to Ivy that maybe if she were to feel it she might get some vibrations off it, then relented and said, no, he was thinking of Editta. The girls told him that wasn't funny and Ivy almost fined him for being so cruel. Poor Editta. What had become of her? What *would* become of her?

As it turned out, Editta had kept all sorts of stuff about Nick in her room. It had been obvious that she'd had a crush on him since that first day of school when he was kind to her, and her obsession had only grown. No one had realized how foolish she could be, though, and her friends were terribly worried. The Moriartys would chew her up and spit her out. It was weird that the teachers hadn't said anything about mounting a rescue operation. Whether that was because they were preoccupied or simply didn't know where to look, the friends didn't know. What they did know was that Editta Sweetgum was Legatum's responsibility and the teachers had better do something fast. Of course that meant finding the Moriartys—a problem no one had solved.

They were worried about David Wiffle too. As much as they didn't like him, he'd been through an awful lot and they felt sorry for him. He'd lost his father, and by destroying the *Detective's Bible* he'd thrown the school into chaos. Was destroying the *Bible* rather than letting Moriarty have it the right thing to do? Maybe the criminal wouldn't have got hold of it anyway. David could have hid it in the boulders or something. Of course Moriarty still could have threatened him and he might have given it up rather than endure more pain, but there was no guarantee of that. It didn't matter now, though. It seemed that Moriarty already had it, or what was left of it. Now the big question was whether he could crack the code and read it. What would David do then?

How had the book come to be in the library in the first place? They now knew that David had found it there and made up a catalog card for it. It seemed that he'd felt that was the proper thing to do for an unlabeled book. Of course if he hadn't, Amanda and her friends would never have figured out that the *Detective's Bible* was the whatsit, so maybe David's OCD had brought about something positive for once. Maybe he wasn't so compulsive after all though. He'd misfiled the card. If he hadn't, they would have figured out what the whatsit was earlier.

Amanda was still wondering what Simon had meant when he'd said he thought Professor Redleaf had seen the Legatum equivalent of Voldemort. Now that things had settled down a bit she asked him.

"I wasn't sure, but I got the idea that she'd seen something shocking," said Simon. "And scary."

"Something to do with Voldemort? That's what you said."

"I didn't mean that exactly, obviously," said Simon. "There's no such thing as wizards."

"Of course not," said Amanda.

"I couldn't get too much out of Scapulus, but he did slip a little and I got the impression that what she saw scared her half to death."

"Maybe, but how do you get Voldemort out of it?"

"I really shouldn't have said that," said Simon. "It's misleading."

"Okay, fine. Forget Voldemort. What did she see then?" said Amanda.

"I think she saw evidence of the most dangerous hacker ever to walk the earth, and you know I don't normally talk that way."

With all the chaos around him, Thrillkill had been able to make at least one decision. He'd hired construction workers to come and fix the school. This work would cause some disruption, but everything should have been fixed by the fall term—should there be a fall term, which no one was sure there would be.

Everyone was so down that the gremlins had taken it upon themselves to lift the school's morale. They had decorated the place in an absolutely royal fashion, and it was drop-dead gorgeous. They were still bickering over silly stuff, though, but everyone seemed to appreciate that they were trying to put a pretty face on a bad situation and help calm people down. Despite their own tendency to squabble, they hated to see people fighting, plus everyone was rattled about the earthquake damage and there was a lot of anxiety over the missing students, although most people, the gremlins included, did not know about the *Bible*.

The décor was beautiful but it looked weird with all the damage. Alexei and Noel had come up with a Downton Abbey theme, and they kept racing around trying to fix flaws. They were having trouble setting priorities, though, and kept arguing over what the most important tasks were. What once would have been horrifying but was no longer so was that that they had hit it off with Amanda's relatives, who were staying at the school for a couple of days with Thrillkill's approval. As great as Despina and Hill had been at the quarry, they were still sticking their noses in everywhere and offering unwanted advice to everyone, including the teachers, who felt that they had to be diplomatic because it was the students' relatives who supported the school.

Then possibly the strangest thing of all happened: Simon and Amphora won the disguise competition. It turned out that Amphora had a real knack for costuming and makeup, Simon had had some great ideas, and they had actually enjoyed working together. They had produced burn victim makeup based on one of the simulations they'd created in Fires and Explosions, taking into account everything from the temperature of the fire to the amount of time the victim had been exposed to it. This accomplishment won them high marks in both Professor Tumble's and Professor Pole's classes and gave the teachers the idea to team-teach some seminars in the fall.

Amanda and Ivy were stunned. Truth be told, Amanda was a little envious. *She* was the one who was supposed to know all about costumes and makeup. Still she was happy for Amphora, who had been having a tough time, and asked Ivy if she thought there was such a thing as a fashion detective. Simon piped up and said Amphora could probably have a great career fighting espionage in the fashion industry. This idea got Amphora so excited that she told her friends she was going to speak to Professor Tumble about it immediately.

Unfortunately Amphora had also managed to get the new cook fired. She was let off with a warning not to become personally involved with the staff. Simon suspected that she had not been punished more harshly because of her family's importance, which made him mad because *he* had been suspended just for cutting a class. Mercifully Ivy declined to fine him for his remark. Later Amphora told Amanda that she hoped she'd see Eustace again. Amanda shrugged. Despite what had happened with Rupert Thwack, the girl hadn't changed one bit. However, one mystery was solved. The last thing the young cook was heard to say as he was escorted out the door was, "Nuts. I forgot my candy stash."

37

IT'S A WONDERFUL LIFE

When Amanda sat down to research where the Moriartys might have gone, she suddenly remembered Darius Plover. She'd been horrible to him, first lying and then ignoring him. She hadn't even looked at the second set of clips. She'd probably ruined their relationship, but she may as well do it and this time tell him the truth.

The second batch was as bad as the first one. She was so upset she briefly thought about pretending she couldn't access them. Still she had said she would tell him the truth, so she opened her mail and wrote the director a note.

Dear Mr. Plover,

I'm sorry it took me so long to get to the second set of clips. I have no excuse and I'll understand if you're disappointed.

I have to say I think they could use some improvements. To be honest, so can the first set. I'm sorry I didn't say this before, but I think the scenes need to be crisper. I feel like I've seen them in other movies. A gimmick might help—maybe some humor or a shock, like the monster exploding out of John Hurt's stomach in "Alien."

I will understand if you no longer want to speak to me. However, I remain your devoted fan.

Sincerely,

Amanda Lester,
Filmmaker.

She reread the message and pressed Send. Oh well. She'd done it now. She'd never have a chance like this again. She'd still make movies but she'd probably never break into the big time. She banged her head on her desk. She was just like G. Lestrade. It really *was* those awful genes again. She wondered if a full blood transfusion would change her into someone else. If that were to happen, would everything be different? Would she lose her filmmaking skills? Would she look different? Would she even still be eligible to go to Legatum? She supposed all of that would happen. Maybe it was better to keep the blood she had.

Ivy entered their room with Nigel and sat down on her bed. "Any luck?"

"What, oh, with Blixus?" said Amanda. Ivy nodded. "Sorry. There was something else I had to do. I haven't started."

"Are you okay?" said Ivy. "Come on up, Nigel." The dog jumped up, turned in a circle, and lay down with his head in Ivy's lap.

"He's so toasty, isn't he?" said Amanda.

"Always," said Ivy. "So?"

Amanda knew exactly what her friend was referring to. "I'm all right. It was awfully weird seeing him though."

She pictured how Nick had looked when he'd got into the white van. His T-shirt had been covered with blood, his jeans were ripped, and a layer of dust had settled all over him, making his dark hair appear gray. She wondered how serious his injuries were. It was she who had zapped him in the gut. Presumably the Moriartys had patched him up. They certainly wouldn't have gone to a hospital, not with all points bulletins out for them.

"Did you ever think he was still alive?" said Ivy.

"No," said Amanda. "I thought the same as everyone: that he had died in the fire. How could he have escaped anyway?"

"Probably a secret exit or something," said Ivy. "It was a pretty big place, wasn't it?"

"Huge. It had several levels. Legatum could have fit inside it. I mean the buildings, not the grounds."

"I wonder where all those criminal kids went," said Ivy.

"I imagine they'll turn up eventually." That was a sobering thought, one they didn't have time to consider now. "You know, Ivy, I'm so mad at him I could spit. Where's he been all this time? How could he let me think he was dead? And how could he be so mean to the crystals?"

She remembered how Nick had stomped on the clock that day in the common room. That was when she'd realized he could be violent. What was wrong with him anyway? Of course, it was obvious: his parents were psychopaths. Still . . .

"And yet," she said.

"What?" said Ivy.

"No matter how bad he acts, I keep feeling that there's good in him. I've seen it." Why else would he have preserved her film for her, as he'd done by putting it into cloud storage and placing an icon on her phone? There was nothing to be gained by that. It was an act of affection, pure and simple. No matter what Nick said, she'd never believe he could be taken at face value. Maybe that was why he'd kept her picture and the film in a secret place.

"I've seen it too," said Ivy. "There's something going on there we don't understand."

"I'm not sure I want to," said Amanda. "By the way, how's your hearing?"

"It's fixed!" said Ivy. "Know what it was?"

"What?"

"Wax. I finally went to see Dr. Wing and she spotted the problem immediately. She cleaned out my ears and I'm fine."

"That's great! I'm so relieved."

"Me too. That was one hidden treasure I could have done without."

That night in bed Amanda thought about Holmes. Obviously the whole thing with him was over. She knew that for sure, although she couldn't quite say why. He was perfect. Not only was he a genius and a nice guy, but he was as attractive as one of Clive's magnets. Plus he stood up for her, which counted for a lot. But he wasn't Nick, and for some perverse reason that mattered.

She wished it didn't. Now that she knew Nick was alive, however, there was a chance she might be able to resolve her feelings about him at last—if she could find him. Would they cross paths again? Maybe all it would take was one more nasty word from him and she'd be able to forget him forever. She needed to figure out where he was and face him one last time.

He had certainly made an impression on Editta. Imagine abandoning the detectives to run off with the Moriartys like that. It was horrifying, but there was something else: now Amanda felt just a bit of rivalry with her friend, even though she was still furious with Nick and probably hated him. This ambivalence confused her. The Moriartys had opened the door of the van to let Editta in. Nick preferred Editta to her. Why? It wasn't looks. Editta was plain and looked like a bird. Holmes had told Amanda she was beautiful, although she didn't agree. Intelligence? Editta was great with numbers. She would be a huge asset to the criminals' organization. But Amanda was smart too, and creative.

And then it hit her: Editta was malleable. She'd do anything for Nick. Amanda stood up to him, to his father. Editta would go along with whatever they wanted.

She sat up in bed. The situation was far worse than she'd realized. Editta was in real danger and had to be rescued immediately. But how?

It was important to go through all the evidence she'd gathered. There had to be clues to the Moriartys' whereabouts. Amanda got out of bed and powered up her computer, careful not to wake Ivy and Amphora. She uploaded all the pictures and videos she'd taken in the last few days to the cloud site Nick had set up for her. How could someone who'd do that be so awful? How could someone who'd invented the Planet Detecto, teased her about the slime mold they'd found eating the pink sugar, would kill a clock to please her, be faking it all? It wasn't possible. He was a good actor, but he wasn't *that* good. Was he?

When she checked her mail in the morning, she was astonished to discover that Darius Plover had written back. She was afraid to read the message, though, and it took her half an hour to get up the courage.

Dear Amanda,

I absolutely love your ideas! I am so excited about them that I'd like to offer you a job. If you could see your way clear to come to L.A. this summer, I would love to hire you as a consultant. If after that you still want to work with Plover Films, I think we can manage some remote work.

Interested?

Your friend,
Darius Plover.

Amanda was flabbergasted. The offer was beyond her wildest dreams. Of course she'd go to L.A., if her parents would pay for the trip. They'd offered to let her live with her aunt and uncle there, so why not? She'd call at once and ask.

She threw on her clothes and tiptoed down to the common room, which was empty, as you'd expect at 6:00 a.m. Was it too early to call home? Probably, but who cared. She brought up her mother's phone number and was about to press the icon when her phone rang. It was her mother!

"Darling, I'm sorry to call so early," said Lila. "I hope I didn't wake your roommates." Her roommates? What about *her*? "I need to talk to you immediately. Are you at breakfast?"

The logic of her being up at breakfast while her roommates were sleeping within range of the ring tone escaped Amanda, but obviously

Lila was so agitated about something that she hadn't realized what she was saying. "I can talk. What is it, Mom?"

"I don't know how to put this, darling. It's bad. Well, it isn't bad, exactly. It's good in a way. Well, you won't think it's good. I think it's sort of good. Actually I don't think it's good at all." Amanda could hear her breathing quickly on the other end of the line. She sat and waited.

"The thing is, well, I'm just going to come out and say it," said Lila. "Your father and I are getting a divorce."

Amanda dropped the phone. Had her mother said that they were getting a horse? They wouldn't even let her get a dog. She felt for the phone under the sofa where she was sitting. It had fallen so far underneath that she had to get down on her hands and knees and reach all the way to the back of the space. When she managed to retrieve it her mother was still talking.

"As you know, dear, he hasn't been the same since the kidnapping. He wants to quit the law and find himself. I'm afraid I can't cope with that, so we've agreed to part. He's out looking for a place to live as we speak." *At six o'clock in the morning? Must be some weird landlords out there.*

Amanda was so shocked she couldn't speak. How was this possible? Yes, her father had been through a lot, but divorce? Her parents had always been on the same page. They agreed about everything, did everything together, plagued their daughter together with their tales of G. Lestrade and Sherlock Holmes. They were like Holmes and Watson. In fact, they were so much like that pair that they'd soon be back together. They had to be. But if they weren't, who would she visit on term breaks? Where would she go at holidays? What if one of them moved back to L.A. and one of them stayed here? OMG, what if this meant she couldn't go to L.A. and work for Darius Plover?

She ran up to her room and found Amphora and Ivy getting ready for class. "I have to talk to you," she said. "My mother, I mean, I just talked to her. My parents are getting a divorce!"

"Oh no!" said both girls together.

"Oh yes," said Amanda. "My dad has gone off to find himself and my mom can't take it."

"I suppose that isn't so surprising considering what he's been through," said Ivy.

"No," said Amanda. "But you'd think she'd be a little understanding. Actually you wouldn't. You've met her. What do you think?"

"She's a great writer," said Amphora.

"Maybe she'll come around," said Ivy. It seemed that neither one of her friends wanted to say what they were all obviously thinking: that Lila Lester was a selfish and foolish woman who always had to get her own way.

"Now that I think about it, I understand my dad's point of view," said Amanda. "And you know what? I'm not as shocked. I mean I always thought they were so much alike, but they're not really. My dad is altruistic. He wants to save the world. My mom wants to make a big splash. It's just that up until now their goals were the same. That's why they got along so well. Now that they're not, they're having problems."

"It happens," said Ivy.

"Unfortunately," said Amphora.

"I wonder if my dad will want me to leave Legatum now."

"Why?" said Amphora, looking horrified.

"Maybe he's disillusioned with law enforcement. He's been doing a lot of yoga."

"I can't see how he'd want you to give up what's always been so important to him," said Ivy.

"No," said Amphora. "I'm sure he'll want you to stay."

"Maybe I should call him," said Amanda. "I don't want to leave. I did at first, but now I don't."

"Of course not," said Ivy. "Why would you?"

"There are other opportunities," said Amanda, thinking of Darius Plover.

"You mean your filmmaking?" said Amphora.

"Yes," Amanda sighed. "My filmmaking."

"First do one, then do the other."

Shortly after this conversation, Thrillkill called Amanda to his office. While she was walking down the hall, she heard two of the maids talking.

"You found some more books in the basement, did you, love?" said Daffy, the one with the red hair piled high. Amanda always thought it looked a bit like a bird's nest. "Put them in the library where they belong. I found one a few weeks ago under a pile of junk and stuck it on a shelf where it would be nice and safe."

"That old thing I saw you carrying?" said Candy, a short, plump young woman with bright pink nails. "I thought it was rubbish."

OMG! They were talking about the *Detective's Bible. That* was how it had got into the library. Something must really be wrong around here if just anyone could pick up Legatum's most important possession and walk off with it like that. If Amanda had already been worried about the school, now she was even more concerned. Their security was in terrible shape.

When she got to the headmaster's office, Thrillkill told her he could really use her help over the summer. There were things he'd like her to work on. He told her about the factions among the teachers and said that he wanted to keep the detectives together at all costs. He explained that the school was in the midst of its worst crisis since its founding in 1887 and could well be destroyed if these problems weren't resolved. Would she be willing to stay and help?

Now she was in a real pickle. She desperately wanted to work with Darius Plover. He'd presented her with a once-in-a-lifetime opportunity. But she didn't want to let Thrillkill and the detectives down, and she was worried sick about Editta. What was she going to do?

Suddenly the answer came to her: George Bailey in the movie "It's a Wonderful Life." George, played by Jimmy Stewart, resented the fact that he had ended up stuck at home working for a boring old bank while his brother, Harry, got to go to college and pursue his dreams. But just as he'd hit rock bottom, an angel came down from heaven and showed him that his town would have been a disaster if not for his efforts. Seeing this, George came to appreciate the life he'd built, even if it hadn't turned out the way he'd planned.

Like George Bailey, Amanda would sacrifice for the greater good. She'd remain at Legatum and help Thrillkill. She could work with Darius Plover remotely. He'd understand. She told Thrillkill she'd be happy to stay. She wished she hadn't, though, because the next thing he said made her want to grab George Bailey by the throat and squeeze.

"Oh, and Miss Lester, I've asked Mr. Holmes to join us. We need his expertise. It's critical that he discover who hacked Professor Redleaf's computer and block them. Apparently it was *not* Blixus Moriarty, he tells me, but someone even more sophisticated.

"Also, the two of you did such a good job on the training film that I'd like you to work together again. We need another film, and this time it will be a bit different. The stakes will be higher. We want you to save the world."

DISCUSSION QUESTIONS FOR YOUR READING GROUP

If you had to sum up the character of Scapulus Holmes in one word or phrase, what would it be? What in the book makes you say that?

What do you think of the décor gremlins, Alexei and Noel? How would you decorate the Holmes House common room if you were one of them?

Is Professor Sidebotham fair? Do you think she's a good teacher?

If you were on that field trip to Blackpool, how would you make sure you remembered every detail? No photos allowed.

What topics would you teach if you were the disguise teacher?

What do you think Professor Redleaf saw on her computer screen that bothered her so much?

Was Thrillkill insensitive making Amanda search Nick's room? Why?

Do you think everyone should know how to program? What is the most important technical skill a person should have—a particular programming language, understanding networks, knowing how computer security works, etc.?

What gift would you give Amanda for her birthday? Why?

Was Amphora right to worry that the crystals might make her sick? Why?

What would you do if you were on a train and found that a couple of clowns had taken your seats?

What would you do with an acoustic levitator if you had one?

Is Simon correct that punishment and revenge are two different things?

Would you feel guilty listening to people's conversations without their knowledge? Why?

What do you think is on the syllabus for Professor Snaffle's secrets class?

How do you feel about David Wiffle at the end of the book?

Who is the most interesting teacher at Legatum? Why?

What's the best kind of skateboard? Why?

What do you think the whatsit contains? Why is it so important?

If a famous director asked for your opinion on some clips and you didn't like them, would you give honest feedback? Why?

What is your favorite scene in the book? Why?

What, if anything, surprised you about the story?

DISCUSSION QUESTIONS FOR YOUR READING GROUP

If you were going to add a new character to the series, what kind of person would it be? What would you have them do?

What do you think happened to the whatsit?

Anything else you'd like to comment on?

ACOUSTIC LEVITATION IS REAL!

Acoustic levitation isn't science fiction. It's real, and it's been used for decades. Whether it could do what Clive does in the book is debatable, however.

The ability of sound to lift things relies on the fact that sound travels in waves and can bounce off surfaces. Those waves can be harnessed to do work.

An acoustic levitator consists of a transducer, which vibrates and makes sound, and a reflector, which causes the sound to bounce back. By placing a reflector in the right place relative to the transducer, you can create a standing wave, which appears to hover in one place but doesn't really, and that is what creates the pressure needed to lift things.

There's a great article on acoustic levitation at How Stuff Works (http://science.howstuffworks.com/acoustic-levitation1.htm). There are even YouTube videos on the subject. Check them out!

Q AND A WITH AUTHOR PAULA BERINSTEIN

Where did you get the idea for the crystals?

I liked the idea of the kids discovering a new life form, and I wanted it to be so unusual that you normally wouldn't think of it as a life form. I also wanted something visually interesting, with lots of color. I researched crystals to see if there is such a thing as living ones, and I found articles that discuss "almost living" crystals. (See http://www.wired.com/2013/01/living-crystal/, for example.) That was good enough for me. Sure, I exaggerated mine, but I often do that. Fiction has to be larger than life.

I've been to Windermere, and there's no Lake Enchanto there. What's going on?

It is absolutely true that I play with geography. In fact, when you read the next book, *Amanda Lester and the Purple Rainbow Puzzle*, you'll see that I do so even more when I send the kids to Penrith, a town near Windermere. I try to retain some semblance of truth, but I change what I need to so that it supports the stories. For example, all my trains and stations are real, although they may not look exactly like they do in the books. The highways are also real, and there really is a sugar mile near London City Airport, or there was. There are still factories in that area.

How did you come up with the idea of using an acoustic levitator to get the kids past the tunnel gates?

I had to get them past those gates, and I thought and thought about how to do it. Those locks are tough! I suppose I could have had them break the locks or get through them legitimately, but that wouldn't have been very interesting. It occurred to me that perhaps I should leave the locks in place but play with the hinge parts of the gates. Then what? Well, there are pins in hinges; what if the kids could remove them. But they're old and rusty and won't budge. You see my reasoning. I just go through various ideas step by step. When I found acoustic levitation on the Web, that clinched it. Clive is inventive. Of course he'd make something like that.

Are you really planning to create a game like *Explosions!*?

I hope so. I've been working with my stepson to design some games based on the Amanda stories, and that's one of the ideas. Once I get the purple book finalized (for publication in November, 2015), I will put together some Kickstarter campaigns to raise the money to get them programmed. I can't wait!

Have you ever skateboarded?

I have! My friend Barbara and I used to go sidewalk surfing. I had a Makaha board. Wish I'd kept it.

Do you know how to program?

I do! I used to be a COBOL programmer at an aerospace company, and I studied Java for a while. I also took a class in assembly language, and although I never followed that up, it allowed me to understand concepts I'd never got my head around before. I can also write

HTML and CSS, although I'm not sure you can consider those programming.

What is it with you and monkeys?

Don't you like monkeys? I hope you do because you're going to be seeing a lot more of them.

Do gingersnaps really settle the stomach?

They do. I used to give them to my dog when we'd go in the car. They work wonders!

ABOUT THE AUTHOR

Paula Berinstein is the former producer and host of The Writing Show (www.writingshow.com). She lives in Los Angeles.

29032439R00236

Made in the USA
Middletown, DE
04 February 2016